MW01088304

THE SECRET OF LILLIAN VELVET

This is an Arthur A. Levine book

Published by Levine Querido

www.levinequerido.com • info@levinequerido.com

Levine Querido is distributed by Chronicle Books

Library of Congress Control Number: 2023931859

ISBN 978-1-64614-261-3

Printed in China

Published September 2023

First Printing

The text type was set in GazetteLTStd Roman.

by

JACLYN MORIARTY

LEVINE QUERIDO

MONTCLAIR · AMSTERDAM · NEW YORK

PART 1

REPORT 1

GAINSLEIGH HARBOR, KINGDOMS AND EMPIRES
—twenty years ago

* * *

This was the time of the Whispering Wars.

Late one winter's night, Jacob and Ildi Mettlestone, fitter than their gray hair might suggest, waited at the docks. They wore overcoats, hats, and sensible shoes. Suitcases stood at their feet.

Their twelve children were gathered around them. Of these, eleven were daughters and one, a son. The eldest, Isabelle, was a grown woman, while the youngest, Patrick, was a child of twelve. The rest were fairly evenly spaced between.

It was very cold. Some stamped their feet to keep warm, others jumped up and down on the spot.

"In half an hour," Jacob told the group, "your mother and I will be collected by a fishing vessel. A week from today, word will come that the vessel was intercepted by Shadow Mages, and that . . ."

He cleared his throat, his gaze drifting across the harbor to the boats that bobbed and swayed in their own tethered shadows. The silence continued.

"And that we were killed," Ildi finished, briskly.

At this, a series of gasps, snorts, giggles, and crinkled brows ran through the huddled group—and somebody began to sob.

"This is necessary?" Isabelle demanded. She exchanged troubled glances with the other grown-up sisters. Although she herself still resided in Gainsleigh—traveling frequently for work—these others had moved away, scattering across the Kingdoms and Empires. Their parents had summoned them home for this meeting—in the midst of the Whispering Wars!—so they'd known something was up. But pretending to be dead? This struck the sisters as excessive.

The younger siblings, however, still lived at home. The Whispering Wars had only faintly touched them—sugar and chocolate could be tricky to find, and newspapers favored big, bold headlines and exclamation marks. That was it really. These siblings assumed their parents' announcement to be a joke, a nonsense, or—in the case of Emma, who was fourteen and prone to melodrama—the greatest tragedy of all time.

"Yes, we are sure it's necessary," Ildi replied, raising her voice over Emma's sobbing. "Look, we won't *actually* be killed," she added, giving this daughter a firm kick with the side of her shoe. (Emma had thrown herself onto the wharf, curled into a ball like an echidna, and was shrieking, "Killed? No! My darling parents! Killed? No!")

"Hush, Emma," Jacob begged, turning away from the harbor at last. "Please. We must avoid attention. You see, children, your mother and I have captured an extremely powerful enemy."

"The enemy is captured?" Isabelle frowned. "In that case . . ."

"The enemy is captured, yes—but not yet fully secured," her mother clarified. "At present, you are all in grave danger. The enemy is determined to exact revenge on us, and would not hesitate to harm or capture our children to this end."

Jacob thrust his hands into his coat pockets. "We must go into deep hiding," he explained. "*All* must believe that we are dead. There will be death notices in the papers. A coronial inquest. A funeral."

Crunch. One of the grown-up daughters, Franny—boots, jodhpurs, and an oversize flannel shirt—had bitten the top off a carrot. Chewing carrots helped Franny think.

"This will all take time," she pointed out.

Her parents turned to her, apologetic. They understood her concern. Franny, the third eldest, had moved the farthest of all the children, to a town called Spindrift, where she was mayor. Spindrift was near the epicenter of the Whispering Wars: Franny's town needed her back as soon as possible.

Briefly, the parents outlined their plan. Franny chewed on her carrot, listening. The other adult sisters added questions of their own.

"We'll return to Gainsleigh the moment the enemy is secured," Jacob promised. "We'll telegram the instant we know."

"So it might not be long?" Patrick checked. "You might telegram tomorrow?" He was the family optimist.

There was a brief pause.

Then: "It could be soon," Ildi agreed, reaching to straighten her son's coat collar. "Tomorrow is . . . unlikely . . . but yes, it could happen at any time."

More discussion. Some of the Mettlestones grew bored with the details and began to drift away along the wharves. Soon, only the three eldest sisters remained. Their questions were insightful and probing. This made their parents proud.

The youngest siblings, Patrick and Emma, skimmed

pebbles across the dark water. Two very organized sisters, Nancy and Claire, argued about whether one had borrowed the other's scarf without asking. The twins, Maya and Lisbeth—both sailors with plans to acquire a boat of their own one day—studied the crafts in dock, observing design flaws. Alys, the musical sister, sat on a bench, tapping out rhythms on the seat back. (Her passion was percussion.) Sophy, the animal lover, crouched by an injured seagull, while Sue, a farmer, studied the kelp that floated on the harbor water, wondering if it might make useful fertilizer.

Eventually, all the children wandered back. They were quiet now, looking out to sea for the boat that would collect their parents.

Mist on the water. The scuttling of a rat. The sound of distant singing from a late-night pub.

"This is going to hit your friends hard," Isabelle pointed out suddenly. "Or do they know it's a ruse?"

Both parents sighed in unison. "It's very distressing," Ildi admitted. "But the *only* people who may know we are alive are you: our twelve children. You must keep the secret. No partners can know. No friends. Not even your own children, should you have any. They must be told that their grandparents died before they were born."

At this, a kind of horror seemed to grip the gathering.

Emma straightened. The melodrama fell from her face like a dropped coat. "Use your wish, Father," she commanded.

There was a startled silence. Their father's wish was never mentioned.

Although Jacob Mettlestone resembled a regular person in every way, he was in fact a Wheat Sprite.

All land-based Sprites possess a unique gift: they can make a single wish in their lifetime.

"Oh, darling child," Jacob replied, his voice low and sorrowful. "I used my wish many years ago."

Emma slumped—they all did.

"I'm sure we don't need to remind you to keep *that* secret too," Ildi said sharply, and her children murmured: "Of course not."

It was universally assumed that Jacob had a wish up his sleeve. This gave him a tactical advantage over enemies in his work—not to mention, a certain panache. (It had also helped with discipline when the children were small.) That he would reveal the truth about the wish now was yet another clue that the matter was serious indeed.

"Anyhow, you'll be back *long* before any of us has a child," Patrick declared. "Long before *I* do, anyway. I'm twelve! A mere child myself! Some might say."

Into the soft laughter that followed this assertion came the long, low note of a foghorn. A fishing vessel crept into the harbor. In turn, the Mettlestone parents embraced their twelve children.

They gathered up their suitcases. They embarked.

PART 2

CHAPTER 1

ON MY TENTH birthday, my grandmother gave me a jar of gold coins.

Earlier that morning, a peculiar noise had woken me. It was a steady slurping, crunching sound, and it was coming from the kitchen. After a while, the sound stopped. Silence fell.

I dozed until it was time to wake up; then I put on my dressing gown, came out to the living room, and sat at the table.

"Many happy returns," my grandmother said, pushing a jar of gold coins toward me.

I hefted the jar with both hands, feeling its weight and its sunlit warmth, and read the label.

ALWAYS FRESH
Est. 1977
Dill Pickles

The edges of this label were peeling, and it was shadowed with water stains. I remembered the slurping, crunching sounds I'd heard earlier.

"Grandmother!" I exclaimed.

She must have eaten a jar of pickles, tipped out the pickle juice, washed the jar, and filled it with these gold coins! It was the effort of this that thrilled me, more even than the coins themselves. As far as I knew, my grandmother didn't even like pickles!

"Eat your toast, child," Grandmother replied, "and I will tell you the plans."

While she talked, I unscrewed the lid of the jar and dug out a coin. In my country, which is called Australia, there are both gold and silver coins. The gold coins represent one or two dollars.

I only wanted to study the coin's engravings, out of curiosity, but Grandmother said, "Child!" in a sharp voice, "I am speaking!" and I dropped the coin.

It fell to the floorboards with a *clang*. Then it spun in place, ringing noisily, before tipping over: *clunk*. I glanced down at it.

I frowned.

It was quite blank.

"Child," Grandmother repeated, more calmly. "Have you understood?"

It was then that the words she'd been speaking fell sideways with a *clunk* inside my mind. Grandmother intended to go out. For the first time in my life, on this, the day of my tenth birthday, she was leaving me home alone.

"I have secured employment," she explained, sounding a little proud. *Secured employment* meant she'd found a job. "Each day, from this day, you will take your lessons here, unsupervised. Upon my return, in the evenings, I will check your schoolwork. I expect it to be of the highest quality. Once you have completed your schoolwork, you may practice piano. You might also . . ." She stood, nudged the fallen coin with her slippered foot, and then, crouching, picked it up and handed it to me. "You might also begin supper preparations. Yes," she decided. "At five P.M. each day, you may begin supper preparations."

After that, she cleared the breakfast table, washed the dishes, and disappeared down the hallway to her room.

CHAPTER 2

BEFORE I CONTINUE, I must say this: I know that I sound strange.

I do not sound like other ten-year-old girls in my country, and possibly even in the world. Here is how I know this.

One Tuesday, my grandmother was teaching me my lessons. She set me a series of geography questions, then rose to make herself a cup of tea.

A moment later, though, she returned from the kitchen and sat down again.

"After lunch," she said, "we will walk to the corner store and purchase milk. The carton in the refrigerator has soured."

"Very well, Grandmother," I agreed. "I am sorry about your tea."

"Continue with your lesson," Grandmother instructed. "Do not concern yourself with my tea."

After lunch, however, Grandmother said, "I feel rather fatigued. I am going to rest for an hour. Complete your comprehension exercise, child." She went into her bedroom and closed the door.

Through the window I could see that the day was pleasant. The sky was blue. Our plum tree was flowering.

I completed my comprehension exercise, using full sentences.

I looked at the clock. Grandmother had been sleeping for thirty minutes. Another thirty minutes of her nap remained.

Crossing the room to the coatrack, I reached into the pocket of Grandmother's jacket and took out her purse. The key was in the front door. I stood on my toe tips and turned it.

Then I walked down the hill to the corner store.

Grandmother and I live on Carmichael Street, a steep road just outside the small town of Bomaderry. Ours is the house with the letter box shaped like a hair dryer. One side of the street is lined with houses; the other has fields with cows or horses. Bomaderry is two hours south of Sydney, and we often hear highway traffic—trucks and tourists—from the M1. Although Grandmother orders our groceries online, when we need something small, such as milk or paper towels, we walk to the corner store.

Two girls around my own age—eight at that time—were sitting on the step of this store, eating raspberry Popsicles.

"Good afternoon," I said. "Isn't it a lovely day?"

The girls stared up at me.

As I stepped around them, one spoke. "Good afternoon," she replied softly.

I bought a carton of milk and stepped around the two girls again. Their Popsicles had stained their chins and their lips raspberry.

I paused.

"May I ask why you are not at school?" I inquired. Most children were in classrooms at this time of the day.

"It's school holidays," one of the girls answered, blinking.

"Of course," I said. "Have you interesting plans for your holidays?"

The girls glanced at each other. "How old are you?" one asked.

"Eight."

"You don't talk like an eight-year-old," the first girl informed me.

"No, you don't," her friend agreed.

I was cradling the milk in my arms, as one might hold a baby, and the carton was cold against my skin.

"I don't?"

They both shook their heads.

I thought for a moment.

"I suppose this is because I live with my grandmother," I told them. "I never see other children of my own age, as Grandmother home-schools me. She worries that schools in this region are too small. In fact, I only know about other children from reading classic children's books. My favorite is *Mary Poppins Comes Back*."

The two girls gazed at me. "Really?" one said.

Encouraged, I continued.

"Really. When I was much younger, my grandmother used to go out to work three afternoons a week and the kindly woman next door—Fiona was her name—took care of me in her home. I *did* like those days. I remember watching a television program with Fiona. It was called *Peppa Pig*. Terrific fun. It did not teach me how other children speak, though, it only taught me how pigs speak. Unfortunately, Fiona moved away. Her husband, Carl, was offered employment in Sydney, as a management consultant, just as their rent here was increased beyond their means. I missed Fiona dreadfully for a while. However, I have grown accustomed to her absence."

There was an even longer pause while my new friends considered all this.

"You should get a TV," one of the girls suggested.

"And an iPad," the other added.

These seemed interesting ideas.

"Where does one acquire these?" I asked.

The girls looked at each other. "At a shop," one said. "Or order it online," the other added.

"Have I enough money?" I opened Grandmother's purse. There were three notes, each worth ten dollars.

One of the girls nodded firmly: "Yes, you do," while her friend squinted doubtfully.

"Well, perhaps I will buy a television and an iPad tomorrow," I said, "but I had best get home now. Grandmother may have awoken from her nap and she will wish for a cup of tea. She will be delighted that I have purchased milk. The carton in our refrigerator has soured. It has been such a pleasure talking to you both."

I began to walk away.

"Bye," one of the girls called.

Then the other shouted, "What's your name?"

I turned around. Nobody had ever asked me for my name before, as far as I could recall.

"Thank you for asking!" I called back, very happily.

(Later, remembering this, I felt embarrassed. "Why didn't you just tell them your NAME?" I scolded myself. "Lillian Velvet!" I could have even asked *their* names.)

Grandmother had not been delighted that I'd purchased milk. In fact, she'd been very angry. After that, she never left the key in the door again, so I never went out to find a shop to buy a TV or an iPad. Of course, I soon realized—from the brochures that appeared in our letter box now and then—that I could as well have afforded a TV and iPad with thirty dollars as I could have taken a rocket ship to the moon.

Anyway, that is how I know I do not sound like other ten-year-olds.

Or I suppose I don't. I suppose nothing has changed since I was eight.

Except that now, on my tenth birthday, everything *had* changed.

Grandmother had given me a jar of gold coins, got herself a job, and was going to leave me home alone.

CHAPTER 3

GRANDMOTHER LOCKED THE door behind her.

I watched through the window as she walked down the path, *clip-clop, clip-clop*. She swayed side to side, very neatly, as if the swaying was part of a dance. She opened the gate, closed it behind her—*clink!*—and set off down the hill to the bus stop.

At once, the house seemed to surge forward, around my shoulders. It was as if the house itself were standing right behind me, breathing in my ear.

Bzzzzzzz.

I turned around.

The *bzzzzz* was the sound of the refrigerator. Or the air conditioner. Perhaps all the appliances were buzzing urgently, wanting to know where Grandmother had gone. "She has secured employment," I said aloud.

How strange my voice sounded! A sudden terror seized me.

I took a deep breath and reminded myself that it was my imagination. The house was not alive. It was just a regular house made of bricks and mortar, regular appliances plugged into its walls. Everyday sounds had become noticeable, that was all, now that I was alone.

I sat at the table by the window and looked at the instructions Grandmother had left.

1. Turn to page 33 of your mathematics textbook. Read the explanation on perimeters and study the examples there. Complete exercises 7.5 to 7.18.

I sighed. Mathematics is not my favorite pastime.

2. *Open your Social Studies textbook to page 57. Read the passage and complete the questions on page 58.*

The instructions continued for the rest of the page and onto a second and third. *Check your answers in the back of the book and mark them,* said one item. Another reminded me to *Make sure your writing is neat.* A gap between items 4 and 5 contained the words

MORNING TEA

Then again between items 8 and 9:

LUNCH

After the instructions, there was a list of don'ts.

- *Don't open the door to anybody, even if they knock loudly (unless it is me—however, it is unlikely to be me as I have the key).*
- *DON'T LEAVE THE HOUSE (although you may go into the backyard).*
- *Don't spend all your gold coins in one day.*

That last one made me blink. I looked at my jar of gold coins. It stood on the table in a patch of sunlight, and glinted.

How could I spend the coins without leaving the house? Actually, how could I even *leave* the house? Grandmother had locked the front door behind her. The back door wasn't locked, but that only led into our yard, which was enclosed by a tall fence. There was no gate in the fence.

I opened the lid of the jar and tipped a few coins into my hand. Just like the one I'd studied earlier, these were all blank.

How could I spend these coins at all?

They weren't even *coins* really, just discs of gold.

At that moment, the little clock that stands on our mantelpiece chimed: *Ding, Ding, Ding, Ding, Ding, Ding, Ding, Ding, Ding.*

9:00 A.M.

Time for school. I slipped the coins into my pocket—quicker than returning them to the jar—and set to work.

At morning teatime, I went into the kitchen. A note on the countertop was headed *MORNING TEA:*

Pour milk into a glass. Take a pear from the fruit bowl. Take a cucumber from the fridge and slice it up.

I followed the instructions, placed my milk, pear, and cucumber onto a tray, and carried this into our small backyard. I sat on the step. It was a warm but overcast day.

A bird flew into the garden, landing on a branch of the sycamore tree.

"Hello," I said to it. "Have you come to wish me a happy birthday?"

The bird made a quick, sharp sound and flew away.

I bit into a cucumber slice.

Then I felt a sensation exactly as if somebody had given me a great shove forward and I found myself—

Well, I was certainly somewhere else.

CHAPTER 4

IT WAS A forest.

The trees were immense. If you tried to hug one, your arms wouldn't even reach halfway around. Great, solid trunks with reddish brown bark, they soared up and up, then flung their branches outward like fountains, forming a canopy of leaves.

Although glimpses of blue sky were visible through this canopy, it seemed to have rained recently. Gleaming droplets stood on the tree trunks and dripped to the forest floor. The air smelled of wet wood with green and tangy undertones. There were faint rustlings—I suppose of lizards and other little woodland creatures—and also the clearer, musical notes of birds calling to each other.

"This is most unexpected," I said aloud.

It truly was.

Nothing like this had ever happened to me before. I'd never even *been* to a forest, let alone been shoved into one. I only knew of them from storybooks.

I placed my palms against a tree trunk, and it had a rough and friendly feel.

Grandmother's list had not accounted for this.

"Hold on!" called a distant voice. "Hold on! I'll be right with you!"

For some reason, that made me giggle. It was the voice of an elderly man, and it was followed by noisy tramping and sharp crackling, and then the man himself appeared between the tree trunks. He propped himself against a tree, getting his breath back. He wore tan slacks, old sneakers, and a woolen pullover.

I waited patiently.

"Well now, good morning!" he said at last. "Mr. Turtelhaze at your service. Just arrived, have you?"

"Good morning, Mr. Turtelhaze," I replied. "Yes. I suppose so."

"And do you wish to stay?"

I considered that.

"I'm not sure where I am," I admitted.

"That's easy," Mr. Turtelhaze replied. "You're in the Luminous Forest on the outskirts of the grand harborside town of Gainsleigh. Do you wish to spend the afternoon here?"

I'd never heard of the Luminous Forest or Gainsleigh, but his tone suggested they were as obvious as the Eiffel Tower. He might think me unworldly if I admitted the truth.

So I focused on his question.

"Do I wish to spend the afternoon here?" I repeated slowly. I realized the truth. "I *can't* spend the afternoon here! I have eight more items of schoolwork to complete! Not to mention supper preparations. In fact, I'm not even allowed to leave the house . . ." I felt suddenly forlorn. "And yet, here I am." Quite by accident, I had disobeyed Grandmother.

That seemed unfair.

"Ah!" The man coughed into his fist. "Therefore, you wish to go home at once?"

"I don't know *how* to go home," I replied. "I don't even know how I got here. I was in the back garden, and I was sitting on—"

"Yes, yes." Mr. Turtelhaze pushed himself off the tree trunk where he'd been leaning. "But you wish to go home at once?" he repeated.

I looked around at the grand trees, the secretive shadows. A bird called suddenly, as if it had just recalled something important. Another bird replied in a low, comfortable tone, perhaps reassuring the first that it already knew the important thing.

"I would like to stay for a *little* while," I told the man, "and explore. I've never been anywhere like this, except in my imagination. Grandmother and I go to the corner store sometimes, but otherwise—"

"You wish to stay for a little while and then return?" the man interrupted.

I nodded.

"Five gold coins," he declared.

That made me blink. I stared at him.

"Take it or leave it," he added briskly.

"But I don't have—" Suddenly I remembered the gold coins I'd slipped into my pocket earlier.

I drew out one of these and offered it to the man. "Would *these* work?" I asked, a little embarrassed. "I know it's not a proper coin. It doesn't have anything engraved on—"

"Perfect," he replied, whisking it away. "Have you four others?"

I counted the other coins in my pocket. Only three.

Mr. Turtelhaze sighed. "Ah well," he said, after thinking a moment. "You can pay the rest tomorrow. Your wish is granted. Enjoy."

He swept the coins into his own pocket, then turned around and began to hurry away, tripping and slipping, disappearing into the trees.

"Wait!" I called. "How do I get back?"

"That will sort itself out," he called.

"And is it safe here?"

There was only the sound of Mr. Turtelhaze's footsteps *tramp, tramp, tramping* through the forest. The tramping grew softer and softer, until I couldn't hear it anymore.

He's not going to answer my question, I thought. A few moments later, however, in a voice that sounded thin and breathless and enormously far away, he yelled: "I very much doubt that it *is* safe! Considering it's *filled with danger*!"

Then there was silence.

CHAPTER 5

NOW IT WOULD be very mean-spirited to take gold coins from a child in exchange for a visit to a danger-filled forest.

I had an idea that there were laws against that sort of thing.

Mr. Turtelhaze had struck me as friendly and law-abiding, and so, I concluded, that must have been a joke.

The forest was not dangerous at all.

"Ha ha," I chuckled to myself, out of politeness.

Still, I resolved to explore in a careful way, watching out for spiders and snakes and—what else was dangerous? Lions, tigers, ghosts, sharks, lightning, quicksand, wicked stepmothers, falling bookcases. That sort of thing. I'd watch out for those.

Very slowly, I began to walk through the forest.

For a while, it was more of the same. Immense reddish brown trees spaced fairly evenly apart, dappled shadows, trickling raindrops. My feet made a soft, scuffing sound on the wet leaves and bark. The sun was warm on the back of my neck, the birds called ideas and thoughts to one another. Altogether it was very pleasant. I began to forget about being careful.

Then I happened to look to my right. I saw a girl.

She was crouched at the foot of a tree, facing away from me, and she seemed to be holding herself very still. One of her hands was slowly feeling around in the leaves, as if she was searching for something.

"Good afternoon," I began. "How—"

The girl spun around, her eyes alarmed. Her finger flew to her lips in the way that means *shhhhhh*. Next, she beckoned me.

I hurried over and crouched beside her.

"Is it a game?" I whispered, but the girl bounced her finger quickly against her lips meaning: *Shhh, shhh, shhh.* So not even whispering was allowed.

For a while, we crouched, only the sound of our breathing and the soft scrabbling of the girl's hand moving around under the leaves again. *Perhaps* she had dropped something?

I was about to ask her, very softly, what she had dropped, and offer to help scrabble around for it, when she suddenly drew her hand up, smiling. She held her palm toward me. Three crimson berries lay on it. I looked at her face. She nodded and held her palm closer to me.

I took the berries and examined them politely.

"Lovely," I mouthed, and made to hand them back.

But the girl shook her head, gesturing at my mouth. She wanted me to eat the berries.

"No thank you," I whispered. The girl seemed to have a good face—round cheeks, strong nose, intelligent eyes—but she was still a stranger. For all I knew, she was the danger that filled this forest. If so, the berries were likely poisonous.

The girl's face contorted in a panicky way. "Eat them!" she hissed. "Quickly!"

I held my ground. "No thank you," I whispered. "I have pear and cucumber at home, which I will eat when I—"

However, the girl's hand was scrabbling frantically in the leaves and bark again and, as I watched, she swept up another few crimson berries and thrust these into her *own* mouth. Then she actually pushed my hand toward my face. There seemed nothing to do but eat the berries.

So I did.

They tasted as bitter as ink.

Definitely poisonous.

But why, I thought, as fuzzy pins and needles trickled in long, sweeping stripes from the crown of my head to the soles of my feet, *why did she poison herself too?*

I felt my eyes begin to close, and—

CHAPTER 6

—AND HEARD THE sudden, highly unexpected sound of stampeding elephants.

My eyes flew open again.

The sound was coming from every direction. And was very close.

Beside me, the girl sat cross-legged on the ground and pressed her fists to her ears.

Now, was that safe?

No.

She'd almost certainly be trampled.

We should . . . what?

We should run!

But where?

The noise was *huge*. It was *everywhere*. It vibrated the air around us! Rattled the leaves and bark!

Stampeding elephants were thundering toward us!

I looked around frantically. A tree! We had to climb a tree!

But these trees soared up and up before sprouting branches. There was nothing to cling onto.

Oh, it was impossible to think with that terrible sound! And I had no *experience* of stampeding elephants! Louder and louder they were too—the booming footfalls of the elephants, the crashes and creaks as they bounced against trees.

I would have to *try* climbing.

And so would the girl! Even if she *had* just tried to poison me, I would not leave her here to be crushed. I grabbed hold of her arm and began to drag her up. "Come on!" I shouted. "Courage! We'll climb a tree!"

The girl's face tilted up at me, horrified. She shook my hand away and pulled *me* down beside her instead.

"This!" she screamed. "Do this!"

Amidst the thundering hooves, her scream sounded as faint as a distant wind. I only knew that it *was* a scream from the expression on her face.

"Do what *I'm* doing!" she shrieked. "*Please!*"

Once again she pressed her fists to her ears.

At this point, the noise was so loud that I'd stopped being me, Lillian Velvet. I *was* the noise. Trembling with it, clamoring with it.

I slammed my palms against my ears and dove down beside the girl.

They were almost here now.

Almost . . . almost . . .

They would trample us . . .

We'd be crushed . . .

They were here—now—now—almost—

And then a great shadow loomed over us, like the shadow of a storm cloud carried by the wind, only far darker, an inky darkness. The stampeding sound became a terrible howl. For a long, terrible moment, the darkness hovered, and hovered, and—and then it slid on, so the air around us lightened. It stopped a short distance away though and draped itself over a cluster of trees.

A sharp intake of breath from the girl beside me.

"Squirrel," she mouthed, pointing.

I could barely make out a little bundle of fur. It had frozen at the base of a tree just outside the shadow. For a long moment, the shadow hovered again. The squirrel held still, held still—and then it gave the tiniest quiver.

Instantly, the shadow plunged toward it. Simultaneously, branches in the surrounding trees began to shudder, as if grown men were sitting astride them and bouncing vigorously. A single branch snapped and plummeted to the ground. The squirrel darted sideways, just avoiding it, but more and more branches were splintering, with sounds like cracking whips.

Each crashed to the ground with a mighty *thud! Crash! Thud! Crash!* The very air shook with it! The poor squirrel flung itself in wild zigzags.

The girl's hands were scrabbling in the leaves. With one movement she had plucked something and was pitching it through the air toward the squirrel. A shower of little . . . stones? No, berries! What was she thinking! A final meal before death? She'd only distract the squirrel and put it off its game! Again and again, she tossed showers of berries while branches fell and the squirrel zipped in hopeless circles, all the time slowing—growing tired—until we could no longer see it amidst all the fallen wood.

Then, abruptly, the shadow skittered away.

Its raucous sound followed it—THUNDERING, thundering, quietening, quietening—

Softer, softer,

softer,

gone.

A long silence.

Then a bird called. "Whoa!" its call seemed to say.

CHAPTER 7

I CLIMBED TO my feet, blinking.

Immediately around us, the leaves had been shuffled and blown about. Otherwise, all was intact.

At the bases of the nearby trees, though, there was a mess of broken branches. The girl rushed toward it—I followed, slowly. I didn't want to see the poor squirrel, squashed.

"Ah!" said the girl, and she pointed.

The squirrel was alive! It was crouched alongside a branch, its little body juddering from exhaustion, but its eyes were bright. After a moment, it darted away into the forest.

"So close," the girl murmured and then, with a shiver, looked back to where we'd been crouched: "So *close*." Next, she gazed critically at the trees around us. They had lost several branches. "But they'll be okay," she told me, nodding her approval.

I stared at her.

"What . . ." I began. I tried to rephrase the question. "What *ever* . . ." I tried again. "I mean to say, what *was* that? A cyclone? A giant, invisible elephant?"

The girl looked at me curiously. "Are you from Gainsleigh?" she asked. "I don't recognize you."

I shook my head. *Don't shake your head! Are you a horse? Manners, child! Full sentences!* I stilled my head. "No, I'm not from Gainsleigh."

"Oh, that explains it. It was a Hurtling. It's been in this forest for the last few days, and everyone's been talking about it—they're so rare. If you've just arrived in town I suppose your family hasn't heard yet. Children aren't allowed to come here until the Hurtling moves on." She was brushing herself down as she spoke. She looked to be around my own age, perhaps a year or two older, but everything about her seemed strong. She was broad and sturdy and self-contained, like a chest of drawers. I felt wispy beside her.

"Where are you from then?" she asked. "What's your name?"

"Lillian Velvet," I replied, just stopping myself from adding: *Thank you for asking!* "And I'm from Bomaderry, which is south of Sydney, Australia."

The girl shook my hand, gripping firmly. "Carrie Mettlestone," she said. "Pleased to meet you, Lillian. I don't know BomaderrywhichissouthofSydneyAustralia. Is it far?"

She squashed the words together to form one long word. That made me smile, but Carrie was waiting patiently for my reply.

"I don't know," I admitted. "I think it must be *very* far. And yet it took me no time at all to get here. What's a Hurtling?"

Carrie rubbed her nose, regarding me thoughtfully. "Do you mind if we walk as we talk? There's something I have to find as quickly as possible, and I *think* it's . . ."

Her voice faded as she marched into the forest. Then she fell to her knees and began scrabbling in the leaves again.

"More berries?" I inquired. "May I ask why you were so eager that we eat those? And the squirrel? I must say, they were not entirely—I would not call them . . . *delicious*. Actually, I thought you were poisoning me. I feel all right now though, so I suppose . . . Of course, I mean no—"

I stopped talking, as Carrie didn't appear to be listening.

"Here!" she said abruptly, and this time she drew a sheet of bark from under the leaves. She shook it free of twigs and dirt and held it up. It was about the size of a magazine, smooth but rough around the edges, and so paper-thin the sun shone through it.

Carrie frowned. "Water!" she said abruptly, and she was off again.

I followed.

She spoke over her shoulder as she hurried through the trees. "A Hurtling is a Shadow Mage," she said.

That was not much help. I was having trouble keeping up, she moved so briskly.

"What's a Shadow Mage?" I called.

At this, Carrie stopped. She turned and waited for me. When I caught up, she was frowning very deeply. She rubbed her nose again, even harder, studying me. Then she carried on.

"Shadow Mages make trouble," she declared as she walked. "True Mages make joy. And Spellbinders deal with trouble by tying it up in nets. Ah, here we are."

We had reached a brook. It was cut deep into the ground although its water was shallow, which explained why we hadn't heard any gurgling as we approached. Even now, the gurgling was soft, as if the brook was only turning over its own thoughts, very secretively.

Carrie crouched and dipped her sheet of bark into the brook. She sloshed it around. I sat beside her to watch.

Then she sat back on the muddy bank and held the bark toward me.

Oh gosh. Now she wanted me to eat bark.

I had to draw the line somewhere.

"Thank you, Carrie, but much as I enjoyed—Well, to be honest, I didn't enjoy those berries—Anyhow, I know you put effort into washing it, but still—"

"Look," Carrie said, ignoring me. She was pointing at the bark. "It's working."

And then, as I watched, words began to form on the bark's surface. First, a scattering of pale letters, then more and more, forming words and lines—the lettering growing darker and more distinct all the time.

"It's directions," Carrie explained, "to the secret burrow of a colony of Sparks. Sparks are a kind of True Mage. You see, with the Hurtling rampaging through the forest, the Sparks are likely in danger. I want to check on them."

"Yes," I agreed.

After a moment, I confessed: "I'm still not sure what a Hurtling *is*, Carrie, and I've never heard of a Spark either. Or anyway, not a Spark that lives in a secret burrow. I know that fire gives off sparks. And welders, when using a blowtorch, must wear a visor because of sparks. Once, Grandmother—"

Carrie was still peering at the bark, but she spoke over me. "A Hurtling is one of the original Shadow Mages," she said. "That's why we can't see them. They're in their purest form—just sound and shadow and energy. Hurtlings *hate* life—whenever they sense it, they try to trample it." She glanced at me. "That's why we had to eat the fridaberries. See, Hurtlings live on berries and will eat any kind of berry except a fridaberry. To Hurtlings, those are deadly poisonous and will kill them within moments. Fridaberries are harmless to us, though, and when we eat them we repel Hurtlings. The squirrel must've eaten one of the ones I was throwing—if it hadn't, that Hurtling would *not* have given up until the squirrel was dead. I agree they taste disgusting, Lillian, but they're the reason the Hurtling didn't stop and crush *us* before it got to the squirrel."

"Oh," I said faintly. "Well, thank you for the fridaberries then."

"Pleasure." Carrie chuckled suddenly, her face becoming warm and dimpled. "I just realized something. You thought I wanted you to eat this bark, didn't you? You're funny."

Almost immediately, though, she was serious again, and back to studying the bark.

CHAPTER 8

HERE IS WHAT was written on the bark.

Be prepared. It's quite long.

Far in the distance, melodies soaring
Oranges falling, my heart is roaring
Longing for teacups that
Lurk in the treetops—
Onward! Onward!
We must fly.
Be the spin on the spinning top,
Rinse the suds from the dripping mop,
Onward,
Onward,
Kites in the sky.
Look for the key at the
End of the beekeeper's
Fanciful laneway
That runs to the market
And
Take the key,
Split the key,
Peel it in two!
Lower it
Into the lock
That you'll find
On a candlestick jammed in the soil.

And . . . away now! Fly now! Like
Kites in the sky.

There was a short silence.

"These are *directions*, you say?" I checked.

Carrie gave a breath of laughter. "I know what you mean," she said. "It reads like nonsense. But True Mages love puzzles and treasure hunts. Sparks are especially secretive True Mages, and make it extra hard to find their burrows—they have a firm policy against visitors. I *have* to check on them though! I'm sure that between us we can figure these directions out."

She squinted at the lines.

Us, she had said. She thought I could help figure it out? I felt a bit dizzy. The words didn't just *read like* nonsense, they *were* nonsense! They couldn't direct a falling apple to the ground!

Perhaps I should pretend to faint? Pretend to be unconscious for a bit?

"Melodies soaring," Carrie began. "That'll be birds, right? So it means we have to look up."

"Mm," I murmured, checking to see if the ground looked soft enough to faint onto. Surreptitiously, I shifted a sharp twig that would really hurt when I landed.

"Oranges falling. So there's an orange tree somewhere. There must be teacups high in this orange tree, as a signal marking the way."

"Mm-hmm," I agreed.

Instead of fainting, I'd decided to murmur sounds of encouragement while Carrie figured it out.

"Now, this bit about being the spin on spinning tops and cleaning suds from dripping mops—that *might* just be general advice for life."

"Hmm!" I changed the tone of my murmur, to show that yes, that *was* a tricky bit.

"Let's skip that and try the next part. Kites in the sky. Just another way of saying we need to look up?"

"Oh, my." The whole thing truly was a mystery.

"After that, it gets clearer," Carrie continued. "We have to find a key at the end of the beekeeper's laneway. There must be a beekeeper around here . . ."

"Mm."

". . . and we have to break the key in two somehow? Strange."

"Strange," I agreed.

"It'll probably make sense once we get the key. Then we have to find a candlestick with a lock in it."

"Mm-hmm. Strange."

"Exactly. Very odd place for a lock. All right, let's start by looking for the orange tree with teacups." She jumped to her feet, so I did too.

"Thanks for your help figuring it out, Lillian," she added, already scanning the trees around us.

"All I did was make murmuring sounds," I confessed. "Once I said *oh, my,* and twice I said the word *strange.*"

Carrie glanced at me. "I like you. You're funny. Do you mind holding the directions while I wade across the brook and check that little thicket of trees? I think they *might* be orange trees. Hang on—"

She handed me the sheet of bark before sitting down to pull off her shoes. They were boots, actually. I haven't mentioned her clothing yet so I will now. A long-sleeved cotton T-shirt, thick corduroy trousers, and suspenders holding the trousers up. I liked her outfit more than my own gingham frock and cardigan.

Once she had her boots off, she pulled off her socks and rolled them up.

I glanced at the "directions" on the bark again.

I blinked.

I looked more closely.

"Of course," I said. "It's an acrostic. Is that important?"

Carrie was rolling up the cuffs of her trousers. "It's a what?"

"From the French—*acrostiche*—which is from the Latin—*acrostichis*—from the Greek—what was the Greek again?" I squinted, which I sometimes find helpful for remembering. It didn't work. "Anyhow, an acrostic is a poem where the first letter or word of each line spells out a message."

Carrie swung around to look at me properly. "It is?"

"Yes." I ran my finger down the lines on the bark, studying the first letters.

(You can flip back and do it yourself, if you like, dear reader. Or wait, I'll just put the letters here for you.)

F O L L O W B R O O K L E F T A T S P L I T O A K

"Follow brook," I read aloud. "Left at split oak."

Carrie gave a hoot of laughter, scrambled to her feet, and slapped my back.

CHAPTER 9

***OF COURSE, IT'S** an acrostic. Is that important?* Carrie kept giggling and imitating me asking that question.

Not in an unkind way. She grinned back at me each time she did it, and she seemed really pleased with me.

We were following the brook, looking for a split oak tree.

"You were so matter-of-fact!" she said. "Even though you'd just *solved* it! If that had been any of my sisters, they'd have been crowing their heads off. But *you* were cool as a cucumber!"

"Well, to be honest," I told her, "my heart was going pitter-patter. I had a *feeling* I'd solved it, but I didn't want to get over-excited in case I was wrong."

Carrie swung around again, smiling even more broadly.

"And then, when it turned out I *had* solved it," I continued, "I felt as if a little fire in a grate was glowing in my belly. I was so happy. I'd worried about not being able to help, you see, especially after you saved me from the . . . whatsit. The Hurtling. Anyway, so—"

"Here," said Carrie. "Split oak."

She pointed to a tree.

It stood close to the brook and was much shorter than the soaring trees around us. Its bark was silvery and deeply ridged, and its leaves had curly edges.

I didn't know if this was an oak tree or not. Of course, I've read about oak trees in my storybooks but they don't usually describe the features. They just say, "by the oak" or "there was an oak tree." Sometimes I ask Grandmother if we can please learn about flowers and trees, but she says no, we must follow the New South Wales Board of Education curriculum.

Still, Carrie seemed sure it was an oak. It was certainly split. A great crack ran down its center, slicing it open so that half of the trunk leaned one way and half the other. You could see the paler, reddish gold flesh of the tree inside.

"You poor thing," I said, and I placed my palm gently on the bark. "What happened to you to split you like this? I wish you could be healed somehow."

I glanced sideways at Carrie, suddenly embarrassed. For a moment, I'd forgotten she was there. When I'm in my garden at home, I often chat to plants, grass, flowers, earthworms, even to clumps of dirt. When Grandmother hears me from inside she leans out the window to shout, "Child! Stop at once! You're making a fool of yourself!"

I braced myself for Carrie to jeer at me, but she only patted the tree herself.

"Yes, you don't look well, do you, old girl?" she said to it. "Lightning struck you maybe? Or the Hurtling? Maybe bacteria in the roots? Well, nothing we can do. Let's go left, Lillian."

She set off into the forest.

I followed, feeling warm of heart. I liked Carrie very much.

After we'd tramped along for some time, Carrie stopped abruptly.

Ahead of us was a clearing between trees. Within this clearing, it appeared as if somebody had been busy laying out an immense bonfire. A huge stack of tree branches was piled helter-skelter like a giant's game of pick-up sticks.

"Oh no," Carrie breathed, and she spun around to look at me, her face washed pale. "Oh *no*!"

CHAPTER 10

AT ONCE, CARRIE lunged toward the wood stack, grabbing a branch from the top of the pile and beginning to drag it down.

"Help me, Lillian," she said, already breathless. "We need to . . . (*puff, pant*) . . . clear this . . . (*puff, pant*) . . . fast."

Thud! The huge branch she'd been dragging crashed to the forest floor, sending up a gust of leaves. She reached for another.

I took hold of a branch and tried to wrench it away myself, but it was trapped and tangled in the stack. I tried a second and managed to tug it loose.

"They'll be under here," Carrie puffed. "Hurry! We might be too late!"

We tugged and dragged—*thud! Thud!* Branches hit the ground and hit the ground, as if *we* were Hurtlings ourselves. The wood scratched and tore at our hands and our forearms. It caught in our hair and tore our clothes. *Thud! Thud!* More and more branches. My palms burned. My muscles ached. Carrie moved faster and faster, and I tried to keep up. The remaining stack sagged.

"Hurry!" Carrie breathed. Although she was panting she was fierce with focus. Her cheeks grew bright red from the effort.

My fingernails bled, splinters peppered my fingers and palms.

We tugged at the branches, then kicked them, pushed them, rolled them, clearing space, clearing space, tugging and dragging.

At last the forest floor began to emerge.

"There! It's there!" With another surge of energy, Carrie kicked aside a few final sticks and leaves.

I couldn't see what she was pointing at.

"We might be too late," she whispered, and I peered more closely, and saw it.

A small opening in the ground, only the size of a cup. This was enclosed by layers of fine bluish thread, a little like spider webbing.

"Sparks?" Carrie murmured. "Sparks? Are you there? Are you there?" She leaned close to the opening and spoke through the web. "Are you there? Sparks? Please be there!"

A long quiet.

"Lillian, I think we're too late." Carrie's voice was soft. She looked up at me, her hair damp with sweat, cheeks grubby, tears in her eyes. "You can't bury Sparks like that. They get snuffed out by darkness. They—" Her voice caught and she stopped, sitting back on her heels, her eyes closing in distress.

I didn't know what a Spark was, or what it was doing inside a tiny hole, or truly why it had been buried under a huge stack of firewood by the Hurtling, but still, looking from Carrie to the spidery thread, I felt that I might cry too.

Then, as I watched, the thread unraveled and a fountain of golden light burst from the ground.

CHAPTER 11

CARRIE SHOUTED WITH joy, and I did too.

"You're alive!" she shouted. (I shouted: "Hurrah!") And she spun me around, crying, "They're all right, Lillian! The Sparks are all right!" Her eyes glinted like raindrops in the sunshine.

When we were both dizzy, we turned back to the little fountain of golden light.

Immediately, the light began to spin, as if copying Carrie and me. Then it scattered into thousands of pieces. Little dashes and dots of light, like fireflies, or like the aftereffects of fireworks. These flitted around us, then glided up toward the tops of the trees.

Next, the lights rushed together again and—Well, the next bit was wonderful but difficult to explain.

Unless you, dear reader, are a mathematician?

Even then, I don't know how to write it. I'll try closing my eyes and thinking it, and if you're a mathematician you close your eyes too, and we'll see if you get the message.

Did it work?

Well perhaps you need to be a very *distinguished* mathematician.

Basically, the lights formed patterns, and the patterns were numbers, and the numbers sounded like music.

I think I mentioned earlier that mathematics is not my favorite pastime. However, nobody had ever turned numbers into beautiful violin or cello sonatas for me before, or into several hundred bagpipers playing all at once.

(You may have heard bagpipes before and found them a bit screechy, dear reader. These bagpipes though? They were like sun-warmed paving stones leading to a turquoise lake.)

I'm not explaining this at all well. Maybe think of it like this. If somebody said to you:

12 + 15 + 11

well, you might sigh and start figuring it out. Or you might say, "Toss me the calculator."

Imagine, instead, that 12 + 15 + 11 was the sweetest melody you ever heard, a melody that skips up a hillside until it reaches 38 (the answer).

Carrie and I sat on the forest floor, our backs to a big tree, while the Sparks played symphonies of mathematics for us. We swayed softly and hummed along.

Somehow, the Sparks wove words into their musical mathematics. They thanked us for freeing them. They told us how frightened they'd been when the Hurtling thundered through and buried them, and how they'd begun falling into unconsciousness right before we cleared the wood away.

"We're just glad we got here in time," we said, and "Ah, you poor things."

Next, the Sparks asked if we often went about saving creatures from Shadow Mages.

I told them no, this was my first time.

"Mine too," Carrie said, and then she looked shy for a moment. "You know," she said, "I've always hoped I might turn out to be a Spellbinder—it's in my family, so I *might* be—and my mother keeps telling me I should start training with her now. I always say there's no point, as I might turn out *not* to be a Spellbinder—and *she* always says, it's worthwhile knowing how to fight Shadow Mages in any way you can. Now I see her point. I think I *will* start studying with her."

The Sparks seemed delighted by this. They showered light over Carrie and told her that if she *did* begin training now, and then she *did* turn out to be a Spellbinder? Well, she would be the greatest Spellbinder of all time.

Carrie seemed very embarrassed and said, “Oh, I don’t know about that.”

A little after this, the Sparks showered light over *me*. It felt tickly like soap bubbles. The light flowed down from my forehead and formed a circle of tiny flickers.

Carrie frowned and rubbed her nose. “They look like birthday candles. Is that meant to be a birthday cake?” she suggested. “Is it somebody’s birthday?”

The circle of lights held still. It hovered in the air right in front of me.

“Oh!” I said, beginning to laugh—

CHAPTER 12

SHOVE.

And I was home.

One moment, I was with Carrie and then—*shove*—I was on the back step in my garden again. The plate of pear and cucumber still beside me.

I heard my own laughter and I heard the laughter cut itself in half.

I wanted to cry.

"No!" I said aloud. "It *is* my birthday! I didn't get to say! I want to go back!"

I ran inside and gathered another handful of coins from the jar, ran back outside, sat on the stairs, and waited to be shoved. I remembered that I'd taken a bite of cucumber when it happened before, so I picked up a cucumber slice and *crunch.*

Nothing.

Crunch.

Nothing.

Crunch.

Nothing.

Until all the cucumber were gone.

I tried the pear then, but there wasn't even a crunch. Just a bit of a mushy sound.

There was a long quiet. I could hear cars in the distance, and a leaf blower somewhere close by. All the fizzing and the music and lights faded out of me.

"Well," I sighed. "Never mind."

And then I was struck by a terrible thought: *It must be* very *late. Grandmother would be home soon!*

I stood up. My dress was torn, my hands were scratched. I

felt my hair. It was knotted and disheveled, and I had lost my hairpins.

I ran inside with the plate and checked the clock on the microwave.

Oh my goodness.

I stared at the display.

That *can't* be the time.

I hurried into the living room and looked at the clock on the mantelpiece there. Same again.

It was half past ten.

Not at night—I knew this because it was still daylight.

No time had passed. Or, no more than a few minutes!

All that walking through the forest, eating berries, the Hurtling, the squirrel, the forest, the sheet of bark, the forest again, the wood stack, clearing it away, playing with the Sparks . . .

All of that had been wrapped inside a moment!

Well, at least that was something.

In the bathroom I washed my face and hands, plucked out the splinters with tweezers, brushed my hair and tidied it with two pins. I changed into a new frock and put the dirty, torn one into a bucket in the laundry to soak.

Then I looked at myself in the mirror.

A fine scratch ran alongside my right eye, and another one, short and deep, cuffed the edge of my jaw. Otherwise I looked just like myself.

I went back to my schoolwork.

Later, when Grandmother's key turned in the front door, I was in the kitchen preparing supper.

"Good evening," Grandmother called.

I came out of the kitchen and watched as she hung her coat and hat on the rack.

"Good evening, Grandmother," I replied. "Did you enjoy your day at work?"

Grandmother studied my face. There was a long quiet. She nodded briskly once, as if she was nodding to herself.

CHAPTER 13

AS SOON AS Grandmother left for her job the next day, I put several coins into my pocket.

Then I settled down to do my morning schoolwork. At first, the arithmetic gave me a jolt of excitement. The questions were singing their answers to me!

5×3 is fifteen! Boom! Boom!

$40 - 5$ is thirty-five!

$8 + 2$ is ten! Tra la la!

I couldn't believe it! I was so excited! The Sparks had magically transformed me! I could hear the music of mathematics!

Only, then I got to question 4:

$4/5 \div 2/3$

—and . . .

It sat there.

No trills. No drumbeats. Not so much as a distant hum. Just

$4/5 \div 2/3$

Waiting for me to figure it out.

I realized that the musical mathematics had been my imagination—combined with the fact that the first three questions were pretty easy. From then on, I had to work out the answers myself, the regular way.

At last it was morning teatime. I sprinted into the kitchen to gather my provisions, skidded out to the back garden, and sat down on the top step.

Crunch.

(That was me, biting into the cucumber.)

Nothing happened.

Crunch.

Nothing.

"Come on," I said aloud.

A bird flew into the garden, landed on a branch, and whistled pleasantly.

Of course!

That had happened yesterday! *Now* it would work.

Crunch!

I braced myself for the shove. Here it came . . . here it came! . . . held my breath . . .

Crunch crunch crunch crunch crunch

(That was me, finishing the cucumber in loud and increasingly cranky *crunches.*)

Next, I ate the banana (not a pear today) hoping that its nutritional value might do the trick.

Again, nothing.

Just the garden being its usual quiet and personable self.

Carrie? I whispered.

A long silence.

Then, quite suddenly: *SQUEEEEEEAK!*

I jumped. (Literally—my bottom lifted into the air and fell back down again onto the step.)

Murmur, murmur . . . "Oh, yes, except that we'd need to tear this up and—" "No, I think we could . . ."

Oh.

It was just the two women who live next door. Their sliding door always *squeeeeaks* when they open it. Although I've never met them, their voices sometimes carry over the fence so I've gotten to know them. The one with the low voice who sighs humorously is named Shahlyla. Her parents emigrated here from Pakistan not long before she was born. The excitable one, who laughs loudly, is Helen. She recently moved here from Northern Ireland and is on a permanent residency visa. (I listen closely.)

This morning they were discussing plans to put in a back patio. They could sit out there on summer evenings, they agreed. Ordinarily, I'd have found this very interesting, but today it was indescribably dull.

Carrie? I whispered again, and I squirmed around on the steps, trying to find the right position. Nothing whatsoever happened. Suddenly, without planning to, I was shouting my new friend's name: "CARRIE! CARRIE! *CARRIE?*"

I stopped.

The silence that followed my shouts seemed shocked and astonished.

One of the women next door softly cleared her throat. "Everything all right over there?" a voice called. It was Shahlyla.

"Perfectly, thank you," I replied, as cheerily as I could manage.

This was the first time I'd ever spoken to them. Another short silence and then "You sure now?" Helen asked.

"Perfectly," I repeated, and I stood up and went back inside.

The last thing I heard as I closed the door behind me was Shahlyla saying, "Well, I suppose we could put a barbecue just *there.*"

After that, the day was like a flat pack.

By that, dear reader, I mean it was like the cardboard box that was once delivered to our house from IKEA. It contained Grandmother's new dressing table broken into several pieces along with a plastic bag of bolts and screws and an instruction booklet.

(To be completely clear, my day felt as if it had been broken into pieces and laid out flat.)

I ticked off the items on my schedule, ate my lunch, completed my schoolwork, and sat down at the piano to practice.

The first thing I usually play is the scale of C major. My fingers had just reached the point where the thumb of your right hand slips under, ready to continue, and the middle finger of your left hand reaches over—similar reason—when I felt it again—a great *shove* from behind and I was—

CHAPTER 14

NOT IN A forest, anyway.

I was standing on a pile of rubble beneath a cold white sky, the wind gusting so fiercely that I swayed.

"Steady there," said a voice, and a hand grasped my arm.

It was Mr. Turtelhaze, the man from yesterday.

"Good afternoon, Mr. Turtelhaze," I said. "This is not the forest!"

"It's not," he agreed.

I gave him a stern look but he wasn't paying attention. He was surveying the rubble.

It appeared to be composed of chunks of stone and plaster, red roof tiles, pieces of upturned furniture, and various household items, such as vases and shower curtains. This mess carried on until it met a wall whose window had been shattered and whose top half had been roughly shorn away.

All around was sky.

"This is a building!" I gasped. "A building that has been . . . ruined! It has encountered a catastrophe! A Hurtling! Is Carrie here somewhere? We must save her!"

Mr. Turtelhaze took a step back and the rubble shifted beneath him. He stumbled then regained his balance.

"Carrie is very far from here," he scolded, "in an entirely other kingdom. Put Carrie out of your thoughts. Do you wish to stay?"

I blinked.

"Do I wish to stay?" I repeated, staring at him. I didn't want to be impolite but honestly, there seemed no reason whatsoever to stay. The place struck me as downright dangerous.

Mr. Turtelhaze tilted his chin, indicating that I should look behind me. I turned and was very surprised by what I saw.

A corner of the building was still more or less intact. There was a room with its door ajar. Inside, a four-poster bed, a chest of drawers, a window with its curtains drawn and . . . a boy.

The boy was standing in front of an easel. He was painting.

"Good gracious," I said.

The boy did not appear to have noticed two people talking in the rubble not far from his bedroom door. Still, the wind was very noisy.

"Do you wish to stay?" Mr. Turtelhaze repeated. "For the afternoon?"

The question had a different complexion now. I was curious to find out why a boy would choose to stand in a ruined building and paint.

"Yes, thank you," I replied. "At least, could I stay for a little while and then return home?"

Mr. Turtelhaze nodded. "Five gold coins," he said. "Plus the six you owe me from yesterday. That's eleven altogether."

I scooped coins from my pocket, something niggling at the corner of my mind. "Six from yesterday?" I asked, realizing what it was. "Didn't I only owe you *one*?"

"Six," he repeated firmly. "Eleven coins in total."

I counted the coins out into his hand—my own hand trembled as I did, because I was sure he was wrong—then I watched him pick his way over the rubble to the broken window. Surprisingly, he elbowed out the remaining glass from the shattered window—*Smash! Smash! Tinkle, tinkle*—and climbed through, disappearing.

When I looked back at the boy he hadn't registered the smashing glass either. He was still painting.

I felt perplexed. Yesterday the man had charged me five gold coins to visit the forest and I'd only had four with me. So that meant I owed him *one*, didn't it? Not six. Paying six meant that yesterday had cost me ten coins altogether. *Today*, he'd only charged me five.

Oh well. Rubble should cost less than a forest, really. I gave myself a little shiver, which is what Fiona next door used to advise me to do to "let something go" and began treading carefully across the rubble.

"Hello," I said softly when I reached the boy's door. I didn't want to disturb him in the middle of an important brushstroke.

The boy carried on painting.

"Hello?" I repeated, more loudly.

The boy swung around, paintbrush in the air. "Now where the jeepers did you pop up?" he asked.

CHAPTER 15

HE LOOKED TO be about twelve years old, had fluffy blond hair and was wearing a paint smock. The starched collar of his white shirt sat over this smock and was much more paint splattered than the smock itself.

He should have tucked it under.

"Sorry for interrupting," I said. "I . . . popped up . . . just out there." I indicated the rubble visible through the doorway.

The boy set down his paintbrush and wiped his hands on a rag. "You're not interrupting! Spiffing to see you! Don't keep me in suspense though, how'd you get up here? The stairs are still buried, aren't they? Wasn't the idea to sit tight until the music worked? Manners though! Where have I put mine? Forgive me but I don't recognize you! Town or country?"

There was a lot in that, and most made no sense to me. However, the boy seemed pleased.

I took a deep breath and told the truth. "I was playing the piano," I said, "when there was a kind of *shove*—and here I was. Then Mr. Turtelhaze charged me five gold coins to stay and visit."

The boy's forehead crinkled. He picked up his paintbrush and twirled it between his fingers thoughtfully. Abruptly, his forehead cleared.

"Ah," he said. "In the tree."

"In what tree?"

"The piano in the tree."

At this point I expect my own forehead crinkled.

"My piano is in my living room," I told him.

"Righto," he agreed. "That's where most people keep them.

However, the piano from the rotunda is in a tree and I thought to myself—I puzzled it out, see?—I thought to myself, *I bet she was playing that piano and felt a sort of shove,* only it wasn't a shove, see? It was gravity. Spilling you out of the tree."

A moment passed. "Except I wasn't in a tree," I said.

"Yes, that's the spanner in the works. As for this Mr. Turtelhaze, never heard of the chap. Running around charging gold coins to visit me, is he? Bit of a scandal, that. Visit me whenever you like! No charge! Tell you what, I'll get you those coins back if I spot the fellow. Don't know him from a bar of chocolate, of course, so I'll need a description. Speaking of, would you like some chocolate? I've got a whole basket of Maywish here."

At this point, I must have seemed openly distressed by my confusion because the boy's eyes suddenly widened. "Jeepers!" he said. "I know what this is! Quick! Sit down!"

He leapt from behind his easel and dragged an armchair toward me.

Obediently, I sat down. The chair was very comfortable, being puffily upholstered in a floral material. The room itself was altogether very comfortable, I realized as I looked around. Thick white carpet (a bit paint splattered), big bed awash with needlework cushions, a grand wardrobe with curly feet and fancy handles. That kind of thing. A small table across the room had the same curly feet as the wardrobe. It was covered in colorful paintings, obviously spread out there to dry.

The boy stood before me, tapping his chin with two fingers. This caused little dots of red paint to appear on the chin. I giggled.

"Yes," he said. "Sudden, unexplained giggling. A symptom, for sure. May I see your eyes?"

That felt like a trick question. I pointed. "Right here."

"So they are." He peered into my eyes. This is an odd thing to happen. You find yourself peering back. His eyes were bright blue. "Pupils . . . dilated," he said. "Or possibly not. Can't recall what *dilated* means, to be honest. Or whether they're *meant* to be dilated or not, if you catch my drift. What's your name?"

"Lillian Velvet."

He chuckled, which offended me. "Sorry," he said quickly. "I'm laughing at myself, not your name. Lovely name. It's only that I'm not faring too well, what? As I don't know your name, I can't tell if you've got it right or wrong! You could be the Queen of Neridgien, for all I know!"

"I'm not," I said. "I'm Lillian Velvet."

"Could be," he agreed.

"Not *could*!" I was growing tetchy, but the boy was on to his next question.

"Headache?"

"No."

"Blurred vision?"

I blinked.

"Ah!" He snapped his fingers. "You *do* have blurred vision! I should have started with that one."

I felt sorry to disappoint him. "Actually," I said, "my vision is quite clear. I blinked because I realized something: you think I have a concussion, don't you? I've read about concussions in the newspapers that Grandmother brings home at times. Rugby players are always getting them. I believe it's to do with the way they slam into other players, or slam each other to the ground. I know about rugby league from when I was small. Well, one evening Grandmother had to go out and she sent me to stay with Fiona and her husband, Carl, next door. This was before they moved away. Anyhow, that evening, an important rugby league game was on the television. I believe it was the third game in a competition called the State of Origin. We had pizza and shouted whenever the Blues scored—the Blues were 'our team,' apparently. Although I was very young, it has stayed in my mind, probably because it was the first time I'd ever eaten pizza or been encouraged to shout at a television. I think the players ought to just make a pact to stop *slamming*, to be honest, and I said to Fiona and Carl—"

"Yes, quite," the boy said, nodding along. "Tell me something, do you know what has happened this afternoon to cause . . . all the destruction?"

"A Hurtling?" I guessed.

"A Hurtling! Golly, no. We don't get those around here. Very rare they are, fortunately. Good guess though. All right, final question. Do you know who I am?"

I shook my head.

"I knew it!" he crowed. "You *must* have a concussion! Not only are you saying any number of nonsensical things—*Television? State of Origin?*—you've also got amnesia! *Amnesia* means you've forgotten things. It often happens with concussion, you know. And you *definitely* have amnesia if you've forgotten who I am! I mean to say, I'm Billy! *I'm the prince!*"

At once, his whole face bloomed bright pink and he scratched the back of his neck. "Jeepers, that sounds conceited, doesn't it?" he said. "Sorry."

CHAPTER 16

AFTER THAT, THERE was no convincing the boy—Billy—that I didn't have a concussion. So I gave up and went along with it.

"You must *not* be embarrassed about having forgotten me," Billy instructed. "Promise?"

I found this an easy promise to make, as I'd never laid eyes on him before today.

"Tell me, Lillian, do you remember the name of our kingdom?"

"I don't remember it," I replied patiently, "because I never knew it."

Billy breathed in sharply but kept his face polite.

"It's the Mellifluous Kingdom," he said, "ruled by my mother, Queen Alys." He watched me closely for signs of recognition.

"Queen Alys," I repeated. "That's a pretty name."

"Is it? Yes, I suppose so. She's my mother so I've always just known her, if you see what I mean. She's very nice and pretty *herself*, although maybe I just think that because she's my mother? No, wait, ignore me. Not just me. She's universally known to be kind and beautiful. I hope you get a chance to meet her but she's busy dealing with . . . Ah." He paused, studying me closely. "You've forgotten, haven't you? You'd better sit down," he added.

"I'm already sitting."

"So you are. Try standing and then sitting again?"

I did as he asked. He himself sat on the bed in case it was important for us both to be sitting.

"This afternoon, a huge storm *whooshed* through our kingdom leaving a trail of destruction."

"Oh no!" I exclaimed.

"Oh yes," Billy countered. "I happened to be in my room here painting. I had a box of Maywish—that's the best brand of chocolate; do you know it?"

Again, I shook my head.

"Well, that could be amnesia or you might just not have come across it before. Anyhoo, happy as a tortoise I was, painting my face off."

I raised my eyebrows at that, which Billy took as a challenge. "I *was* painting my face off! See! Look at all the paintings I did!" He rushed over to the table where paintings were drying and began to wave them in my face.

Although I didn't get to look at each for very long, as he only waved each of them once before grabbing another, it was enough to see that the paintings were very good.

"You clearly have *not* painted your face off," I scolded Billy while he carried on flinging papers, "given that you still *have* your face. However—"

I paused. Billy had frozen, his expression surprised and a little hurt. I thought back over what I'd just said.

"Sorry," I said. "My voice sounded sharp then, didn't it? I was going to say that your paintings are *brilliant*!" I stood and stepped over to the table so I could admire them more closely. "Look at this one of a slice of cake. I can *taste* the cake! Its frosting is so creamy and sweet! Look at this one of a crimson rose. I can *smell* this rose, Billy!"

The hurt slid away from Billy's face and he beamed. "Truly? I'm overjoyed! I started painting after my aunt Emma sent me this easel and paint supplies for my birthday—she's an artist, you see. I have *ten* aunts and one uncle, so it's not surprising that one is an artist. You get practically every occupation when you've that many. Anyhow, Aunt Emma told me she *sensed in her bones* that I had talent. I couldn't be sure if she was just being herself though, if you get my drift. Well, to get my drift you'd have to know that Aunt Emma is a very dramatic sort.

Once, when she visited us, I offered her a cup of tea. 'Billy,' she said. 'A cup of tea would be my dearest dream come true. A treasure trove of joy. I love you more than anybody in all the Kingdoms and Empires for offering me a cup of tea.' I mean to say, it was just a cup of tea. But turns out, I do love painting! I lost myself in it today—that's why I was in here while everyone else was outside enjoying the sunshine. It was beautiful weather right before the storm. Do you truly like my paintings? You seem like an honest sort of person."

"Yes, I really think these paintings are excellent, Billy," I replied. "Look at this one of a lovely, fluffy dog! Oh, I can *feel* its soft fur! I want to *hug* this dog!"

Billy's face lit up even more brightly. "I'm especially glad you like that one," he said. "I'm allergic to dogs, you see, so I painted this fellow to be my own pretend dog."

"He *does* feel like a real dog!" I said. "Oh, I wish you weren't allergic and that this dog was your real dog! I can *see* him sitting down on his haunches, tail wagging excitedly, head looking from you to me and back again, waiting to see what we will do."

The blush was back on Billy's face. "I'm awfully glad you're visiting, Lillian," he said. "I hope you'll visit again—oh, I've got entirely offtrack, haven't I? I was telling you about the storm. Let's sit down again. Right, so I was painting my face—I was painting, happy as a tortoise—when I heard a distant wind—*wwwwooooohhh*. Suddenly, rain was *hammering* and . . ." Here, unexpectedly, he began leaping about the room, shouting the following noises:

BOOM! BAM! SMASH! PCHOW! KERRRRRPWIOUCH!
CRASH! PFFFWOARRRR! BOOOOOM!

He sat down again, breathless.

I felt a little breathless myself, just from watching, and also relieved he had stopped. My ears were hurting.

"And that was the storm?" I asked.

"No, that was the housekeeper doing a really good job mopping the floor," Billy replied.

Then he broke into a grin. "No, it was the storm. Scared the jeepers out of me, didn't it? Castle roof had collapsed, what? Nobody but me was on this floor at the time, thank goodness. Most were outside, as I mentioned—most people in the *kingdom* were out of doors. Lots of damage—it's a mess out there. I was able to shout down to my mother in the garden, and we agreed I should sit tight and wait until the music worked. Don't want people wasting time trying to rescue me when they could be gathering instruments. More important than ever today, if you get my drift."

I wove my fingers together. "Actually, I *don't* get your drift, Billy. What do you mean about music and instruments?"

"You've forgotten about the instruments," Billy said, nodding. "Of course. Should have twigged. I think perhaps it's easiest if I *show* you." He stood and walked to the window. "Only just closed the drapes as the sun was in my eyes. Are you ready to see your kingdom, Lillian?"

I nodded, feeling stately. *Are you ready to see your kingdom, Lillian?*

Billy flung open the curtains.

CHAPTER 17

"OH, I WISH it *was* my kingdom!" I cried. "It's so beautiful!"

I was so loud that Billy jumped. At once, I felt my cheeks flare. Grandmother says it's like living with a jack-in-the-box, living with me—the way words suddenly fly out of my mouth, no warning, top volume, scaring her out of her wits.

However, Billy gave me a friendly punch on the shoulder. "Does a world of good to hear you say that, Lillian," he said. "Must be almost worth a knock on the old noggin and a spot of concussion, what? To see the Mellifluous Kingdom as if for the first time? It *is* beautiful, isn't it? Even if it *has* been rather beaten and battered today."

As soon as he said that, I began to see the damage the storm had done. At first, I'd only got a general impression of a town laid out in neat rows of picturesque cottages—parks and gardens between—and beyond that, neat rows of orchards—ponds and lakes between—and beyond that, golden fields of sunflowers, and beyond *those*, gentle hills, lit up silvery pink by the late afternoon light.

Now it was like when you do those spot-the-difference puzzles. At first, you think, *Why, these two pictures are exactly the same!* Then the differences start popping out at you, and they're so obvious it's embarrassing.

Now, in a similar way, I spotted roofs of houses where tiles had been torn away or chimneys toppled. On the streets, there was an overturned carriage here, a smashed window box there. Branches and upturned swing sets were strewn across the gardens and parks. Parts of the orchards looked muddy and bedraggled, as if they had been trampled by zigzagging schoolboy giants. Even the distant sunflower fields struck me as wearily hunched.

"Where are the people?" I wondered. In the town, a man was coaxing a horse to come down from a terraced lawn, and a woman was chasing a flock of sheep along a laneway, but otherwise the streets seemed empty.

"About half of them are in the castle grounds," Billy replied, and he turned the handles, opening the window outward. At once, the noise of a crowd sounded and all I had to do was lean forward to see the grounds of the castle—people everywhere.

Down there, the mess was even more obvious. Muddy puddles and leafy twigs were scattered across the grass and the curving driveway, along with many more unexpected objects. I counted several pairs of trousers, three barrels, purple papers blown around, a boot, a standing lamp (only now it was lying, rather than standing), an unhinged door, a set of wind chimes, a pineapple, and a large plush penguin.

A small child was sailing a paper boat in a puddle, but otherwise, everyone—from elderly folk to tiny children—was scurrying about. As far as I could see, they were busy picking things up, putting them down, and then darting toward other objects. They kept disappearing out of sight, around the sides and backs of the castle, and then reappearing, still doing the same thing. As I watched, a woman shouted, "Here! A bassoon!"

"Excellent," Billy muttered. "That's almost all of them."

The woman crouched, picked up a long wooden object—a bassoon—and shook it free of dirt and mud, before holding it high.

People nearby cheered, and the woman, to my surprise, began to run. She darted between people—most of whom called "Well done!" as she passed—water splashing up beneath her pounding feet, until she reached a raised marble rotunda.

I hadn't noticed this rotunda yet—it was well across the lawn.

In the rotunda, people were setting up chairs and mopping them down, or fiddling with musical instruments. Violins, a cello, saxophones, trumpets, a set of drums—and here came the woman, waving the bassoon, and a cheer rose up.

A voice shouted, "Drago! It's here! The bassoon is here!" and the group parted for a young man to dart forward. Spotting the instrument, he embraced the woman, hugged the bassoon, and then began studying it closely, tilting it this way and that.

"The Mellifluous Kingdom is built on music," Billy explained. "Each evening, as the sun sets, the ancient Mellifluous instruments are played. The music keeps our kingdom in good repair."

If I hadn't met the Sparks yesterday, I might have said, "Well now, Billy, I'm very sorry but that makes no sense." Actually, it did occur to me to say that. However, I stopped myself because if mathematics could become music, then why should not *music* become repairs?

"Obviously, it's more important than *ever* that the instruments are played today," Billy continued. "The music will repair the storm damage. Trouble is, the storm sent the instruments flying from the rotunda and scattered them all over the castle grounds! That's why half the people are here. They're locating and repairing the instruments. Mother made top priorities the rescue of people and animals, and instrum—Oh, there she is! Look!" Billy pushed the window wider and leaned right out.

A tall woman, dressed in a simple knee-length frock and gum boots squinted up at him. "Still okay up there, Billy?" she called.

"Spiffing!" he shouted back.

The woman laughed. This made her face even lovelier than it already was. "You're tremendously brave and patient!" she yelled. "I'm proud of you!" (*He's just painting pictures in a pleasant room,* I thought. *Why be proud of that?*) Billy's mother turned and hurried across the lawn, calling instructions or questions to various people she passed. Her tone seemed measured and kind.

"She *is* beautiful," I said.

"Thanks," Billy replied. "She's worried though. I can tell.

She hides it well but something's up—and I can tell you exactly what it is. See over there?"

He pointed to the sharp right. I had to turn side-on to the window to see. As soon as I saw, I gaped.

There, lodged very high in the branches of a tree, was a piano. A number of people were gathered around the trunk with ropes and other equipment, looking up at the piano, conferring, and looking up again.

"A piano in a tree," I murmured.

"It was *quite* the storm," Billy said. "Pianos don't belong in trees, of course—we already established that—they belong in living rooms. However, *that* piano belongs in the rotunda. Some think they can get it down with ropes and pulleys, others say we should send the pianist up to play it *there,* in the branches, at sunset. Both options are dangerous—piano or pianist could very easily fall from the tree and smash to pieces. Yet sunset will be here very soon!"

I realized something. "You thought *I* was up in the tree playing the piano?" I said. "And somehow fell and landed outside your room?"

Billy nodded. "That was me putting two and two together and getting a bag of cheesy crisps. It was my mind, see? I'd been painting the piano when you arrived." He pointed to the easel. Clipped to it was a perfect depiction of the piano stuck in the tree.

We turned back to watching the tree. Now and then somebody would try clambering up and then would come sliding or crashing back down. Heated discussion would follow.

I looked back at the rotunda. It was already much tidier. Musicians were seated with their instruments and were polishing or tuning them. The people who'd been scurrying about had now gathered around the rotunda watching or were drifting over to the piano-in-the-tree.

"Seems they've recovered all the instruments," Billy muttered. "Spiffing."

"And they need to play at sunset?" I checked. "Which will magically repair the damage to the kingdom?"

He checked a clock on the wall, nodding. "In about five minutes."

"Can't they just skip the piano," I suggested, "and play the other instruments extra loudly? Or postpone playing until tomorrow, once the piano is safely down? I mean to say . . ." I didn't like to offend him or his kingdom, but still. "I mean to say, in *other* places, people get to work and repair things themselves. They roll up their sleeves and use buckets and mops, hammers and nails. They don't wait around for music to do it."

Billy glanced sideways at me. "There's a bit more to it than that, Lillian," he said gently. "Music is the essence of this kingdom, if you catch my drift. Repairs don't . . . well, they don't *take* without the music. As for playing tonight's concert without the piano, that's a cracking idea, and we'd *ordinarily* get away with it, but each Mellifluous instrument has a specialization. When they're played together there's a general polish and shine, but it's the trumpet that keeps the cherry orchards healthy, the violins do the roads, and the piano . . . well, you asked before where all the people are? And I said that half are in the grounds?"

I nodded.

"The other half were injured in the storm," he said gravely. "Many are critical. Do you see that building?"

I looked in the direction he was pointing. Just outside the town, the building was large and squat, and resembled a block of vanilla ice cream with a dollop of chocolate melting all over it.

I blinked. Its roof had caved in.

"That's the hospital," Billy said gravely. "Behind the building, there's a field and that's where the injured people are waiting. Several need urgent surgery. They need to be in the hospital. And that can't happen"—his eyes swung back to the clock—"unless somebody plays that piano in the next few minutes."

CHAPTER 18

THE MUSIC STARTED then.

A single sweet note drifted up from the rotunda—I think it was an oboe. The crowd hushed. The note repeated itself, hesitantly, and then became a melody, soft and thoughtful.

Meanwhile, the sun was setting in soft, thoughtful clouds of pink.

Other instruments joined the oboe—flutes, clarinets, a piccolo—each weaving through the melody, while the pink billowed and grew in the sky.

I checked the tree. The piano was still firmly lodged in its branches. A handful of people remained at the tree's base. Their heads tilted back as they watched a man climb. Ropes had been flung over one of the higher branches, and the man was rigged up in a harness. Grimly, hand over hand, foot after foot, he rose.

At the podium, stringed instruments joined the music, gentle at first, then faster and more rhythmic, the violinists and cellists sawing back and forth like pounding footsteps.

Suddenly, the entire rotunda of instruments burst into life! Trumpets, trombones, tubas! Snare drum, bass drum, tambourine, triangle! Chimes and castanets! The music swelled in a way that made my chest and face catch fire! (That's how it felt.) It was as if an elegant afternoon tea had transformed into a giant parade!

In the midst of all this excitement, I realized that the person perched at the drum kit—drumsticks flying, hair tossed about as she played—was Billy's mother, the queen! I laughed aloud in amazement.

The music drifted from one mood to another, each dissolving into the next—from sweet to ominous, from sorrowful to ferocious—and the sky seemed to do just the same. Pale mauves deepening into searing purples, the pink forming a vibrant orange glow as the sun settled deeper in the distant hills.

"It's working," Billy said.

I was confused for a moment. Then I looked up and over the kingdom. The most extraordinary thing was happening.

In the town, an overturned carriage rocked slowly back and forth on the road, lurched to a standing position, and shook itself down. Broken windows grew new glass. Chimneys leapt up as if from a nap, and tiles slotted into place in all the gaps.

Down below, the puddles were drying up, the grass turning a bright lime green, while the mess of scattered objects flew low and fast just above the surface of the ground, presumably returning to where they belonged. Suddenly:

KER-BANG! CLATTER, CLATTER, CLATTER—

I shrieked. I couldn't help it. That noise was coming from just outside the door!

"It's all right," Billy said, with a reassuring pat on my shoulder. "Just the castle repairing itself."

He was still staring out the window—at the hospital, I realized.

That building remained exactly as it was.

The roof still melted. Windows gaping holes. Front door dangling on hinges.

The music soared in the rotunda, the town and fields were magically repairing—but the hospital drooped in place.

Crack!

Across at the tree, the rope had snapped. The climbing man came tumbling down. People at the base reached and caught him.

Obstinate, the piano sat in the branches.

I glanced at Billy's painting. He had caught that strange *stuckness* in the image. You could *feel* it. That piano was *not* coming down.

The sun was sinking further and further into the hills. The sky was alight with the vibrant reds of a fading sunset.

"Billy," I said.

My eyes were back on his painting. You could *see* the scratches on the piano's clawed foot, you could *feel* the gloss of its keys, *smell* the muskiness of its old wood—but you couldn't hear it.

A strange sensation crept up my throat and became words: "Somebody has to play it," I said.

"Quite," Billy agreed, distractedly.

"Billy, paint somebody playing it."

Billy blinked. He looked at his painting. His face was puzzled and worried, and then he gave a shrug.

"Can't hurt," he said. "Only how can I . . ."

Then he turned and dragged the armchair close to the window. "Sit here," he ordered. "Pretend this chair is your piano stool. Pretend the window ledge is the keyboard. And *play* for me." Rapidly, he squeezed paints out of tubes onto a tray, dipped a brush in water, and hovered, waiting for me to do as he asked.

I placed my fingers on the cool wood of the window ledge, and—I played.

Specifically, I played Mozart's Piano Sonata no. 11 in A Major.

Tap, tap, tap went my fingers on the wood.

Billy, beside me, painted—*flick, flick, flick*—a pause as he studied me—*twitch, twitch*—another pause—*scrape, scrape, splash, slide,* and so on.

As I played, I watched through the window. In the rotunda, the music was slowly fading. In the tree, the piano remained lodged while the people below clambered, fell, clambered, and fell.

The town itself was in glossy repair, its flower boxes neat and blooming, its windows gleaming. Only the hospital sagged.

In the distance, the mountains were lit up gold with the final touch of the sunset.

My fingers still tapping on the window ledge, I glanced quickly sideways. Billy was adding a dab of color here, a shadow there, but there *I* was in the painting now. You could see the concentration on my face, you could feel the tension in my shoulders, you could—

You could hear the piano playing.

Mozart's Piano Sonata no. 11 in A Major.

You could hear *me* playing it! You could hear my rhythm losing its pace (the way it always does at that point), you could hear the bits where I get the notes tangled. I carried on playing, half-watching Billy's painting as I did, and *hearing* the music, truly *hearing* it.

Of course, I knew it was my imagination, yet it was so real!

And then I glanced through the window again.

The musicians in the rotunda were staring up at us. The queen was standing at the drum kit, her hand over her mouth. The crowd that had been facing the orchestra had all turned, and were gazing toward Billy's window. Even the people at the tree were motionless.

Was it *not* my imagination? Was it real?

"Keep playing," Billy whispered, as he added dab after dab of paint. "It's working."

As I played, I took a chance and looked out toward the hospital again.

Still the same.

Still the same—and then the front door climbed back onto its hinges, the window glass snapped into place—*snap, snap, snap*—and the roof gathered itself together, stretching like a waking dog.

CHAPTER 19

AND THEN I was home.

A violent *shove* and I was sitting at my own piano.

This time I felt the disappointment land dully in my stomach. I knew there was no point grabbing coins or crunching cucumber to try to get back to the Mellifluous Kingdom, yet I longed to be there still. I wanted to watch as a stream of patients filed from the field into the freshly repaired hospital, some limping, some leaning on the arms of doctors and nurses, some carried on stretchers—all of them relieved. I wanted to see Billy hold his painting to the window, the paper rustling in the wind, and shout to the crowd: "I painted it and it *played*!"

I wanted to hear the crowd cheer for him!

I wanted to *say goodbye* to Billy!

"It's *rude* not to say goodbye!" I said aloud, swiveling on the piano stool to glare at the jar of gold coins on the table. (In my head, the jar was Mr. Turtelhaze. A squat, glassy little Mr. Turtelhaze.)

Turning back to the piano, I began to play Chopin's Nocturne in C-sharp Minor, as that's the saddest piece I know. I played everything I know that's in a minor key and I was lost in a mournful pianissimo section when a key turned in the door.

I swung around in surprise. "Grandmother!" I said. "You're early!"

She hung her coat and bag on the rack.

"Did your boss allow you a special early—" I began to ask, but I was looking at the clock as I spoke.

It was half past five.

The exact time that Grandmother had arrived the previous day.

"Child," she said, enunciating clearly. "Have you begun supper preparations?"

I scrambled to my feet. "Not yet! I'll do it now! I'm ever so sorry, Grandmother! I got lost in my piano playing! I was *planning* to . . ."

"Hush," Grandmother said, rubbing her temples with her fingertips. "Begin preparations. We must eat soon." She glanced at the clock herself and then, to my utter astonishment, she added: "I'm expecting company tonight."

CHAPTER 20

AFTER SUPPER, GRANDMOTHER baked a cake.

I watched as she stirred the mixture with a wooden spoon. I'd never seen her bake before.

"What sort of cake is it, Grandmother?" I asked. "Shall I guess? Is it chocolate fudge? Is it a rainbow cake? Is it a spiced apple cake? Is it—"

"It's a butter cake," Grandmother replied, spooning the batter into a tin. She placed this tin in the oven, closed the oven door, and turned to me. "Please go and prepare yourself for bed."

"But, Grandmother," I began, and faltered. "Aren't we having company for the first time ever? Shouldn't I—?"

"*We* are not having company," Grandmother said. "*I* am having company." She was frowning distractedly into an open cupboard. "Nor is this the first time I've ever had company." Now she was taking teacups and saucers from the shelf and setting them in a row on the bench top. "On occasion, I have guests for tea. They simply arrive after you have fallen asleep. Tonight is no different. Bath, teeth, and bed, please."

I did as she asked, only far more slowly than usual.

"Are you delaying on purpose?" Grandmother asked, watching through the bathroom door as I slowly squeezed toothpaste onto my toothbrush.

I considered. "Not on purpose," I replied. "I just feel that my body has slowed itself down. I think it's disappointment. May I ask why I'm not allowed to try the cake or meet your guests? I've never had cake before, only read about it. And I rarely meet anybody new."

"Quicken your pace," Grandmother ordered, turning away.

There's never any point asking Grandmother about her decisions. She only ignores me, or grows very angry. I'd been foolish to ask. In bed, I tried to keep my sighs of sadness soft so she wouldn't hear them and shout. I was determined to stay awake, though, until the guests arrived. I lay in the darkness listening to Grandmother dragging the couches around in the living room.

After a while, my eyelids became eager to close. I decided to stare through the window at the streetlight outside as a way of discouraging them. That was a mistake. It only put me in a trance. My eyelids begged for me to let them close. Well, they could have a short break, I decided, closing them. That was an even greater mistake. I fell asleep.

Some time later I woke abruptly to the sound of a burst of laughter.

"*Shhhh,*" said several voices.

I sat up, my heart beating quickly.

Low adult voices sounded from the living room. Clinks of spoons and teacups.

"Absolutely vital that it be moved from this house," a woman's voice said, and then *mumble, murmur, mumble.*

"There are risks either way," another voice offered—-*mumble, murmur, mumble.*

"It *must* be destroyed,"—*mumble, murmur.*

I swung my legs over the side of the bed. How would Grandmother react if I went out to the living room? And said, "Good evening, everyone! I am Lillian"?

She hadn't expressly forbidden this, had she?

Still, it was probably understood.

Here's what I'd do! I'd pretend to be sleepwalking! I'd wander into the living room, gazing about me in a confused, unfocused way.

"Oh, hello," I'd say. "What are you all doing in my bedroom? Good gracious! I'm not *in* my bedroom! Where am I?" Then I'd rub my eyes.

Was I brave enough to do it?

At that moment, I heard a voice say very clearly, “Well, I’m off,” and another said, “Yes. Look at the time.” Chairs scraping. Footsteps headed toward the front door.

Last chance, Lillian.

I hopped off the bed—and there was a giant shove sideways.

CHAPTER 21

I WAS ON a field.

A silver moon shone in a big sky that was scattered with stars and wisps of pale cloud. The air was crisp and I shivered in my pajamas.

Lively music was playing nearby, tambourines clashing. There was a rapid tempo, lots of brass instruments and pounding drums—the kind of music that fills you with excited anticipation. I turned in the direction from which it was coming—and gasped.

It was a circus!

Across the field, an immense tent stood, striped in blue and gold. Its roof was strung with fairy lights that radiated out from the central peak and ran all the way to the ground, as if anchoring the tent there. Alongside were splashes of golden light from little stalls selling doughnuts and toffee apples, popcorn and corn on the cob. People wandered between these stalls, made their purchases, and then disappeared into the tent carrying paper bags. Closer to me, in the darkness, horses nickered and whinnied amidst the deep shadows of caravans and other small structures and enclosures.

"Cold night for it!" said a voice, and Mr. Turtelhaze strode through the darkness toward me. He was dressed smartly this time, in shirt and tie, and seemed to be brushing crumbs from his collar.

"Good evening, Mr. Turtelhaze," I said politely. "Yes, it is chilly! This grass is like ice beneath my bare feet. If I'd known it was going to happen again, I'd have—"

"Do you wish to stay?"

I looked at him carefully. "I have no coins," I said. "I *do* wish

I could stay, of course, although I'm in my pajamas, which means, first, that I'd be cold and embarrassed, and second, that I have no coins with me. Mr. Turtelhaze, I'm afraid I don't understand what is happening. One moment I'm home and the next—*shove!*—I'm somewhere completely different. Then you appear and I pay you gold coins from the jar my grandmother gave me. Perhaps this happens to everyone when they turn ten? I haven't read about it in any of my books, though, and—well, I have no experience with it. I'm bewildered. That's my favorite word for confused. Not that I don't appreciate it, of course—it's been marvelously fun. However, if there is any way you could explain to me what—"

"You can pay me tomorrow," Mr. Turtelhaze said. "Do you wish to stay?"

Oh.

Well, I'd better focus.

I gazed at the lights of the circus only a few minutes' walk away. Perhaps if I jogged there it would warm me up? And if I lurked in the shadows nobody would notice my pajamas? On the other hand, Grandmother was *right* down the hall. What if she happened to check on me?

"Just for a *very, very* short time," I decided. "Yes please."

Mr. Turtelhaze was silent, and I glanced up to check if he had heard, or if perhaps he was fuming, annoyed with my slow decision making—but he had vanished.

I was alone in the field.

Taking a deep breath, I set off across the grass. It crunched slightly beneath my feet, and I realized it was covered in a fine layer of frost, glinting here and there in the moonlight. No wonder it had felt like ice. It *was* ice.

The lights grew stronger, sounds louder, and tent larger as I approached. A thrill swept through me, part excitement, part fear, and for a moment I could hardly breathe.

I slowed down. I had reached that cluster of smaller structures now, and the sound of horses was more marked, mingling with the circus music and the chatter and calls of the stallholders and customers.

A bell was ringing and people were streaming toward the circus tent. Could I get *into* that tent? Watch the circus somehow? I had no money, of course, for a ticket. Perhaps if I crawled under a tent flap?

"Back it up here!" called a voice and I swerved away, hiding in the shadow of a caravan.

A lantern swung into view. It was held aloft by a man striding along, followed by a horse and cart. The man stopped.

"Back up!" the cart driver instructed his horse, and it stopped and began, slowly, to walk backward, causing the cart to roll back behind it. I almost expected to hear the *beep beep beep* that trucks make as they reverse.

As the cart entered the light of the lantern, it became clear that it was stacked high with gravel. It was reversing toward one of the structures—a kind of garage on wheels.

"Halt!" shouted the man with the lantern.

"Halt!" the driver repeated. The horse stopped, twitched, and began munching on tufts of grass.

The cart now stood at the opening of the garage. The driver leapt down, and both he and the man with the lantern studied the load of gravel. They began fiddling with some kind of lever on the side of the cart. Slowly, the cart itself began to rise.

Oh, they are going to tip the gravel into the garage, I realized. It was not a garage but a kind of storage container.

While the men were distracted by their work, I decided I should carry on to the circus. Softly, softly, I crept by them. The horse glanced up at me, chewing noisily. I looked quickly at the men, but they were intent on the cart, raising it higher and higher. Any moment now the gravel would fall thundering through that opening and fill up the space.

It was irresistible; I had to watch. I wanted to hear the explosive clattering that the load would surely make. I stopped. I looked at the opening of the storage container. Back at the cart. Would all that gravel fit in there? It would be a tight squeeze. *Creeeaak,* the cart was almost vertical. The gravel was on the *verge,* the very *precipice* of falling.

A flash of blue caught my eye.

The blue was in the storage container. I could just make it out in the darkness as the lantern light swayed across it. An object was lying on the floor. Whatever it was would be buried by the gravel. I hoped it wasn't important—just some old towels or rags perhaps.

I squinted, trying to see exactly what it was.

The blue was—a jacket of some kind? Was that also a rolled-up trouser cuff? Was that a *little foot*—?

"It's a person," I murmured, in astonishment. "It's a little boy lying on the floor."

The gravel began to topple forward.

I gasped. "Stop!" I cried, but my voice snagged, coming out only as a rasp. I took a deep breath, preparing to *scream* the word and—

Shove.

I was back in my room.

CHAPTER 22

"STOP!" I BELLOWED. "STOP! STOP! THERE'S SOMEBODY *IN* THERE!"

But I was shouting at the walls of my own bedroom. I pounded on my pillow and screamed again. "TAKE ME BACK! TAKE ME BACK! *MR. TURTELHAZE!*"

I screamed and screamed. Vaguely, I was aware of a shuffling in the living room, footsteps, the front door slamming.

I jumped up, ran out to the living room. The jar of gold coins still stood on the table. I grabbed it, twisted off the lid, and poured coins into my hands. Several fell to the floor.

"MR. TURTELHAZE!" I shouted. "*MR. TURTELHAZE!* I NEED TO GO BACK TO THE CIRCUS! IT *WASN'T LONG ENOUGH!* I NEED TO GO BACK *RIGHT NOW!*"

I stamped in fury. My vision rushed with color.

"*MR. TURTELHAZE!*" I absolutely shrieked the name.

"*Child!*" Grandmother was standing in front of me. The echoes of my own screams sounded in my ears.

"Grandmother!" I said. "A little boy! Gravel! Hurry! Hurry!" I forced myself to breathe. "Since you gave me the jar of gold coins, I've been *shoved* into other places," I said. "I just saw a little boy about to get crushed by gravel. And then I was back here! Too late to shout a warning! I need to get back!" I rattled the coins around noisily and called again. "Mr. Turtelhaze! Mr. Turtelhaze!" I was sobbing.

"Child," Grandmother said coldly. "Your shrieking has scared my guests away. Control yourself. Do *not* allow a dream to—"

"No! It was *not* a dream! I promise!"

"Hush at once. Go back to bed. It is late. I am tired."

No matter how much I pleaded—describing the colors of the circus tent, the volume of gravel in the cart—desperate to convince her that I was *not* inventing—Grandmother still insisted I was dreaming and sleepwalking.

"No," I begged. "It's *real.* I was *going* to pretend to sleepwalk so I could meet your guests! Only, I wanted to see a *little* of the circus! I should've stayed longer! And I'm awake now! *This* is not sleepwalking! A little child's in danger!"

"The only child in danger," Grandmother muttered, "is *you.* You are in danger of provoking my wrath. You read too many storybooks and it has befuddled your imagination. The very idea of pretending to sleepwalk so you could meet my guests! How duplicitous! I am ashamed!"

I tried to argue longer, but my voice was fading. Too much time had passed. The gravel would have fallen. It was too late to save the boy.

Eventually she sent me back to my room, where I lay crying, thinking desperately of that child in the blue coat, that enormous load of gravel, and how I'd failed to convince Grandmother—in fact, I'd made her angry yet again; I seemed to do that every other day—until, I suppose, I fell asleep.

PART 3

REPORT 2

THE PALACE, MELLIFLUOUS KINGDOM, KINGDOMS AND EMPIRES
—Tuesday, May 1

* * *

It was late.

Queen Alys was in her study. A tap dripped somewhere. She stood, moved out into the corridor, listened carefully, then entered the guest bathroom. She changed the washer in the tap, tightened the faucet, and returned to her desk.

A week had passed since the great storm. Now, a storm rampaged in Alys's heart.

She blinked, embarrassed by that metaphor. It was not like her to be dramatic. Alys had always been a composed sort of person. When crises arose, calm billowed up from somewhere deep within her, bringing with it clarity of purpose. She also had compassion and humor. (All this made her an excellent queen.)

At the moment, though, calm seemed out of reach. A telegram sat on Alys's desk. It had arrived earlier that evening and was from her eldest sister, Isabelle.

Here is what it said:

They're back. Arriving in Gainsleigh, Friday, May 25. Want to see us all & meet the children. Come to my place, Thursday, 24th, & stay for a week? Inviting everyone.

"Who's back?" Alys had muttered, frowning as she read the telegram. Then the hammering, like driving rain, had started in her heart, and the wind had seemed to howl through her mind, tearing up her thoughts at their roots.

Her parents.

Her parents were coming out of hiding.

Over twenty years ago, she had stood on the docks at Gainsleigh Harbor, along with her sisters and brother, saying farewell. None of them had believed their parents would be gone for long. A month at most, they'd imagined. They'd playacted through funerals, memorials, condolences—and Alys had found it unbearable.

She was a deeply honest person and hated to lie.

For years after that, Alys had been angry with her parents. She knew they had to pretend, for their own and their family's safety, but she'd blamed them for choosing their dangerous work, missed them desperately, worried, and longed for their return. Eventually, time had lifted her in its strong arms and carried her into her own future. She became a professional drummer. With her rock band, she toured the Kingdoms and Empires, fell in love with the Mellifluous Kingdom, applied for and won the position of queen, and welcomed her son, Billy, into the world.

Billy didn't even know he *had* grandparents. He was a lovely, trusting, sunny-natured child, and now she'd have to tell him she had lied to him.

Sighing, Alys reached for her diary and turned to Thursday, May 24. She flicked through the pages, switched some appointments around, and picked up the telephone.

"Yes," she said. "A telegram to Isabelle Mettlestone, Gainsleigh, please. From Queen Alys of the Mellifluous Kingdom. Just this. *Extraordinary.*

Stop. We'll be there. Stop. Got it? Thank you." She hung up and reached for her stationery.

She was going to write a letter to Isabelle and expand on that *Extraordinary.*

Instead, she found herself writing *these* words:

Dear Emma.

Alys put the pen down. Her brow creased.

Emma? Why was she writing to Emma? Emma was one of her youngest sisters, an artist who lived far away on tiny Lantern Island.

Raising her eyebrows, Alys carried on writing anyway.

I suppose you have heard the news about our parents (she wrote). *How are you feeling? I must say, I feel very odd. I feel there is a storm in my*

Ah. That's why she was writing to Emma. Again she stopped, only this time it was to smile to herself. Of all her sisters, Emma was the most likely to understand the storm in Alys's heart. Emma tended to reside in a storm of her own making.

For the next ten minutes, Alys enjoyed dissecting her own emotions, imagining Emma nodding vigorously, and Emma exclaiming, "Yes! Exactly! That! Only worse than that! Much worse!"

Alys grew calmer. She felt herself resuming her position as the sister with composure. Soon, she was able to move on to other topics. She described the *literal* storm that had stunned her kingdom recently, the collapse of the palace roof, her terror about Billy, her relief when it turned out he was safe—although trapped—in his bedroom, the damaged hospital, the scattering of the Mellifluous instruments. She skipped the part where she herself had been outside, hiking, and had come within a whisker's breadth of being hit by a terra-cotta pot. (The wind had knocked it from the balcony of a country inn.) Instead, she told how Billy had painted a picture of a piano and that this had saved the day.

It's all thanks to you (she wrote—giving credit where it was due, another aspect of her character that made her queenly). *You gave Billy the easel and painting supplies for his birthday. I can't thank you enough! I think he has inherited some of your talent too—I believe he's very good. I'd love your opinion? I'll enclose his piano painting for your interest (if Billy doesn't mind). You'll see he has painted a girl playing the piano: she is apparently a local but I don't recognize her.*

Alys was growing tired. She tapped the pen against her head and wrote:

Listen, what do you think I should do? Ever since the storm, Billy has been begging me to get him a dog! I suppose it's a reaction to the trauma—he really is lucky to be alive. He's allergic to dogs, of course, but he's got it into his head that he's suddenly "over" the allergy. I guess that's possible—remember how Claire was allergic to peanuts and grew out of it?—but if I get him a dog, and he starts sneezing and wheezing, he'll be heartbroken! Also, it wouldn't be fair to a dog, to bring it into our home and then

She stopped. She knew exactly what to do about the dog situation, and did not need Emma's advice. She would simply take Billy into town and let him play in the park with some of the local dogs. It would quickly become clear whether he was still allergic or not.

"Ah, never mind," she wrote, before adding a few lines in which she asked about Emma's art and her life on Lantern Island, and then, almost asleep now, she told Emma how much she looked forward to seeing her, and the rest of the family, in Gainsleigh, on the twenty-fourth of May, for a week together.

The return of our parents must be bringing up a lot of complicated emotions for you, Emma. I hope you are all right. Please let me know if I can help.

Much love,

Alys. Xoxo

She sealed the letter into an envelope, addressed it, and placed it in her out tray. There was a stack of work in her in tray, including letters from some of her other sisters—written before this news of her parents' return—but she would answer those tomorrow. As she reached to switch off the desk lamp, she felt perfectly serene.

Her hand froze.

Rushes of heat and cold plunged from her scalp to her toes.

Just as quickly, the moment ended.

She forced herself to breathe deeply and sat back in her chair.

"What was *that?"* she asked herself. "Am I still distressed about this news of my parents?"

The answer came quickly: *No, it's more than that.*

Her instincts were trying to tell her something. Something had snagged her subconscious just as she reached to switch off the lamp.

For a long time, she sat and stared into space, thinking. Nothing came to her. She stood up and went to bed.

* * *

The next evening, Queen Alys returned to her study.

She sat down, switched on her lamp, and studied it.

It was an ordinary lamp—well, a stylish lamp, with an elegant shade. Tentatively, she held her hand toward it, as she had the night before. Her skin became luminous pink in the light. Again, she froze. This time the rushes of heat and cold were more subdued, allowing her to consider. She stared at her hand for a long moment.

And she knew what it was.

That strange pink glow. It was similar to the glow that had preceded the great storm. She'd been pulling on her boots, about to go for a hike, and she'd sensed the change in the light. She'd looked out the palace window and seen a sudden rush of clouds before the sunlight returned.

There was something in that moment. The faintest flicker—

She reached for her telephone.

"Yes," she said into the receiver. "Telegram to the Association of Spellbinders, please. From Queen Alys of the Mellifluous Kingdom." A pause and she continued. *Recent storm in Mellifluous Kingdom was NOT a storm. Stop. Repeat NOT a storm. Stop. Request investigation. Stop. URGENT.*

Another pause. "Can you read it back to me? Yes, exactly. Yes, I do want the repetition of *not a storm,* thank you. Please put the words *not* and *urgent* in capitals. And that will go out at once? Thank you. Yes, that will be—"

She hesitated.

Her eye had caught the stack of correspondence from her sisters on her desk. All the letters had been newsy, but now that she considered it, had they all also referred to a storm of some kind? Her mind ran back over their words. Her sister Claire had written about being almost swept off the road by gale-force winds. Franny had mentioned a typhoon that caused her barn roof to collapse. Sue had described taking shelter in a barrel when a "peculiar storm" hit their family orange orchard.

Once again, Alys's heart began thudding as quickly as rain.

"No, wait, please, that's not all," she said in a rush. "I want telegrams sent to *all* my ten sisters and my brother. You have their details, yes? Are you ready?" In her panic, she pressed her mouth closer to the phone. "Are you ready?" she repeated. This was not like her. She forced her breathing to slow. "Yes. It must say this. All caps. *BEWARE. Shadow Magic storms may be targeting Mettlestones. Seek shelter. Seek Spellbinder protection URGENTLY.*"

She tapped her fingernails rapidly, waiting as the telegram operator read it back.

"Exactly. Thank you so much. You'll send those immediately?"

She replaced the receiver.

For a while, she sat back in her chair, allowing the quiet of the palace to calm her. She had done what she could. For now, that would have to suffice.

She turned to her in tray and began working through palace administration.

Half an hour passed. She stopped and rubbed her shoulder. The telephone rang.

"Late," she murmured, and answered.

"Your Majesty," said a voice. "It's me from the Mellifluous Telegram Office again. We spoke half an hour ago and you asked me to send two telegrams for you—one to the Spellbinders, and one to multiple recipients?"

"All my siblings, yes."

"Well, there's a problem."

Alys tensed, clutching the receiver. "A problem?"

"They simply won't go through! None of them! I'll keep trying, of course, but I thought you ought to know they'd been delayed. It's the strangest thing—never happened before! Oh, hold on, there's somebody here. That's odd! Hello?"

Abruptly the call was cut off.

Alys frowned. Something was very wrong.

Footsteps sounded in the corridor. *Oh good,* she thought. It must be her night guard, doing the rounds.

"Harry," she called, rising from her seat. "Could you arrange for someone to check on the Telegram Office at once? I'm worried about—Oh!"

The figure in her study doorway was not Harry.

"Who are you?" she asked, bewildered.

* * *

The following morning, Queen Alys was not at breakfast.

PART

4

CHAPTER 23

SATURDAY IS CHORE day in my home.

I woke up feeling as bedraggled as a wrung-out old rag. You could have used *me* to do the housecleaning.

Maybe the boy woke up and cried out in time, I told myself. *Or somebody saw him and stopped the gravel falling.*

In my heart, though, I feared that hadn't happened.

At breakfast, Grandmother read the newspaper, not mentioning the night before. Ordinarily, I might have chatted, but I ate my toast in silence. Then Grandmother and I put on our aprons and rubber gloves and set to work.

My first job is always the mirrors. Usually, I love cleaning mirrors. You spray them with Windex and then you wipe them with paper towel and all the streaks and smears disappear! The mirror glass jumps out at you, so crisp and clear, as if beaming with delight to be clean. (It's much better than doing our baseboards. These are chipped, with peeling paint. You never quite feel you've achieved anything.)

Today, though, when my reflection jumped back from the hallway mirror, I saw my own pale face looking miserable. Scratches still there from when Carrie and I freed the Sparks. Dark, puffy shadows under my eyes.

From the living room came the *squeak* and *slosh* as Grandmother mopped the floor.

I reached up to polish a smear on the glass and—

CHAPTER 24

SHOVE.

My first thought was *Gosh, I'm going to need a lot more Windex.*

This was because, immediately after the *shove*, my reflection became very blurred.

It was not the mirror in the hallway though: it was a lake.

I was standing on the shore of a huge lake and a breeze had just sent ripples across my reflection. As I watched, the lake settled into glassy stillness and there I was, crisply reflected in the blue, surrounded by grand pine trees. I swiveled on the spot, my feet pressing into earth and twigs. Here and there, tucked between the trees, were log cabins with gardens and porches. Beach towels hung over the porch railings. To my left, a jetty jutted out into the water. To my right, the lake curved around into a cove hidden by trees. Sounds of laughter and splashing carried back to me from the cove.

The sun was warm on my shoulders.

"Morning," said a gruff voice, and there was Mr. Turtelhaze. He was wearing a dressing gown and slippers, and he stood alongside me, squinting at the water. "Wish to stay?" he inquired.

"Oh yes," I began, "only—"

Mr. Turtelhaze sighed. "Only you don't have any coins?"

I shook my head. "Well, no I don't. But I was going ask about the child. Did they stop in time? Please tell me he wasn't crushed by the gravel. I feel *terrible*. I made a dreadful mistake asking if I could stay for only a very short time and now I wish—"

"Would you say," Mr. Turtelhaze interrupted, sounding tetchy, "that you generally *do* wish to stay when this happens to you?"

"This? The shove, you mean?"

"Whatever you want to call it."

I hesitated. So far, I'd been shoved into a forest, the rubble of a castle, a circus and now a lakeshore. The only time I'd regretted my choice was the previous night, when I'd regretted *not* staying for long enough. On the other hand, what if I found myself shoved *into* a lake, rather than onto a lakeshore?

Or into a volcano?

"Let's say the next *five* times it happens," Mr. Turtelhaze suggested, "would you wish to stay?"

Ah well, if I were shoved into a volcano, I'd be done for by the time Mr. Turtelhaze turned up in his dressing gown anyway.

"Yes please," I decided. "For this, and the next five times I get shoved, I wish to stay for a little while and then return."

"Righto." He nodded. "I'll keep an account. You can pay what you owe when I see you next—after this and the next five trips."

Here, I grew worried. "I don't know how many gold coins are left in the jar," I admitted. "I haven't counted them. So I can't be certain I'll have enough, considering"—I wanted to be polite yet honest—"considering the cost seems to *vary*. I'd feel dreadful if I ran out of coins too soon."

Unexpectedly Mr. Turtelhaze smiled. It was a strange, secretive sort of smile. "No need," he said, and then he was gone.

I was alone in a picturesque setting. The scent of fresh pine needles filled the air; murmurs and laughter drifted on the breeze from around the cove; the soft plashing of the lake at my feet seemed to be making shy contributions to the conversation.

"Hello there!" called a voice.

I turned around. The voice was that of an elderly woman. It seemed to have come from the log cabin directly behind me, only I could see nobody about. Two rowboats stood upright on the porch of that cabin, one leaning against the wall, the other against the front door.

"Hello? Could you come here please?"

I looked to the side of the house, to its roof, along the—Ah, there she was. A window was slightly ajar, and I could just make out the shape of a woman behind the glass. She was crouched down, her head side-on so that she could call through the gap.

I ran up the path to the house, admiring the garden—a profusion of daffodils, tulips, crocuses, and peonies!—as I passed.

The woman had white hair that was pulled softly back from her face into a ponytail and held by a ribbon. As I stepped closer, her face broke into a delighted smile.

"Oh!" she said. "I'm awfully sorry, I thought you were one of the grandchildren!" She giggled in an infectious way. I caught it and giggled back. "You're staying in one of the cabins around the lake, are you?" she continued, and then before I'd answered, "May I ask a favor? I seem to be stuck! We've been renovating, you see, and the equipment has blocked off the back door. The windows were painted recently and they're jammed shut—I only just managed to get this one up *a little*—so I can't climb out the window. And my grandchildren have accidentally leaned a boat against the front door! It's wedged into the doorframe so I can't move the door no matter how I try. Could you drag the boat aside so I can get out? I've been baking bread but now I'd like to swim around the lake to join the others. Spend some time playing in the water with the children."

I stared, baffled. The grandchildren had locked her in the house yet she seemed so *sunny*. She wanted to *play* with those children! This woman was a mystery.

"Of course!" I told her, gathering my wits and moving toward the porch. "And no, I'm not staying in a cabin. I've just arrived. Or *appeared*, really, if I'm honest, and this will sound odd, but I might disappear suddenly at any moment. So I'll shift this boat straightaway before—"

"*Lillian?*"

My arms were already stretched around the rowboat, hands gripping the sides, and I had steadied my legs ready to begin dragging when the elderly woman spoke my name. The way she said it—*Lillian?*—reminded me of a three-note chord played on the piano—one of the notes, high and sharp, another low and dramatic, and the third sort of in the middle.

I turned to stare at the face in the window. "You know my name?"

"Stay there," she said quickly. "Don't move the boat yet. Stay exactly where you are—no, come back here to the window actually, and wait."

She disappeared into the dim light of the cottage—I could hear her footsteps hurrying, and the sounds of her scuffling around in there. I really did want to move the boat, before I was whisked away, but I obeyed her. It made me agitated though.

There was a quiet during which the woman called, "Are you still there, Lillian? Just a moment! Please!"

"Still here!" I replied. Ordinarily I might have carried on chattering, explaining how I couldn't promise that I *would* stay, and about how fresh and warm the air was here, and how fragrant the garden, and also to wonder about how she'd known my name—had she overheard my conversation with Mr. Turtelhaze? But had Mr. Turtelhaze spoken my name? I didn't think he had, actually. Did she *know* Mr. Turtelhaze?

That sort of thing.

However, there was something so serious and urgent in her tone that I stayed quiet, looking out over the lake. In the distance, a bird swooped, skimmed along the surface of the lake, and flew high into the sky again.

"Here," said the woman's voice, a little breathless. She was back at the window, crouching again. She pushed an envelope through the gap.

"Will you keep this in your pocket?" she asked. "And if you ever meet a girl named Bronte Mettlestone, will you please give it to her?" She froze suddenly, still holding the envelope. "*Have* you met a girl named Bronte Mettlestone?"

I considered the question.

"I cannot say for certain," I said. "I know I've met a girl named *Carrie* Mettlestone. I liked her very much! And two years ago, when I was eight, I recall meeting two girls at the corner store when I went to buy milk. Now, those girls did not tell me their names. One of them could easily have been named Bronte Mettlestone. I simply do not know. I remember they asked what *my* name was, and that would have been the—"

"It's all right." The woman was smiling again. "Here, take this envelope and always keep it in your pocket? Promise?"

I promised.

"Thank you," she said, and she sighed a deep sigh of relief. "Now, if you wouldn't mind shifting the boat for me, I'll come out and say hello properly! If you like, I could lend you one of the girls' bathing suits and we could swim around to the others?"

I jumped up and ran to the porch, chattering now as I did. (She seemed more relaxed and the air less suspense-filled, so it was as if I'd been set free to be myself again.) "I've never swum in a lake! When I was small, and Fiona next door used to look after me, she took me to a local swimming pool once and taught me to swim! She said I was a fish! Because I was so happy to be in the water. So I believe I *can* swim. You know though . . ." I paused in my pushing and dragging of the boat. I was taking care not to scratch any paint. "You know, though, what if I get shoved home and I'm in the bathing suit? I don't know how to get *back* here, you see, and that would be like I'd stolen it! Not to mention, I wouldn't have my own clothes with me, I suppose. They'd still be here. So I wouldn't have your envelope in my pocket! How *do* you know my name anyway? And may I ask who this Bronte Mettlestone is? Is she related to my friend Carrie? How will I recognize her? There, I've done it now. The door is clear. Of course, Grandmother might be—"

Shove.

I was home again.

CHAPTER 25

I'D BEEN GOING to say that Grandmother might be cross if I turned up in somebody else's bathing suit, dripping lake water and with my own clothes missing—even if they were only my housecleaning clothes.

Instead, I was gazing at myself in the hallway mirror.

"*That* wasn't very long, Mr. Turtelhaze," I muttered to myself. I felt a little mutinous. These adventures were interesting, but they did not have the depth or breadth of the adventures in my storybooks. They were costing me who knew how many gold coins from the pickle jar, but really they were cut-price adventures. First-chapter adventures. The sorts of adventures you can't get your teeth into.

During lessons, Grandmother once taught me about the Greek myth of Tantalus. Having behaved wickedly in some way—Grandmother was vague about how exactly—Tantalus was punished by having to stand in a pool of water directly beneath a fruit tree. That sounds pleasant enough, except that Tantalus was very thirsty and he could never *quite* reach the water (even though he was standing in it), and very hungry yet he could never *quite* reach the fruit.

The story of Tantalus is where the word *tantalizing* comes from. It means getting a glimpse of something precious before it's whisked away from you.

This is how I felt about Carrie in her forest and Billy in his castle—and now the kind old woman in the cabin. They were tantalizing glimpses. If this were one of my books, I'd have set off on a lengthy, complicated adventure with my new friends by now. Probably we'd have eaten bread and cheese while trekking through countryside, and we'd have stayed in a roadside inn with mice in the rafters, squabbled over some little thing, vowed eternal friendship, and I don't know—it depends on the storybook. Slayed a dragon. Solved an ancient riddle. Found a lost city of cats. *Something more* anyway.

As for the boy at the circus who was about to get buried by gravel, well! In a *storybook*, the hero would have saved the child! The hero would have shouted, "Ho! Desist at once!" (*desist* means "stop") to the men with the cart. Or the hero would have zoomed forward and scooped the boy up *just* before the gravel fell.

Perhaps I was not the hero?

Perhaps I was just a passerby in somebody else's storybook?

That idea made me feel better about the boy—surely the hero would have saved him after I'd "passed by'—yet it also depressed me.

"I *want* to be the hero," I murmured.

"What are you babbling about, child?" my grandmother's voice called from the kitchen. "Which chore are you up to?" Her footsteps sounded in the hallway and then stopped. "Why are you dillydallying over that mirror? It is time to commence the laundry. Surely you know we need noon sunlight to dry the clothes?"

"Grandmother," I said bravely. "I apologize. I was just now *shoved* sideways into a lakeside location, where a friendly—"

"Child," Grandmother said. Her voice was like the low growl of a lion, warning other creatures to stay away from its lair.

"Yes, Grandmother," I said. "I'll do the laundry at once."

While Grandmother polished the silver, I took the envelope that the woman had given me and put it in my dresser drawer, to keep it safe while I cleaned. Then I carried the hamper into the laundry room, sorted the clothes into whites and colors, tipped the whites into the machine, turned on the taps, added the detergent, selected the water level and temperature, and pressed START.

I watched for a moment, as the machine started itself up in its usual self-important way, sloshing and frothing, and—

CHAPTER 26

SHOVE.

For a splinter of a moment, I felt both happy and ashamed.

Happy because I was standing up to my knees in water. I must be back at the lake! A second chance to spend time with the kind lady and perhaps go swimming with her family!

Ashamed, because I'd just been feeling grumpy about never getting second chances, and here I was—getting one.

Almost at once, though, I saw that I was *not* back at the lake. This was *not* a second chance.

In fact, I was standing in the *ocean.*

The ocean!

Sea spray splattering, the powerful smell of salt and seaweed, white water frothing and sloshing around my knees—and now I was awash with excitement!

I *had* seen the ocean before, by the way. Fiona next door used to take me to Tilbury Cove sometimes, back when she took care of me. There I had paddled by the shore, or collected sea grapes and interesting stones. Tilbury Cove is sheltered, though, with gentle waves—the sort that stroll toward the sand at a leisurely pace and say: *Hello there, sand—plash,* before politely sliding away.

Once, when I was even smaller—perhaps only two or three—Grandmother took me to Seven Mile Beach, which is a twenty-minute drive from Bomaderry. I can only remember that day in flashes. A wintry sky. Grandmother in an overcoat. The roar of the ocean and the *SMASH!* of waves. Grandmother instructing me to sit over there and dig in the sand, please. The cold grittiness of sand in my fingernails. Watching Grandmother far across the beach from me, speaking to a man in a woolen hat. Their faces were very serious. Their coats blew about in the wind.

That was all I recalled.

Anyhow, here I was today, standing in frothy white water. Currents tore around my legs, and I pushed my toes into the sand to keep my balance. Behind me, toward the shore, a mess of rocks was set against a steep cliff wall. In front of me, the frothiness stretched out to where truly *huge* waves crashed and smashed, creating a haze that hid the horizon.

This was exhilarating! Wonderful!

Dangerous, also, I supposed. I began to wade toward the rocky shore, keeping an eye out for Mr. Turtelhaze. I would tell him I definitely wanted to stay, I decided, even though I had no coins with—

Wait. Mr. Turtelhaze would not be here. I'd already agreed that I wished to stay for my next five visits.

Well. I'd be all right. I just had to get to those rocks.

I was *dragging* myself through the water now, and it somehow felt as if I was dragging myself through noise. A rough ocean makes such a racket! It's like a constant hissing, but with a crackling behind it. Like a giant box of breakfast cereal being poured into a huge bowl: the wax paper rustles, the angle of the box is adjusted so that the cereal pours faster and louder, then back to a steady pouring, then a rush again. And so on.

Drag, drag, wade, wade.

This is exhilarating! I reminded myself.

Still, if Mr. Turtelhaze were here I might have asked him to direct me to the safest place, please. It's true that I was drawing closer to the shore, but now I could see that waves were pounding against the cliff, and water was pouring into inlets and caves. The shore was not much of a . . . *shore*.

Never mind, I'll climb onto a rock, I told myself. *That one there.*

My chosen rock was tall with a good flat surface on its top.

I could sit up there and watch the sea. I kept my eyes fixed on it. *Wade, wade, drag, drag.*

CRASH! A wave leapt high, smashed down hard, and my chosen rock disappeared beneath a whirl of white.

Well, I'd choose another rock.

Wade, wade, drag, drag.

An object brushed against my bare leg, and I jumped.

It's all right. It's just seaweed.

Another object rushed by me on the surface of the water—that wasn't seaweed. It was a wicker basket! It bobbed side to side as it skimmed along.

Wade, wade, drag, drag.

Something else hit my knee hard. *Ouch, what is that!* I swerved and let the object pass me, bobbing to the surface as it did.

It was a long wooden handle with a spiked metallic end . . . Good gracious, it was a rake! A gardening rake! What was that doing in the ocean?

Wade, wade, drag, drag.

Now flowers floated on the surface. Some nudged by me, some caught around my legs for a moment and then rushed away on the current. More and more skimmed by, scattered across the water, dipping under, twirling around—huge blue flowers, they were, like paper lanterns or scarves, or like hats drooping from hooks.

This is exhilarating, I told myself doubtfully.

Only, why were all these objects being tossed about on the sea? Baskets, rakes, flowers—here came another wicker basket! Oh, there went a *chair.* An iron chair. Tumbling by me.

That wasn't normal, was it? Had there been some kind of a . . . flood? Had the ocean taken a mouthful of the shore?

Crash! Crash! the waves shouted excitedly.

"Yes, all right," I shouted back. "Well done, waves."

It seemed to me that the water was getting *higher* the closer I got to the shore, rather than lower.

I looked down. The water was about waist level.

I felt my forehead crinkling.

This was, by no means, exhilarating.

I hunched like somebody fighting through a gale-force wind. Water splashed at my bare arms and *thwacked* against my shoulder blades.

"Mr. Turtelhaze!" I called. "I changed my mind! I *don't* want to stay!"

The waves foamed and frothed. My eyes stung with salt; *splat, splat,* the water dashed against my face. I opened my mouth in surprise and swallowed a gulp of sharp salt water. The sea was almost at my shoulders!

I blinked hard trying to see a likely rock to climb.

That big one was a bright green color—covered in slimy algae. I'd never be able to get a grip.

A cave was set into the cliff face beyond the rocks. If I could just reach that. Only, it seemed to be blocked by—

I squinted. What was that?

It was a dark brown object with evenly spaced slats—a garden gate! A gate was wedged up against the narrow opening of that cave. The water was jostling it about a little, I thought—

No.

It wasn't the water.

There was a figure behind the gate. A person was in that cave. A *person* was jostling the gate around—trying to escape.

CHAPTER 27

ALL THAT MATTERED now was freeing the trapped person before I was shoved home.

Not again. That would not happen again.

I plunged into the ocean and *swam* toward the rocks, my clothes immediately dragging me back, like reluctant companions. Objects swarmed around me—another wicker basket even thwacked into my face, bruising my lip—but I drove through it all.

Impossibly, I reached the rocks. I waded between them in neck-high water—jutted my elbows out, fixed my eyes on the cave, and dug in one foot after the other.

I scrambled over some rocks and sidled between others. The soles of my feet hit sharp pebbles and slid on slimy surfaces, causing me to trip and splash into the water.

At last, I reached the water below the cave, which was set up in the cliff wall. But a jumble of rocks formed a kind of hillock, and I was able to clamber onto them.

Here, it was much quieter. I paused, gasping for breath, a sharp freshness in my lungs, cold ocean wind against my wet skin.

Then I crawled along the last few rocks to the gate.

In the darkness behind it I could just make out the figure. A bearded man. Both of his hands were on the gate, jostling it. He hadn't noticed me.

"Good morning," I said.

The man sprang up so fast he hit his head.

"I'm sorry to startle you," I said. "I saw you from down in the sea, and feared you were trapped."

Rubbing his head, the man squinted through the slats in the gate. "That's all right," he said faintly.

"The water is rising quickly! We should hurry before it gets this high. Here now . . ." I was studying the gate. "If you push it to the left *there,* and at the same time, I lift it up *here,* I think we can do it."

"All right," the man agreed, and we jostled, lifted, huffed, and gasped until the gate sprang free. I prized it out and lay it on the flat rock beside me.

The bearded man crawled out, got to his feet, and smiled warmly at me. "Thank you," he said.

"A pleasure," I replied. "I spotted you from the water. I'm sorry it took me a while to get here—the waves are rough and the current strong. And the sea is full of objects! Baskets, flowers, rakes—well, just one rake—but a chair! And so many flowers! Large, blue flowers! They're lovely, but I've never seen anything like them in my own neighborhood. Perhaps they are common around here—I do not know where I am, you see."

The man was peering down at the wild ocean now, his hands in his coat pockets. "This is the Kingdom of Kate-Bazaar," he said, absentmindedly. He turned back to me, focusing. "And, yes, the flowers *are* common here. They're called blue elouisas—there are fields of them on the cliffs, and the Faery children use wicker baskets to collect them. A tidal wave has just now swept many baskets away—along with other objects, including the garden gate that was wedged in the opening of the cave. I believe the Faeries saw it coming and got to higher ground."

"A tidal wave!" I cried. (In my head I added: "*Faeries!*")

"Or anyway, it is believed to be a tidal wave," the man said, rather cryptically. "The ocean remains very unsettled."

"It does seem unsettled," I agreed.

He looked at me curiously. "You're cold," he decided—it was true that I was shivering. He took off his coat—a tweed jacket—and placed it around my shoulders. "It was very kind of you to help," he said slowly. "But you ought not to have broken the rule."

My chin swung up in surprise. "Rule? You mean my grandmother's rule? Do you know Grandmother? I must say, I never *purposely* break—"

But he was shaking his head. "I don't know your grandmother," he said, "or her rules. I mean the rule of travel in time. You are clearly of another time—I can see time scribbled all over you. Did the Genie who assisted your travel not explain the rule?"

As he spoke, many different thoughts came bobbing to the surface of my mind. Perhaps they'd been there all along, swimming around, and the man's words were like a current nudging them up for me to see.

Of course!

The coins, the wishes-to-stay, his sudden appearances—Mr. Turtelhaze must be a Genie! I'd read about Genies in my storybooks, only I'd never known before that they were real. Also, the Genies in my storybooks behaved somewhat differently to Mr. Turtelhaze.

Wishes, though: those were the gist of what Genies did.

I smiled, understanding at last.

For my tenth birthday, Grandmother had given me a pickle jar filled with Genie wishes.

I was so lost in this happy thought that it took me a moment to recall that a bearded man was standing right beside me. "The Genie never told me any rules," I said. "He never tells me much of anything, to be honest. Are there rules?"

Here, the man's face became grave. "He ought to have told you," he said. "Come, let us sit here on the rocks and I will explain. Do not reveal your Genie's name to me, or I will be obliged to report him. I do not like to report other Genies—not least because there's too much paperwork." He chuckled wryly.

"All right," I agreed, sitting beside him.

He was wearing a thin shirt and the wind tugged at it. "Would you like your jacket back?" I asked. To my relief, he shook his head.

"When you travel in time," he began, and then he paused. "May I know your name?"

"Lillian."

"Thank you. I am Reuben. When you travel in time, Lillian, you must never alter the inevitable. By that, I mean don't change things that would *not* have changed but for your actions. Do you see what I mean? Let's say you arrive in another time and a carriage is speeding along a track. The track runs along the edge of a cliff. You see the carriage. You see that another carriage has become bogged in the mud, just around a bend. Disaster is inevitable—the horses will rear up in alarm when they reach the bogged carriage, or they'll attempt to swerve around it. Either way the carriage will crash. Perhaps even plummet off the cliff? It's very difficult, but you must not shout a warning. You may only stand and observe."

"Why is the track so close to the cliff's edge?" I asked.

"That's not the point. The point is, you cannot help. You could do untold damage to the time line otherwise—upset the universe; tip the very sky into the land, or vice versa. If you see somebody in trouble, I'm afraid you must leave them to the trouble."

I considered all this.

I sat beside Reuben, pretending to be calm, but my heart was going *pitter-patter, pitter-patter* like an upturned can of pebbles.

For one thing, I had not known that I was "traveling in time" when I was shoved. I'd only known I was going to a different place—you could hardly miss that—but how could I have known it was also a different time?

For another thing, I'd been doing a lot more than just "observing." I'd helped Carrie set the Sparks free. I'd helped Billy play piano music that repaired a hospital. I'd moved a boat to release a friendly woman from a cottage by a lake.

The only thing I *hadn't* done was rescue the boy about to be buried by gravel, and, well—

"I'm afraid that's not possible," I told Reuben. "Thank you for telling me the rule, but if I ever *could* break it, I *would*. Certainly, if I saw a carriage about to crash? And I could warn the driver in time? I would do so."

Reuben pressed his palm to his forehead. He seemed distressed. "Lillian," he said, his voice low and gravelly.

"Are you suggesting I should have left *you* trapped behind that gate?" I demanded, suddenly angry. "The ocean is rising! You could have *drowned* in there! Are you honestly suggesting I could be so cruel as all that?"

"I'm afraid—" Reuben began, but I hadn't finished.

"Why don't you get back *into* the cave then!" I spat at him. I grabbed ahold of the gate and swung it up in front of him. My voice lashed at the air: "Get back into the cave and I'll trap you in there again! Go on! Get in with you, *man*! If you're so sure that the *sky* is going to *tip* into the land, if . . ."

At this point, I felt a large hand resting gently on my head. I was silenced. There was something strangely and instantly calming about the warmth of Reuben's hand on my wet hair. I still trembled, and there were still angry tears in my eyes, but my heart rate slowed and slowed.

"Lillian," Reuben said, speaking very softly and sadly. "Who speaks to you in this way?" He paused and then continued: "And how does it make you feel when they speak to you this way?"

I stared at him, very surprised by his words. He gave a little shiver as if he'd just walked through a spider's web and was shaking himself free. Then he began again, in a slightly different tone: "I understand your anger," he said. "You're a good person. You can't imagine *not* helping somebody in trouble. However, dear child, if you are unable to follow this time-travel rule, you must not travel. Upon your return, tell your Genie this. Tell him you're too good a person for travel in time. Don't worry about having helped me just now—I am Reuben, and outside time and space. You, however, should never time-travel again. Do you understand?"

He raised his hand and pointed to some rocks. "See that gap?" he said. "Climb through and you'll see a ledge. From there a track will take you safely to the top. There's nobody around—they're all sheltering, so you should be able to stay out of trouble until your return. On the remote chance that you *do* encounter a person who requires help? *Please* do not help anybody. No matter how much danger they are in—in fact, the more danger, the more harm you could do. Thousands, even millions of people, could be injured or even killed. Do you see? Resist temptation. Turn your gaze away. Can you promise me that?"

I looked at Reuben's face. His eyes were filled with sorrow, and I felt the sorrow deep in my heart.

I nodded. "I promise."

Reuben gazed at me a moment longer and then, suddenly, he was gone.

CHAPTER 28

MY HEART WAS thrumming.

This is why I didn't immediately climb to the top of the cliff, as Reuben had instructed. Instead, I sat on the rock to think.

Here's why my heart was thrumming.

If these visits were time travel, it meant perhaps I could go *back* to that little boy in the circus. Back to the time before the gravel fell on him. It *wasn't* too late. This time I could save him.

I just needed to ask Mr. Turtelhaze. Not ask. *Demand.* I'd pay as many gold coins as it took. I'd use the whole jar.

"Mr. Turtelhaze?" I called, looking around.

I knew that wouldn't work. I'd just have to wait until the next time I was shoved and then—

The thrumming stopped.

My heart froze.

Once again I'd forgotten that I wasn't seeing Mr. Turtelhaze for another five visits. I shook my head. I couldn't wait that long.

I'd have to figure out how to contact Mr. Turtelhaze.

I'd ask Grandmother. She must know. She gave me the gold coins.

Of course, I'd just promised Reuben not to help anybody, but he hadn't stood in a field watching a cartload of gravel about to fall on a tiny boy.

Also (I argued with myself), that had happened *before* I'd met Reuben, so technically the promise didn't apply.

If there were a way to save that little boy, I would save him.

And after that, I would tell Mr. Turtelhaze: "No more visits, thank you. I cannot obey the rule."

I might also be a bit snappy with him. "You should have *told* me that it was time travel!" I'd say. "You should have *told* me about the rule!"

Still, I was glad he hadn't told me. Imagine if I'd followed Carrie through the forest, refusing to help her! Pretending not to notice the acrostic poem? Or watched silently as Carrie cleared the branches to free the Sparks? The Sparks might not have been saved in time!

Not to mention, Carrie would have thought I was extremely rude and lazy.

Same with Billy and the piano—if I hadn't suggested painting the piano, would the hospital have remained unrepaired? People could have died!

As for the lady in the cottage, imagine if I'd said to her, "No change, lady. Not moving that boat for you. Deal with it."

Not as vital as the other examples, of course, and I'd probably have spoken more politely than that—yet, still, it would have been a curiously mean-spirited thing to do.

On the other hand, if Reuben was right, what trouble had I *caused* by doing these things? Had thousands been harmed? Maybe the elderly lady had been trapped in her cottage by a boat *on purpose*, because she was a rampaging murderer!

Perhaps I *hadn't* changed anything though? Perhaps Carrie would have saved the Sparks without me, and Billy the hospital, and even the lady in the cottage might have managed to climb out the window.

I sighed. So either I'd caused terrible harm or I'd made no difference. What sort of adventurer was I?

One who'd be finished with adventuring once I'd saved the circus boy, anyhow. That was a shame. Even if they were only cut-price, first-chapter adventures, they'd made my life interesting for the last few days. However, I would *not* break my promise to Reuben, which meant I would have to stop adventuring.

I squinted toward the rocks that Reuben had pointed out. Yes, I could see a way through them.

"Goodbye, ocean," I told it, taking one last look at the wild white waters. Blue flowers still tossed and turned on the waves, along with other objects I could not identify. Dark shapes and light, in all sorts of colors, plunged beneath the water and leapt about on its surface. That shape there looked almost like a person—a small person, a little child. Oh, there was another similar shape beside it.

Two tiny, childlike shapes thrashing around, grabbing at each other, little feet kicking, dipping under the water, popping back up again.

What could they be?

What objects looked *exactly* like tiny children?

On the wind came the clear sound of a child coughing—gasping for breath—yelping in fear—

Two tiny children were drowning down there.

Little hands reaching for one another.

I leapt to my feet. How to rescue them? Panic radiated from my shoulders to my fingertips. I might be able to gather *one* child from the water and carry it to shore—but *two*?

"*Eli!*" one tiny voice called from down below.

"*Taya!*" spluttered the other. They were calling each other.

I looked around frantically for signs of another person—someone, anyone who could help!

Ah! The garden gate! I could tow them in on that! I snatched it up from the rock and scrambled back down the rocks toward the water. As I ran, I tore off Reuben's coat so it wouldn't slow me down.

"Hold on," I muttered. "Hold on, little children." Eli and Taya, they had said. "Hold on, Eli and Taya! I'm coming."

I splashed and swam, splashed and swam, dragging the gate behind me. Reuben's voice returned to me: Please *do not help anybody . . . Resist the temptation. Turn your gaze away. Can you promise me that?*

I'd made the promise. I had *meant* it with all my heart.

Should I keep it?

I laughed aloud, swallowing a mouthful of salt water as I did. "Sorry, Reuben," I said to myself as I plucked the children, one at a time, from the water and up onto the gate. "Not a chance."

CHAPTER 29

SHOVE.

I was back home.

"*Not again!*" I shouted, stamping in fury. I *hadn't* towed the children—toddlers really—to shore! True, they were up on the gate now, but would they get back to land? Would a wave wash them from the gate?

"I need to go *back*!" I sobbed. "Let me back!"

The laundry door flew open and here was Grandmother, her eyes bright with anger.

"*Child!*" she hissed. "The *noise*! You know very well that—" She stopped, reeling as she took in the sight of me.

I looked down at myself. I was soaking wet. My knees and palms were bleeding. My lip felt swollen. Water dripped and splashed onto the laundry floor.

Behind me, the washing machine chugged away, still only getting started—so once again, I hadn't been gone for any time.

Grandmother's voice became icy. "Have you been laundering your*self* instead of the dirty clothes?" she demanded.

For some reason, this made me giggle. I did look exactly as if I'd hopped into the washing machine.

Grandmother, however, did not find it amusing, and she instructed me to change my clothes at once and continue with the chores.

"Excuse me," I said bravely, as I followed her out of the laundry, leaving a trail of puddles. "Could you please help me, Grandmother? I need to see Mr. Turtelhaze. Could you telephone him for me? Ask him to come see me? I *must* get back to the boy at the circus and save him."

Grandmother did not reply. I had reached the bathroom and was collecting a towel to dry myself. I turned back to her in the hallway. She was glaring at me. There was a long silence, so I carried on speaking.

"Thank you so much for your birthday gift, Grandmother," I said. "It's very special—I didn't know it was time travel though! Or that I'm not *supposed* to change things! I don't think I can resist—No, I *know* I can't resist helping. I don't mean that to sound . . . conceited . . . I really don't see how *anybody* could stand by and watch people in trouble and just . . . whistle a tune and look away! It's too much to ask! Which means I have to stop traveling. Once I've saved the circus boy. And maybe checked on those little ones on the garden gate. But I need Mr. Turtelhaze, please. You see, I told him I wished to stay for the next five visits, and that means—"

"Mr. Turtelhaze?" Grandmother snapped. "I have never heard of the man. A ridiculous name. You have invented him. Once you have changed into dry clothes, we will start on the windows. As usual, I will wash the outside, while you wash the inside." She stopped suddenly and blinked. "However," she added, "you may leave my bedroom windows for today."

She strode back down the hall.

"Grandmother?" I called—my voice sounded forlorn to me.

"*Child,*" she snapped, spinning around. "Enough!"

CHAPTER 30

WELL, I THOUGHT dully, as I dipped a sponge in soapy water and raised it to the kitchen window. *Perhaps the circus boy was saved in time. Perhaps the little children will wash up on a beach somewhere, safe and well on the gate?*

It was too late to help them now. I would just have to wait through five more visits until I saw Mr. Turtelhaze again. Then I'd go back in time and save them.

I stared through the glass at Grandmother, who was outside uncoiling the garden hose ready to aim it at the window. Usually, I like this part of chore day. The *splat* of water from the hose is so startling, even though I know to expect it—I almost jump in fright. And then there's a wonderful waterfall effect running down the glass.

Today, though, I only stared through the window and—

Shove.

I was somewhere else again.

A different window was in front of me. Through it, I could see a quiet street. An old-fashioned motorcar slid by, followed by a horse-drawn cart. Across the road was a row of shops: a butcher, a bakery, a haberdashery.

Brrring! sounded from behind me and I spun around. I was in a small grocery store. Rows of shelves led to a counter where a woman in an apron was serving a teenager. The *brrring!* had come from an old-fashioned cash register.

"Mr. Turtelhaze?" I whispered hopefully.

Nothing happened.

This was tricky. I knew that I had to be careful not to help anybody, or change anything.

Perhaps if I stayed in this store, watching the street through the window? I could surely avoid doing any harm that way. I peered to the right.

A cage was sitting in the middle of the footpath.

It was filled with rabbits: fluffy, white rabbits.

Well, it couldn't hurt to say hello to some rabbits, could it? I'd always wanted a pet rabbit (and Grandmother had always said, "*Child!*" when I proposed it).

I walked out of the grocery store—*jingle!* said the door—and hurried along to the rabbit cage. There was nobody about.

I crouched. "*Hello,* rabbits!" I said.

There were about eight of them pressed together, little pink eyes darting about, ears back in nervous apprehension.

I looked up and down the street, wondering why a cage of rabbits was standing on the footpath, and that's when I noticed the meadow. It was just along the street, where the row of shops ended. The grass was a lovely lime green. Bees hovered amidst dandelions. Around the edges of the meadow, willow trees cast dappled shade.

"*That's* where you belong," I told the rabbits. "Not in this cage!"

Abruptly, something occurred to me. This has probably already occurred to you, dear reader. Remember, though, that I was living *inside* the story, and for me it was filled with details and emotions—those tend to crowd out more sweeping observations.

Here was the sweeping observation: every time I'd been shoved somewhere, a person or thing had been trapped.

The Sparks were trapped underground; Billy was trapped in his room; the child at the circus was *about* to be trapped by gravel; the nice elderly woman had been trapped by a boat lodged against her front door; Reuben, trapped by a gate—and now?

Eight rabbits trapped in a cage.

Again, I looked up and down the street. A few people were

window-shopping; a mother and son were arguing about whether they should get a milk shake; a man stepped out of a doorway, picked up the mat, and gave it a good shake. Dust flew out into the quiet day.

Nobody was paying any attention to me.

"If I set everybody else free," I told the rabbits, "why should you not be free too?"

It was surely my job. Anyway, how could it hurt for a few rabbits to run free in a meadow?

I picked up the cage, walked to the meadow, set it down, and opened it. The rabbits glanced up at me. Their little whiskers quivered. Little noses twitched.

I took a few steps back so they would not be afraid, and then, as I watched, the rabbits edged out of the cage. One by one, they sprang away into the meadow.

Smiling, I turned around, my eyes running along the row of shops again.

That's when I saw the hand-painted sign, dangling from hooks, right above the spot where I'd found the cage:

PET SHOP

"Oh," I said—*shove.*

I was back in my kitchen and *SPLAT!!!* went the hose water against the window.

This time I really did jump.

CHAPTER 31

THE REST OF the day was the usual Saturday—chores, piano, a walk to the corner store with Grandmother to purchase a new bulb for the living room lamp—with no more unexpected "shoves."

Something strange did happen though. It was while we were cleaning. After I'd done the windows in the kitchen, living room, and my room, I refilled the bucket with soapy water and carried it into Grandmother's room.

Oh that's right, I remembered, *she told me not to worry about her windows today.*

I glanced at her bedroom windows. Between the drapes, I could see smudges here and there on the glass. A spider's web was even forming at the top of one of the frames. The windows really did need a clean. It was unusually kind of Grandmother to excuse me from washing them, but I would surprise her by doing them anyway.

Pressing the drapes to the far ends of the curtain rod, I turned to squeeze out the sponge, ready to begin cleaning, when

BANG

I gasped in fright and swung around to the window. My first thought was that an animal had accidentally flung itself at the glass. Was it hurt?

It was not an animal though. It was Grandmother's fist. She was still outside with the hose. She curled her fist a second time and banged again:

BANG!

Her face was absolutely furious. *Livid.* "GET OUT!" she mouthed at me. "GET OUT! GET OUT!" and each time she spoke, her face contorted and she thrust a pointed finger in the direction of her bedroom door.

It was very surprising.

"You want me to leave your room?" I checked.

Grandmother raised her eyes to the sky and began again with the furious "GET OUT! GET OUT!"

I picked up the bucket, glanced back at Grandmother—still gesticulating frantically in the direction of her door—and began to leave the room.

As I passed her wardrobe, though, I felt something peculiar. It made me stop still. It was as though someone had flung the loop of an invisible rope over my head, let it fall around my waist, and tightened it sharply. Then a bubbling sensation began in my stomach, similar to when the dishwasher is running and the sink begins to gurgle. It was equal parts frightening and exciting. I reached my hand out to the wardrobe door and—

"*CHILD!*" Grandmother was striding down the hall. I hadn't heard the door open as she came inside.

I hurried out of her room and met her in the hallway.

"Well, why don't you go back *in there*?" Grandmother hissed, gesturing behind me to the open door of her bedroom. "Back into my room that I specifically told you not to enter! No, no, go on in and wash my windows! Even though I *specifically* told you *not* to do the windows! Go on then! Do them! Do *all* the things I've *ever* told you not to do! Go on, child!"

I knew she didn't mean that, of course. It was her way of being angry.

"I'm very sorry, Grandmother," I said, hefting the bucket to my other hand. "I thought you were giving me a break from your windows, as a treat, and I decided I'd surprise you by doing them anyway."

"A *treat*!" she exploded. "When have I *ever* given you a

treat?" She continued being very angry for some time and then, as I said, the day carried on as usual: chores, piano, a walk to the store.

Later, while we were eating dinner, there came the strange roaring sound that we often hear at dusk. Our road is popular with local skateboarders. The roaring is just the sound of their wheels on the path.

"*Yes, yes,*" Grandmother muttered, as she often does when we hear the skateboarders. "Make that dreadful racket and disturb the neighborhood. Yes, yes, keep it up."

Again, she didn't mean it. It's her way of being angry.

She used the tongs to heap more beans onto my plate, but I was lost in thought.

What a wonderful thing it must be, I thought, *to be flying along on a skateboard.*

This was followed rapidly by another thought, one that surprised me. It was a memory, more than a thought. It was the voice of the bearded man named Reuben, who'd been trapped in the cave. *Lillian, who speaks to you in this way?* his voice said again, this time in my head. *And how does it make you feel?*

I recalled with a jolt that Grandmother had just added beans to my plate. "Thank you, Grandmother," I said. "The beans are very good."

PART 5

REPORT 3

A FARMHOUSE, LIVINGSTON, KINGDOMS AND EMPIRES
—Thursday, May 1

* * *

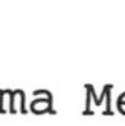

Emma Mettlestone, the renowned artist, was writing a letter to her sister Isabelle.

She was sitting cross-legged on a camp bed in a cramped, overcrowded storeroom. The room was in the farmhouse of another Mettlestone sister, Sue. A large patch of mold, in the shape of a lion's head, stretched across the ceiling.

Emma rested her notepad on her knees and began.

Dearest Isabelle (she wrote),

You will not believe what has happened! Or perhaps you will believe it because I expect it has been in the news.

Actually, you will definitely believe it because I already telegrammed everyone about it.

Anyhow! Here it is! I have escaped with my life by a whisper! By a hair's width! From the wildest, most dramatic, most terrifying, horrifying STORM of ALL TIME!!!

I'll tell you something eerie. In the last few weeks I've experienced (1) the astonishing news of our parents' return, (2) a letter from Alys that mentioned a storm in her kingdom, and (3) this.

THREE storms! First, the hurricane in my heart about our parents, second the storm in my mind's eye from Alys's description, and now the dazzling reality of reality!!

Honestly, it was the dreadfulest night of my life. I wish there was a way to fill a letter with sound effects (BOOM! WHOOOOOOH! PATTERPATTERPATTER etc.) or even the actual physical sensation of wind that pays no mind to your possessions or the neatness of your hair! And the thundering rain that shatters the air, as if an immense toolbox filled with nails and other little bits and pieces of metal has been violently upturned in the sky! Truly!

Because then you might understand! As it is, you cannot.

It is merest luck that Chief Detective Riley set out in his galoshes and raincoat and rounded up the island's inhabitants, directing us to shelter in the library, just as the storm was beginning.

"Thank you but I'll stick it out in my cottage," I told him.

"You'll stick that attitude and come along with me right now," he replied. "Mark my words, your cottage won't be standing by morning."

Well, I thought, that was a bit melodramatic of him, but I gathered my most valuable possessions, popped them in a wheelbarrow, covered that with a tarpaulin, and pushed it to the library—through the wind and rain—as instructed.

Everyone else had already arrived, along with their most treasured possessions, and this will surprise you but it turned out to be the loveliest night of my life. It was like when we were children and gathered for midnight feasts in your room, Isabelle. Or before our parents went into hiding, when they took us on holidays to the mountains, and we all bunked in together and watched the snow falling in the moonlight outside.

The library is a good, solid brick building, with shutters, so we knew we were safe, and there were tins of biscuits and cakes. One of our island teens, Bidisha, had brought along her guitar, and she played songs for the younger children. Outside, the storm crashed and banged like Mother used to in the kitchen when she was cross with Father, and we did worry about our homes, of course—but mostly it was as cozy as scones with jam and cream.

Anyhow, the next morning, when the sun returned, we emerged to see the worst. And it was worse than the worst. The storm had bludgeoned my darling Lantern Island. All our houses were in pieces. Roofs torn asunder, windows shattered, furniture strewn about, darling old trees cracked or felled across roads.

Chief Detective Riley told us to get ourselves off-island for a few weeks, until the engineers and contractors could make the place safe.

My darling friend Barnabas offered to take Sugar and me to the mainland in his little boat. Sugar, as you know, is my dearest friend in all the Kingdoms and Empires. Well, I brought along my most valuable possessions, and Sugar brought hers, and the boat was rather heavy in the water. We all had a go but could not *make the boat move. Barnabas cursed us and our valuable possessions and there was a bit of an argument about the meaning of* valuable*—and then, splash! Rising from the water like magical fountains came our sublime Water Sprite friends, Serfpio and Cyphus. They are my dearest friends in all the Kingdoms and Empires. Being very muscular they'd no trouble towing us across the water to the mainland. Problem solved.*

Sugar and Barnabas are staying in an inn, and I

am staying with darling Sue and her family, of course, here in Livingston.

The good news is that Sue has said I can stay in her storeroom for as long as I need, and the splendid news is that I am going to come and stay with you instead.

If that is all right?

It really is wonderful here! I love it! I am in raptures, chatting with Sue and her strange Livingston accent (she says everything twice!) and her husband, Josh, and their boys, my darling nephews, Sebastian, Nicholas, Connor, and Benjamin, and their various dogs, cats, hamsters, ducks, etc. (Honestly, they have pet ducks. I couldn't bathe last night for the ducks in the bathtub.) I do love the boys, especially little Benji—oh, he wants to be known as Benjamin now that he's started school. He's always wandering off on his own, claiming he can "take care of himself." I read a story to him last night and he curled up on my lap and fell asleep with his thumb in his mouth. It was the darlingest thing that has ever happened to me.

Anyhow, but he quickly woke up and joined in a soccer game with his brothers. The boys play soccer twenty-four hours a day! In the house! Using anything they like as the ball—a tin pot, say, or a laundry basket—and they hoot and holler as they play, often slamming into each other, or the furniture, or the wall.

It's not that I don't love it, it's more that I can hardly bear it.

More generally, farm life itself seems frenetic: chickens, lambs, pigs, orchards, etc. all needing to be fed, washed, trimmed, weeded, moved about from this pen to that . . . I don't know. I can't keep up. (Have Sue and Josh bitten off more than they can chew with this farm? I know they bit it off many years ago and have been chewing away ever since—but their jaws must be awfully tired.)

They seem happy though.

Anyhow, the big reunion is coming up and we'll ALL be coming to you then—so you won't mind if I arrive early? Your apartment is so large and elegant. I cannot paint at ALL here, but I could sit in your conservatory, or your sunroom, and paint all day, couldn't I?

I've been to the post office this morning and arranged to have my most valuable possessions packaged up and sent to you. So they should arrive tomorrow morning, then I'll arrive tomorrow afternoon, and this letter should reach you the day after that.

Ha! That's no good! No, I'll run back to the post office and have them express this to you. Then you'll be expecting me.

Cannot wait to see you! It will be the best thing that has ever happened to me.

Much, much love,

Emma

* * *

A PENTHOUSE APARTMENT, GAINSLEIGH, KINGDOMS AND EMPIRES
—Friday, May 11

Isabelle Mettlestone was eating breakfast.

The Butler entered the room, carrying the post on a tray.

"Good morning," she said.

The Butler set the tray before her, pulled up a chair, and joined her for breakfast.

"Ah," said Isabelle, as she scanned the first of her letters. "It seems that one sister is arriving sooner than expected . . ."

She read Emma's letter aloud, she and the Butler both laughing fondly at Emma's flair for dramatic hyperbole.

"It's the artistic sensibility," the Butler suggested.

The doorbell rang. The Butler rose to answer it.

"Telegram," he said, returning and handing a paper to Isabelle. "More sisters. This is from Lisbeth and Maya."

Lisbeth and Maya, the twins, cocaptained a cruise ship together.

Isabelle took up her spectacles again and peered at the paper.

"Well now," she murmured, and she read it aloud:

Ahoy. Whopper of a storm here on the Oski Coast. Never seen the like. Miracle we stayed afloat. Passengers shook up. Ship in for major repairs. Can we come to you early? L&M

There was a silence.

"Strange," the Butler said eventually. "Emma mentions that Alys had written to her of a storm. Emma's storm. And now Lisbeth and Maya. Three immense storms, each in a different part of the Kingdoms and Empires, each affecting Mettlestone sisters."

"And three of those four sisters," Isabelle murmured, "are *not* prone to exaggeration."

"I wonder if we should contact your other siblings," the Butler suggested. "See if it's happened to them too? See if there's a pattern?"

Isabelle bit her lip.

For a while, the pair sat at the table, sipping

tea and buttering toast, each deep in thought. Eventually, Isabelle set down her cup. "I'm sure it's just a coincidence," she decided. "It's only three storms. Weather happens! Let's not worry about it."

PART

6

CHAPTER 32

THE FOLLOWING MORNING, Grandmother and I were enjoying our usual Sunday breakfast of scrambled eggs with parsley when a note appeared under the front door.

I know this happened. I was chattering about eggs, and how a fried egg feels to me like a person wearing sunglasses and jeans, whereas scrambled eggs are more like people dressed up in bright clothes for a party, and a boiled egg—

"Child!" Grandmother said. "Eggs are not people!"

"And a boiled egg," I continued, "is wearing a cardigan, don't you think, and perhaps woolen socks? As for a poached egg—"

"Child!"

I gazed around the room, trying to decide about poached eggs, and that's when the piece of paper slid under the front door.

"Oh!" I said, rising from my chair. "What's that?"

"Sit down," Grandmother ordered. "Concentrate on breakfast. I am going to make myself another cup of tea."

On her way to the kitchen, she detoured swiftly by the front door, swept up the piece of paper with her left hand, pressed it into her pocket, and carried on to the kitchen.

When she returned to the table she set down her cup of tea and picked up her fork again.

"What was the note?" I asked.

"Note?"

"Yes, the note that slid under the door."

"What nonsense, child," Grandmother said. "There was no note under any door!"

I thought about this. "In that case, why did you take such a circuitous route to the kitchen?" I asked.

"Good gracious, child," Grandmother muttered.

Then she told me she had to go out for a short time. I was to read one of my books or play the piano. The usual rules about not leaving the house, or opening the door, would apply, and she would be back in time for lunch.

As soon as Grandmother had left, locking the door behind her, I ran into her bedroom.

Yes, I was surprised too, dear reader. I'm usually very obedient.

However, I had not stopped wondering about that strange sensation I'd experienced when I walked by Grandmother's wardrobe the previous day. Even while I was talking about eggs, and notes under doors, the wondering was there, ticking away at the back of my mind like a very noisy clock.

Also, I *knew* I'd seen a note pushed under the door. I *knew* Grandmother had picked it up. Yet Grandmother had told me this was nonsense.

Somehow, this suggested that Grandmother's worldview had got a bit broken, if you see what I mean, and that it should—for today, at least, and only while she was out of the house—be ignored.

So I ran into her bedroom and stood by the wardrobe.

Nothing happened. No sensation of a rope tugging me, no tingling, no prickling. Just the sound of my own breathing—and of a lawn mower somewhere down the street.

I tried different parts of Grandmother's room, but still nothing happened.

Then, quite suddenly, I wanted to be in the back garden.

This made no sense. It was a damp, chilly day. Yet before I knew it, I had rushed into my room, taken my jacket from its hanger, zipped it up, and skidded down the hall to the back door.

Just as I was about to go out, I remembered the letter that the elderly woman at the lake had given me.

Always keep it in your pocket, she had said. *If you ever meet a girl named Bronte Mettlestone, will you please give it to her?*

Yet I had put it in my drawer. In my mind, that had seemed a safe place to keep it until I met a girl named Bronte Mettlestone. I don't know when I imagined that would happen—I think I was picturing an invitation to a birthday party. Or Grandmother enrolling me in school at last.

I wasn't thinking straight.

I'd never been invited to a birthday party, and Grandmother had always glared or rubbed her temples when I'd suggested school. On the other hand, I'd been shoved into another world several times lately, and I'd met *Carrie* Mettlestone there, as well as Billy and Reuben—not to mention the elderly woman who'd given me the letter herself! I'd practically met more people in the last three days than I had in my whole life.

Who was to say the next person would not be a girl named Bronte Mettlestone?

So I skidded back *down* the hall, found the envelope, pushed it into my pocket, ran toward the back door—the tingling was back! The rope was tightening!—turned the handle and . . .

CHAPTER 33

SHOVE.

CHAPTER 34

I GAVE THAT "shove" a chapter all to itself, as I was annoyed with it.

I wanted to be in my back garden! Not on another adventure! I didn't know *why* I was so frantic to be in my back garden, only that the urge was overpowering.

My hand was still turning a door handle and pushing a door, only now it was an ornate brass handle and a big oak door, not my own ordinary back door.

Whoosh went the door, and I stepped into a room.

It had shuttered windows, a wooden floor, a ticket counter, and was lined with long, low benches. NICHOLAS VALLEY COACH STATION, said a sign nailed to the wall.

At the ticket counter, a thin, bespectacled man sat behind a glass screen.

On one of the benches, a boy sat, hunched over, a backpack at his feet and a skateboard resting against his knees. He was spinning one of the skateboard's wheels. The room was quiet except that I could hear rain falling outside, a quiet clinking from the ticket seller counting coins, and the faint whir of the skateboard wheel.

"Hello," I said, boldly.

The boy looked up and I realized just how bold I'd been: he was very handsome—dark eyes, dark hair, brown skin—and about twelve years old.

"Hi," he replied, looking at me curiously.

I strode over and sat down beside him—truly amazed at my own boldness now. I couldn't seem to help it though.

"Look," I said. "I'm awfully sorry but I wonder if you might help. I keep being *shoved* to different places, you see, and then I'm shoved back home once I've sorted out somebody being trapped. Today, I want to get home as quickly as possible as I've a powerful urge to be in my own back garden. Yes, I see from your expression that you find this odd. Me too. But have you any idea who might be trapped? Are *you* trapped? I mean, the door *was* open when I came in just now so you could . . . go out? I think it's raining though and perhaps you have no umbrella? Is that it? Does that make you *feel* trapped? Or the ticket seller—is he stuck behind the glass, do you think? Ought I to break the glass for him? Or your skateboard—is *it*, sort of, trapped? Well, that's unlikely. I'm trying to think outside the box. I'm babbling as I'm anxious to get this sorted out. Oh, sorry, my name is Lillian Velvet."

By this time, a dimple had appeared in the boy's right cheek. In fact, he was trying not to smile too broadly.

"Hey, Lillian Velvet," he said. "I'm Oscar Banetti. If the ticket guy's trapped in there he hasn't mentioned it to me. Still, you could try smashing the glass and see what happens?"

His face was serious but the dimples jumped back into his cheeks.

"I see that you are making a joke," I said, and smiled to show my appreciation of his humor.

"Don't you go breaking any glass," the ticket seller grumbled, not looking up from his coin counting.

"As for my skateboard," Oscar continued, lifting it up in the air. "Free as a—Wait, you know what this is?"

"Your skateboard? Certainly!" I replied. "I've never ridden one, nor even seen one up close before. However, my road is popular with skateboarders and often, around dusk, I hear them riding by. It's noisy! The wheels on the path moving at high speed. Sounds like an approaching thunderstorm! Grandmother always says—"

"What street do you live on?" Oscar asked.

"Carmichael Street. In the house with the red letter box shaped like a hair dryer. It's just outside of Bomaderry," I added, as he was looking confused. "Bomaderry is two hours south of Sydney."

Now his eyebrows shot up like grasshoppers. "You're from my world!" he said. "Bomaderry's near Shoalhaven, right? Mate of mine has a holiday house there. I'm from Sydney."

All my eagerness to rush back home dissolved. He must have been *shoved* here as well! He might be able to explain what was happening to me!

"You don't talk like someone from my world though," he added, his brow crinkling slightly.

"As to that," I said. "I live with my grandmother, and only ever—"

I was about to give my explanation but Oscar said, "Hold on. Do you mind watching my stuff for a minute? My coach—it's like a horse-drawn carriage really—but it'll be here soon and I just remembered I promised to get my mates some fudge from the place they like. I'll be two minutes—it's right next door. Don't go anywhere. I want to hear your story."

He was out the door in a flash.

"I can't promise I'll still be here," I called, but the door had already thudded closed.

I want to hear your story, he had said. Nobody had ever asked to "hear my story" before. I felt a warm glow and hoped I wouldn't be shoved back before I'd had a chance to tell it. Only, what exactly *was* my story?

While I waited, I studied Oscar's skateboard. I even experimented by placing it on the floor and standing on it. It wobbled and began to slide out from under me, and I tripped sideways with a great clatter that made the ticket seller look up sharply.

"Sorry," I said.

The ticket seller nodded and went back to his clinking.

Oscar returned, shaking his head so that rain droplets scattered everywhere.

"I got extra," he said, offering me a piece of caramel fudge as he sat down. "Start at the beginning."

So I did. I ate the fudge—the most astonishing, delicious thing I'd ever tasted—and started with the pickle jar of gold coins. While I talked, Oscar flicked at the wheel of his skateboard, only glancing sideways at me now and then.

Grandmother would have snapped, "Stop fiddling and *pay attention*, child!" I almost did snap that at Oscar. However, I stopped myself.

I was glad I did. When I finished talking, it turned out he *had* been paying attention, in his own way.

"I don't know what's up with the shoving all over the place," he said, "but that bearded guy named Reuben you met in the cave? I think he might be a Genie mate of mine. And you say you've got a letter for a girl named Bronte Mettlestone? I could bring that to her if you like. She's one of the mates I got the fudge for. I'm on my way to see Bronte and her cousins right now."

I jumped, and Oscar looked around to see what had scared me.

"No, I'm only startled by the coincidence," I explained. "You know Reuben! You know Bronte Mettlestone! How can this be?"

Oscar glanced at the clock on the wall. "We've only got a few minutes before the coach to Katherine Valley gets here," he said. "So I'll try to keep it short."

CHAPTER 35

THEN OSCAR TOLD me *his* story.

It turned out that he'd been skipping school one day when—

"Skipping school?" I asked, confused. "You mean you're allowed to go to school and yet you choose to skip it?"

Oscar tilted his head.

"It's strange to me," I explained. "I'd love to go to school. Imagine learning with other children! Imagine a teacher giving you homework!"

"Imagine," Oscar said, raising one of his eyebrows high.

He carried on with his story. He'd been skipping school and he'd gone to the skate park, and—

"Do you also skate in other places?" I checked. "I might have even *seen* you if you ever came to Bomaderry and skated down my hill! I don't recognize you, but the skaters are shadowy figures at dusk, so—"

"No offense, but we don't have long," Oscar said, scratching the side of his thumb and looking at the clock again.

I agreed that I would save my questions until the end.

Oscar said he'd been at the skate park and kids had told him he could get to "the best skate park ever" if he looked at a mirror—

"The best skate park ever? So your own skate park is not—"

"Lillian," Oscar said.

"Sorry."

Oscar hadn't believed it, but he'd looked at the mirror and it had worked. Or "kind of worked." Suddenly he'd found himself in an entirely different world.

"Not a skate park," he said. "They don't have skateboards in this world—but a city of Elves. And I met this family of sisters, Imogen, Esther, and Astrid, and their cousin, Bronte—"

"Bronte Mettlestone!"

"Right. And—"

"And a girl named Carrie Mettlestone?" I cried.

"No. Although that name sounds familiar. They keep telling me names from their family, but I sort of zone out. Too many of them. No, I was going to say there was also their friend Alejandro. Anyway, we spent five days on a rescue mission to save Elves—"

"You spent five whole *days* on your adventure with your new friends!" I exclaimed. "That's like a *book*! My adventures are just first chapters of books."

"Okay," Oscar agreed, not seeming to get my point. "And there was this dude named Reuben helping us out—"

"Reuben!"

"Reuben, yeah. Maybe there are heaps of Genies around named Reuben, but the way you described him talking about time and that? And how he didn't want to report another Genie? It kind of sounds like him."

Something occurred to me. "He told me that I traveled in time. Is that happening right now? What year is it? What date?"

Oscar blinked and pointed to a standing chalkboard. It listed coach times and had the date scrawled at the top.

"Oh, same year—but Thursday, twenty-fourth of May? Is that today really?"

I might have been speaking too fast. It took Oscar a moment to think and then he said, "Thursday, twenty-fourth of May." He nodded to himself: "Yeah. That's today. I'm going to Katherine Valley to meet the girls now and we head to Gainsleigh this afternoon."

"Thursday, twenty-fourth of May," I repeated. "How strange. That's my birthday."

"Happy birthday," Oscar said promptly.

"Thank you, but it was three days ago."

Oscar's brow crinkled briefly then cleared. He told me that

when *he* goes back and forth between worlds, time doesn't change—it stays exactly the same.

"And what *is* this world?" I asked.

"It's called the Kingdoms and Empires. It's like our world but more old-fashioned. Plus they have magic. The main thing to remember is that Shadow Mages are bad, True Mages are good, and Spellbinders can bind shadow magic. Genies are sort of wise, I guess, and outside everything."

I registered what he'd said a moment earlier: "When you come back and forth? Are you saying you come and go as you please?"

He nodded. "Reuben put a wish on my skateboard. I just say the address in either world and ride through. I can take a friend along too, if they're on a board. Mostly we stay in this world, though, cause there's not much for me at home. My parent situation is not . . . perfect. Actually, I think Reuben set up the thing with the mirror and the skate park so I'd find my way to this world, and make new friends, and . . . get a new family. He tells me Genies can choose specializations, and he likes helping kids whose parents aren't . . . up to scratch."

I nodded. "Lovely of him," I suggested.

"Yep. So now I go to boarding school here in Nicholas Valley with my mate Alejandro, and the girls are at school in the next town over—Katherine Valley. Imogen, Esther, and Astrid have been students there awhile and Bronte joined her cousins there last term. So we see each other a lot. The Mettlestones have sort of . . . made me part of the family."

At that moment, the ticket seller knocked on the glass and called, "Coach is about to arrive, Oscar. You going to get *this* one?"

Oscar's smile faltered.

He hunched over and began spinning his skateboard wheel again. I had to concentrate to hear him as he was murmuring softly. "I skipped the first coach of the day," he told me. "Not sure I really want to go, see?"

A pause. Outside, the rain poured on.

"You don't want to see your friends at the other boarding school?" I asked.

Another pause.

"Yeah, I want to see *them*—I love those guys—but this time we're all going away together for a week. To a place called Gainsleigh for a big family get-together. Their long-lost grandparents are coming back or something. The whole Mettlestone family want to welcome them."

He glanced sideways at me.

"Well, that's wonderful," I said, hesitantly. "The whole family!"

Oscar cleared his throat and started counting on his fingers. "One set of long-lost grandparents, eleven aunts, an uncle, a butler, a Whisperer, and a whole bunch of kids."

There was a pause. He had spoken the guest list as if it was a list of recent climate catastrophes. I didn't know what a "Whisperer" was but it sounded fairly harmless to me—quiet, anyway. "And you're nervous that it will be too crowded?" I suggested.

"Nah." Oscar shifted around on the bench. "Well, maybe, yeah. It's more—the aunts have a lot of different occupations, see? One of them is a queen! There's also a farmer, an artist, a dragon vet, a couple of cruise ship captains." He was counting on his fingers. "I don't remember the rest. It wouldn't've been so bad if Alejandro was coming—he's sort of part of the family too—but he's off traveling with his parents."

"Oscar," called the ticket seller. "You should head outside if you *are* going—the coach will depart any moment."

"A *queen*!" Oscar repeated, almost talking to himself now rather than to me. "How are you meant to talk to a royal person?" He swiveled toward the ticket seller, cleared his throat, and spoke up. "Yeah, I don't think I'm going to take this coach either," he called. "In fact, I'm not going at all."

"Suit yourself," the ticket seller replied. "You want a refund for your ticket?"

"Yes please."

Oscar stood, picking up his skateboard and backpack, and

took a ticket from his pocket. “It was good to meet you, Lillian,” he said. “I guess I’ll head back to school.”

I rose myself, confused. “I don’t understand why you’re not going.”

“It’s like I told you. They’re not my kind of people. As well as the queen, I hear there are four boy cousins who live on a farm and play soccer. See, I live in a city and play rugby league.”

“Rugby league!” I exclaimed. “I know that game! People get concussions when they play it.”

“Well, but the point is, I can’t talk to soccer people.”

I frowned. “I’m talking to a skateboarder right now,” I said. “I wouldn’t have thought skateboarders were *my* kind of people. I’d never even met a *skateboard,* let alone a skateboarder, before today.”

“A skateboarder?” Oscar tugged on his ear, chuckling. “That’s different. I’m just me.”

I pressed my fingertips to my temples, the way Grandmother does when she’s frustrated. “Oscar,” I said. “Every single person is just themselves. Really, in their heart, even when they’re pretending to be somebody else. Not only that but every single person is a story! All day at home, I *long* for new stories and adventures—I’ve read all my books several times, and Grandmother just says, ‘*Child!*’ when I ask her to tell me about her life, or to get me another book. So to me it’s very strange that you wouldn’t take a journey to meet the other members of your family, and hear their stories.”

At this, Oscar’s face seemed to melt into sadness. He looked directly into my eyes. “They’re not really my family,” he said.

“Oh, as to that, I’ve read plenty of books where people choose new families! There’s no such thing as a *real* family! My grandmother found me in a basket at her front door when I was a baby! Which means she’s not my *real* grandmother—but she is certainly *real*! Now, it sounds like you are fond of *some* of the Mettlestone family? So why don’t you give the rest a chance?”

“Last call,” the ticket seller said, this time speaking quite mildly. He was leaning forward, right up to the glass, listening to our conversation.

"Plus you bought fudge for your friends!" I urged. "The most delicious thing I ever ate in my life! You'd better bring the fudge to them! Go on! Get the coach!"

Oscar chuckled.

"Ah, fair enough," he said, swinging his backpack onto his shoulder. "You reckon I can still make it?" he asked the ticket seller, taking a step toward the door.

"If you run."

"Okay, give me that letter you wanted me to pass on to Bronte, Lillian, and—"

Shove.

I was home again.

CHAPTER 36

THAT WAS A *strange one,* I thought.

I was back in my hallway, hand resting on my own back doorknob.

I hadn't freed anybody. All I'd done was have a conversation. I hadn't even had time to give Oscar the letter meant for the girl named Bronte Mettlestone!

I turned the doorknob and stepped out into the garden. It was cold and I drew my jacket closer around me. At once, that strange sensation returned: a tickling, prickling, excited feeling. A sensation like someone was tugging at me urgently—as if I was about to take a dog for a walk and it was straining on the lead, frantic to tear off down the road.

But where was I being tugged?

There was nothing new in the garden. It was still just the small, neat lawn that Grandmother mowed each weekend, the garden bed in which pansies grew, alongside mint and parsley, the sycamore, the old mulberry tree.

I stood in the center of the yard, my heart bouncing about with all its anxious urging that I . . . Well, that I do *something*!

That *something* was right here in this garden! *Hurry! Hurry! Hurry!*

Over *there*!

To the garden bed!

It was like several hands beckoning me. Reaching up and pushing me along.

I ran the short distance, skidded to a stop, and looked down at the pansies. They seemed disheveled. The dirt around them appeared to have been scraped and turned over.

Hurry! Hurry! Hurry!

Hurry and do what? I wondered.

Then I became aware that voices were speaking next door.

Murmur, murmur, "how about a pergola?" *murmur, murmur,* "no, but if we do that, we can't get the hot tub," *murmur, murmur,* "should the patio end here?"

Oh, the women next door were discussing the renovation of their backyard again. I let their voices drift by, staring down at the dirt.

"Trapped by indecision!" said a voice—it was Helen, the Irish one, her words full of laughter.

"Trapped by indecision!" I repeated aloud, without meaning to.

Louder than I realized, I suppose, because there was a rustling, then the sound of some object being dragged, and two heads popped over the fence.

"Hello!" they both said, at the same time.

I'd had very clear pictures in my mind of what these neighbors looked like—Helen would have frizzy red hair and Shahlyla would be short and plump—and my pictures were completely wrong. In fact, Helen had short white-blond hair and wide-set eyes, and Shahlyla had an angular face and long hair that tumbled past her shoulders.

"Good morning," I replied. "I'm so sorry about copying you like that! I meant no offense. The thing is, I was just talking to a boy who was waiting for a coach. He'd been invited to a party, you see, and he couldn't decide if he should go. When I heard you say the words *trapped by indecision,* I thought: *Oh, that's like Oscar! He was trapped by indecision!* And I've been—"

I stopped. They might not want to hear about how I'd been shoved to another world to help free trapped people fairly regularly lately. They were adults, and would think I was inventing.

"Sorry," I repeated.

The two women were both smiling at me. They seemed very friendly.

"Nothing to be sorry for," Helen said. "Did your friend decide to take the coach in the end?"

I was pleased that she was calling Oscar my friend and

decided not to correct her by explaining that I'd only just met Oscar.

"I think so," I replied. "He was running to catch it when I left. He was worried the people at the party weren't *his* kind of people, you see, and that he wouldn't know how to talk to them."

"Ah," said Shahlyla. "Nervous? Trapped by *fear* as well then?"

"Oh yes! I think you're right. He had a skateboard, but I suppose even people with skateboards can be afraid."

"I suppose so," Helen agreed solemnly. "I'm Helen, by the way, and this is Shahlyla."

"I know," I said. "I've figured that out from when you're talking and—" I smacked my hand to my mouth. Now they knew I eavesdropped!

They laughed though. They seemed not to mind at all.

"Yes, we're always out here yammering on about how to change our backyard," Helen told me. "We are *trapped by indecision* because we can't afford all the things we'd like. Just *one* thing really—but which? You must get sick of hearing us."

"Not at all," I insisted. "I enjoy your conversations very much. I wish you *could* have all the things you want for your backyard—the hot tub and the pergola, the patio and rosebushes, the herb garden! Everything!"

"That's very kind of you," Helen said. "Will you do me a favor and tell us your name?"

"I always forget to say my name!" I cried, and both women laughed again. They really seemed lovely. Their laughter was loud and strong, but came out at different pitches—Helen's up high and Shahlyla's down low.

"I'm Lillian Velvet," I said. "Pleased to meet you."

"Lovely to meet *you*," they said, very seriously.

"And don't worry," Shahlyla added. "We knew your name was Lillian. Helen here has just forgotten it. She's very forgetful. Helen would forget to open her eyes again after blinking if it didn't happen automatically."

"I would," Helen agreed, contentedly.

"Lillian, your grandmother knocked on our door and

introduced herself to us just the other morning," Shahlyla continued, "and *she* told us your name. A package had been delivered to our house by mistake and she'd come by to collect it. She said it was your birthday and she seemed very excited about that fact. That was Thursday, I think? Happy birthday for Thursday!"

I stared at Shahlyla. I think my mouth must have been wide open. Imagine Grandmother introducing herself to the neighbors! Imagine her telling the neighbors my name! And that it was my birthday! And being *excited*!

After all this time!

I had a sudden thought: *were* they *her visitors the other night?*

The two women were watching me with interest, and I remembered to close my mouth.

"Have you seen Grandmother since then?" I asked. "Did you come over for cake the other night?"

"Cake!" said Shahlyla. "Oh, I love cake. But no, we haven't been at your place for cake. I saw your Grandmother last night though, around midnight."

"You did?" I asked.

"You did?" Helen said at the same time, looking at Shahlyla curiously.

She nodded. "Yes, I woke up and remembered I'd left my scarf out here, so I came out to get it. I didn't want it getting wet if it rained. And I heard sounds coming from your garden, Lillian, and looked over the fence, to check there was no intruder."

"You didn't tell me any of this!" Helen complained.

"You were fast asleep," Shahlyla told her calmly. "I wasn't going to wake you and tell you that I'd seen the neighbor gardening. That's what the noise was, Lillian. Your grandmother was digging in the garden. Right about where you are now, in fact." She pointed just past my feet and we all looked down at the pansies. "I called out hello, which startled her, and she told me that moonlight gardening suits her very well. Then I said good night, and I said that moonlight *sleeping* suits me very well, and she said, 'All right then,' and I picked up my scarf and went back inside to bed."

There was a lot to take in. Grandmother had had two conversations with the neighbors. Grandmother enjoyed *moonlight gardening*?

"I didn't know she liked moonlight gardening," I admitted. "It sounds like something from a book. *Tom's Midnight Garden*."

Helen said how much she had loved *Tom's Midnight Garden* when she was a child, and then they both said, well, they had to run, as they were very late for a barbecue. They still hadn't made the salad that they'd promised to bring along. There was a brief, funny argument between them about whether to add toasted pecans or toasted walnuts to the salad, and then Helen said, "I hope we can chat with you again, Lillian!"

Their heads disappeared, *squeeeeak* said their sliding door, and they were gone.

Shaking my head in wonder at it all, I looked down at the pansies again.

Suddenly, powerfully—as if it had been waiting impatiently throughout my conversation with the neighbors—the sensation was back. The tingling intensified.

Something important has been buried here, I realized, and a second thought flowed right through my body: *I need to dig it up.*

I fell to my knees, heart hammering, plunged my hands into the dirt and—

"CHILD!" Grandmother shouted. "Get up out of the dirt at once!"

I turned around. She was standing in the doorway, her hands on her hips. She must have returned from her errand already.

Very, very reluctantly, I stood up.

"Come inside," Grandmother said. "And wash your hands *immediately*."

Her voice vibrated with anger.

CHAPTER 37

IT STARTED RAINING not long after that. Grandmother and I put on our wet-weather gear and set out for a lengthy walk around our neighborhood.

It's a very hilly neighborhood. By dinnertime, I was exhausted. The tugging sensation grabbed me each time I ventured down the hallway, becoming almost unbearable whenever I was near the back door. This added to my weariness. At one point, the sensation grabbed ahold of my feet, seeming to *push* them, more and more aggressively, as if a grown adult was on the floor prodding at me.

My knees buckled.

I could not resist a moment longer. Grandmother was in the kitchen, and I made a snap decision.

I would dig up the garden.

I skidded to the back door, grabbed the handle, turned it— and it was deadlocked.

This was both surprising and confusing: the back door is never locked.

"Child," Grandmother called. "Come and set the table."

"Coming," I called back. I paused, though, looking down at my feet. "What's going on with you, feet?" I whispered. They stood on the carpet, silent, not answering, and—

Shove.

I only had a moment to register that I was now standing on a *rug*, not my hallway carpet, when . . .

. . . the most extraordinary sensation hit me. A cruel, ceaseless pressure was coming from every direction—from outside my body and *inside* it too. At the back of my neck, the inside of my forehead, at my shoulders, and deep within my toes.

"Stop it!" I shouted—or tried to shout. My voice wouldn't work. I curled my shoulders down, huddling into myself, squeezing my eyes shut. "Stop it! Stop it!"

I could hardly breathe! My body shook, I gasped for air.

From somewhere deep inside my mind, a word crawled out:

Cold.

That's what this was.

Coldness.

The most intense cold I'd ever experienced. A terrifying, violent cold. The kind of cold that burns and sears. A scream froze in my throat.

I forced my eyes open.

I was in a small enclosure made entirely of thick, blue ice. The walls of the enclosure rose up from the rug and closed together just above my head. Around me, the air was thick with white mist.

I forced myself to turn a slow circle, my movements jittery, my teeth chattering wildly. All blue ice and mist, blue ice and mist—a tangle of knotted black and red thread pinned to the ice wall, a half-formed net of green-and-gold lying on the rug—ice and mist, ice and mist, and then—I gasped.

A girl stood in the mist behind me.

She had dark hair and wore a yellow dress. Her eyes were squeezed shut, her face creased with lines of distress, her shoulders hunched against the cold, and both her hands were twirling in the air.

"Hello there," I forced myself to say—only it came out, "He-e-e l-o-o the-e-r-e" because the cold shook my words like a hand rattling stones.

The girl startled, her eyes opening wide.

"Who-o-o are yo-u-u?" she asked. Her words, like mine, were filled with shivers and shakes. Her eyes were very frightened.

"Where are we?" I managed to ask. "How do we . . . get . . . out?" It didn't seem important who I was. I touched my palm to the ice wall and pushed, but the cold sent shots of flame through my body that made me want to burst into sobs.

"I think it's sh-sh-shadow magic," the girl said, looking at the ice walls. "Only I c-c-an't . . . *see* it to . . . bind it." Her body juddered. She closed her eyes again, and again her hands made quick, jerky movements.

"T-try opening your eyes," I recommended. "If y-you need to see."

"It's sh-sh-shadow magic—I can only s-s-see it with cl-cl-osed eyes."

I looked around the enclosure again. The only things in here were the girl, me, and—well, that tangle of thread and that half-formed net, but they were just rubbish, weren't they? Nothing to do with "shadow magic"? I shouldn't disturb the girl in her hand-twirling, should I?

This was her strange world, and I should be patient.

Try to be patient.

Try.

Hurry, I thought. *Hurry. Hurry. Solve this, g-g-girl in yellow dress.*

Even my thoughts shivered and shook.

Only, as I watched the girl, her face grew ever more bluey gray, her hand movements jerkier and smaller, and then they slowed, and slowed.

They slowed so much they stopped. She roused herself and moved them again.

This is dangerous, a voice whispered in my head. I was so sleepy. What was that called? Hypothermia. When you grow too cold, your body shuts down. You fall asleep.

It was very important not to fall asleep. But it was somehow *warmer* not to be awake. I was sinking into the warmer core of myself, into the pleasant space of my own mind.

I glanced at the girl, and her movements had stopped altogether again. Her face had relaxed. Her head was bowed. She was falling asleep.

You need to stay awake!

That was a panicked thought, not words out loud.

How do I speak again?

I had forgotten.

I had to make conversation. What could I talk about?

"Is this black and red thread important?" I managed to ask. "Or . . . this . . . net of green and g-g-gold?"

The girl's head was slumped forward. She hadn't heard.

Oh, perhaps I should just let her sleep. Perhaps we could both sleep.

No! Lillian, wake up!

I pushed the girl's shoulder, and her head snapped up. She looked at me, dazed. "Wh-ho are you?" she whispered.

"Th-this th-thread," I heard myself say. "This n-net. Are they important?"

The girl blinked hard, straightening up. "Are y-y-ou a Spell-binder?" she asked. "Can you s-s-ee the shadow magic?"

"No. I just . . ." I pointed to the tangle of thread pinned to the ice wall. "Th-this?" I said.

She looked where I was pointing and frowned. "What?"

I reached out to touch it. "Oh!" I said surprised. "I can't f-feel it—my h-hand goes straight through it. B-but it's there. It's black and red thread."

"Point to it," the girl said. "P-p-point to exactly where it is."

She fixed her gaze on the place where I was pointing, then closed her eyes tight again, her hands moving quickly in the air.

"Oh, the net is f-f-floating in the air now!" I said. "It's moving up t-toward the tangle!"

The girl opened her eyes. They were bright.

"Close to the t-t-tangle?" she asked, teeth chattering. "To the right or left of it?"

"Just below, and to the l-l-left."

Her eyes closed and her hands moved. "Talk me th-through it," she said. "We want the net to go around the tangle. The t-t-angle is the shadow magic. The n-net will bind it."

"It's getting close now," I told her. "No, you've gone t-too f-far to the right. It's-it's . . . You almost had it. Now j-just a *tiny* bit up and . . ."

It was frustrating. I wanted to reach out and do it myself—it was so close! Right there! But each time I tried, my hands went through the net.

I took a deep breath and tried to be patient.

"Okay, you've got it n-n-now—up a bit, up a bit, up and . . . And . . . and . . . NOW!"

Snap!

The net closed around the tangle, pulled tight, and *snap!* . . . disappeared.

Instantly, the ice began to melt.

And there it was—

I'd almost forgotten it existed.

Warmth.

Oh, beautiful, beautiful warmth.

CHAPTER 38

WE WERE IN a room.

The ice enclosure had melted into nothing.

(Ordinarily, ice melts into a puddle of water, of course. I'd worried that the rug would become wet and smelly. But no, the enclosure simply vanished, and the rug was dry beneath my feet.)

I looked around the room—a row of single beds, two large wardrobes, a corkboard on the wall—and was about to ask the girl what had just happened and where we were when a terrible burning sensation gripped my fingers, my toes, my cheeks, and my ears.

"Oh!" I cried, horrified, clutching my hands to my ears and then together and then to my cheeks. "Oh! What now?"

The girl pulled a quilt from the bed and wrapped it around me. "It hurts, doesn't it?" she said grimly, taking another quilt for herself. "I think it's the sensation returning. Move your fingers and toes if you can."

And so we sat side by side on the edge of a bed, both wrapped in quilts, wriggling our fingers and toes. It hurt so much that tears began to run down my cheeks. The girl moved closer to me, putting an arm around me. Tears were in her eyes too.

"It'll stop, don't worry," she said, shaking her hands, stamping her feet on the rug. "I think it's called frostnip."

My hands and feet grew pink, then alarmingly red, and they burned and burned, and I tried not to cry aloud.

At last, ordinary color began to return to our skin, and the burning faded. We both sighed deeply, then we turned to each other and, for some reason, we laughed.

I think it was the shock. And the strangeness of experiencing something so terrible with a stranger.

"I don't know who you are," the girl said, "but you just saved my life. I was falling asleep—I think it was hypothermia." She grinned at me suddenly. "Thank you!"

"No, you saved *mine,*" I argued. "Doing that thing with your hands! You made the net float in the air and wrap around the tangled thread! Which made the ice disappear! Thank *you!*"

"I couldn't *see* the shadow magic until you pointed it out," she replied firmly. "So *you* saved my life."

"No, no," I began, and the girl giggled, threw her arms wide, and hugged me.

I had never been hugged by another child in my life. In fact, I hadn't hugged anybody at all for some time—Fiona next door used to snuggle on the couch with me when we watched television, drinking warm, frothy milk and eating her freshly baked banana and chocolate chip muffins. Also, she would pick me up and hug me when I hurt myself.

Grandmother, however, has always declined my offer of a hug. And if I hurt myself she says, "Child! Be careful!" and turns away.

So I hadn't hugged anyone for years.

That might explain why I began to cry again when the girl hugged me. She thought I was frightened, though, because she murmured into my hair, "It's all right. It's definitely gone now."

Then she climbed right up onto the bed and crossed her legs. "Everyone else is at assembly downstairs," she said. "I only ran up here to get the poem I was meant to be reading out; it's my grade's turn to present at assembly, and I'd forgotten mine. I suppose you're a new student? I've been here a term now, and I promise that's the first shadow attack that's happened since I started—I've no idea how it got in. There's a Spellbinding around the school so it's usually safe. And there aren't many Shadow Mages in the mountains these days."

I decided to be quite honest, as we'd just saved each other's lives. "I'm pretty confused by all that," I said. "You see, I'm not a new student, I'm actually from another world. I believe we are in a place called the Kingdoms and Empires? This is a school, is it?"

The girl studied me curiously. "Yes, this is the Kingdoms and Empires," she agreed after a moment. "We're at a boarding school called the Katherine Valley Boarding School. My cousins go here and I asked to try it this term. That black and red tangle you saw was a shadow spell—those are made by Shadow Mages such as Witches or Sterling Silver Foxes—and the green-and-gold net was a Spellbinding that I made, as I'm a Spellbinder. That's a secret, by the way—please don't tell anyone. Usually, I can see magic with my eyes closed, but for some reason I couldn't just now. Whereas you *could* see it—with your eyes open! Are you sure you're not a Spellbinder?"

"I don't think they exist in my world," I said. "I'm Lillian Velvet, by the way," I added, remembering to introduce myself. "May I ask your name?"

She smiled. "I'm Bronte Mettlestone," she said.

CHAPTER 39

OF COURSE, THE first thing I did was scramble to get the envelope out of my pocket and thrust it into her hands.

"So lucky it was still in my pocket!" I cried. "So lucky I got shoved here before bedtime so I wasn't in my pajamas!"

Bronte looked from the envelope to me, and back again. I was impressed that she kept her confusion to a tiny little crease in her brow.

"I'm sorry!" I said. "I'll explain!"

Worried I'd be shoved back any moment—after all, I'd already helped two trapped people (one of them myself)—I babbled my explanation. It was a summary really: pickle jar, gold coins, shoving back and forth, elderly woman in cottage by lake.

I skidded to a stop and looked at Bronte.

She looked back, that little crease still above her eyes. Then she shrugged. "I can't think who the elderly woman could be," she said. "You didn't open the envelope to see what was in it?"

"Of course not," I said, surprised. "It's for you."

She smiled at that and opened the envelope. I turned away so as not to accidentally read over her shoulder, while hoping she'd read it out loud. I was very curious.

However, time ticked by and she did not speak. In fact, there was such a deep silence that I looked back at her.

She was gazing at the paper with a very peculiar expression. Slowly, she folded it and put it back in the envelope.

Then she leaned against the headboard, tapping her fingertips together. She kept glancing over at me and then down at her fingertips.

There was a chest of drawers beside the bed. Abruptly, Bronte leaned over, pulled open the bottom drawer, drew out an object, and held it up.

I had never seen anything so beautiful. My heart stopped completely for a moment and then began fluttering like a garden filled with butterflies.

The object was a bottle: a graceful, swooping, cobalt-blue bottle, about the size of a wine bottle, and decorated with patterns in pressed gold foil.

"This is a Genie bottle," Bronte told me, her voice solemn. "It no longer holds a Genie."

I accidentally giggled at that. I had met a Genie named Reuben—and perhaps Mr. Turtelhaze was one too—and I got a sudden picture of Reuben, who's a fairly large, broad man, trying to squish himself into this bottle. Bopping his head against the opening. Maybe trying to feed his beard in first, and then getting stuck when he reached his chin. Or sticking in his little toe and waving the bottle around, jammed onto the end of his foot.

Bronte waited patiently through my giggles, then shuffled around on the bed and continued. "Around two years ago, when I was ten," she said, "I bought this bottle from a stall at the Lasaftk Markets on the Oski Coast. The Genie herself appeared beside me suddenly, while I was deciding whether to buy it or not. She was dressed in many layers of clothes, all of them shades of lipstick red, and I remember I thought her elegant and mysterious. I think she'd had a romantic connection with the man selling the bottle. Anyhow, I bought it. It has a magical power. Shall I tell you what the power is?"

"Yes," I said, "you shall." (I was embarrassed about adding *you shall* like that. I'd meant it to sound solemn, but it came out imperious.)

There was a glint in Bronte's eye. "If you put this by your bed at night," she said, "you will dream the dream you are supposed to dream."

"How marvelous," I breathed. "And it's so beautiful."

"It's yours," Bronte said, and she placed it in my hands.

CHAPTER 40

I GOT INTO a real panic then.

It was *not* my bottle; it was Bronte's! Much too generous of her to give it to me! On the other hand, I wanted it! Very much!

That's why I got into the panic. These two separate and opposing ideas were wrestling each other in my head.

Bronte had paid money for the bottle in a marketplace! I imagined putting it on the window ledge in my bedroom, and gazing at it. Bronte had met the Genie it had belonged to, a woman dressed in different shades of lipstick red! I imagined carrying it around the neighborhood with me, on my walks with Grandmother, and enjoying the admiring gazes of passersby. Bronte kept it in her bedside drawer, where it allowed her to dream the dreams she was meant to dream! I imagined—

I put my foot down hard on the floor. No more imagining. I must be polite. Firmly, I placed the bottle back in Bronte's hands.

"I could not possibly take it," I began.

"You must," Bronte insisted, returning it to my hands. "That's what the letter says I have to do: give you my Genie bottle. Here, just a moment . . ." She rummaged in the chest by her bed again, pulled out a drawstring bag, took the bottle from me, and placed it in the bag. Next, she looped the bag's handle around my wrist twice. "Now you *can't* return it," she said.

We both looked at the handles looped around my wrist. Quite honestly, I could have just unlooped them.

"I don't know why that person by the lake wanted me to give it to you," Bronte said, "but it's all right, I've had it for over two years. The dream magic only works *once* per person, and I've already used that long ago. My best friend Alejandro has used it, and so have each of my cousins, and all my new friends here at boarding school. It's your turn."

"Still!" I began—and then several voices sounded from outside the door and the room filled with people.

Not filled, exactly. It only felt that way for a moment. Three girls had arrived, all talking at once. They looked very similar, except that they were different sizes—large, medium, and small—and they all wore their hair in braids.

"Bronte, why didn't you come back to the assembly?"

"We missed your poem! Esther's was great though."

"Oh, you liked it? Thanks!"

"It's morning tea now."

"They've got cupcakes in the dining room!"

"No, the cupcakes are tomorrow."

Those were the sorts of things the girls were saying as they poured into the room.

Seeing me, they stopped abruptly, bumping into each other.

"Hello!" they said, blinking. They glanced at the drawstring bag hanging from my wrist.

"This is Lillian," Bronte told them. "Lillian, these are my cousins Imogen, Esther, and Astrid Mettlestone-Staranise." She pointed to each in turn, and each bowed her head, so that their braids bounced. "People always call them the braid girls, but they prefer to be called the Staranise sisters, if you don't mind."

"Not at all," I agreed. "Pleased to meet you, Staranise sisters."

The girls giggled.

"Lillian just saved my life," Bronte added. "There was a shadow spell in the room."

At this, there was such a chorus of gasps from the Staranise sisters that I thought someone had switched on a ceiling fan. However, when I looked up there was no ceiling fan.

The girls gathered close, and Bronte outlined what had happened—how she'd come into the room to fetch her poem and found herself freezing to death inside an ice cage instead. She'd been sure it was shadow magic yet had not been able to *see* the shadow spell to spellbind it.

Then I'd appeared (she continued). She made me sound like a hero, which was kind. I tried to interject, explaining that I hadn't done much at all, but she shushed me.

The sisters shook their heads in horror and kept interrupting to hug both Bronte and me—so there I was being hugged again; the bottle in the bag kept bumping against them but they politely didn't mention this—and to call us "darling," or "oh, you poor darlings."

When the story ended, the girls draped themselves over the closest beds, and engaged in an intense conversation with Bronte. It was all about spellbinding, Spellbinders, Shadow Mages, and shadow magic. How had the "shadow spell" found its way into the school? (they all wondered). "Maybe it was stuck to the bottom of somebody's shoe?" (one of them suggested). Why had Bronte not been able to see it? And why had *I* been able to see it? Was I sure I was not a Spellbinder?

"Maybe Lillian could see it because she's from another world?" Bronte said eventually. "I forgot to mention that."

I expected her cousins to be at least as shocked by this news as they had been by the ice cage, but they only turned to me calmly.

"You are? Wonderful. Welcome to our world," said Imogen, the biggest one.

"Interesting," the middle one, Esther, added, tilting her head at me. "What's your world called, Lillian?"

I wasn't sure how to answer that. Planet Earth? The Milky Way?

I settled on this: "I'm from Australia."

"Oh, that's Oscar's world!" the smallest one, Astrid, exclaimed. "You must know our friend Oscar!"

"As a matter of fact I do know Oscar," I replied. "I just—"

But the three sisters were nodding again, as if it made perfect sense that I should know Oscar. They were assuming that everyone in Australia knew each other.

"My world—my country, I mean—is *very* big," I said cautiously. "A *lot* of people live there. It's a remarkable coincidence that I know Oscar."

"All right," they replied, but I could tell they were just being agreeable.

"In fact," I added, "I only met Oscar for the first time this morning, here in your world. He was getting a coach at the Nicholas Valley Coach Station. He's bringing caramel fudge for you!"

At this, the sisters—and Bronte—gasped like ceiling fans again.

Good gracious, I thought. *I've put my foot in it somehow. I wonder what they have against caramel fudge?*

But it turned out it wasn't about the fudge. It was about the timing. Their voices overlapped as they said the following:

"You saw him this morning?"

"About to come here?"

"Oh no!"

"He's supposed to come *tomorrow*!"

"He must have got the day wrong," Astrid concluded forlornly, and to me she explained: "We're all traveling to Gainsleigh tomorrow, you see, and staying there for a week. If Oscar is on his way *now* he'll just have to turn around, go back, and come again tomorrow!"

Well, that wouldn't work.

Oscar was already reluctant enough about this trip. They couldn't be sending him back.

The girls were all talking again—wondering if they should walk into town to meet the coach, as Oscar would be expecting them—or perhaps, if they didn't go, he'd realize he had the wrong day? And then he could return without being embarrassed? It was only a short coach trip after all.

What if he *didn't* realize, though, and walked up to the school, looking for them? Would the school principal think he was skipping class? But why had he been allowed to leave Nicholas Valley Boarding School in the first place? Surely he only had permission to leave *tomorrow,* not today?

Something went *plink!* in my head.

Oh, I thought.

"What date is it today?" I asked.

Bronte looked across at a calendar pinned to the corkboard. "Wednesday, twenty-third of May."

"Ah." I was very embarrassed. "When I say that I met Oscar this morning, I really mean that I met him tomorrow morning."

There was a long silence. Imogen put her thumb and index finger to her lower lip and twisted it, squinting at me carefully.

"I seem to travel to different times when I move between worlds," I explained. "In my world, it's next week already. When I met up with Oscar this morning—*my* time—he told me it was Thursday, twenty-fourth of May. Which is tomorrow in *your* time, of course. Confusing, I know. I'm very sorry to have caused you needless worry. Although, I'm also relieved, because . . . well . . . ?" I paused.

Should I say this? I decided to be brave. "Can I tell you something else please?"

"All right," they agreed. They were watching me curiously.

"Oscar is anxious about meeting the Mettlestone family," I said. "I understand you have a very *large* family? Well, Oscar missed the first coach this morning—I mean tomorrow morning—because he wasn't sure he should come. He only got the second one after much hesitation. I hope it's not a betrayal of his confidence to tell you this. I'm new to the world of friendship. Only, you all seem kind-hearted so I thought you might want to know just to . . . keep an eye on him."

The girls glanced at each other.

"Poor Oscar," Esther said. "I had no idea."

"You did the right thing telling us, Lillian," Bronte put in. "And don't worry. We'll make sure he feels welcome. He has to come! We're meeting our grandparents for the first time!"

"Spiffing!" I said. Then I felt odd about saying that and changed it to "Marvelous."

They didn't seem to notice my choice of exclamation. They told me they'd just discovered that their grandparents had been in hiding for the last twenty years.

"We're very interested to meet them," Astrid said. "Especially our grandfather. He's a Wheat Sprite!"

"A Wheat Sprite? Is that a"—I tried to remember what I

knew about magic here—"a True Mage, a Shadow Mage, or a Spellbinder?"

"True Mage," Bronte told me. "So they can do bright magic, which means they can cast spells for things like healing, love, gold dust, and fine foods with subtle flavors. But land-based Sprites are different from other True Mages because they can *also* grant a single wish in their lifetime. Land-based Sprites rise up out of nature when it's feeling at its happiest, and nature gives them the wish—as a kind of celebration, or birthday present. They're pretty rare. We've met Water Sprites before but never a Wheat Sprite."

Her cousins all murmured their agreement. "Yes, but our long-lost grandparents are still just old folk from *our* world—no offense to old folk generally—whereas Oscar is from *another* world! The family will be just as keen to meet *him,* maybe more!"

"Plus Oscar does tricks on a thing called a skateboard," Esther said. "He's been teaching us. We take skateboards everywhere now."

They all giggled, supposedly at the idea of carrying skateboards around.

"*And* Oscar can fly," Astrid added.

"He can *fly*?" I turned to her doubtfully. She might have got the wrong end of the stick about Oscar's and my world. It's true that we have machinery that allows us to fly, dear reader, such as airplanes—but without one of those? Not a chance.

"Yes, Imogen can fly too," Bronte agreed. "She takes us flying around the school sometimes—she can take up to three people, as long as we link hands. We get in trouble for it, but we tested it first, going up by increments, and always over soft things like pillows or the lake. Shall we take you flying after school?"

My head was spinning. "Oscar can *fly*?" I repeated, abstractedly.

"It's because he got made an Elven king when he was on his first adventure with us," Astrid explained. "Imogen was made Elven queen."

"He didn't mention that," I said, trying not to mind about how truly superior Oscar's adventures were to mine.

"He's humble about his achievements," Bronte said. "So are my cousins." She pointed to the middle sister. "Esther defeated an ancient Ocean Fiend not long ago. Look, she's blushing—she's so embarrassed when anyone mentions it. If I was her, I'd be finding ways to bring it into conversation whenever I could."

Esther rolled her eyes. Her cheeks really were pink. "You would not, Bronte. *You* defeated the evil Whispering king and *you* never mention that."

"That's not to be sneezed at!" I said. "I don't know what a Whispering king is, but still, bravo, Bronte!"

Again, the four fixed me with interested expressions.

"Was that not the right thing to say?" I checked. "I know I speak strangely. My grandmother home-schools me and I have almost no experience with other children—or not until recently, when I received my pickle jar of gold coins. You see I've mostly learned about life from classic children's books, such as *The Phantom Tollbooth* and *A Wrinkle in Time,* which—"

I stopped. I was accustomed to being interrupted. Bronte and her three cousins, however, were listening closely, nodding along, brows crinkling when I mentioned the book titles—I suppose they don't have those books in this world, poor things. I felt both moved and embarrassed by their attention and wanted to shift focus.

"Anyhow, you all seem very talented," I said faintly. "Imogen is a flying Elven queen, Bronte defeats evil kings, Esther defeats . . . water features?"

Bronte grinned. "Water Fiends. You're talented too, Lillian—you can see magic. Plus, we missed Astrid." She pointed to the smallest Staranise sister. "She only needs to look at someone to be able to tell exactly how they're feeling. A valuable talent."

Astrid shrugged. "And I'm not modest about that at *all*."

The girls all laughed, and, after a moment, I joined in.

Esther turned to me. "Would you like Astrid to say how *you're* feeling, Lillian?"

That made me laugh again. I already knew how I felt. People tend to, don't they? As it's them, doing the feeling.

"Yes, please," I answered anyway, to be good-natured.

At that moment, a bell began to ring. It was a deep, low sound:

GONG! GONG! GONG!

"That's class time," Imogen told me, and all except Astrid began to gather themselves to go to class. "And we haven't eaten any morning tea. We'll swing by the dining hall on the way. Do you want to come, Lillian? You could join one of our classes for today. I'm sure the school would love to have a girl from another world drop in. Maybe Astrid's class?"

But Astrid was sitting on the edge of the bed staring at me.

"You're frightened," she told me. "That's how you feel."

"Not surprising." Bronte spoke up from the mirror where she was brushing her hair. "She just got trapped in an ice cage and almost perished. Or at least almost lost her fingers and toes to frostbite."

"Perhaps she's nervous about going into a classroom," Esther suggested sympathetically. "You don't have to, Lillian—we could come back to see you at lunch?"

I smiled. They were very thoughtful girls. "I've almost forgotten the ice cage now, Bronte," I said, "and I'm excited about the idea of being in a classroom. I've always longed to go to school. This is a dream come true."

Astrid remained perfectly still, hugging her knees and gazing at me. "It's bigger than that," she said quietly. "You really are frightened, Lillian."

I laughed—a little too loudly in the sudden silence of the room. "Not at all!"

"That's the thing," she said. "You're the most frightened person I've ever seen, yet you do not know it yourself."

Shove.

And I was home again.

CHAPTER 41

MY FEET WERE back on my threadbare bedroom carpet.

Ah well. No visiting a classroom after all. Somehow I'd known that wouldn't happen. I sighed, trying not to mind, and then I felt a weight pulling on my wrist.

The Genie bottle, still in its cotton drawstring bag.

A smile rose up from my chest.

I have a Genie bottle.

I hugged the bag, delaying the moment of opening it and drawing the bottle out, feeling the glass against my palms—

"*Child!* Set the table!" Grandmother's voice was sharp. She dislikes having to repeat herself.

"Sorry! Coming!" I called back, and scrambled to hide the bag under my bed. As I ran out to the dining room, I realized something surprising: that tugging and dragging sensation had vanished. I no longer yearned to rush out into the rain and dig up the garden. In fact, the idea seemed ridiculous. My feet sprang down the hallway like the hooves of a gazelle.

Later, when I'd said good night to Grandmother and climbed under the covers, I leaned over the side of my bed to look at the bag. There it lay, quiet in the shadows.

I had imagined taking the bottle on walks around the neighborhood with Grandmother. Now that I was home, though, I knew I would not do that. In fact, I would hide it from Grandmother. I'd never hidden anything from Grandmother before, so why now? *Hush,* said a voice in my head. *Just hide it, Lillian.*

Still, if I wanted to "dream the dream I was supposed to dream," I had to place it "by my bed." What if Grandmother entered my room in the night and saw it there?

I decided to leave it in its bag on the floor, *just* adjacent to the bed, hidden by the edges of my bedspread.

First, though, I peeked into the bag.

Hello, Genie bottle, I whispered, and my heart lit up the way a full moon lights a starry sky.

Then I pulled the cord tight again, set the bag amidst the bedspread folds, and lay my head on the pillow.

Quite quickly, I fell asleep.

CHAPTER 42

I DREAMED THE color red.

It drifted around me in all its many shades—tomato red, fire engine red, Illawarra flame tree in autumn, waratah blooming in spring. There was the crisp red of an apple, the gloss of a ladybird beetle's shell, the brightness of poppies and strawberries, the warmth of cherries and red peppers, the glow of a ruby or a fireplace.

I reached my hands out to touch a strand and it ran across my fingers, glowing, soft as silk.

"Hello, Lillian," said a voice, and I realized that it *was* silk I was touching—a silken scarf.

A woman stood beside me. She was very beautiful. Her eyes were dark, her hair was long and a rich dark color, and she was draped in many layers of red clothing—a long skirt, a blouse, a cardigan, several scarves, several shawls, beads, and belts, all in shades of red.

"Hello," I replied. "How do you know my name? I'm sorry for touching your scarf. I thought it was just a sort of whirling shade of red, abstract rather than concrete, and—" I stopped, and frowned to myself. "You remind me of someone—or something . . ." I bit my lip, thinking.

The woman waited patiently.

"It's all these shades of red," I explained. "They are somehow familiar. Like different shades of . . . lipstick! It was the girl named Bronte Mettlestone! She told me that the Genie who once belonged to her bottle had been dressed in shades of lipstick red! Are *you* a Genie? Are you *that* Genie?"

"I am," agreed the woman, still watching me. Her expression

was complicated—she seemed intrigued and amused by me, yet also sad. Not sad in herself, I mean: *sad for me.*

"I'm all right," I found myself telling her, a bit snappily, but that only made the sadness grow in her.

I pursed my lips. "Is this the dream I'm supposed to dream?" I asked.

She grinned. "It's about to be," she said, and she placed both her hands on the small of my back and—

CHAPTER 43

SHOVE!

"Hey!" I shouted, outraged. "You shoved me!"

Or had she? Perhaps I'd been shoved in the regular way at the exact moment she'd placed her hands on my back? *Could* I be shoved inside a dream?

These questions distracted me briefly, so then I gave myself a shake and looked around.

I was quickly baffled.

I was in a large room, the size of a community hall. It was dimly lit so I squinted, trying to make it out. Its floor was of concrete, its walls lined with doors. Each door was slightly ajar and each had a sign fixed above it.

WILD ANIMALS, said one sign.

DEAR FRIENDS, said another.

LOST TOYS, said a third.

"How odd," I murmured. From somewhere in the distance I could hear sounds—music and voices—but there were no windows and I couldn't see outside. Abruptly, the sign above one of the doors lit up.

RANDOM PEOPLE WHO WORK IN STORES, it said.

That door swung open and a man emerged, strolling into the room. Behind him, the door swung closed again.

He was a youngish man with a scattering of pimples across his cheeks, and he was dressed in good gray trousers, a collared shirt with a name badge, and a wide orange tie.

"Excuse me," I said, stepping up to him. "I wonder if you could tell me where I am? I was dreaming, you see, and—"

The man strolled right by me. His eyes didn't even flicker in my direction. It was very rude. I'd been going to ask if I was still dreaming or if I was awake and in the Kingdoms and Empires.

A second sign lit up—BELOVED PETS—and a border collie ran through that doorway, barking. The young man crouched, petting the dog.

A third sign: MOODS. That door opened and a flagpole jutted out at an angle, its fluttering banner declaring ANNOYED.

I looked back at the young man. His face was now creased with irritation. "Whose dog is this?" he shouted. "What's this dog doing here in the—?" He froze.

Across the room, another light: SETTINGS. A flagpole poked out of this doorway, wobbling a little; then its banner unfurled to reveal the word CLASSROOM.

"—the classroom!" the young man exclaimed. "What's this dog doing here in the classroom?"

To my amazement, the space around him grew busy, filling with objects and shapes—rows of wooden desks, an inkpot on each, a chalkboard, several children in smocks and long socks. The children gathered around the dog. The young man vanished.

The SETTINGS door lit up again. SEASIDE, said the flag. Now the dog was running along a sandy beach!

A door labeled MY FAMILY opened, and a man, woman, and four boys stepped out holding buckets, spades, and beach towels. The MOODS door flung out the word WORRIED. Immediately, the family bit their lips. The mother held a hand to her forehead, peering out at a stormy sea. The dog whined.

PARTY, announced the SETTINGS door. The family sported fancy, old-fashioned clothes now—long skirt and ruffled blouse, hats and jackets. EXCITED, said the mood door. They jiggled up and down, beaming at each other.

Flash! Flash! Flash!

All around me, doors lit up and flew open. I could no longer keep up. Scenes changed constantly, sometimes merging, sometimes vanishing. Two horses *clip-clopped* right by me, pulling a wagon. People skipped or danced or lay side by side on the floor—which became grass, and then dirt, and then a boat on a lake—pointing at the ceiling—which became a starry sky and then a man riding a broomstick. The broomstick swooped over my head so close the man's sandals brushed my shoulder. I screamed.

A woman sat beside me in an armchair, knitting a cardigan. "Children," she said sternly. "A piano is no place for a duck."

The family group vanished and returned several times, splitting into different formations—the boys climbed trees, the adults roller-skated sedately in a park. The original dog wandered about with a friendly expression and wagging tail. A schoolteacher stood in a corner, one arm wrapped around an octopus, the other scooping toffee sauce onto her own head.

"That's just *not* acceptable," the teacher scolded, as the sauce melted down her forehead.

The octopus squirmed from the teacher's arms and became a cat. It shrank down to the size of a pin. The knitting woman in the armchair picked it up, held it on the palm of her hand, and dropped it into a saucepan.

"This is too strange to be real," I decided. "I must still be dreaming."

And then, as I looked at doors flying open, strangers running around unfamiliar places, dogs, cats, teachers, parents, a knitting woman in an armchair—I understood.

This was someone else's dream.

CHAPTER 44

THE MOMENT I realized this, my eyes landed on a door marked: EXIT.

It was in the far corner of the hall. I made my way toward it, thinking: *Yes. It is not polite to wander around somebody else's dream.*

As I reached the door, though, I hesitated. If a Genie had *shoved* me here, shouldn't I stay?

Still.

Dreams are private. I'd seen the exit. I'd better use it.

I pushed open the door and stepped through.

It slammed behind me with a gust of air and a *bang!* I was not outside though. I was in a long, narrow corridor with a low ceiling. It was very quiet, although a thrumming energy emanated from the closed door behind me and, more distantly, the music and voices I'd noticed when I first arrived.

Tentatively, I followed the corridor. It ran straight for a while and then began to curve. It also sloped slightly downward, I realized—my knees had to bend at each step. Around another curve I walked and *blam!*

The walls opened up and the ceiling shot so high it almost disappeared. Now I seemed to be in an immense warehouse. Rows and rows of shelves, each stacked with boxes and baskets. Some of the passages between shelves were as wide as a street, and some were so narrow you'd have to turn side-on to squeeze along them.

Two things happened suddenly. First, one of the shelves rolled itself up like a snail shell, while several of its baskets and boxes spilled onto the floor. Second, a metal claw swooped down from the ceiling, plucked a basket, and sent it flying into the air.

The room fell still again.

Was I still in the person's dream then?

After a long moment, I crept closer to one of the shelves, very afraid that it might suddenly roll itself up, or that a claw might swoop down and throw *me* into the air. The shelf stayed where it was though, like an ordinary shelf, and I stayed where I was, like an ordinary girl.

I inched closer and noticed that the boxes were labeled. Here is what I read:

UNPLEASANT SMELLS

LOVELY SMELLS

DANGER SMELLS

SAD SMELLS

ASTONISHING SMELLS

SMELLS OF MY BROTHERS' FEET

SMELLS OF ANGIE

SMELLS OF ANGIE AFTER SHE HAS A BATH

SMELLS OF ANGIE AFTER SHE HAS ROLLED IN SHEEP POO

After that, the labels were too far away to read, disappearing into the shadows.

Well, I thought, standing back from the shelf.

Smells.

In boxes.

Well, I thought again.

My mind had nothing further to add. Just *Well.*

Come on, mind, I prompted it. *Why are boxes filled with smells lined up on a shelf?*

My mind shrugged.

And then it gave a little jolt and said: *Wait. Lillian. Where are dreams made?*

Of course! Dreams are made inside your mind! A dream takes bits and pieces of memories and thoughts and throws them together to create wild new stories. I hadn't just been inside a stranger's *dream;* I'd been inside their *mind*! By exiting the dream I'd only found my way into another part of the dreamer's mind! The part that stored all the smells they recognized!

I shuffled sideways toward the next shelf along and read some labels:

LITTLE WORDS
BIG WORDS
NEW WORDS
CONFUSING WORDS
IMAGINARY WORDS
WORDS THAT MAKE ME GIGGLE
WORDS THAT MAKE MOTHER GIGGLE
WORDS THAT MAKE ANGIE PRICK UP HER EARS
WORDS THAT MAKE ANGIE WAG HER TAIL
WORDS THAT MAKE ANGIE GROWL
WORDS THAT ARE IMPOSSIBLE TO SPELL
WORDS THAT ARE IMPOSSIBLE TO SPELL AND YET I KNOW HOW TO SPELL THEM, WHICH MAKES MOTHER PROUD
WORDS TO KICK YOUR TOE ON

Not just smells, then, also words.

I was getting an idea of the person whose mind I was inside. For one thing, it seemed to be a child, perhaps quite a young child. The child had brothers, parents, and a dog named Angie. Maybe Angie was the dog I'd seen running through the dreams?

On the next shelf, some of the boxes were half-open. One of these was labeled PRECIOUS MOMENTS, and I took a chance and moved close enough to peer inside.

It was very strange—inside the box were images, and each one took me inside itself. There was seaweed strewn on sand and I was there, for a moment, touching the seaweed, breathing salty air, sea breeze on my cheek. Then I blinked and saw a pair of wet woolen mittens—I could feel their weight and damp softness on my hands. A basket filled with apples in an orchard. A man painting a farmhouse door. The sun setting over a field.

A woman's voice murmuring, "Go back to sleep—you're not well—we'll do the milking today."

The child lives on a farm, I decided, *and once went on a holiday to the seaside.*

The next shelf held a series of open baskets, the first of which was labeled TO KNOW FOR TEST TOMORROW.

The child has been studying for an exam at school tomorrow. Lucky child, going to school.

This one was filled with scraps of paper. I picked up a handful. There were both writing and pictures:

Spellbinders weave nets that bind shadow magic (a picture of a figure wearing a cape)

Examples of common Shadow Mages: Witches, Sterling Silver Foxes, and Radish Gnomes (picture of a tall, thin, bearded man with sharp, pointy ears, labeled sterling silver fox)

Examples of rare Shadow Mages: Hurtlings and Toasted Clips (unexpectedly, there was a picture of a toaster oven and a jar of peanut butter)

I dropped the papers back into the basket.

Spellbinders. Shadow Mages.

The child lives in the Kingdoms and Empires.

So I *had* been shoved into the Kingdoms and Empires—only this time I'd been shoved from my own dream into the dream of a sleeping Kingdoms and Empires child.

I stood back again, gazing at the rows of shelves. Those faint, distant sounds continued. A clash of tambourines. Trumpets blaring. Voices shouting and laughing.

A child was sleeping and dreaming and these noises were carrying on around the child. Perhaps the child was asleep in a bed while their parents had a party? Or perhaps the parents were watching television? Did they have television in the Kingdoms and Empires? I thought maybe not. It seemed an old-fashioned sort of world.

Something was itching at me. A half thought. A question.

I was inside a child's mind. The big hall contained the child's dreams. This warehouse held the child's memories. But even when I'm dreaming, or remembering, I'm always *there* somehow. I'm the one doing the watching, the listening, the . . . *thinking*.

So where was . . . well, where was the *child*?

CHAPTER 45

AS SOON AS I had *that* thought, I noticed a door at the far end of the warehouse. Once again, it was marked EXIT.

I sighed and hurried toward it. It was a great distance away. Faster and faster I walked, until I was half-jogging. When I finally reached it, I threw it open.

It led into another low corridor, which once again curved and curved—definitely sloping downward now, quite steeply. I almost tripped, it was so steep. I didn't slow down though. In fact, I found myself running fast. Around and around and around.

I passed spiral staircases. Slides. Cupboards. Pipes.

The sounds from outside rose and fell. "Come on!" I heard a woman's voice call. "It's starting!" The music stopped for a moment and then resumed. More tambourines. Applause.

I was sprinting now.

What's the hurry? I asked myself—and only sprinted faster, stumbling, catching myself, and running again.

The curves of the corridor grew tighter and tighter—it was coiling itself more and more narrowly. I was running on a constant curve, into a deeper and deeper darkness, dizzy and dazed.

There! I thought.

There!

Up ahead, the corridor stopped abruptly. Another doorway. Not labeled.

The child is behind the door.

I don't know how I knew this, I only knew I had reached the center. The child would be here.

I skidded to a stop and knocked.

Nothing.

I pushed my ear to the wood of the door. No sound from inside.

The noises from outside seemed more distinct though. "Let's get toffee!" I heard. "Quick, it'll start again soon." Hurrying footsteps that faded. The music swelled. A horse neighed.

The child is sleeping somewhere in the outdoors, I realized. *The child is at some kind of outdoor event—a fair?*

I knocked again, thudding with both fists until they ached.

Still nothing.

Close by, a soft whistling sound—the wind? More footsteps. The voices of men. Further away, the roar of a crowd.

I grabbed the door handle and turned it.

Locked. I jiggled, but nothing.

Again I knocked, calling, "Hello! Child! Hello! Wake up!"

Tried the handle again; still locked.

Maybe I could use a hairpin to pick the lock? I touched my hair. Of course, I was asleep in bed myself—in my pajamas, no hairpins.

I knelt at the door to try to peer through the keyhole.

That's when I saw it—stitched around the door handle and crisscrossing the keyhole itself.

Red and black thread.

It was this—this thread that had sewn the door, locking it. I reached out to tear it open, but my hand felt nothing at all.

So strange! Yet somehow familiar.

Of course, it was the kind of thread I'd seen inside the ice cage with Bronte. This time it was not tangled though, but very neatly stitched.

I frowned, trying to remember what Bronte had said. Was this *shadow magic*?

Had shadow magic locked the child deep inside his own mind? Was shadow magic keeping him asleep?

Another distant blast of music. Another blast of applause.

Closer to: the whickering of a horse.

A man's voice: "Back it up here!"

"Back up!"

"Halt!"

"Halt!"

A long, slow creaking sound—

And I knew where I was.

The circus.

The men with the wagon piled high with gravel.

Boy asleep in the enclosure.

I was inside the mind of that sleeping boy.

"WAKE UP!" I roared, pounding on the door. "WAKE UP!"

Absolute silence from behind the door and—

Shove.

I was back in my own bed.

PART 7

REPORT 4

A SPACIOUS PENTHOUSE APARTMENT, GAINSLEIGH, KINGDOMS AND EMPIRES —Thursday, May 24

* * *

It was 10:30 p.m.

Rain had been falling steadily all day and the streets were slick and shiny under moonlight.

Isabelle Mettlestone stood at her study window, gazing absently into the night. Her home was almost full. She fancied she felt it stumble a little, under the weight of its many guests.

Isabelle had one brother and ten sisters. These, along with her brother's wife, Lida—the only partner attending, the others being busy at work—and all the children, would be staying with her for a week. The adult guests were still up and about—she could hear coffee being made in the kitchen, laughter from the living room, the *clonk . . . clonk* of snooker being played in the games room.

To calm her mind, she ran through the sleeping arrangements.

First, the adults.

- Carrie—liked space to work on her Spellbinding; a mattress in the ballroom.
- Franny—liked sleeping rough and intended to bunk down in the garden shed.
- The twins, Maya and Lisbeth—had been sharing the library since they arrived ten days

earlier, a storm having damaged their cruise ship.

- Nancy and Claire—the organizers; twin foldout couches in the games room (they'd almost certainly get the correct game pieces sorted into their correct boxes).
- Sue—the farmer; air mattress in the conservatory (she'd definitely revive some of the wilting plants while she was staying).
- Alys (when she arrived—she was late)—chaise longue in the music room. As queen of a musical kingdom, Alys was soothed by the presence of music.
- Emma (along with several boxes of her "treasured" possessions)—had been occupying the studio (and painting joyfully) for the last twelve days, having fled her storm-wrecked Lantern Island.
- Sophy—at her own request, the stables. Sophy was a veterinarian and ordinarily slept in a barn filled with dragons.
- Patrick and his wife, Lida—lavender guest suite.
- The parents (guests of honor, due to arrive tomorrow morning)—

Isabelle stopped. She clunked her head against the window glass.

Her parents would sleep . . .

Where?

How had she forgotten *her parents*? The entire week was for them! Should she put them here in the study? What about bedding! Cushions from the living room? But they were elderly! What was she—

Oh.

What was wrong with her?

The Grand Rose Suite had been ready for her

parents for over a month. Immediately after reading their telegram, in fact, before she'd even telegrammed the others, she had entered the suite and begun to make the bed. To relax her racing heart, she had plumped the cushions. To make their return *real,* and not a dream, she had turned down the covers, placing fresh towels at the end of the bed.

All right. The children.
Asleep—or in bed, at least.

- The girls—bunk beds in the hibiscus room. The girls consisted of Bronte (technically Patrick and Lida's child, but Isabelle and the Butler had raised Bronte—the hibiscus room had been Bronte's *bedroom*—they missed her desperately now she'd chosen to attend boarding school) along with Nancy's lively daughters, who always wore their hair in braids: Imogen, Esther, and Astrid.
- The boys—bunk beds in the daffodil room. The boys consisted of Sue's boys (Sebastian, Nicholas, Connor, and little Benjamin), their cousin Billy (arriving with his mother, Alys, any moment), and Oscar—the boy from another world.

Again Isabelle stopped, smiling this time. Oscar had arrived with the girls that afternoon, nerves in his tightly held shoulders. She'd seen him give his shoulders a good shake, trying to shake loose those nerves. She'd seen Bronte offer an encouraging pat on the back, and he'd grinned at her, embarrassed and grateful.

Then Sue's boys had swarmed him, hammering him with questions about life in his world. They'd offered competitive tales of their own, about life on their family farm. Soon, the boys were belting each other with cushions from Isabelle's couch.

The girls, being protective of Oscar, had rushed to intervene. Cushions had flown. A vase had been smashed. Various adults had shouted.

Isabelle hadn't minded. The vase had been an odd shape—it always made flowers jut out at the wrong angle. She was relieved to see it broken. More to the point, the cushion fight had been exactly what Oscar needed. He was part of the family now.

The children had fled downstairs to the gardens, arguing loudly about whether the city or the country, soccer or rugby league was superior, and feverishly discussing the schedule for the next few days. (Isabelle was proud of her schedule: she'd arranged concert and circus tickets, picnics and hikes.)

Now they were safe in their rooms, Billy being the only child missing. He was a sunny-natured boy, but she felt he would hold his own with a cushion should another battle erupt.

For a third time, Isabelle stopped. She peered down at the street, searching for signs of a carriage. Billy and Alys had been supposed to arrive by now. Something urgent must have come up in Alys's kingdom.

Well, Alys was a queen, after all. Things were always coming up.

So why was Isabelle's heart racing like a locomotive?

An answer came like a shot of ice: *What if it's too soon for our parents to come out of hiding? What if the danger hasn't passed?*

Almost at the same time, a voice spoke up from behind her. "*Scintillate,*" said the voice. "Your turn, Isabelle."

Isabelle blinked. She turned from the window.

The Butler, seated at the desk, was looking at her expectantly. She was supposed to be playing Scrabble with him, and with her sister Franny. Having traveled a vast distance to be here, Franny was exhausted. She was slouched in an armchair, eyes closed, feet up on the desk. You might have assumed she was asleep, except that she was holding a carrot, from which, occasionally, she took a great, crunching bite.

Also, now and then, she spoke.

"Nope," Franny said now, eyes closing again. "Nice try building on the *late,* but *scintillate* is spelled with two *l*'s."

"She's right." Isabelle rejoined the Butler at the desk and studied the board. "Try again."

"My apologies." The Butler tugged at his own ear. "I know how to spell *scintillate.* I must be distracted."

Crunch, said Franny, taking another bite.

Isabelle and her sister Franny were very similar, although their appearances suggested otherwise. Isabelle was dressed correctly, hair in a neat twist. Franny, on the other hand, had wild gray curls and wore an oversize shirt, jodhpurs, and dusty old boots.

The Butler nudged one of these boots aside so he could adjust his word. "*Tinsel,*" he said, with a sigh. He looked at the clock and blinked. "I believe I know why I'm distracted," he announced.

The others waited. The Butler continued. "While it is common for your sister Alys to be delayed," he said, "it is extremely uncommon for her to be delayed without sending word."

At this, the shot of ice hit Isabelle again, this time straight in the chest.

"You're right," Franny said, eyes springing open. Her boots swung down to the floor.

PART 8

CHAPTER 46

AT BREAKFAST ON Monday morning, Grandmother spoke to me sharply.

"Are you ill, child?" she demanded.

I wasn't surprised by her question. I'd just seen my face in the bathroom mirror. My eyes were puffy and bloodshot.

"Thank you for asking, Grandmother," I replied, drawing my seat up to the table. "I am only tired after having a dreadful dream last night."

"A nightmare, you mean," she corrected. "Be precise."

"Well, I don't know that it *was* a nightmare," I responded vaguely. I picked up my knife and tilted it so that it caught the morning sunlight. Grandmother's hand shot out and plucked the knife from my fingers, replacing it on the table.

I looked up at her. "Most of the dream was fun," I explained. "I was inside somebody *else's* dream, you see. At the very end, though, I realized that it was the dream of the little boy at the circus—the one I saw about to be buried by gravel—and so here was another chance to save the child's life. Only, I failed! Again! When I woke up, I couldn't stop crying. It was shadow magic, you see, I know that now, and—"

"Go and splash water on your face," Grandmother told me, pouring tea from the pot into her cup. "I am going into work early today and must leave in a moment." She glanced at the clock on the wall and set to work finishing her breakfast.

The moment that Grandmother had closed the front door behind her, I picked up the jar of gold coins, unscrewed the lid, and filled both my pockets with coins. Then I added a few more. My pockets sagged. When I moved, the coins bumped heavily along with me, clinking and thudding against my legs.

The Genie bottle had sent me the "dream I was supposed to dream"—a dream that had *shoved* me into the boy's dream. I'd been meant to wake him—to release him from the spell that was locking him into sleep—in time to save him.

Only, I hadn't done that. I'd failed.

Moreover, that was my last chance. Bronte had said the Genie bottle would only work once. I had used it up.

My eyes filled with tears again. I blinked hard, trying to stop myself. This was the time to concentrate.

The fact was, if the dream shove counted as a regular shove, my five visits were complete. I counted the visits on my fingers to be sure.

First, the wild ocean scattered with flowers in the Kingdom of Kate-Bazaar. I had met Reuben there, promised not to help anybody, then helped two little children, Eli and Taya, by placing them onto a gate.

Second, the rabbits in a cage that I'd freed before noticing they'd been outside a pet shop. They'd probably been purchased by somebody who'd gone to fetch their car—or more likely carriage, in that world—to take the rabbits home.

Third, the skateboarder named Oscar waiting at a coach stop, who had shared caramel fudge with me. He was a better adventurer than I.

Fourth, Bronte Mettlestone, trapped in a cage of ice, who'd given me a Genie bottle and introduced me to her cousins, the Staranise sisters. (I should never have accepted the bottle. I'd used it wrongly. Also, how could I ever return it to her?)

Finally—if it did count—the dream shove last night.

Therefore, the next time I was shoved, Mr. Turtelhaze should be back. I would be ready for him with my pockets full of coins.

Mr. Turtelhaze was going to get more than a few coins though.

He was going to get a piece of my mind.

CHAPTER 47

IT WAS DIFFICULT concentrating on my schoolwork that morning.

My mind seemed to have fallen into my pockets, where it jangled and clinked amongst the coins.

75 – 36 (a question asked).

Jangle, clink, jangle? (replied my mind).

I kept doodling in the margins of my schoolbook and then erasing the doodles, brushing away the eraser dust—and drawing doodles again.

At last it was time for morning tea. I carried my sliced apple and my oatmeal bar into the garden. Two things struck me immediately.

First, Grandmother's boots were standing on the back steps, covered in mud. A muddy shovel leaned against the wall beside them.

Second, the part of the garden that had been disheveled the day before had now been tidied and patted down.

I walked across the grass and stared at the smooth earth. No tingling, frantic sensation of any kind. It was clear to me that whatever had been buried here was no longer buried here. Grandmother must have engaged in moonlight gardening again, and dug it up.

I glanced over at the fence, wondering if the neighbors were home and—*shove*.

I was somewhere else.

I straightened my shoulders, ready to give Mr. Turtelhaze a piece of my mind.

Instantly, though, I noticed I was somewhere very pretty. This was disconcerting. It's difficult to feel fierce and bold when you're standing on a grassy slope bright with drifts of fallen autumn leaves. What's more, the slope ran down to a sandy cove. Blue sea reached out to the horizon beneath a curve of bright blue sky. *Plash*, said the sea. *Plish*, said a dolphin rising from the water, turning a graceful curve. Close to shore, the air shimmered and rippled like soap bubbles.

"Give me a moment," said a voice, and I turned to see Mr. Turtelhaze crossing the grass. This time he was dressed in a suit, its trouser legs rolled up. His tie had been loosened and his feet were bare. Leaves drifted around his ankles as he scuffed through them.

"Take off your shoes!" he advised, smiling broadly. "Grass is soft against the soles."

I smiled back and was about to pull my shoes off when I remembered myself. At once, I changed my smile to a frown.

"Mr. Turtelhaze," I began, "you did *not* tell me that my visits took me back in time! You did *not* tell me that I couldn't help anybody without causing harm! I'd already broken the rule when Reuben told me about it. And I keep doing it! Over and over! I can't help it! I *cannot* keep visiting the Kingdoms and Empires if I'm not allowed to help people. No offense to you or to Grandmother, but that is the worst kind of adventure. Therefore, I must, with sadness, discontinue my visits. However, first I *must* help the little boy at the circus. I need to go back there, please. If I had known he was about to be buried I'd never have asked for a very short visit the first time, and now the dream shove has—"

"Oh, you can't wish to *go*," Mr. Turtelhaze said absentmindedly.

I blinked.

He was gazing out at the dolphins—there were five or six of them rising and falling in the water now. He glanced back at me and smiled.

His reaction was very unexpected.

I had supposed he would be shocked, offended, or chastened by my lecture. Instead, he hardly seemed to have noticed it.

"You can't wish to go," he repeated. "You can only wish to

stay. As for this Reuben and his rules? Nonsense. Do what you like. Help whomever you please. Have you got the coins you owe? And you wish to stay today?"

I stared.

My mind had been feeling like a cupboard, cluttered with questions and emotions. I'd planned to take each out, one at a time, to present to Mr. Turtelhaze—only he'd reached in and swept all the clutter to the ground.

"Was the dream shove an actual shove?" I asked faintly—snatching up a random question.

"You've visited the Kingdoms and Empires five times since I last saw you," Mr. Turtelhaze said, still sounding sunny. "They all count. Why shouldn't they? Do you wish to stay on this visit? And shall we say the next . . . ten visits?"

Now it seemed as if the clutter was being shuffled about so I could hardly make out what was there.

"I truly can't wish to go back to the circus? Even if I used *all* my coins?"

"You truly can't."

"Was the little boy okay?" I asked hopefully instead. "Perhaps somebody saw him in time?"

Mr. Turtelhaze tucked his hands in his pockets and didn't reply. Perhaps he didn't know.

"I can *really* do what I like?" I asked. "My actions won't cause terrible harm?"

"Such nonsense!" Mr. Turtelhaze scoffed. "Oh!" he added softly—but that was because he was gazing out to sea again. I believe he was still admiring dolphins.

"Reuben was wrong?" I checked.

"Reuben was wrong. Do you have the coins? Do you wish to stay? Today and for the next ten times?"

I scooped all the coins from my pockets and held them out to him. "There's *no* way to go back to the circus? Is there nothing I can do to help the—"

"Right, so that's for that, and that's for that, and that's . . ." Mr. Turtelhaze was muttering to himself, plucking coin after coin from my hands. "Oh, and that and—oh yes, *that*—which means—yes, that . . ." The coins were almost gone. "Last chance," he added. He sounded businesslike now. "Wish to stay for a little while and then return home, as usual? For this and the next ten times?"

What else could I do?

"I'm not sure I have enough coins left in the jar," I whispered, "but if I do, yes please."

"Righto," he said. "You'll owe me." He squinted to himself. "I'd say you have *just* enough in the jar for ten more visits. After that, no doubt, you're done."

He swept the last coins from my hands. He was gone.

CHAPTER 48

ALMOST IMMEDIATELY I heard a solid, rhythmic sound like marching boots. At the same time an urgent voice cried: *"Get down!"*

I ducked down, close to the grass.

"Stay still! Stay quiet!" the voice ordered next. It was a girl's voice. She sounded confident, like a fifteen-year-old.

And she wasn't speaking aloud. She was speaking inside my head.

"Is it a Hurtling?" I asked her, also speaking inside my own head.

"A Hurtling? No, it's not a Hurtling! It's soldiers! Can't you see them? They're right above you!" There was a short pause and then: *"How did you just answer me?"*

I swiveled—

"Stay still! Didn't you hear me? Stay still!"

Moving slowly, I t-u-u-u-u-r-n-e-d around, and c-r-a-a-a-a-n-e-d my neck to see. The voice had been correct. On the hill above me, soldiers were marching in pairs. A path ran along the hilltop, but I could only see a section of it, curving around the headland. Soldiers in uniforms and peaked caps, buttons gleaming, arms swinging, feet marching, *one-two, one-two,* appeared and disappeared, appeared and disappeared along the path.

If any soldier looked down the hill, toward the sea, they would see me.

"Shhhhh," the voice in my head reminded me, although I'm sure I hadn't made a sound.

"What does it matter if they see me?" I asked the voice.

"You're not a Whisperer, are you?" it demanded. *"Even though you're answering me?"*

"No," I replied. *"I mean, certainly, I know* how *to whisper. You just make your voice go soft and . . . whispery. It's like speaking with air, instead of with your voice. So if that means I'm a Whisperer then I suppose I—"*

"I mean you're not from around here, are you?"

"No."

"Then stay still! Stay perfectly still! Do NOT let them see you!"

She had not answered my question, but I crouched lower. To pass the time, I counted soldiers.

"How many more are there?" I asked once I'd reached a hundred and twelve. By this point, I was very tired of crouching.

"Not many. Poor things." The voice had become wistful.

"Poor things?" That was confusing. *"I thought we were afraid of them?"*

"YOU'RE afraid of them," the voice snapped. *"I'm not! I'm trying to protect* you! *But look at them! So skinny, so wounded, so ragged, so few . . ."* Her voice seemed to stumble, as if she might cry.

So *few* of them? I thought (to myself—not to her). There were over a hundred and twelve.

I was about to reply: *"They seem very well to me! Backs as straight as doors! Swinging arms!"* when I noticed one soldier's wrist. It caught my eye because it was wearing a frayed armband, red and black. The wrist was thin and knobbly. The next soldier along was wearing the same armband on a similarly thin wrist. And the next. So many thin, swinging arms, all with frayed armbands. One soldier's arm was in a sling. (That arm jolting up and down as she marched.) Another sling. An eye patch. A bandage covering an ear.

The faces were thin too, I realized, eyes set deep. The edges of the trousers were worn, a rip or a hole here and there.

"Oh," I said. *"You're right. They don't look their best. What happened to them? Did they lose a battle?"*

My legs were beginning to burn from staying in this position. I should have started out by sitting down rather than crouching. Tentatively, I tried lowering myself onto the grass.

"*Be still!*" hissed the voice, and then it became very withering. "*Did they lose a battle? You must be joking. A battle? They lost the whole war! We lost the war! They've trapped us behind a Spellbinding! To punish us! We are PRISONERS in our own kingdom! Who ARE you? How can you not KNOW this?*"

I decided to return to counting soldiers. I'd missed a few, so I started again at one.

. . . three, four, five, six . . .

My legs ached and moaned, begging me to let them fall onto the grass. "Can't we just sit down?" my legs pleaded. "Look how soft the grass is!"

Surely I could just quickly drop?

. . . twelve, thirteen, fourteen . . .

It was never-ending! My thighs were on *fire*! Not actual fire, but that's how they felt.

. . . seventeen, eighteen . . .

THUD.

I hit the grass with a gasp. My legs had made the decision for me.

Up on the crest of the hill, several heads swung in my direction.

CHAPTER 49

"BEAUTIFUL DAY FOR a march!" cried a voice.

It was the voice in my head. Only this time it was speaking aloud, somewhere up on the hill.

The soldiers' heads swiveled away from me, toward the voice.

"Princess Lida," they chorused, sweeping off their caps. "Good morning, Your Highness, happy birthday!" and they bowed. I couldn't see the girl herself—she was out of sight, beyond the soldiers. It turned out that all the soldiers' caps had been hiding great piles of hair. This hair had been wound up and neatly pinned in place.

"*Hide!*" the girl's voice barked in my head, at the same time as I heard her say loudly to the soldiers: "Good morning to you. How are your moods? How is your energy?"

Hide? Where?

I scrambled across the grass on all fours, like a scuttling crab, and dove into a pile of leaves. It crunched noisily.

"*HUSH!*" she wailed, at the same time as she practically shouted: "AND, CORPORAL ARMSTRONG, HOW IS YOUR SPRAINED ANKLE TODAY? YOU SEEM TO BE GETTING ALONG ALL RIGHT ON IT?"

I squirmed into the leaves, as quietly as I could—which was, in fact, very loudly—until I was more or less covered.

Then I waited, heart thudding.

"Please, I do not wish to delay you any further," the girl's voice was saying to the soldiers. "The remainder of your battalion are well ahead now. I apologize. You'd best march on and catch them. No, no, I do not require assistance. Thank you but I am only out for a stroll. My best wishes to you all."

A short pause and then voices chorused: "Thank you, Your Highness, happy birthday again!" and the *thud-thud, thud-thud* of marching feet resumed.

Thud-thud, thud-thud.

Thud-thud,

Thud-thud.

Silence.

More silence.

More silence.

"Have they gone?" I asked. *"Can I come out?"*

"Hold on."

A long, long quiet. The breeze. The plashing sea. A distant bird's call.

And then quick footsteps ran toward me and there was the girl's voice, directly above me: "All right, get out of there and explain yourself!"

CHAPTER 50

EXPLAIN MYSELF?

That felt like a tall order.

I burst forth from the leaves like a sprinkler system—that's what I imagined I was like anyway; I suppose I was less splashy than that, as I'm not made of water—and faced the girl.

She was very beautiful. Smooth, brown skin (with only two little pimples, one high on her right cheek, the other to the left of her chin), bright, dark eyes, a fine sharp nose, and the longest hair I have ever seen. It was dark and shimmery and it flowed almost to her ankles. Yet she never once tripped over it. I kept an eye out for that.

"Thank you for distracting the soldiers for me," I said, brushing leaves from my own hair (which is very short and cut in a straight line, in what Grandmother calls a "bob"—I keep it tidy with two hairpins). "I was crouching, you see, and I couldn't hold still for another moment and—"

"How did you escape?" the girl demanded, hands on her hips, the long hair shivering behind her back. "And how were you able to answer me when I whispered you just now?"

"Whispered me? Do you mean when you spoke in my mind? I don't know how *you* did that, let alone how I did! I mean, I just . . . answered. How did I escape? I didn't escape! I'm from another world, you see. I was *shoved* here. I get shoved to different parts of the Kingdoms and Empires, and into different times. As a matter of fact, be prepared: I could be *shoved* back at any moment."

The girl reached out and plucked a couple of leaves from my dress. She was frowning deeply. "Shoved?" she repeated. "Do you mean you were magically transported here from another world?"

"Magically transported. That's a better way to put it. Thank you. Anyway, I don't even know what this place is, I'm afraid. It seems beautiful though."

I looked around, and the girl did too. The ocean with its arcing dolphins, the strange shimmer in the air, the golden leaves.

When she turned back to me, the girl's face had softened. "It *is* beautiful," she agreed. "It's the Whispering Kingdom. The most beautiful kingdom in all the Kingdoms and Empires, with the kindest, gentlest people. We are Whisperers, which means we can whisper thoughts into people's minds—that's how I spoke to you. But people *cannot* usually reply like you just did." She pursed her lips. "Some of us also hear whispers from the future, telling us what's going to happen—but I never heard a whisper about you."

"That must be handy," I suggested, and then I remembered myself. "My name is Lillian Velvet. I heard the soldiers calling you Princess Lida and also they called you *Your Highness*. Should I call you that? I've already met a prince in my travels—Prince Billy—do you know him? And I've met people from a family called the Mettlestones. Do you know the Mettlestone family?"

"I am Princess Lida, yes. Just call me Lida though," the girl—Lida—replied. "I don't know a Prince Billy or anyone named Mettlestone."

"What about Carrie Mettlestone? She was in the Luminous Forest on the outskirts of the grand harborside town of Gainsleigh. Or Bronte Mettlestone? She was at a boarding school. There were cousins too. They were Mettlestone-Staranises, which is a form of Mettlestone. Do you know them? Imogen, Esther, and—"

"I don't know *any* Mettlestones." She was sounding cranky again. "Never heard of them. Saying Mettlestone over and over won't change that, Lillian Velvet."

"Anyway," I continued, "it all started on my birthday, when Grandmother—oh! I forgot! It's *your* birthday today—I heard the soldiers saying happy birthday! No wonder you look cross—I haven't said happy birthday! Many happy returns, Lida!"

At this, Lida turned away from me abruptly, a number of expressions crossing her face. Dejection, bewilderment, distress. None of these seemed birthday appropriate.

"It *is* your birthday today, isn't it?" I checked.

"Yes. That's why . . ."

"Why what?"

"Come with me," she said suddenly, and she began striding down the hill toward the little beach. I followed, trying to keep up.

"I turn fifteen today," she said, her long hair floating behind her like a veil, "and—"

"Fifteen! That's exactly what I guessed," I cried. "When you spoke to me in my head, I thought to myself: that sounds a confident voice, like a fifteen-year—"

Lida stopped and swung around to look at me, intently.

"Sorry," I said.

"I am fifteen today," she repeated, beginning to walk again. She had reached the sand and was scuffing along it at high speed, "and that means I have to start wearing the armband all the time. Never take it off. I already wear it *sometimes,* but I don't *want* to wear it all the time! It makes me so snappy! You might have seen the soldiers wearing them—black and red armbands? It's compulsory once you turn fifteen. So I'm leaving."

"Why is it compulsory?" I asked, puffing a bit. Her legs were longer than mine. "And why does it make you snappy? Is it rough against your skin? Perhaps, as you're a princess, you could get an exemption? Have you asked to be—"

Lida had stopped again, only now she sighed and without answering any of my questions pointed at the ocean: "See that hideous, dastardly, evil Spellbinding?"

"Spellbinding?" I murmured. All I could see were ripples of foam as the breeze crossed the water, the distant haze of ocean spray, blue sky dipping to the horizon. There was that shimmering in the air, of course, very close to the shore. Actually, if

I turned my head slightly, it almost appeared as if a curtain were suspended there.

I tilted even more and realized that it *was* a sort of curtain.

It was transparent, like plastic, and was decorated with a diamond pattern. Very pale thread, green-and-gold, was stitched into this curtain, forming a long fine rope that ran horizontally along the water, just where the curtain touched the sea.

"That shimmery curtain there?" I asked. "Is that the Spellbinding? With the green-and-gold rope?"

"It's like a shimmery curtain, yes," Lida agreed. She was following the curve of sand now, still at a brisk pace, but she stopped and glanced back at me. "There's no green-and-gold rope though."

I paused, frowning.

There was definitely a green-and-gold rope.

I let it go and resumed following her.

"What's it there for?" I called after her.

"Didn't you hear me?" she called over her shoulder. "We lost the war. *All* the Kingdoms and Empires ganged up against us. They locked us in, using that Spellbinding. It goes right around our entire kingdom. Which means our kingdom is now a prison. Although"—she screwed up her eyes, staring at the curtain (and its green-and-gold rope)—"there are supposed to be gaps here and there. Some people have been able to escape. Here. Help me with this." She had stopped at a great pile of bracken and seaweed, and she began lifting clumps of it and setting these aside. I pitched in.

"We were actually doing quite well in the war," she told me as we worked, "until the *Spindrift children* infiltrated and stole state secrets."

"Spindrift children?" I wondered what they were. They sounded frightening.

Or perhaps it was just the way Lida lowered her voice and infused it with horror, as if *Spindrift children* were venomous cockroaches.

"Most people in my kingdom know nothing of them," Lida

continued, working diligently. “But I live in the palace with my father, the king, so I overhear important conversations—with generals and advisers and so on. Sometimes I even sneak into the war room and look through the filing cabinets. So *I* know about the *Spindrift children*.”

This time she made the children sound like plantar warts.

I dragged a tangle of rubbery seaweed aside, wondering what we were doing. Perhaps there were Sparks buried under here? Would they start singing mathematics to me again when we set them free? I was about to ask Lida this question when she swept aside a huge prickly bush and there it was.

A boat.

A little blue rowing boat, its oars lying crossed on its floor.

“I’m escaping,” Lida told me. “Today.”

CHAPTER 51

“OR ANYWAY, I’M going to *try* to escape,” she amended, regretfully. “I’m going to search for a gap in the Spellbinding and if—*when*—I find it, I’m rowing far, far away. Here, help me clean this out.”

Along with the oars there was a mess of twigs, leaves, and pieces of seaweed—the residue of the greenery that had concealed the boat.

As we scooped out detritus and flung it aside, Lida explained the *Spindrift children* to me. “They’re seven children who helped defeat us in the war. Some of them infiltrated our kingdom—undercover—and discovered the secret about our armbands. We have files on all seven in the war room.” She stood back and counted off names on her fingers, slapping each as if the children were now mosquitoes perched on her fingertips. “Finlay. Honey Bee. Hamish. Glim. Victor. And the twins: Eli and Taya.”

“Dreadful,” I said. “What wicked children, helping to defeat your kingdom.” I was a bit out of breath, reaching in and out of the boat. “It must be—”

I stopped.

“Eli and Taya,” I murmured.

The names were extremely familiar. They were important in some way.

“Yes, the twins,” Lida replied. “According to their file, they’re Faery children, probably from the Kingdom of Kate-Bazaar. Most likely swept away in a tidal wave when they were tiny and washed up in Spindrift. That’s where they met the other children and became part of the evil Spindrift gang.”

"Kate-Bazaar?" I repeated, a little blankly. Puzzle pieces were falling together in my mind.

A wild ocean. Blue flowers. The Kingdom of Kate-Bazaar.

Tiny children's voices: "Eli!" "Taya!" "Eli!"

"Yes, it's a kingdom that's famous for a flower called the blue elouisa."

I leaned over the rowboat trying to hide my face, and my excitement.

"So . . ." I said, keeping my voice as casual as a picnic. "Eli and Taya were safe? They were washed away but they made it to another kingdom on the gate?"

"On the what?" Lida snapped.

I cleared my throat. "I mean, the twins must have been on some kind of *raft* if they were washed all the way to another kingdom when they were tiny. Such as a . . . gate."

"If you like," Lida accepted.

Just as quickly, though, my elation evaporated. "Wait," I said. "If they *had* drowned right there in the sea at Kate-Bazaar rather than being safe on . . . let's say a gate . . . then *you* might have won the war?"

Lida's face grew thoughtful. "We might have." She nodded. "Of course, I wouldn't want any little children to drown. But *thousands* of our soldiers have died since the Spindrift children carried out their dastardly plan. Many more have been wounded, as you saw just now. There are shortages of everything here—fuel, flour, fresh vegetables. People are weary, hungry, *and* imprisoned by a Spellbinding." She glared at the sea again. "So yes. It would be better if they'd drowned."

We'd stopped working now, as the boat was more or less clean. Lida was reaching under the seat. She pulled out a cloth shoulder bag hidden there.

"Provisions," she told me, holding it up and dropping it onto the floor of the boat.

"You've been planning your escape for a while," I said. I was feeling distracted. There was a pounding in my head, as if someone had got in there with construction equipment.

Reuben had been right. Mr. Turtelhaze was wrong.

I'd gone back in time, saved the twins, Eli and Taya, and that had led to the loss of *thousands* of lives. This whole kingdom was imprisoned—because of me.

Lida had now taken a pair of scissors from the bag. This was unexpected. What did she plan to do with those? She gathered her long, long hair together, held the scissors steady and *snip*.

Cut it off.

Even more unexpected.

She'd cut it about waist height.

"Had to do that," she said grimly, tying the cut-off part together and slipping it into the boat. "It would give me away out there. Whisperers are known for their very long hair. I should probably cut it even shorter, but I just can't—my hair is too tied up with my whispering. Here, help me bring the boat to the water."

We dragged the boat along the sand, not speaking.

"And *all* the Kingdoms and Empires ganged up on you in this war?" I double-checked, eventually. If so, perhaps they'd have lost the war anyway? Perhaps Eli and Taya did not play a big role? It sounded like a very unfair and unbalanced war. "You had nobody on your side at all?"

"Well, we did have some allies," she admitted, grunting with the effort of dragging the boat. "A lot of Shadow Mages helped us."

Shadow Mages?

I frowned, thinking back over what I'd learned in my time in the Kingdoms and Empires.

Shadow Mages make trouble, Carrie had said in the forest.

Shadow Mages are bad, Oscar had told me in the coach station.

Hadn't a Shadow Mage almost frozen Bronte and me to death?

"And they're pretty powerful," Lida continued, as the boat began to splash against the water. "Plus we had the armbands. Also very powerful. We'd have won the war if it wasn't for the Spindrift children."

She stopped, breathless, holding the boat with one hand.

"Why *are* the armbands so powerful?" I asked.

"They're made of thread from ancient shadow mines," Lida replied. "So they're like shadow magic bands. When we wear them, people can't resist our whispers. They have to do exactly what we tell them."

"Oh," I said, faintly.

"My father, the king, made it law that all Whisperers have to wear them so that we could control the Kingdoms and Empires. The armbands make everyone cranky—you might have noticed how irritable I am? I'm not usually like this, only I had to wear the armband all morning because my father was watching me. I only took it off when I came out. It's the shadow thread. You know how shadow thread is . . ."

Her voice faded, and she gazed moodily at her own wrist.

"Is what?" I prompted. "Shadow thread is what?"

"Well, it's a cruel sort of magic, shadow magic. That's why we have to kidnap children from all over the Kingdoms and Empires. We send them down into the mines to get the thread for us. You need little children's fingers to pluck it. They get very sick, though, if they pluck it for long. The Spindrift children rescued hundreds of those children, but Whisperers still escape the Spellbinding occasionally and kidnap extra children to bring here. I thought you were one of them." She frowned at me. "That's why I was telling you to hide. So the soldiers wouldn't recapture you and send you back to the mines. But you say you're from another world?"

"I am from another world," I agreed.

The pounding in my head had stopped. I was staring at her. She looked away quickly.

"I can't *think* straight," she complained. "It's the armband! Even though I'm not wearing it now, I can still feel the shadow magic coursing through my bloodstream! The Spellbinding stops shadow magic—so it won't let me out. It will sense the shadow magic in me. Still. I'm going to try," she added fiercely.

"Lida," I said. My voice sounded odd to me. "Are you trying

to escape so you can kidnap children and bring them to work in the mines?"

She stamped her foot. "Of course not! I'm going far from here and never returning! I don't want to hurt children! I protected you, didn't I? Will you be all right if I leave now? Can you get back to your world?"

I nodded slightly. "I always get shoved—magically transported—back," I said.

We'd reached the water now, and together pulled the boat into the sea. Then we waded along, one of us on each side of the boat. The water was almost at waist height when we reached the shimmery curtain—the Spellbinding. Cautiously, Lida pressed her shoulders against it—and was jolted back.

She sighed deeply.

"This is what happens," she muttered. She stepped sideways, pushed forward again—and bounced back.

As she carried on trying, I studied the curtain. The green-and-gold rope was like a long, fine line running along the water's surface. Whenever Lida hit that rope she bounced back. My eyes followed it to the right as far as I could see, then to the left. At one point, a good distance from us, the rope was slightly split. Two frayed ends dipped into the water, a gap between them no bigger than my hand. From there it picked up again and carried on, strong and taut.

"There's a gap there," I told Lida, pointing.

"You can't see gaps," she said shortly. "You just have to keep trying." She carried on pressing herself at the curtain and being repelled. Push—*jolt!* Push—*jolt!* Push—*jolt!*

"The green-and-gold rope," I told her. "It breaks, just over there."

"There *is* no green-and-gold," Lida complained. She kept on, side-stepping along the curtain and surging at it. Push—*jolt!* Push—*jolt!* It was a little annoying to watch, to be honest.

"There *is* actually," I told her after a moment. "You keep walking into the green-and-gold. It's a little annoying to watch, to be honest."

I hadn't meant to say that aloud.

Abruptly, Lida swung around. "You can *see* a gap in the Spellbinding?" she demanded.

"That's what I've been trying to tell you."

"Show me."

"Here. Follow me."

I waded through the calm water, Lida behind me, towing the boat, until we reached the gap.

"It's there," I said, pointing.

"Right there?" She was doubtful.

Slowly, slowly, she took a step toward the Spellbinding. Another step. Another. A tentative movement of her hip—and the green-and-gold rope fell away around her.

She was through.

She whipped back around, staring at me in wonder.

"I did it!" she gasped. Her hand was still on the boat. She tugged it a little and it slipped through easily.

"I'm on the other side! I can't believe it! I can't believe it!" She appeared radiant with joy, staring down at herself in the water, back at the spellbinding curtain, at herself again, laughing aloud. "Thank you, Lillian! Thank you!"

Abruptly, she stopped laughing. She held the side of the boat as it bumped up and down in the water, and looked down at her hands.

"You're really going away?" I asked. "And not coming back?"

"I'll go down the coast to Colchester, or Nina Bay," she replied, "and make my way from there. I'll start a new life somewhere completely new, far from here. Maybe the place you mentioned earlier? The grand harborside town of . . . where?"

"Gainsleigh," I filled in.

"Yes. There. I'll start a new life there."

Another long pause.

"Lida," I said. "Won't your parents be sad that you're running away?"

"My mother died when I was a baby," she replied. "There's just my father, the king."

"All right, your father. Won't he be sad?"

"Oh, he's been sad all my life. I don't think he can get any sadder."

"But won't *you* be sad leaving him?" I persisted.

Lida was facing out to sea. "Of course I'll be sad," she said, her voice strong and clear. "This is my kingdom. I love my kingdom. It's the most beautiful kingdom in all the Kingdoms and Empires. I love my father. I love my friends."

I frowned. "Then why . . . ?"

"Lillian, haven't you been listening?" she asked softly. "My kingdom steals children and makes them work in mines. My kingdom formed an alliance with Shadow Mages. My kingdom wants to control *everyone*. My father, the king, insists we wear shadow magic around our wrists. We might once have been a good and gentle people, but we're not anymore—we are led by an evil king, and our blood is poisoned by shadow magic. It's *lucky* that we lost the war and are trapped here now! We deserved to lose! Of course I don't want to leave!" She stopped, and her last words seemed to drift across the ocean. "But of course I have to leave."

When she turned back, her face was proud and bold but tears slid down her cheeks. Wind gusted by and blew the hair around her face.

"You're sure you'll be okay?" she asked me. "You'll be able to go back to your own world?"

I nodded.

She climbed into the boat, set the oars into the locks, and *shove—*

I was home again.

CHAPTER 52

IF I WAS having trouble concentrating on schoolwork before that visit, you should have seen me afterward.

My mind was like a tree filled with chattering birds at dusk.

I sat at the table, trying to read a passage about the Victorian Gold Rush of 1851 to 1868 but actually just drawing circles all over the page.

This was probably because my mind was spinning in circles. According to Reuben, anything I did could change the time line, possibly causing thousands of people to die. According to Mr. Turtelhaze, that was nonsense. According to Lida, the two little children I'd rescued in the ocean, Eli and Taya, had grown up to help defeat the Whispering Kingdom, causing thousands of soldiers to die.

So Reuben was right!

Yet, the Whispering Kingdom had been kidnapping children and working with Shadow Mages, so actually it was *great* that they'd lost the war. Which meant, in a way, that Mr. Turtelhaze was right. Although, he was also wrong. Perhaps he was wrong about my being able to travel through time, back to the little boy at the circus? Perhaps I'd be *shoved* there again! It would be *wrong* to leave that boy to be crushed by gravel if I could get to him, just as it would've been wrong to let Eli and Taya drown. Yet Reuben was *right* when he said that it could change—

And so on.

Around and around went my mind.

I also remembered somebody—Esther?—saying that Bronte had defeated the evil Whispering king. Had she defeated Lida's father? Where did that fall in the time line? How far back in time had I traveled when I rescued the twins and when I helped Lida escape? It'd only been a few days back when I met up with Bronte and her cousins. Were Lida and Bronte enemies? Would Lida forgive Bronte for defeating her father?

I began to draw little faces in my circles.

I'd agreed to visit the Kingdoms and Empires ten more times. The next time I was *shoved*—or magically transported, as Lida had described it—should I stay perfectly still, not moving a muscle?

Apart from anything else, that sounded dull. Also I might get a crick in my neck.

No. I would not stay perfectly still.

I glanced over at the pickle jar of coins. It was down to its bottom third. Depending on your mood that was either a solid number of coins—a solid number of adventures—or hardly any.

(When I'm reading one of my books and I'm nearing the end, I feel sorrowful that the book is almost over. I try to reassure myself by holding the remaining pages between my thumb and forefinger and thinking: *still a good chunk left!* Yet I know that the chunk will be too small, will end too soon—that there is very little story remaining. This felt similar.)

Just how hollow would my life be when the visits to the Kingdoms and Empires were over?

It was definitely something to worry about.

Then I looked back at my worksheet and saw that my worries were much bigger.

I had ruined my worksheet.

Circles, circles, circles, little faces, little faces, little faces.

The sheet was a mess.

I grabbed the eraser and began rubbing out circles and faces, brushing aside the dust, rubbing out again, brushing aside dust. Faster and faster I worked. I lifted up the sheet, gave it a good shake, and set it down.

It was covered in gray stains where the eraser had not been able to lift all the pencil markings. It was also covered in little rips and tears where the eraser had broken through the paper.

I began to cry.

I tried to erase the gray stains. It didn't work. I tried taping the rips together. That didn't work.

My teardrops were spilling everywhere now, adding their smudges to the paper.

All right, I thought, taking a deep, calming breath. *Think of a solution.*

The solution was to answer the questions at the end of the worksheet using formal language, complex structure, and my neatest handwriting. When Grandmother saw that, she might not notice the mess I had made of the worksheet.

Right.

First, read the text.

Only, my eyes kept leaping from the words to the smudges. Grandmother would *definitely* notice those! I could not see for the tears!

At one point I forgot to breathe for a moment. This alarmed me.

I pushed my seat back from the table.

I bit my lip.

Breathe, child, breathe.

Abruptly, I stood up, walked down the hall and into my bedroom. I crouched, reached for the Genie bottle, and drew it out of its pouch.

The moment my fingertips felt the cool glass surface, the moment my eyes landed on the intricate foil design and the graceful swoop of the bottle's neck, the moment I held it up into the air—a beautiful calm fell over me.

I wiped my eyes.

I carried the bottle out to the table, set it down beside me, and got to work. I read the passage about the Victorian Gold Rush of 1851 to 1868 and answered the questions neatly. I redid the mathematics I'd rushed in the morning, and embarked on my other schoolwork. I worked through my lunch break, eating a sandwich at the table.

The whole time I was working, the bottle stood by my elbow. It seemed to me to carry inside it the world of the Kingdoms and Empires—new friends, Carrie Mettlestone and Bronte Mettlestone; Prince Billy and Princess Lida; the kind elderly woman by the lake; Reuben, the bearded Genie; and new places too, the Luminous Forest outside Gainsleigh, the castle in the Mellifluous Kingdom, the cottage by the lake, a wild ocean strewn with blue flowers in Kate-Bazaar, a placid ocean with graceful dolphins in the Whispering Kingdom.

It was all there in the bottle beside me, and I imagined that it murmured gently: "There now, Lillian, it's all right. It's going to be all right."

CHAPTER 53

BY THE TIME Grandmother arrived home, I had completed my schoolwork, hidden my Genie bottle under the bed again, and was playing scales at the piano.

"Have you begun supper preparations?" Grandmother asked, as she closed the front door behind her.

"Yes, Grandmother. I have peeled and diced the potatoes, washed the lettuce, sliced the beans, and—"

"No need for details." Grandmother hung her coat on the rack and strode into the kitchen. To my surprise I heard the sound of water running and a pan clanging onto the stovetop. Usually, she checks my schoolwork before she cooks.

"We will eat supper immediately," she said from the kitchen. "I'm expecting company again. You will need to be asleep before the guests arrive."

I did not inquire whether she planned to bake another cake. Later, when I saw that she *was* baking a cake, I did not ask what flavor it was, or whether I could have a piece. I did not plead to stay up so I could meet the guests. I knew that it would be no use. Also, any of that might have reminded her of my existence, which in turn might remind her of my schoolwork.

Once again, I tried to stay awake. Once again, I fell into a deep sleep.

I woke to the sound of Grandmother's voice calling, "Lift it to the right and then push hard."

There was a jiggling sound and then a *bang*.

Our front gate sticks sometimes. You have to lift it to the right and push hard.

"Got it," called a stranger's voice. "Good night then."

A few other voices chorused, "Good night. Until we meet again."

The *thunk* of our front door closing.

Grandmother's guests were leaving. Grandmother had just seen them off at the front door.

I slipped out of bed and across to my bedroom window, twitching the edge of the curtain. People were streaming through our front gate. I counted seven of them, all wearing coats and hats.

When the last of the group had stepped through, closing the gate behind them, they formed a huddle on the path. They appeared to be speaking but, in the darkness, I could not see their faces. Nor could I hear their voices. A moment later the huddle broke apart, with nods and tips of their hats, and they scattered in different directions. Three crossed the road, one in a straight line, two at a diagonal. Three stopped alongside parked cars, reached into their coat pockets—*bip-bip!* of keys—and climbed in, and drove away.

The seventh person, a tall man, remained on the footpath, watching as each of the others departed. Eventually, this person began to walk, rather slowly, to the left. As he passed beneath a streetlight, I caught a glimpse of his face.

It was Mr. Turtelhaze.

CHAPTER 54

I STARED AT the empty street.

Grandmother had told me she did not know Mr. Turtelhaze. Her exact words had been: "Mr. Turtelhaze? I have never heard of the man. A ridiculous name. You have invented him."

Yet here she'd been, eating cake with Mr. Turtelhaze. Here *he* was, walking away from our house into the darkness.

Of course, she could have met him since I mentioned him, I supposed. Perhaps he was a new colleague at her job? If so, though, it might have been kind of her to say to me: "Lillian, it seems I was mistaken. You did not invent Mr. Turtelhaze after all. He is a new colleague at my job. Isn't it a coincidence? I'm inviting him to tea along with my other mysterious friends tonight. I apologize."

Admittedly, Grandmother did not ordinarily—or ever—speak to me in this manner.

I knelt at the window ledge, pressing my forehead to the glass. If my window weren't locked, I might have opened it, climbed out, and run onto the street, chasing Mr. Turtelhaze. "Who *are* you?" I would have demanded. "How do you know my grandmother? And why did you tell me that Reuben's warning had been nonsense? It clearly *wasn't* nonsense!"

I still didn't know what I was meant to do the next time I was sh—

Shove.

That's exactly how it happened.

I was thinking about the next time I was shoved, when I was actually shoved.

I chuckled in surprise. It was as if I'd *caused* the shove to happen—thought it into being.

I was still kneeling, and gazing at a light—but I was kneeling in wet, muddy grass and looking at the moon.

The sky was like a parade of windblown clouds. Pale gray clouds, torn and ragged at the edges as if they'd just fought a battle. They streamed overhead, carried by a strong wind, heading home to rest.

I peeled my knees from the grass and stood up. Cold gusts of air blew my pajamas against me, and my feet squelched in icy rainwater. I appeared to be in some kind of rough countryside where a wild storm had just passed. In the darkness around me were several clusters of broken trees, some with cracked or fallen branches, some even lying full-length on the ground. Behind me, a narrow country road appeared half-flooded. It was crisscrossed with more fallen branches and trees. Beyond this road I could see a wide, scrubby lawn and a driveway leading up to a huge barn. Lights shone from windows at the front of this barn. Its roof was scattered with clumps of debris. Rainwater rushed from its eaves. All around me, in fact, was the sound of clattering, running, dripping water, and rustling, skittering leaves and bark, and the low, haunting hum of the wind.

I was glad I hadn't been shoved just a few minutes earlier. The very air seemed to be weighted and shivering, and the trees and bushes seemed to blink in shock, or to chatter in excitement and distress.

Well, I thought. *Even if it were safe for me to pull little children from wild water and place them on a garden gate—it's nighttime and there's nobody about.*

Shivering, I took a few splashy steps toward the road. To the left, this road was a tangled mess of branches and fallen trees, impossible to pass. To the right, though, there was just the one huge tree lying across, then a great puddle of floodwater stretching along a large part of the road's surface. After that, it appeared clear. If I climbed over the trunk, and skirted around the puddle, I could follow the road and see where it led me.

Deep shadows crossed the grass whenever the clouds crossed the moon. Each time this happened I slowed my pace, and each time the moonlight returned I could see more of the road, still a fair distance away.

Squelch, squelch went my feet. Another plunge of darkness. *Squelch . . . squelch . . .* A glow of soft moonlight. *Squelch, squelch.*

I was almost at the road's edge. Water droplets gleamed on the leaves and branches of the fallen tree. That stretch of floodwater was a deep dark shadow that glittered and winked as if scattered with jewels. There must have been a ditch in the road, I decided, and it had filled with rainwater.

Squelch, squelch and I was on the road.

That fallen tree I planned to climb over was immense. It must have been growing close to the roadside and the storm had torn it up by its roots. If a carriage or car had been passing when it fell, the vehicle, and anybody inside, would have been crushed.

The puddle of water started on one side of the fallen tree and stretched out along the road on the other side. I approached the trunk, trying to see where I might be able to scramble over it. As I did, I glanced sideways at the puddle.

I looked back at the tree, reached up my hands to climb—and stopped.

I turned to the puddle.

There was something very strange about it. It had an unexpected shape and texture. It was too solid, too dense, for water. Mist or perhaps steam was rising from it. It seemed to be emanating warmth. I took a step closer, holding my arms tight around me, and peered down.

The puddle opened its eyes and peered back.

CHAPTER 55

I TOOK IN a great gasp of air—*whoosh*—and tripped backward. Landed on my bottom.

The road was wet and hard. Still, I scooted as far from the puddle as I could. A high-pitched squealing sound was coming from the back of my throat. That embarrassed me. What was the point of it? I see the point of a scream. It alerts others that you're in danger. It might even scare away an attacker. However, there is no value in the faint, high-pitched sound I was making.

My mouth was wide open. I put my hand to my chin and forced it upward, snapping it closed.

Then I breathed deeply, so that my shoulders rose almost to my ears. That's how I calm myself.

Or try to.

I didn't feel calm.

Slowly I forced myself to look at the puddle.

It clearly wasn't a puddle. It was a creature.

I squinted, trying to make out the creature's features in the moonlight. Its eyes were staring at me. They blinked slowly.

I yelped.

The creature stopped blinking and carried on staring at me.

Its eyes were enormous. A deep, liquid gold color, with green flecks. Lashes as long as pencils.

I forced myself to stand and to move slowly, slowly toward it.

It blinked again. I scuttled away.

It stared at me.

I moved toward it.

The closer I got the more the truth became clear. The puddle was not "a creature." The puddle was a creature's head.

I could make out a long snout. Hoods above its eyes. A raised ridge across its forehead. Steam drifting from its nose.

A slow realization prickled over me.

The creature was pinned to the road by the tree.

Its head was on this side of the tree, the tree was across its neck, and its body—its vast, impossible body—was stretched along the road like floodwater.

"Oh!" I cried. "You poor darling!"

I crept a little closer. Even though I thought the creature was a poor darling, I was still frightened. Both things can be true at once.

I could hear the creature breathing now, a hoarse, gravelly sound that stopped now and then. More wheezing than breathing. Each time it emitted a sound, a burst of warm steam blew toward me. I could smell a strong leathery scent, and smoke, and something musky like the sweat of an animal.

I looked into the creature's eyes.

The eyes gazed steadily back. They were deeply, desperately sad.

"Don't worry," I murmured. "We'll get this tree off you."

I studied the tree trunk. It looked to be about as heavy as a semitrailer.

"When I say *we,*" I began, but the creature's eyes had closed.

"I'll be back with help," I promised, swiveling on the spot. Lights still glowed in the barn windows. I set off running as hard as I could.

A small sign was nailed to the barn door. I could just make it out:

STRAW BRIDGE ANIMAL HOSPITAL

VETERINARIAN: DR. SOPHY METTLESTONE

An animal hospital! Perfect.

I pounded on the door.

Immediately a woman's voice called, "Yes? Who is it?" Her voice was both alert and edgy.

I wondered how late it was here. Footsteps approached from inside and there was silence.

"Hello!" I called. "Sorry to disturb you! My name is Lillian Velvet. There's a creature on the road out here trapped by a fallen tree! I think it's badly hurt. The tree is huge! I can't lift it. I mean, I haven't *tried* lifting it, but I suspect that—"

The door swung open. A woman stood before me in a dressing gown and slippers. Her face was kinder than her voice had been, although it was thin and grayish, the bones sharp, and her eyes were pinched.

"You're a child," she murmured, and then she asked, "A creature? What kind of creature?"

What kind of creature?

This was a good question.

What kind of creature was lying out there beneath the tree, its eyes hooded, its forehead ridged, its mouth a long snout that steamed when it breathed, its vast body stretched along the road, smelling of leather and sweat and smoke?

"I think it's a dragon," I said, to my own astonishment.

CHAPTER 56

THE WOMAN KICKED off her slippers and reached for a coat on a hook by the door. Her wrists and shoulder blades seemed very thin.

"Come inside," she instructed me, "and wait in the warmth."

She pulled on a pair of boots, grabbed a little black bag, and stepped outside. On the doormat she paused and looked back at me.

"Make yourself at home," she said. "It's on the road just out the front here?"

I nodded.

"Don't worry about the noises out the back," she added. "The animals are restless from the storm. I'll be back as soon as I can and we can discuss why a little girl is wandering about on this stormy night!" She smiled suddenly in a way that made me smile myself. Then she closed the door behind her and was gone.

I moved to the window and peered out into the moonlight. The woman's figure raced along her driveway, coat flying behind her. She had a very determined pace. As she neared the road, she disappeared into shadow so that I could no longer see her.

I turned around. The room was a small kitchen. Two flowerpots stood on a ledge above the sink, and a faded navy tea towel hung from the oven door handle. A table was scattered with empty mugs, plates of toast crusts, envelopes, papers, and three or four bottles of pills, each with a printed label. The room smelled of boiled potatoes and peas, cinnamon and cocoa. A potbelly stove stood in the corner, glowing with warmth.

I realized that I was shivering and stepped across to the stove, warming my hands and feeling waves of jitters as the cold faded from my body.

Sophy Mettlestone, I thought.

The woman was another Mettlestone. When she returned from helping the dragon, I could ask if she knew Carrie or Bronte. Or the Staranise sisters.

Make yourself at home, she had said. I wondered what that meant exactly. That I was supposed to behave as if this were my own home? In that case, I should wash up the dirty mugs and plates.

I did that, drying them with the faded tea towel.

As I turned back to the table there was a sound like several paper bags being crumpled. It was coming from behind the door at the back of the kitchen. I froze. A chittering sounded next and then scrabbling claws, hissing, and three rapid *Eek! Eek! Eek!* sounds.

This was followed by silence.

I remembered that Sophy had told me not to worry about the noises. *The animals are restless from the storm*, she had said.

What sort of animal sounded like crumpling paper bags?

My eyes fell on the papers on the table. It appeared that Sophy had been opening her mail: there was one stack of loose pages and one of torn envelopes. The stacks were messy. I straightened them up.

Most of the papers seemed to be marked *Electricity Bill* or *2 Tonnes Kibble*, but one tipped sideways from the stack as I straightened it. This paper was thick and creamy.

Dearest Sophy, it said, in beautiful calligraphy.

A personal letter. I would certainly not read it.

As I slid it back into the stack, though, a word leapt out:

circus

Circuses had been on my mind, of course, because of the little boy and the gravel, which is probably why it leapt out. I picked up the letter again and read the paragraph around the word.

Oh, Sophy, I'm so sorry you won't be able to come along to welcome our parents back. You sound very ill, and I'm worried about you. Perhaps you should be at the hospital? I know you trust your local doctor, but maybe you need a second opinion?

I looked up from the letter and across at the pill bottles. The woman *had* seemed very pale and thin. Frowning to myself, I carried on reading.

If you do get better in time (please do!), I know it will be strange seeing our parents after so long—you were just a teenager when they left. It might take a while for us all to relax and become a family again. Therefore, I've planned activities throughout the visit, to try to minimize awkwardness (and to make it as fun as possible for the children). There will be picnics, concerts, hikes, and boat rides. One exciting development is that the circus is coming to the Gainsleigh Showground on Friday, May 25. The very day that our parents arrive. I have acquired tickets for the whole family.

That's where I stopped reading. Not because I remembered my manners but because I heard the most extraordinary sound.

Once again, it was like crumpling paper bags, only this time it was more like

CRUMPLING PAPER BAGS

By that I mean it was like a paper bag the size of an apartment block being crumpled. I jammed my hands over my ears in horror.

The sound seemed to be coming from *everywhere* now, from the sky, the earth, the trees!

I threw open the front door.

Here is what I saw.

A sky filled with dragons.

At least a hundred of them: immense dark shadows, wings outstretched, hovering just above the road. The sound was coming from their open mouths along with blasts of fire that turned the air purple and the trees, the ground, the road an eerie orange.

As I watched, five of the dragons swooped in unison, landing in a row on the fallen tree, and digging in their claws. Now their wings beat hard and fast. I felt the mighty gusts of air from where I stood.

Slowly, slowly the five dragons rose into the air—their wings straining with the effort—and slowly, slowly the great log rose in their claws. Up and up they flew and then with a *thud* they dropped the log onto a field and returned to lighting up the sky.

Sophy, a tiny figure now, rushed forward to the dragon that still lay sprawled on the road. I saw her stroking its head. I saw her open her bag and offer drops of something.

I heard the dragon make a sound like a long groan and then, as I watched, it slowly stumbled to its knees and, with a great lurch, to its feet. It shook out its wings.

"There now!" came Sophy's voice, while the sky lit up like a vibrant sunset with celebratory flames.

Shove.

I was home again.

CHAPTER 57

I WAS STILL on my bedroom floor, kneeling in front of the window.

I could hear Grandmother moving about between the living room and kitchen, clearing the teacups and cake plates left by her guests.

Although I was sleepy, it was a special, glowing kind of sleepiness. I sat back onto the carpet by my bed and smiled to myself: that storm of oranges and reds, the dragon shaking out its wings, the joy in Sophy's voice as she cried, *There now!*

A little part of my mind argued, "But what about Reuben and his warning? You traveled back in time and freed a dragon! Now it might rampage through the countryside, setting houses alight and gobbling up little children!"

I flicked those thoughts away. I'd seen kindness and intelligence in Sophy Mettlestone's face. She would not have set a dangerous dragon free to cause harm.

More than that, I had looked into the dragon's eyes. There, I had seen sadness and pain, but also much more: I felt that I had seen the dragon's soul. Its soul was formed of strength and humor and generosity. It was an old dragon, I thought, a wise dragon. It would not rampage through the countryside. In fact, I could more easily imagine it sitting back in a rocking chair with a pipe and a book, a rug over its knees, a glass of whiskey at its elbow.

It would have to be a very large rocking chair, of course. An enormous pipe. A tremendous book. Gargantuan rug. Immense . . . anyhow, you get the point.

The glow inside me began to fade and change shape. It was

still a glow, but it was drifting toward sadness. Soon I would run out of coins. I'd have to stop visiting the Kingdoms and Empires and seeing astonishing things such as Sparks and dragons, and meeting members of the Mettlestone family. There'd be no hope for that little boy at the circus . . . My chin began to tremble and my eyes to fill with tears.

Hush, I urged myself. *Hush! Don't cry! Grandmother will hear and throw open the door and be angry to see you are awake!*

In a panic, I reached under the bed and drew out the Genie bottle. It glinted in the streetlight from my window. Once again, I felt the beautiful calm. I felt my face smooth and my shoulders relax. Once again, I sensed that the bottle carried the world of the Kingdoms and Empires inside it.

This must be why the woman by the lake had asked Bronte Mettlestone to give it to me. Somehow she'd known that I am sad sometimes—and that I'd be even sadder once my visits stopped. She'd sent me the bottle as comfort, and to remind me of the Kingdoms and Empires.

It was strange that an empty bottle could be so powerful. In a storybook, it might have been filled with a magical potion you could drink for invisibility, say, or superstrength. Or with an actual Genie, of course. This one, though, seemed to take its power from its emptiness. If it had been filled with a potion—or a tiny furnished room where a Genie lived—then it would not have had the space for my memories of the Kingdoms and Empires. As it was, there they were, safely collected.

I decided to peer into the bottle and *see* the memories. I knew I was being fanciful, probably because I was sleepy, yet I put my hand on the cork stopper and drew it out.

And instantly, there they were. Spilling from the bottle and drifting around me like living music, in all their colors and sounds and smells: my Kingdom and Empire memories.

I sat back, breathing them in. There was Oscar spinning the wheels of his skateboard in the coach station. The sound of the ticket seller clinking coins behind his window. There was the rowboat wedged against the door of the cottage by the lake. The scent of pine needles. There was the cage standing open in a meadow, the freed rabbits hopping leisurely through the grass. It all reminded me of Prince Billy's paintings—how you could *taste* his picture of a cake, and *smell* the fragrance of his roses. In the same way, I felt almost certain that I could *feel* the soft, soft fur of a rabbit. I even reached out my hand toward it—

And, with a very gentle *shove*—more a nudge, actually—there I was.

In the meadow, reaching out to stroke a soft, white rabbit.

CHAPTER 58

THE RABBIT HUNCHED close to the grass, nose twitching, and allowed me to stroke it. It was even softer than I'd imagined. After a moment it shook itself and bounced away.

"Come back!" cried a voice. "No! Please! Come back!"

A small girl was running across the meadow. She looked about six, wore denim overalls, had very untidy black hair, dark brown skin, and ran like a gazelle. Zipping here and there, all elbows and knees.

She was chasing rabbits. As she sprinted by me, I saw that tears were coursing down her cheeks.

"*Please* come back, rabbits!" she wailed. "You'll have a fantastic life! Out here you might get eaten by a fox!"

Oh.

There was the cage standing open. There were the rabbits, scattering in every direction.

I myself must have just been here, moments before, releasing these rabbits before being shoved back home.

The rabbits must belong to this girl. Perhaps her parents had purchased them for her from the pet shop where I'd found the cage? As a birthday present?

Now her birthday present was escaping.

"I'll help!" I called. "Let me help you!"

She paid no attention. I began to chase rabbits. They were surprisingly nimble. Also, I kept pursuing one rabbit only to be distracted by another, and changing direction. This meant that I was running in zigzags, wearing myself out.

In a very short time, all the rabbits had disappeared into the trees at the far end of the meadow.

The little girl stood still, sobbing. Her shoulders rose and fell with her sobs.

Slowly, I approached her.

I reached out and touched her arm. She flinched, spun around, frowned, and resumed sobbing.

"I am so sorry," I said. "You see, it was me who set your rabbits free."

The girl squeezed her eyes tight at that. She clenched her hands into fists, hiccupped, and swung around again. "Why?" she demanded. "*Why would you do that?*"

"I didn't realize the rabbits came from a pet shop," I explained, "or that they belonged to you. I thought it was my job to set them free."

A frown flickered across her face. She thought I was speaking nonsense, and I did not blame her.

"I'm so very sorry," I repeated.

Her anger fell away suddenly, replaced by a weary sorrow. She was as tiny as a little twig, and the sadness on her face was the size of a continent. There was something familiar about it.

"Please," I said. "Is there anything I can do to help?"

"It's not your fault," she began, trying to smile—and then she tensed, turning toward the trees again. Again, she reminded me of a gazelle, only this time one that has been alerted to danger. She was poised, frozen, peering hard into the forest.

There was a *snap!* as if somebody had stepped on a stick.

"*Witches*," she muttered, and to me: "Run!"—and she set off running once again.

CHAPTER 59

SHOVE.

I was back in my bedroom.

I was also confused. The girl had been sprinting toward the trees rather than away from them. This seemed the wrong decision. *Witches*, she had said, very clearly.

In my world, dear reader, Witches live in storybooks and are cackling, wicked sorts with brooms and black hats. In the Kingdoms and Empires, I seemed to remember, they were Shadow Mages.

Either way, they should probably be avoided.

If I hadn't been shoved back home, I could've followed the girl and tried to help her. Now I didn't have that option.

Or perhaps I did?

The Genie bottle was still open on the floor, and my Kingdoms and Empires memories still drifted around me in all their colors and songs, sounds and smells . . . could I find a new memory of what had just happened, reach out, and dive inside it?

I thought of the tiny girl's sorrowful face. Perhaps I should first return to an earlier point, find my*self*, and stop me from releasing the rabbits? Then the girl wouldn't be in the meadow in the first place, actually, chasing the rabbits, and hearing the Witches.

Was that possible? Could I meet myself in the past and change my own actions?

My head started spinning slowly, like a creaky old merry-go-round. Dear reader, if you are confused by all my jumping around in time, imagine how I felt.

Well, I thought firmly. *Put your confusion aside and TRY going back to help—*

That's when my heart started pattering, my fingertips tapping, and my eyes flickering from image to image.

If I *could* go back and help somebody, *this* was the person I'd help first.

CHAPTER 60

"WHERE ARE YOU?" I muttered. "Where are you?"

From Billy painting at his easel, to Bronte brushing her hair, to soldiers marching to—There!

The circus tent.

I reached for it with both my hands, plunged toward it as if diving into a swimming pool, and—*shove!*

There I was.

Standing in the middle of a field, looking across at a big blue-and-gold tent. Closer by were the caravans, the sheds—and yes! There was the structure I'd mistaken for a garage, which was actually a storage container.

I took off, running. This time I would save the boy! I knew he was sleeping—trapped by some kind of shadow magic, deep inside his own mind—so I might not be able to wake him. Never mind! I would drag him out of there! I'd shout at the men with the horse and cart to help me!

The wind seemed to fly along with me as I ran, just as excited as I was. It streamed through my hair, tearing up my eyes. I was going to save him! I was going to save the boy!

I skidded up to the storage container—and stopped.

Empty. No boy in a blue jacket. Just some scattered clumps of dirt, some loose pieces of gravel.

I scratched the back of my head.

I felt warmth on my shoulders. Looked up at the sky. It was blue.

It was daylight.

I was here at the wrong time.

CHAPTER 61

I FELT LIKE a mixing bowl into which somebody has poured one cup of disappointment and two tablespoons of embarrassment.

Of course it was the wrong time. The fairy lights on the circus tent were not lit. The food stalls were shuttered. No tambourines or brass instruments or drums, no smells of butter popcorn or toffee. No crowds—just the buzz of a fly, the distant sound of low, slow voices, a handful of people wandering amidst caravans and sheds, birds cheeping.

It was very obvious. Yet there I'd been, flying along with the wind in my hair and elation in my heart. What was the matter with me? The grass was dry and sun-warmed beneath my feet—and I could *see* that grass as clear as day. I could see beyond the field too: a country road, a grassy hill, meadows and fields.

An extra teaspoon of embarrassment landed in the mixture: *thud*.

Was it even the same date as my first visit? Hadn't there been frost on the grass when I was here?

Well, I thought. *I'll go back to my bedroom and try again.*

Only, how did I return to my bedroom? Could I *dive* back, the way I'd dove here? Must I wait to be shoved?

I tried stretching my arms up, running a few steps, and plunging.

Landed on my stomach hard and bumped my chin. My teeth clashed together.

A woman walking by, leading a goat on a rope, raised a quizzical eyebrow as she passed.

Thud, thud. (Huge scoops of embarrassment being loaded in.)

"Excuse me," I called after the woman, sitting up with as much dignity as I could muster.

She turned back, looking amused.

"Please would you tell me what date it is today?"

"Friday, May twenty-five," she answered.

Friday, May twenty-five? That was the day after my birthday. I'd been shoved to the circus that very night. So I *did* have the right day, just the wrong time of day!

Or did I? Just because I'd *visited* here the day after my birthday, did not mean I'd *arrived* on that date. I usually traveled in time.

"Are you sure?" I called after the woman, suddenly doubtful. "It's very warm!"

Her eyebrows flew so high they seemed to be scrabbling to leave her face. "The warmth of the day," she declared, "does not alter the date of the day. It is, indeed, Friday, twenty-fifth of May." She tugged on the goat's lead, shaking her head, and carried on.

Then perhaps she took pity on me because she called over her shoulder: "It'll get colder when the sun goes down. There'll be frost on this grass later tonight!"

I scrambled to my feet.

I did have the right day!

I just needed to find the boy and warn him! Or find the man who delivered the gravel! I could even tell the woman walking the goat!

Of course, she already seemed to have a low opinion of my intelligence and might not react appropriately if I chased her to warn her that a child would be buried by gravel tonight.

I chased her anyway, composing a speech in my head. I wanted it to sound as if I was a very sensible girl who happened to enjoy diving onto grass sometimes.

"Excuse me?" I called, once I had my speech clear in my head.

The woman had stopped to allow her goat to munch on a patch of clover. She turned to me.

"Yes?"

Shove.

I was back home.

CHAPTER 62

FIVE MORE TIMES that night I tried.

Each time it was easier to travel. By the fifth, I only had to flick through the images until I found a circus memory, and then reach my fingertips toward it. It was as if I was in a shop, stretching for bread on the top shelf.

Each time, though, something went wrong. On the first attempt, it was noon, the sun high in the sky. Circus folk sat on barrels munching sandwiches, lettuce and onion spilling to the grass. On the second, the sun was just beginning to rise, the circus tent in gray darkness, food stalls shuttered and silent, sounds of snoring all around me.

During the noon visit, I spoke to people—a woman shoveling horse manure; a man eating fried potato slices from a paper bag—and the people were confused, or annoyed, or said, "Go and play with the other children" or "The circus doesn't open until later, dear."

During the dawn visit, I woke a few people up. Most did not enjoy that. One man in a nightdress was so irritated his face became a swarm of angry lines—as if I'd prodded open a nest of snakes.

On the third and fourth attempts, I arrived at the correct time. The fairy lights were lit, tambourines clashing. Those were the worst. On both occasions, I was in a ditch on the far side of the field. I scrambled out and sprinted across the hard, cold grass. "There's a boy!" I shouted, my arms waving wildly. "There's a boy!" My voice sounded thin as a breeze against the circus music.

I could even see the cart of gravel rolling toward the storage container; I even caught another glimpse of the blue jacket. "There's a boy!" I screamed, still too far to be heard, my feet pounding hard. The driver's head didn't turn. I needed to be closer! If only I could get closer—*shove*, I was home again.

On my fifth attempt, I saw the boy himself.

It was late morning, the sun growing warm. The boy was in the distance, moving quickly. He was shrugging off his blue jacket as he jogged and tying it around his waist. He disappeared behind the circus tent.

Once again, I ran across the field, my heart beating wildly. I was worn out by now, of course, half-asleep, my legs aching from all the sprinting. But the sight of the boy himself gave me fresh energy. I pelted along, darting sideways now and then as if I might be able to duck away from a shove back home. A stitch grabbed at my side. My breath rasped. I skidded to the edge of the circus tent.

I was still here!

And there he was. There was the boy!

"Excuse me!" I bellowed.

The boy did not turn. He was running toward a group of adults.

"Excuse me! I need to warn you!"

He only ran faster. "GET AWAY FROM HER!" he shouted, and then: "HELP! SOMEBODY HELP! IT'S STERLING SILVER FOXES!"

A glimpse of the woman with the goat in the midst of tall strangers—the boy tearing toward her—and *shove*.

CHAPTER 63

AT THAT POINT, I fell asleep.

I remember trying to reach out one more time—a jumble of confused thoughts in my mind. Sterling Silver Foxes were Shadow Mages, weren't they? Shadow Mages were attacking the woman with the goat? Perhaps *they* were the ones who would cast the shadow spell on the boy, causing him to fall asleep in the storage container? Maybe my job was to save him from *them*, and save the woman too (and her goat)? But if I couldn't—if I couldn't even—What about the rabbits in the meadow? Would the foxes eat the rabbits? The sterling silver rabbits? The Witches eat the foxes? *Lillian, wake up, you're thinking nonsense, try again.*

Yes. All right. Try again. I could just—

My eyelids closed, hands drooping by my sides.

Next thing I knew I was waking with a start in the morning. I could hear Grandmother moving about in the kitchen. I was lying on the floor by my bed, images of the Kingdoms and Empires still floating from the open bottle.

"Child!" called Grandmother's voice from the hallway.

I slammed the stopper into the bottle, shoved it under the bed, and leapt up onto the sheets—right as my door flew open.

"Child," Grandmother repeated sternly. "Why are you not up?"

"I'm very sorry, Grandmother," I replied. "I did not sleep well last night. I had dreams that—"

"Get up at once," Grandmother said, withdrawing from the room. Her footsteps thudded down the hall and back into the kitchen.

When Grandmother set off for work, I watched her through the window. She swayed side to side, as usual. She clinked the gate closed behind her and disappeared down the street.

I felt very strange.

I frowned, trying to understand this strangeness. Partly, I knew it must be tiredness, along with despair that I'd failed to save the boy (and now, also failed to save a woman and a goat, not to mention the lost rabbits, and the girl running toward Witches).

However, it was also something to do with the way I'd felt as I watched Grandmother walking. And the way I'd felt when she disappeared down the street. The first feeling was like someone taking your skin between their thumb and forefinger and giving a sharp little twist—that exact feeling, only deep in my belly. The second feeling was like the person had let go.

You're the most frightened person I've ever seen.

Where had I heard that sentence? Ah, it was Astrid, the smallest of the Staranise sisters at the boarding school.

Why had her words jumped into my head just now? I was not a frightened person. I was Lillian Velvet.

I sat at the table and looked at my stack of schoolwork and instructions. Although she had remembered to place today's work here, Grandmother had still not checked yesterday's work. Therefore, she had not seen the state of those worksheets.

I thought about how I had sobbed yesterday.

Well, I admitted, perhaps I am frightened *sometimes.* Only when I have good reason to be frightened though. It had been my own fault. I ought not to have doodled all over my work.

I set to work completing the morning's exercises as neatly as I could. I did not allow myself to glance at the jar of coins or to think about the Kingdoms and Empires.

At morning tea, I took my apple, cheese slice, and crackers outside to the garden. A big part of me wanted to run into my bedroom, take out the bottle, and dive back to the circus, to try to save the boy.

However, I needed to think.

First, I counted up my most recent visits to the Kingdoms and Empires. There was: the trapped dragon; the rabbits and the Spellbinding girl; and a total of six trips to the circus. (Mr. Turtelhaze had said that every time I visited the Kingdoms and Empires it counted. Therefore, I supposed, it made no difference that I'd dove into my own memories rather than being shoved. Those trips all counted.)

Altogether then, I had made eight recent visits to the Kingdoms and Empires.

Only two left.

Two more chances to save the little boy.

I had to use them very, very carefully. I could not throw them away arriving at the wrong part of the circus, or the wrong time of day, begging people to take me seriously, and being shoved back.

I needed to truly *think* and *plan* and—

Squeeeeeeak!

Ah, that was the sound of my neighbors opening their sliding door. I liked Shahlyla and Helen very much. They'd been sensible when I'd told them about Oscar, and funny about things like moonlight gardening, and whether to put roasted walnuts in their salad. Perhaps they'd be able to help me decide what to do? Perhaps I should tell them the whole story?

I stood and began to cross to the fence, ready to call their names. Then a voice spoke.

It was not Shahlyla's or Helen's voice. It was the deep, gruff voice of a man.

"Yeah, I reckon we can do it," he said. "They're back Friday, yeah?"

"Yep," another male voice agreed. "Gone up the coast, apparently. You lot can do the whole shebang by then? Hot tub, barbecue, terrace? And what was the other thing? The pergola."

"Yeah, and Rob reckons he can get in some nice established rosebushes up there, plus the herb garden. It'll be tight, but we can do it. Gonna be stunning out here."

This time the voice of a woman—a stranger—agreed. "A *huge* improvement. It looks pretty rubbish at the moment, which is ideal. Let's get the cameras rolling for the before shots."

There was a great deal more chatting and banging about, the door squeaking open and closed.

At first I'd thought they must be intruders, and I planned to confront them: "Ahoy!" I was going to shout. "Get out of my neighbors' yard! Avast ye!" (I thought pirate talk might help them fear me.) (Remember, dear reader, that I was very tired.)

However, the more I listened the more it became clear that the people were actually the crew of a television show, the sort that renovates people's yards for them as a "surprise" while they're away. Shahlyla and Helen must have gone on a short holiday "up the coast," and when they returned they were going to be astonished by the transformation.

I considered calling, "How wonderful! It sounds like you are doing all the things my neighbors have dreamed of doing! They will be so happy!" However, they would then know I'd been eavesdropping. They might not take that as well as Shahlyla and Helen had.

Also, I reminded myself, I needed to think.

It was wonderful about the garden, but it would be more wonderful if I could save the little boy.

I returned to my bedroom. Sitting on the floor by my bed, I reached for the bottle and took it from its pouch. I held it in my hands.

Once again, beautiful calm ran down my spine and along my arms to my fingertips.

That calm will help me think! I realized.

And almost at once, it did.

PART 9

REPORT 5

A SPACIOUS PENTHOUSE APARTMENT, GAINSLEIGH, KINGDOMS AND EMPIRES
—Thursday, May 24 to Friday, May 25

* * *

In the kitchen, the *thud-thud* of Franny's boots made Carrie Mettlestone pause.

Carrie was the second eldest Mettlestone sister. She was a large woman, and her bright and flamboyant clothes matched her bright and flamboyant mood—she was elated to be welcoming her parents back the next morning. But Carrie was also a Spellbinder, one of the most powerful in all the Kingdoms and Empires. She was always alert for trouble.

After a moment, though, she tuned back in to the conversation. She was with two of her younger sisters, Sophy and Emma Mettlestone, and they were making tea and coffee.

"And how is the poor darling now?" Emma asked, setting a soapy mug on the drying rack—she was washing mugs that had been used earlier.

"The poor darling is healing up nicely," Sophy replied, smiling. "I was worried there might be an infection in his wing stitches, but I only had to persuade him to stop nibbling them."

Sophy was a veterinarian, based in Straw Bridge and specializing in dragon care. She had just told her sisters the tale of how, two weeks earlier, a storm had blasted through her neighborhood. A tree had crashed down onto Dragon Great Damian. He was a noble old dragon, and a particular friend of Sophy's.

"If it wasn't for a little girl finding him, and fetching me, he'd never have survived the night," Sophy continued. "I don't know what she was doing out in a storm—she'd vanished when I went back inside. Funny little thing. Do you know, she *washed my dishes for me* while she was there? Hold up, it was three peppermint teas, Carrie, not two?"

Carrie removed a tea bag. "And Claire wanted coffee?" she checked.

"So did Nancy," Emma agreed. "But what about *you,* poor darling Sophy? It sounds like you've been *very* ill!"

"Yes, we didn't expect you'd be able to come along at all," Carrie agreed, studying her younger sister. "You look well now—good color, nice round cheeks."

Sophy smiled. "Didn't you hear? The reason Dragon Great Damian was out in the storm was that he was bringing me a spell to cure my illness. He'd been telling an ancient dragon friend of his about my symptoms, and she'd diagnosed me with a rare shadow influenza. The *only* cure, apparently, was the spell. Damian had memorized it, and he rasped it out to me the moment he was free, poor old thing. According to his friend, the ancient dragon, I only had a day or two left to live at that point."

Emma and Carrie both stopped and stared at her. "So if Damian had not survived the storm," Emma breathed, "we could very well have lost you?"

"*Shadow* influenza? Where'd you get that?" Carrie demanded at the same time.

Sophy shrugged. "The local Spellbinder says she hasn't sensed any Shadow Mages or shadow magic in our region for months. Maybe fell from a Witch's broomstick as it flew very high overhead?"

Carrie looked unconvinced. "Your local Spellbinder sounds like she's not focusing," she said. "She should absolutely have recognized shadow influenza."

"Thank goodness for the little girl!" Emma murmured fervently.

All three nodded. Then Emma frowned. "Speaking of near misses, do you realize that *five* Mettlestone sisters—Alys, Lisbeth and Maya, me, and now Sophy—have all been struck by dangerous storms in the last few weeks? Isn't that tremendously, suspiciously, and alarmingly bizarre?"

Her sisters chuckled. They were accustomed to Emma's melodrama.

Abruptly, though, Carrie grew serious again. She pursed her lips.

"Five is a lot to be coincidence," she admitted, "along with this shadow influenza of Sophy's. Especially given the timing of our parents' return. We know they went into hiding because they'd brought down a powerful enemy—I assume a very powerful Shadow Mage. Maybe that Shadow Mage is *still* not properly secured, even though they think they're safe? And it's coming after us now?" She scratched at her arm absentmindedly. "There's been no sign of shadow magic in the storms, though, has there?"

Her sisters shook their heads. "The local Spellbinder did a check on my storm," Sophy replied, setting the mugs onto trays, "as it was so unusual. She found nothing though."

"Hmph," said Carrie.

But Emma was nodding. "Same with the Lantern Island storm," she said, "and the twins say theirs was not a shadow storm either." She lifted the tray. "I'll bring these in and ask the *others* about their recent weather."

Sophy tilted her head, listening. "Something's going on out there," she declared.

Carrie and Emma listened too.

Footsteps ran along a corridor. A door slammed. Isabelle's voice called, "I'm making one more call," and Franny demanded: "Where's Carrie?"

* * *

"I'm here." Carrie stepped into the corridor. The others followed.

Franny strode toward them. "It's Alys and Billy," she said. "Gone missing."

"Missing?" Emma gasped. She was still carrying the tray. It rattled in her hands. "Since when?"

"Weeks," Franny replied. "Well, Alys disappeared weeks ago, apparently, and Billy not long after. Turns out, the palace guards have been sending messages everywhere about it, not realizing they weren't getting through. They've been receiving fake replies; fake people have been answering their phone calls. Turns out, communication around Mellifluous has all been shut down. Isabelle and I have been calling in some serious favors just now, trying to get through to the kingdom."

"But this is impossible!" Emma cried. "How can a *queen* go missing!"

Franny nodded slowly. "That's part of the problem," she said. "In the last couple of days, the palace, getting desperate, sent out a couple of messengers on horseback, to bring the news of Queen Alys's disappearance to the K&E Alliance, investigative branch. The messengers were shut down by bureaucracy. You know why?" *Crunch.* She chewed hard on her carrot. "According to the official records, Alys is *not* queen of the Mellifluous Kingdom."

A stunned silence.

"She's *not*?" Emma breathed. "Then who is?"

"Officially?" Franny said, raising an eyebrow. "A person named Lillian Velvet."

Carrie started. "Lillian Velvet?" she repeated. "That name is familiar."

"It's familiar to *me,*" Sophy declared. "That's the child who told me the dragon was trapped!"

Now the others blinked. "A *child* is queen of Alys's kingdom?" Emma murmured.

Franny rolled the carrot between her palms. "Let's get everyone together," she decided.

* * *

In the hibiscus room, Bronte Mettlestone lay awake, listening to the sounds of her cousins sleeping while the adults thudded around upstairs.

The grown-ups in this family became very excitable when they got together. All night there'd been cackles and shrieks from aunts, booms of laughter from Bronte's father, Patrick, and the Butler, lively shouting and teasing from everyone, and slamming doors.

Now the noise had changed its tone, Bronte thought. Laughter had ceased. Footsteps were quicker; deeper silences were followed by briefly raised voices.

She sighed and turned over in bed.

"Certainly not," said her cousin Astrid from the bunk below hers.

"Certainly not what?" Bronte asked.

"Certainly not the tomato sauce! It's a cat!"

Ah. Astrid was talking in her sleep. She did that often.

"All right," Bronte agreed, "not the tomato sauce."

"I mean to say," Astrid grumbled.

Imogen snored. Esther breathed deeply.

Bronte sat up. It had grown very quiet above her, so perhaps the adults were preparing for bed.

She could no longer wait until morning. She needed to speak to her aunt Carrie.

With all the hullaballoo since her arrival that afternoon, she had not had a chance for a private conversation with Aunt Carrie. She wanted to tell her Spellbinder aunt about the ice cage that had trapped her at boarding school—and, especially, about her own inability to *see* the shadow magic. Was something going wrong with her spellbinding? Her eyesight?

Also, that letter that Lillian Velvet had given to her. It had seemed exactly right to Bronte at the time, to hand over her Genie bottle. Had she been wrong though? Had she made a terrible mistake?

Outside the room, the grandfather clock began to chime. She counted along. It stopped at twelve.

Midnight.

She slipped out of her bunk, and crept out of the room.

Halfway up the carpeted staircase, a shadow fell across her.

"Oh!" said a voice.

PART

10

CHAPTER 64

DEAR READER, I made a mistake.

My idea had been to return to Bronte at her boarding school.

How did I come up with this idea? Well, first I decided it would be foolish to waste my final two trips visiting incorrect times and incredulous people—people who didn't believe a word of my warnings, I mean—at the circus.

Who do I know in the Kingdoms and Empires who *might* believe my warning, and might be able to get to the circus and save the boy? (I asked myself.) If only I knew more about the circus, though, such as *where* it was, and—

That's when my mind leapt to its feet.

The letter on Sophy Mettlestone's table! The one I'd seen while she was outside helping the dragon!

I'd forgotten it. Now, though, I remembered the lines I had read.

One exciting development is that the circus is coming to the Gainsleigh Showground on Friday, May 25. The very day that our parents arrive. I have acquired tickets for the whole family.

The entire Mettlestone family were going to the circus on Friday, twenty-fifth of May. It *must* be the same circus. It was the same date, after all, and Mettlestones had featured in almost all my visits.

Which new friend should I tell? A child, I thought, rather than an adult—adults would think I was inventing or dreaming. Carrie Mettlestone had been the first child I'd ever made friends with (if you didn't count the two girls eating Popsicles when I bought milk for Grandmother's tea). I liked the idea of seeing Carrie again; however, she had not mentioned going to a Mettlestone family gathering.

Bronte, however, was definitely going.

She would also believe my warning. She and I had escaped from an ice cage together. That sort of thing forges a bond, I think.

Bronte was the one.

I took the stopper from the Genie bottle, found my memory of chatting with Bronte—after we'd escaped from the ice—focused all my attention on her face, reached out toward her—

—and arrived on an elegant staircase.

CHAPTER 65

"WHERE AM I?" I asked.

Bronte blinked. She seemed surprised to see me.

"This is my aunt Isabelle's house," she replied politely. "Hello, Lillian, where did you come from?" She wore a nightgown and slippers. The window behind her was dark but I could hear voices from upstairs.

"What date is it? What time is it?" I demanded, a little rudely.

"It's Thursday, twenty-fourth of May," Bronte replied promptly. "Oh, no it's not. It's Friday, twenty-fifth of May, actually, as it's just past—"

"Friday!" I cried.

"Technically," Bronte told me. "As the clock just struck midnight."

Relief shot through me. "So you haven't been to the circus yet?"

Frowning, she shook her head. "We're going to the circus tomorrow evening—*this* evening, I mean, as it's Friday now. How did you know?"

"Listen quickly," I told her. (Her brow crinkled. I could see that she was wondering how one listens quickly.) "I could be shoved back at any moment and I must tell you something *awfully* important before then. At the circus, I swear to you, a cartload of gravel will be dumped onto a little boy."

Bronte's face turned the color of the grout between our bathroom tiles. She was clearly taking my news to heart, which pleased me, until she whispered: "Why would you do that, Lillian?"

"I don't mean *I'm* going to bury a child beneath gravel!

I mean I saw it happen on one of my visits! Remember I mentioned I travel in time when I come to your world? Well, I saw gravel about to bury a little boy. I think he's under a shadow spell that's keeping him asleep. He's . . ."

What did I remember about him?

"He's tiny, around six years old, and he's wearing a blue jacket," I told her. "I think he lives on a farm. And that he has three older brothers."

Bronte reeled back as if I was a lion surging toward her. "You mean *Benjamin*? My cousin Benjamin? *He* lives on a farm! He's six years old and has three older brothers! He has a blue jacket!"

"I don't know if his name is Benjamin! That's all I know about him! And I've only ever seen him from a distance! The Genie bottle gave me a dream, as you said it would, and that's how I learned more about him!" I paused, thinking fast. "Will you please *promise* me you'll watch your cousin Benjamin? And more generally . . . look out for cartloads of gravel? And a storage container where Benjamin might curl up and fall asleep? Oh, and earlier in the day a woman at the circus gets attacked by Sterling Silver Foxes and the boy tries to help her! Please? Please say you believe me!" My words had become like a crowd of joggers on a narrow footpath, all bumping into each other, tripping over other joggers' feet.

For a moment, Bronte gazed at me. Then she nodded. "I believe you," she said. "And I promise. I'll go up and tell the adults." She pointed up the stairs to where I could hear the low murmur of several adult voices talking at once.

I felt so relieved that my legs went wobbly. I sat on a step. Its carpet was soft and springy. Placing my palms on it, I let the softness run through me, along with the relief.

It was going to be all right. Bronte and her family would save the boy.

She sat beside me. "Benjamin does wander a lot," she told me. "I can imagine him getting lost at the circus, trying to save someone from Sterling Silver Foxes and then falling asleep under a spell. Thank you for warning us, Lillian." She paused and her voice grew practical: "Perhaps we should go to the circus early and do a precheck for Shadow Mages—there are two other Spellbinders in my family besides me, so between us we'll be able to sense any shadow magic. We should also find that storage container and put a warning sign on it. Make sure people know of the danger in case it's actually another boy, and *not* Benjamin. Can you tell me where the container is located?"

I couldn't answer, as I was trying not to cry. Bronte was taking my warning so seriously and sensibly! My relief had billowed out into emotion.

Eventually, I explained all I could remember about the storage container, and the gravel. I also told her how I'd been trying to get back to the circus, using the images in the Genie bottle.

"I only have one more visit left," I finished. "I'd like to meet you at the circus and *show* you where the storage container is, but I always seem to land at the wrong time."

Bronte tapped her fingertips together, thinking.

"We're leaving for the circus at six P.M.," she said, and she swiveled and pointed to the window behind her. "Can you see the street down there?"

I peered through the glass, trying to see beyond my own reflection. Below was a broad, paved street, shining in the rain and moonlight. Glowing patches of raindrops swirled around each lamppost. Elegant buildings lined the opposite side of the street, each approximately eight stories high, each with tall, ornate windows, balustrades, and, at street level, porches with columns.

"Those are apartment buildings like this one," Bronte explained. "Some have businesses on the ground floor—see the fancy jeweler down there, directly opposite us? With the pillar-box out the front of it?"

I could see the shuttered windows of a jewelry store and, in front of it, a red letter box, deep in shadow, hunkering down against the rain.

"That's where our carriages will be leaving from," Bronte

continued. "Fix that image into your mind perhaps, and maybe . . . maybe write *Friday, May 25, 6:00 P.M.*, on your hand? Don't let my aunt Isabelle see ink on your hand though. She doesn't like that."

I must have looked doubtful because Bronte bit her lip. "If it does work," she said, "you can ride with us to the circus and take us directly to the storage container when we get there."

I doubted it would work. And even if it did, I could get shoved back home before we even reached the circus.

Still, Bronte had my warning now, and this was just a kind of backup plan. And perhaps it would work and I'd even get to watch the circus with the family?

"All right," I decided. "I'll try."

At that moment, the noise from upstairs, which had dimmed since I first arrived, grew louder. Voices were raised. There was a *thump* and the sound of an adult saying, "Hush. We must not wake the children."

Bronte glanced toward the landing at the top of the stairs. "I don't know what's going on up there," she said. "They do always get overexcited when they're together. Come up now and I'll introduce you and you can tell them your warning yourself?"

We both stood and had taken two steps—Bronte leading—when a woman's voice rose above the chatter. "You say that Alys is no longer queen of the Mellifluous Kingdom?" the voice demanded. "And that a person named *Lillian Velvet* has taken over?"

Bronte stopped. She turned to me, eyes wide.

Shove.

I was home again.

PART 11

REPORT 6

A SPACIOUS PENTHOUSE APARTMENT, GAINSLEIGH, KINGDOMS AND EMPIRES —Friday, May 25

* * *

Slowly, Bronte Mettlestone climbed the stairs.

She was lost in thought.

When she entered the living room, it took a moment for the adults to register her presence. They were squished on couches, perched on window ledges, cross-legged on the floor. Bronte's mother, Lida, lay flat on her back on the rug, eyes closed, brow creased in thought, long hair splayed around her, as if she'd decided to lie down in a puddle of black ink. (Lida lay down whenever she wanted to think. This caused awkwardness in the supermarket and during parent-teacher meetings at school.)

Teacups and coffee mugs were scattered over every surface. A wine goblet lay on its side on the floor.

Several people were talking intently—either in small groups or to the room at large. Few appeared to be listening.

The Butler noticed Bronte first. He was by the sideboard. "Bronte," he said in his low, resonant voice. "Dear child, you had best return to bed."

The room fell silent. Everyone looked at Bronte. She folded her arms.

"I don't think she means to return to bed," one of the aunts murmured.

Aunt Franny spat out the end of a carrot. "It's bad news," she informed Bronte. Franny did not believe in honey-coating for children. "Your aunt Alys and cousin Billy are missing. Most likely in serious danger." Raising her chin, she addressed the next part to the room at large. "Authorities are en route to the Mellifluous Kingdom as we speak, to investigate. For now, we need to figure out if the disappearance is related to our parents' return."

"Or just a political issue in Alys's kingdom," Aunt Isabelle added.

"Also, a person named Lillian Velvet is registered as the queen of Alys's kingdom," Aunt Carrie put in. "But nobody at Mellifluous knows who she is. The name is familiar to me though."

Again, several people began to speak at once. Bronte's father wanted to assure Bronte—and everyone—that all would be well. (Patrick's natural optimism had frayed over the years but generally persisted.) Aunt Sue wanted to ask if her boys were making trouble downstairs ("and are they, and are they making trouble, is it the trouble they're making?") and if that was what had woken Bronte. Aunt Emma wanted to express her distress by gasping and moaning (a little like a ghost). Aunts Maya and Lisbeth were both of the view that here was a "top-notch mystery like that sea monster we had to slay more times than we can count." Aunt Nancy wanted to proclaim that Lillian Velvet was most likely an invention or a red herring, while Aunt Sophy argued, reasonably, that it was neither an invention nor a red herring that had knocked on her door and told her about the trapped dragon.

"*I* know who Lillian Velvet is," Bronte declared. "I just now saw her on the staircase."

Another silence fell, this time punctuated by a *clang* as a teaspoon fell into its saucer.

Bronte spoke as quickly as she could, conscious that she would lose her audience to its whirlwind of words any moment. "Lillian Velvet is from another world. She appeared in my dormitory the other day, and saved my life. Just now, she warned me that a little boy—who sounds a lot like Benjamin—is going to be crushed by a cartload of gravel at the circus tonight, if we don't prevent that happening."

As she'd guessed, her audience flew into its whirlwind. Aunt Sue sprang to her feet, demanding to know what her little son Benjamin was doing under a cartload of gravel instead of in bed. Several adults were keen to hear how Bronte's life had been in danger in her dormitory, and why she hadn't mentioned this earlier. Several demanded an explanation as to how Lillian Velvet had broken into the apartment, where she was now, what she had done with Aunt Alys and Billy, and why she'd taken Aunt Alys's kingdom.

"OY," Aunt Franny shouted. "Quiet down, the lot of you. Let's hear Bronte's story. Okay, Bronte, start with the dormitory."

So Bronte told the group about the ice cage, how she could not see the shadow magic to spellbind it but then Lillian Velvet had appeared and pointed it out to her.

"You couldn't *see* the shadow magic?" Aunt Carrie frowned. "Then . . . how did you know it was shadow magic?"

Bronte faltered. "I just knew. And Lillian *could* see it. She told me where to spellbind, and that saved us."

Aunt Carrie rubbed her nose. "So Lillian Velvet appeared at the same time as this ice cage, and Lillian Velvet then claimed it was shadow magic?"

"She didn't *claim* it was shadow magic, she . . .

It *was* shadow magic . . . I've been wanting to tell you, Aunt Carrie—there's invisible shadow magic."

But Aunt Carrie was exchanging worried glances with the others.

"So after Lillian Velvet *appeared* to save your life," Aunt Franny began.

"She didn't *appear* to, she did save my life."

"After that," Aunt Franny persisted, "what happened? Did she want information from you? Did she ask questions about your family?"

"No! *She* was as frightened as I was! She didn't want anything from me! . . . Oh, well. I mean . . ." Bronte frowned and bit her thumbnail. ". . . I mean, she had a letter . . . but that was . . ."

"What? What letter?" numerous adults asked at once.

"It was a letter to me . . . and it asked me to give her . . ."

"To give her what?"

Bronte found herself reluctant to tell them.

"To give her my Genie bottle."

A great intake of breath, all around the room.

"All right, take it easy, everyone," Aunt Claire said. "I'm sure Bronte didn't give her Genie bottle to a stranger. She's far too sensible for that."

Bronte winced.

"Oh, Bronte," murmured Aunt Isabelle. "You gave away your Genie bottle."

Bronte was beginning to feel a very strong mixture of emotions: confusion, irritation, and, also, dread that she had made a mistake. She buried this dread beneath defiance. "You don't understand! *I* was finished with the Genie bottle! The letter told me to . . ."

"Who was the letter from?" someone demanded.

Bronte pretended not to hear that. "The thing is, she just now visited us to warn us about the circus! She wanted to make sure that Benjamin is safe from the gravel in the storage container!"

"It's a trap," Aunt Nancy declared. "Lillian Velvet wants us all locked up in a storage container. For some reason."

"I'm inclined to agree that it's a trap," Aunt Franny said grimly. "Think about it. Mysterious weather patterns everywhere. Lillian Velvet appears in the middle of a storm at Sophy's place—"

"To tell me about the dragon!" Aunt Sophy protested.

"And then you left her alone in your place, didn't you? For all we know, she could have *caused* the storm in order to gain entrance to your place. To find out more about our family."

Sophy blinked. "Oh," she said, thinking. "There were letters and things on my table. I did notice that she had straightened the stack—as well as doing my dishes. And the papers included Isabelle's letter telling about the plans for this weekend."

Several adults nodded sternly. "She'll have found out about the circus that way," they agreed.

Aunt Sue, who had already leapt to her feet, now sprang into the air. "Look at us, and the sight of us, sitting around here *talking*? This Lillian might still be in the house! Indeed, she might be in the house! The children!" She ran from the room, and they all listened as her footsteps thudded down the stairs. Doors opened and closed. A few moments later, she returned.

"All fine," she said, panting a little. "No extras. Aye, and don't they all seem fine?" (Her sisters usually made fun of Sue's accent, but now did not seem the right time.)

"Of course they're fine!" Bronte cried. "Lillian disappeared back to her world! She's a *child*! She's nice! She saved me from invisible shadow magic, remember?"

"There's no such thing as invisible shadow magic," Aunt Carrie told Bronte, as gently as she could. "That's what being a Spellbinder is—it's being able to *see* and bind shadow magic—and you, Bronte, are a very skilled Spellbinder. Sounds more like this Lillian Velvet tricked you into believing it was there. She must have a strong power—perhaps from her own world—and she used this to create an ice cage, then made you believe it was shadow magic. Gained your trust that way so she could take your Genie bottle."

"I wonder what she wanted with the Genie bottle?" Aunt Isabelle murmured.

Aunt Emma, in dramatic form, was visibly trembling. "Lillian Velvet is the enemy our parents tried to capture! The enemy *who sent them into hiding*!"

"It's possible," Aunt Claire agreed. "Especially as she's now taken control of Alys's kingdom."

Bronte felt a temper tantrum building. She pressed her palms to her cheeks, trying to secure the tantrum safely inside her.

"I truly believe that Lillian Velvet—" she began. But did she truly believe this?

Bronte's mother, who had been lying flat on the floor through the entire conversation, sat up. Her hair fell into place around her shoulders, running to the floor like a stream.

"I met Lillian Velvet on my fifteenth birthday," she announced. Her voice, as usual, was tranquil and soft. "Lillian Velvet helped me escape from the Whispering Kingdom."

Another burst of voices, including Bronte's own.

"There!" Bronte cried. "Lillian Velvet is a *good* person!"

The rest of the adults, however, seemed to see Lida's revelation as troubling—although they were hesitant to express this.

"No offense, Lida," Aunt Nancy said, overcoming her hesitancy—"but the Whisperers were the *enemy* when you escaped. That was right after the Whispering Wars, wasn't it? Whisperers were still working with Shadow Mages and kidnapping children then, remember? So helping you escape is actually—no offense—another mark *against* Lillian Velvet."

Lida shrugged. "Perhaps," she said simply, "but I liked her very much. That was a difficult time and I've tried, over the years, to bury it deep within my memory. I've been lying here trying to figure out why I recognized Lillian's name. It just now returned to me."

"Perhaps I should lie on the floor too then," Aunt Carrie said, and she shuffled between the others and flung herself down. "Oof," she said, as she landed. She closed her eyes.

Again, the whirlwind of voices resumed, growing louder and more agitated.

When the *brrrrriiing!* sounded, it was very much as if the telephone, sitting on the sideboard, had suddenly tired of all their noise and was screaming in frustration.

The Butler answered.

Everyone watched him. Aunt Carrie sat up from the floor.

"He is?" the Butler said. "Downstairs? Alone? Yes, by all means, send him up. Send him up at once."

Ignoring all their questions, he hurried away to the front door.

When he returned, a few moments later, he paused in the doorway and announced: "Prince Billy."

"And his dog," Billy added, stepping into the room. A dog trotted in behind him.

PART 12

CHAPTER 66

OH (I SAID to myself).

I was back on my bedroom floor. I replaced the stopper in the Genie bottle and leaned back to think, palms flat on my carpet. It was much rougher and more threadbare than the staircase carpet I'd been sitting on.

You got the warning through! I reminded myself. *You should feel light with happiness!*

I did not though.

The words I'd just heard still sounded in my ears.

You say that Alys is no longer queen of the Mellifluous Kingdom? And that a person named Lillian Velvet has taken over?

So the Mettlestones knew Queen Alys? Was Billy all right if his mother was no longer queen?

More important, who was this person who had taken over their kingdom and who had my name!

It seemed a *very* peculiar coincidence.

I shuffled around, growing increasingly itchy and uncomfortable. It was more than the carpet itself, I realized. It was the way Bronte's eyes had widened when those words were spoken—right before I disappeared.

There had been *doubt* in her eyes.

Surely Bronte didn't think that *I* had taken Queen Alys's kingdom? Did she imagine I'd staged a coup d'état, led an army to victory, and was now busy running a kingdom? I was ten! (And only just too.)

I wouldn't know the first thing about running a kingdom.

Yet if Bronte thought I *was* the sort of girl to steal kingdoms, she might doubt my story about a child being buried by gravel.

Suddenly, I felt very tired.

It was impossible to save the boy. I had tried everything. Perhaps I should give up—let time take the course it was supposed to take. Hadn't Reuben warned me that changing things could cause untold harm? As sad as it was, it had *happened,* and I had to let it go.

Even as my mind ran through these thoughts, though, fierceness seemed to grow within me. It rose in my throat like dragon fire.

I was *not* going to come this close and not save that boy!

In fact, I would not wait another moment. I'd use my final visit right now. I'd go straight back and make certain that Bronte still believed me.

I wrenched the stopper back out of the Genie bottle, watched as images poured into the room, waited, waited—and there it was.

Bronte and I talking in the stairway. Bronte pointing to the window. Me peering through the glass at the rainy darkness below. Paving stones. Pillar-box.

I pinned it all in my mind and squeezed my eyes closed. The window, the paving stones, the rain darkness. Window, paving stones, rain darkness. I reached out my hands.

PART 13

REPORT 7

A SPACIOUS PENTHOUSE APARTMENT, GAINSLEIGH, KINGDOMS AND EMPIRES
—Friday, May 25

* * *

Prince Billy of the Mellifluous Kingdom did not look his best.

His face was dirty and scratched. His hair was as fuzzy as a dandelion wish. His good shirt was stained in grass greens and tomato reds, his trouser hems were muddied, and he only wore one shoe. On the shoeless foot was a dirty sock, a huge hole at the toe. His dog also looked shabby, burs knotted into its fur. The dog sat very neatly at Billy's feet, as if trying to make up for their messiness.

"Good evening, everyone," Billy said, sounding breathless. His cheeks, they saw now, were gaunt, face behind the dirt almost translucently pale. "I apologize for . . ." He swayed, then straightened and raised his voice. "I apologize for interrupting. Might I prevail upon you . . . I mean to say . . . could you please . . ." His voice trembled.

"Oh, Billy," several aunts said at once, and "Billy, old chap," his uncle Patrick added. Several adults moved toward him, arms out.

He waved them away. "You are very kind but I must pull myself together. I need your help, please. I need you to . . ." Again, he gathered himself and spoke in a rush: "Please rescue my mother." Deep intake of breath. "She's being held just across the road."

And he collapsed onto the carpet.

There was a burst of commotion, ending with Billy scrambling back to his feet, wiping away tears, and repeating: "My mother is being held just across the road! There's a jewelry shop. She's in there. Please rescue her."

The commotion grew louder.

"Hold up, Billy!" Aunt Maya cried. "Ease the mainsheet! You've been across the road all this time?"

"Top-notch news that you've escaped," Aunt Lisbeth put in. "We'll power over there and get your mother. What can you tell us about the scabby sea bass that captured you?"

Billy shook his head. "I *didn't* escape," he said. "I *wasn't* captured! Look, when my mother went missing, I was desperately worried and even more so as palace security made no headway. Then I noticed that my new dog, Theodore'—here, Theodore stood, wagged his tail briefly, and sat down again—'well, that Theodore had a fine sense of smell. He tracked down my lost scarf! In the billiard room. And the chef's lost pair of tongs! In the laundry hamper. So, I said to myself, 'Jeepers, Billy! Why not let Theo sniff your mother's jacket?' And then say to Theo: *'Find my mother, find her!'* "

Thus, Billy explained, he had run away from the palace.

He had followed Theodore's lead to the railway station, onto a train, and next to a coach station, and onto a coach, and a ferry wharf, a ferry—and so on, through various forms of transport—until they had arrived—after three days and nights without food or sleep—in Gainsleigh, at the jewelry store right across the road from Aunt Isabelle's.

A strange quiet fell over the living room. All the amazement and hope that had flourished when

Billy announced his mother was across the road dwindled into nothing.

"Oh, Billy," several people murmured.

"Yes," Billy agreed. "It's been tough, but, pip pip, never mind. I'm sure you can help me rescue her. Let's go at once though. We mustn't dillydally."

Another quiet.

"Billy," Aunt Isabelle said gently, moving to put an arm around her nephew's shoulder. "I'm sure that Theo here is a good dog, skillful at finding scarves and tongs." Theo thumped his tail, apparently agreeing. "However, a dog could not track a missing person onto a train, a coach, and across water! The trail would have been long lost! Darling, I'm glad that Theo has brought you here to us, where we can keep you safe, but—"

Billy flung her hand aside, looking at her incredulously. His face turned violet. A deep breath. And then, at the top of his lungs he bawled: *"MY MOTHER IS ACROSS THE STREET! WE NEED TO RESCUE HER AT ONCE!"*

Theo looked up at his owner with concern.

The whole room shared Theo's concern. Billy was such a sunny-natured boy, such an easygoing, gentle child. Nobody had ever heard him raise his voice, let alone screech like that.

"All right," Aunt Isabelle said, making a swift decision. "All right, Billy. Someone will go and check the jewelry shop."

Billy nodded. "Thank you, Aunt Isabelle. I do apologize for my shouting just now. May we go at once?"

"You will stay here," his aunt told him firmly. "Have something to eat and drink, Billy, and we'll get something for Theo too. Perhaps Aunt Claire could take you into the kitchen and . . ."

Claire was already stepping forward, but Billy frowned.

"You're not taking me seriously," he realized. "My mother is across the road, most likely being held by Shadow Mages." He took a deep breath, preparing to scream again, and Aunt Carrie hurried to his side.

"We are taking it very seriously," she promised Billy. "How about this? The three family Spellbinders will head over immediately. I don't believe there *are* Shadow Mages in the neighborhood—I'd have sensed their presence. However, if there are, we will bind them and rescue Alys."

Bronte spoke up. "There *could* be shadow magic in the neighborhood," she countered. "The *invisible* kind that was used in my dormitory." She looked across at her cousin. "Billy, if your mother is there, I promise we'll bring her back."

The three family Spellbinders—Aunt Carrie, Uncle Patrick (Bronte's father), and Bronte herself—reached for their coats.

At the last moment, Lida (Bronte's mother) insisted on coming too. She could do reconnaissance, she said. She could slip across, peek into the windows of the jewelry store, and then whisper her observations back into the others' minds.

Billy visibly relaxed when he heard the word *reconnaissance*. They *were* taking this seriously.

"Meanwhile, we'll stay and keep an eye on the children here," Aunt Franny said, "and make sure that Billy is fed and . . ."

She had been going to say that Billy would be bathed and put to bed himself but, seeing his expression, she thought better of that.

"Good luck, everyone," she said, instead.

The group of rescuers put on their coats and set out into the rain.

CHAPTER 67

WINDOW, PAVING STONES, rain darkness. I reached out my hands and—

Window, paving stones, rain darkness.

I was on the staircase again, at the window, looking through the darkness and the rain, at the paving stones and pillar-box below.

How much time had passed? Adult voices still sounded from upstairs. Was I brave enough to enter a room noisy with adults? Was Bronte with them now?

I turned back to the window, thinking, and blinked.

Colors and shadows moved about on the street below. I pressed my forehead to the glass, trying to see. In the lamplight, a man, a woman, and a girl—was that *Bronte*?—were standing in the middle of the street in the rain.

A woman was descending the jewelry store staircase. She gestured at the others as she moved toward them. Her face caught the lamplight. She was very beautiful. Smooth brown skin, bright dark eyes, a fine sharp nose, and the longest hair I'd ever seen. Shimmery in the moonlight, it flowed down to her ankles.

Lida, I thought at once. That's Lida.

Only this was a grown-up woman, whereas my friend Lida had been a teenager of fifteen.

I peered harder. Grown-up Lida had joined the others in the middle of the road. They huddled together, apparently talking.

Automatically, I glanced left and right along the street. No cars or carriages. Only soft rain falling, silvery and crossed with darts of color.

The darts of color were black and red.

My frown deepened. The darts of color twisted. They flew through the air, braiding together as they moved in a smooth, curving motion. My eyes followed them back up, squinting to find their source, and there—an open window, high above the jewelry store. I could just make out a figure inside the window, hands moving rapidly. The red and black darts flew from those hands. My eyes roamed along the building and there—another open window. Another figure weaving the air, more red and black darts. Directly above that window, a figure held a broom and moved it in swift circles, creating more of the darts.

Altogether I counted seven windows. Seven strands of red and black darts which, as I watched, poured down and plaited together, forming a thick rope that grew and grew—and snaked its way in a low, slow circle around and around and around the group in the middle of the road.

REPORT 8

SOUTH END OF LONGFELLOW STREET,
GAINSLEIGH, KINGDOMS AND EMPIRES
—Friday, May 25, not long past midnight

* * *

They had gathered together in the middle of the street, astonished.

"You're *sure*?" Carrie hissed, for the second time.

"I'm as surprised as you." Lida brushed the rain from her eyes.

None of them had believed that Alys would be in the jewelry store.

Descending in the elevator, Carrie had said: "Billy probably subconsciously led the dog to Gainsleigh himself, wanting to be with his family."

The others had nodded in agreement.

Still, they'd said they would investigate properly—that way they could honestly tell Billy they'd tried. Lida had slipped across the street and up the stairs of the jewelry shop in order to peek through the cracks in the shutters.

She'd expected to see a counter, and shelves of jewelry. Instead, she'd seen a bare room with a mattress in the corner. A woman was asleep on the mattress.

"Alys?" she had whispered, in disbelief, and Alys had sat up, looking around in confusion.

"It's me, Lida. We are here to rescue you. Wait there."

Through the crack, she'd seen Alys nod quickly.

Lida had not bothered with any more whispering. She'd slipped back down the stairs and joined the others in the road.

So now here they were, rain dripping down the collars of their coats, exchanging amazed glances.

"Do we just go straight in and get her?" Patrick wondered aloud.

"I'll crack the lock," Carrie said softly. "If that doesn't work, I'll smash the window."

"And I'll fetch her out," Patrick said, nodding. "Lida, you and Bronte keep watch."

Lida was surveying the street and buildings. "There are a few open windows up there," she said, squinting. "Strange for a cold, wet night. Are you three sure there's no shadow magic around?"

She turned to the Spellbinders. Carrie and Patrick both nodded. "We're sure."

Bronte hesitated. "As far as I can *tell,*" she said.

"Right." Carrie turned to Patrick. "Let's go."

Before they took a single step, though, the ground beneath them shuddered—and began to split.

CHAPTER 68

"*NO,*" I WHISPERED.

It was just like the circus again.

Danger too far for me to reach.

The street below shuddered and so did my whole body. The ground around the group rose like a waking bear. The little figures were flung to the road. Around them, cracks formed like smashed glass, each crack gaping open to form a deep, black crevasse.

They scuttled away from the edges and clambered unsteadily to their feet. The street immediately lifted itself and shook them back down again, like a picnic blanket shaking itself free of crumbs.

Any moment one of them would fall into those gaping holes.

Two of the adults and Bronte were trying to spellbind, weaving their hands in the air even as they stumbled and fell. Green-and-gold nets kept forming, but the nets caught nothing, slipped to the ground, and disappeared.

They couldn't *see* the red-and-black braiding to bind it.

It was *there* though! The shadow magic was right there, at shoulder height!

I wrenched open the window and leaned out.

Too far away. They'd never hear me.

If only I could somehow speak into their minds!

I blinked.

Lida? I thought.

Yes? Her reply shot back at once. Down below she grabbed the man and pulled him to his feet before slipping over herself.

It's me! Lillian Velvet! You can hear me?

Her reply was a little snappy: *Can't chat just now, Lillian. Oof.* She'd fallen again.

Tell the Spellbinders I can see the shadow magic, I said.

A pause.

Then, as I watched, the man slipped into a crevasse. Caught the edges with his fingertips. The others rushed toward him and hauled him back up.

Tell me, Lida said sharply. She sounded breathless and frightened. *Where is the shadow magic?*

I forced myself to remain calm. *It forms a ring,* I said. *All around you. It's shoulder height.*

Lida fell hard on the ground.

Shoulder height? Whose shoulder? she asked after a moment. Her voice was very shaky.

I peered amongst them, frantic. The Spellbinding man was crawling on the ground. *His,* I replied. *The Spellbinder man. When he's standing.*

That's my husband, Lida murmured. *Patrick.* I watched as Lida pushed herself up by her elbows, and made her way across to Patrick. She pointed up.

He nodded. From the ground, he began spellbinding again, directing his hands skyward. Bronte and the Spellbinding woman crawled over, and Lida spoke quickly to them. Green-and-gold nets formed rapidly. They shot up in the direction of the shadow braid—and missed.

"HIGHER!" I shouted aloud, forgetting myself. "A LITTLE HIGHER!"

Higher, I said in my mind, instead. *A tiny bit higher.*

Lida took her husband's arms and nudged them upward. *Here?*

Too high.

She nudged them down.

Here?

Yes. That's it!

Thudding footsteps and raised voices sounded behind me. My shouting had alerted the adults upstairs.

"THERE'S A CHILD HERE ON THE STAIRS!"

"A STRANGER!"

I swung around briefly.

"Is that her?" several voices asked. "Is that Lillian Velvet?"

"GET AWAY FROM THAT WINDOW AT ONCE!" a voice boomed. Three or four adults thundered down the steps toward me.

"Please!" I cried, turning back to the window. "They need me! I have to do this!"

It's working! I told Lida. *Tell them to keep going at that height. Wait, tell them they should all face different directions! It's a circle!*

"Get away from that window!" several stern voices repeated. I glanced back over my shoulder. So many adults crowded together scowling at me like a great gray thundercloud. I trembled.

Then I bit my lip. "I'm trying to *help* them down there!" I cried. "They need me!"

The adults frowned, deeply skeptical, and began to swarm even more determinedly toward me.

"STEP BACK FROM THAT WINDOW—" they chorused.

And then quick, light footsteps came scampering between the adults, and there was my friend Billy.

"Jeepers!" he said. "It's Lillian Velvet! Stay back, everyone! Lillian, what do you need?"

"Billy! They need to leave me be," I pleaded, turning back to the window. And while Billy stood right behind me, occasionally bellowing, "STAY AWAY FROM LILLIAN VELVET!" to the adults—who scolded, begged, reasoned with, and commanded him to get out of their way—I carried on directing Lida.

A little lower—now to the right—tell Bronte she almost had it then, just a teeny bit higher and to the left—while down below the figures slid this way and that, scrambled to their feet, carried on spellbinding, and slowly—raggedly, messily—that red-and-black ring was swallowed up by nets, and swallowed up by nets—the darts growing weaker, finer, petering away like the final drips of a tightened tap.

And then it was gone.

The road fell perfectly still.

To my surprise, rather than pausing to catch their breath, the people down there leapt to their feet and ran toward the jewelry shop.

Lida sent a final, breathless thought at me: *Thank you, Lillian, thank you! Now we can save Alys! Queen Alys! She's in the jewelry store!*

She followed the others. One of them kicked open the door, the rest stormed inside, and—

Shove, I was home again.

PART

14

REPORT 9

A SPACIOUS PENTHOUSE APARTMENT,
GAINSLEIGH, KINGDOMS AND EMPIRES
—Friday, May 25

* * *

It was early morning and everyone was talking at once.

Everyone was also rushing about. The guests of honor—the long-lost parents—were due to arrive any moment. Food was being prepared, the table laid for the welcome breakfast. Pancake batter bubbled, coffee simmered, oranges were squeezed, extra chairs brought into the dining room, napkins folded, and voices raised.

At the heart of the commotion was a fierce disagreement. The subject of the disagreement?

Lillian Velvet.

Half the people believed that Lillian Velvet was a hero. In the middle of the night, she had saved a group of Mettlestones from a terrifying shadow attack. Queen Alys had been rescued, and a gang of Witches and Sterling Silver Foxes, lurking in the apartments upstairs, had been captured. This gang was linked to several recent attacks on Mettlestones—storms, illness, ice cages. Somehow they could hide their shadow magic. When they'd intercepted Alys's telegram, they'd realized she was onto them, so they'd captured her and brought her here. Their plan had been to attack other members of the Mettlestone family when they came to rescue her.

Now, though, Alys and the Mettlestones were safe—and it was all thanks to Lillian Velvet.

Hooray for Lillian Velvet!

The other half believed that Lillian Velvet was a villain. She had *caused* the attacks, including the one on the street last night. She was the mastermind behind the gang of Sterling Silver Foxes and Witches, and had probably taught them how to hide their shadow magic, using tricks from her own world. She had ordered them to capture Queen Alys, installing herself as the Mellifluous queen instead. She was cunning, *pretending* to help members of the Mettlestone family, so that she could steal valuable items, like the Genie bottle, and gain their trust. Meanwhile, she was scheming to destroy every one of them.

Boo for Lillian Velvet!

"By golly, she's *certainly* not a villain!" Billy fumed. He had not left his mother's side since her rescue, so he kept his voice to the volume of a fume, rather than screeching again, not wanting to distress her. Alys appeared to the others to be her usual composed self, but Billy knew better. He was moving about with her as if they were participants in a three-legged race. His dog, Theodore, kept winding between their legs, as if he wanted to sabotage the race. (Nobody minded. Theodore could have got away with eating the antique candelabra. He had tracked down Alys. Theodore was 100 percent a hero.)

"I never heard any of my captors mention the name Lillian Velvet," Alys said in her soft voice. She gave her son's shoulder a squeeze.

"They wouldn't, would they?" Franny called from the corridor. She strode into the room carrying a bowl of fresh fruit and placed this on the table. "Lillian will have instructed them *not* to reveal her identity. There's no doubt she's the powerful enemy who sent our parents into hiding twenty years ago." Franny took a carrot from her pocket, frowned at the lint that was clinging to it, and bit into it anyway. "They're coming out of hiding too early," she added through a mouthful.

"She's a child," Lida protested from the other side of the room, where she was arranging flowers. "She does have otherworldly powers—she can travel in time; she can speak into my mind even though she's not a Whisperer, and she can *see* magic even though she's not a Spellbinder. However, she's not an evil genius. She's a frightened child who has helped me when I needed her—twice."

"She's saved me twice now too!" Bronte called from the kitchen. "She's absolutely a hero!"

"She saved our whole *kingdom,*" Billy argued from the table, where he and his mother were now seated side by side, buttering a stack of toast. "Or anyway, she saved everyone seriously injured in the storm. She's the one who suggested I paint the piano! And the piano music rebuilt the hospital! She even modeled in the painting for me, which was *awfully* sporting of her!"

"Oh yes, I've seen that painting," Emma piped up. (She was polishing the mirror over the fireplace, and had been for some time. She kept finding new smudges.) "Your mother sent it to me, Billy. It's a marvelous painting! Breathtaking! Best I've ever seen. The girl playing the piano looks sweet too, even though she *is* an evil genius. You're the most talented child in all the Kingdoms and Empires, Billy, and the favorite of all my nephews."

"HEY!" exclaimed her other nephews—Sue's four boys—in unison. (Their job was meant to be dusting, but they were kicking the dusters around, as if they were soccer balls, instead.)

"You're *all* my favorite nephews," Emma told them placatingly. "You boys are the best little farm boys in all the Kingdoms and Empires! And Oscar is the best boy from another world I've ever met! Where is Oscar anyway?" She turned from the mirror, but Sue's boys had lost interest and were out in the hallway wrestling.

"I'm here," Oscar replied. He was under the table. Isabelle had asked him to fit rubber covers to the legs of the extra chairs so they would not scratch the floor. "And I *like* Lillian Velvet."

"Emma, did you just say you have a painting of Lillian Velvet?" Carrie demanded, her voice rising above the commotion. She was banging down place mats—*thwack, thwack, thwack.* "I wish I could see that painting. I was out on the street last night when you lot saw her, so I don't know what she looks like. I still don't know why her name is so familiar."

"But you *can* see it, my darling sister," Emma replied. "It's here! It was one of my most valuable possessions, of course, so I saved it in the storm on Lantern Island. I'll fetch it for you!"

She darted from the room.

Oscar, meanwhile, was feeling defensive about Lillian: she was from *his* world, after all. These people didn't get her the way he did. He crawled out from under the table. "She's a bit weird but in a cute and harmless way," he said. "I mean, she said that her grandmother had found her in a basket on the doorstep, and that she got a pickle jar of gold coins for her tenth birthday. Basically though, she's a regular kid. I've never seen someone go off the way she did about caramel fudge."

There was some confusion about whether Lillian Velvet was a kind of cheese—Oscar had to explain that *go off* meant "get excited"—and then the argument took flight again.

Emma returned, ducking to avoid a flying teapot—one sister had flung it at another in a temper. She handed the painting to Carrie.

"Yes, she does look sweet," Carrie agreed, studying the painting. "Still don't recognize—"

She sat down suddenly with a thump. Fortunately, there was a chair right behind her. Her finger traced the image of Lillian in the painting.

"It's *Lillian Velvet,*" she whispered.

"Well, *yes,* we've established that," her sister Nancy said acidly.

Carrie's face had taken on a strange glow. "Lillian Velvet, how did I forget you?" She tapped the painting gently, then looked around at her family, who had (more or less) fallen quiet, awaiting her explanation. "I met her when I was a child," Carrie murmured. "She helped me save a colony of Sparks who'd been buried by a Hurtling. That incident changed my life, actually. And I liked her so much!" She looked up from the painting. "I'm switching sides," she announced. "Lillian Velvet is a *hero*!"

Another burst of heated arguing, which grew and grew, louder and shriller—"You mark my words, there's a secret about Lillian Velvet and nobody's safe until we find out what it is!" Nancy bellowed—until a pair of hands was clapped together sharply and a stern female voice demanded: "*This* is how you behave now?"

"As for this Lillian Velvet," a softer male voice added, "I've got an idea what *her* secret might be."

And the entire family stopped, as one, to stare. Two figures stood in the dining room doorway.

Jacob and Ildi Mettlestone. Long lost, now returned.

REPORT 10

A SPACIOUS PENTHOUSE APARTMENT,
GAINSLEIGH, KINGDOMS AND EMPIRES
—Friday, May 25

* * *

Isabelle spoke first.

"You're here," she whispered. She cleared her throat. "How long have you been standing there?"

"Long enough," Jacob replied.

There was a quiet in the room that felt full of sound, or full of pounding heartbeats anyway. As if everyone was running a sprint race—arms and legs pumping—while simultaneously standing quite still.

Franny raised a carrot toward her mouth, then lowered it without taking a bite. "You know who Lillian Velvet is?" she asked.

"I know who she *might* be," her father corrected. "You see, when I was at university, I did this course." He scratched the side of his chin thoughtfully. "It's a small, secret course—only Sprites are allowed to do it. I'm a Wheat Sprite, of course. Anyhow, I really only chose the course because it was conducted via singing, painting, and sleeping. Sleeping! I mean to say, what normal university student *wouldn't* choose such a course!" He chuckled.

Beside him, Ildi gave a brief chuckle too. "I slept through all my classes anyway. Lucky you were taking those and gave me your notes."

"So I did," he agreed. "But you wrote my essays for me."

This was extremely strange.

Here were their long-lost parents—or long-lost grandparents—and they were standing in the doorway reminiscing about university days?

It now felt as if the room were swaying gently side to side. Or as if the people in the room were trees, rooted to the ground, their branches swept to and fro by a haunting wind.

"Anyhow," Jacob continued, comfortably, "it was a course about strange and otherworldly things. For example, we learned about a certain kind of child. As a baby, this child is taken to another world and left in a basket at the door of a person or family. The child grows up not knowing their true identity. On their tenth birthday, the child receives a stack of gold coins. For the next week, the child is transported into different places and times within the Kingdoms and Empires. There, they encounter people who need help. The child is allocated a guide who appears now and then to advise them."

Several people in the room were making small sounds of recognition. "That sounds like Lillian!" "That's what happened to Lillian!"

"Yes." Jacob nodded. "If I've heard you all correctly, Lillian Velvet was found on her grandmother's doorstep. It was Oscar who mentioned that—you're from another world, aren't you, Oscar, and have become part of our family? In that case, you're one of our grandchildren! Welcome to our world! Welcome to the family! All right, I also believe that Lillian . . ."

Jacob went on to list the facts about Lillian Velvet he'd overheard. Lillian received a pickle jar of gold coins for her tenth birthday, he said

("I don't remember pickles from my studies," he added, "but I might have slept through that bit—ha ha"). Lillian was regularly "shoved" to different places and times within the Kingdoms and Empires. Lillian had helped various people in trouble. Lillian had mentioned a man named Mr. Turtelhaze, who advised her—like a guide.

"But what's it all *for*?" Bronte asked, wonderingly.

"Excellent question, Bronte," her grandfather replied. "It's a test. It lasts for exactly a week after the child receives the coins. The coins represent wishes, you see—each wish costs five coins, if I remember correctly. The wishes cannot be used to determine when and where the child is transported—that's prearranged—but *may* be used to determine the length of any stay. That's so the child can wish themselves back quickly if they're in danger, say. The child can also spend wishes for other purposes, such as to help the people in trouble. However, the idea is for the child to use their own wits and intuition to solve problems—ideally helping the people to help themselves. It's a pretty easy test. To pass, the child only needs to have at least one wish—or five coins—still remaining at the end of the week."

"And then what happens?" little Benjamin demanded. "If they do pass the test?"

Jacob clasped his hands together and tapped his chin with two raised forefingers. He looked exactly like a professor. "First, let me ask *you* all something. Another thing I've heard people here say is that Lillian Velvet can *see* magic, although she's not a Spellbinder. And that she can *speak into the minds* of Whisperers, although she's not a Whisperer herself. So tell me: who else do you know that can see beyond reality? Who else can speak inside of minds?"

Most of his family stared at him, baffled. Some shuffled and looked at their feet.

"Let's put it another way," Ildi spoke up from beside Jacob, a little impatiently. "Who can move around in time and space? Who grants wishes but prefers to help people to help themselves instead?" She *tched,* exasperated. "Come on! You know it! Who else would be *drawn to a Genie bottle,* and who would use a Genie bottle to get themselves around?"

Heads snapped back. Eyes and mouths opened wide.

"Jeepers," said Billy. "You're talking about . . ." He stopped, still not quite believing it.

His grandfather looked at him. "Genies," he said. "If this Lillian Velvet passes the test? She's a Genie."

REPORT 11

A SPACIOUS PENTHOUSE APARTMENT,
GAINSLEIGH, KINGDOMS AND EMPIRES
—Friday, May 25

* * *

"So you can stop arguing about her," Ildi declared. "And you can stop blaming her for the trouble you've had with Shadow Mages lately."

Beside her, Jacob nodded. "Lillian will have been transported here to *help* you with all that."

"And somebody said something about Lillian warning you about danger coming?" Ildi frowned. "We didn't catch *everything* you said."

"You appear to have caught most of it," Isabelle said faintly.

"Anyhow, the point is—listen to Lillian's warnings." Jacob nodded. "Whatever they were. She's certainly *not* a villain."

Nancy Mettlestone, who was well known for being meticulous, double-checked: "Well, but *could* a Genie be a villain?"

Her parents exchanged swift glances. "Practically impossible," her father replied, very seriously. "A Genie child is pure starlight."

At this, a softness, like the light at dusk, or the clinking of teaspoons during afternoon tea, began to drift around the room.

Lillian Velvet is a Genie child.

After a few moments, though, this mood was replaced by awkwardness.

Jacob and Ildi still stood in the doorway like strangers! Regarding them, their adult children thought: *They're so old! Look how frail and lined and gray they are!* (The Mettlestone grandchildren thought: *These two seem pretty young and fit to be grandparents, to be honest.*)

Meanwhile, nobody was moving to welcome Jacob and Ildi, let alone invite them in for breakfast—or ask them how they'd been.

Jacob studied his fingernails. "I have a question," he said suddenly. "I heard Alys saying she somehow knew the storm in the Mellifluous Kingdom was *not* a storm? How did you know that, Alys?"

Alys blinked. She reached down and stroked Billy's hair, and then patted Billy's dog. "I just knew," she said. "The light of my desk lamp reminded me of how the light had changed when the storm was approaching. And suddenly I felt the storm's rhythm again—and I realized it was not the rhythm of a normal storm."

Both Jacob and Ildi smiled broadly. "Oh, Alys," they said, their next words overlapping: "You were always our musical child!" "You always had that wonderful sense of rhythm!"

And they stepped forward and hugged Alys tight. Then, as if in a dance, they moved around the room hugging everyone in turn.

This dance, although heartfelt, had a graceful formality. Little Benjamin could hardly bear it. He could sense overwhelming emotion—so much loss, so much joy—within all the politeness. So when his grandparents reached him, he burst into sobs.

The others murmured, "Oh, Benjamin, darling," and then *all* the adults began to cry. This made them laugh. They cried and laughed at the same time.

"Our parents are back!" Carrie exclaimed. "And Lillian Velvet is a *Genie* child!"

At which, for some reason—the disbelief, perhaps, or just the astonishing twists and turns of life—they shouted with laughter while they hugged their parents again, tears streaming down their cheeks.

* * *

Later, while they were enjoying breakfast, Bronte asked a question.

"What if Lillian *fails* the test?" she asked.

Everyone looked across at her, interested.

"Oh yes." Her Aunt Franny put in. "If she *does* spend all the wishes and cannot become a Genie? Does she turn into an ordinary child? Or will she get a second chance?"

Jacob's mouth was full. He chewed quickly, shaking his head. "Nope," he replied eventually. "No second chances. A Genie child who fails the test ceases to exist."

Heads swung in his direction. "Ceases to *exist*?"

"Like a flame blown out on a birthday cake," he declared.

A moment of startled quiet, then: "Jeepers!" Billy exclaimed. "I hope Lillian's being careful with her wishes!"

"I'm sure she is," his grandfather said. "She'll know how important it is. Her Genie guide will have made that *very* clear to her. And sounds to me like she's been using her *wits* to help people, rather than her wishes, which is exactly right. Can somebody hand me the maple syrup? These pancakes are perfect!"

PART 15

CHAPTER 69

AFTER I'D RETURNED from watching the Mettlestones survive the shadow magic attack, my heart fluttered about like flying insects on a lawn.

Butterflies, you mean, I told myself sternly.

No, I argued back (passionately), *any insect at all! It could be a moth or a dragonfly or a—*

I took a deep breath. I was being silly. It was the shock of having just watched a street toss and turn like a feverish sleeper while people slipped and fell toward gaping holes.

I returned the stopper to the Genie bottle and leaned back against my bed. Slowly, the fluttering transformed itself into a smile.

It wasn't just shock making me silly. It was *relief*!

I had saved them! I'd saved them!

All right, be modest now, I reminded myself. *This is unseemly.* I tried to make my face serious. The smile jumped right back.

I remembered how Lida had sent her hurried, final thought to me—*Thank you, Lillian, thank you! Now we can save Alys!*—and how they'd all rushed at the building—*stormed* the building!

So determined. They must truly love Alys. That was nice.

It was the perfect ending to my adventures in the Kingdoms and Empires. Not only had I saved the people on the street but now the Mettlestone family would *definitely* trust me! Lida would tell them how I'd helped her! They'd know I was not the sort of person to steal kingdoms! That doubt in Bronte's eyes would disappear. The adults would no longer want to come rushing—*storming*—down the staircase toward me.

Instead, they'd believe my warning and they'd make sure nothing happened to the little boy at the circus.

All would be well.

I stood up, still smiling, and walked back down the hall like a balloon bobbing on a string. "Hello, schoolwork!" I said, sitting down. "Hello, jar of gold coins!" The jar seemed to glint proudly at me.

"So you should be proud!" I told it. "You were the *perfect* birthday present!"

It was difficult to believe that my birthday had been only five days ago. So many (short) adventures had taken place in those five days!

I reached for the jar so that I could pour the last of the coins into my pockets. Most likely, I'd be *shoved* at some point and then Mr. Turtelhaze would appear, collect the coins I owed, and send me straight back home. There'd be no coins left for me to "wish to stay."

I tilted the jar from side to side, in a jangly way, for a moment. What if there weren't enough coins to pay for these last few visits? What would happen then? The jar still felt quite heavy though. Perhaps I'd end up having *more* than enough? Maybe I'd have one or two visits remaining!

I was being too optimistic. I jiggled my shoulders to calm myself, placed my hand on the lid ready to open it—and somebody knocked on the front door.

CHAPTER 70

I WAS SO shocked that I jumped to my feet and my chair toppled backward. It hit the floor with a CRASH.

Nobody ever knocked at our door. *Don't open the door to anybody even if they knock very loudly,* Grandmother's rules said, *unless it is me.*

Was it her?

If it was her, she'd have a key! She must be testing me!

I crouched down, breathing quickly.

Knock, knock, knock. Three very firm knocks.

"Hello?" called a woman's voice. A familiar voice. Not Grandmother's though.

All right, it was definite then. I must *not* answer the door.

Knock, knock, knock.

Another long silence.

Footsteps moved across the porch, down the stairs, and onto the path.

I breathed out in relief, and then, even louder: KNOCK! KNOCK!

This time I was so startled I fell over backward onto the floor myself.

The new knocking was coming from the *window*!

The person had not carried on down along the path, they'd moved to the front window!

I stood up in wonder and stared.

A woman was standing in the window. She waved at me and smiled.

Good gracious. It was Helen from next door!

I stared. Grandmother had not told me the rules for when people knocked on windows.

"Hello, Lillian!" she said. She crouched down and spoke into the open gap at the bottom of the window. That window is kept very slightly ajar for the fresh air, although it is locked in place so that intruders cannot enter along with the air. "Is your grandmother at home?"

I shook my head.

"Ah, so you're being a good girl and not opening the door to strangers!" she said. "I heard a crash in here after I knocked—is everything okay?"

I nodded. Everything *was* okay. Or, at least, as okay as it could be when a neighbor astonishes you by knocking on your window.

"I've come by to ask *you* a favor anyway," Helen continued, still crouched there. She shifted about a bit—perhaps her legs were hurting from holding the crouched position. I had experience of that. "You won't believe it, Lillian, but a TV station has surprised us by renovating our back garden!"

"Oh yes." I moved closer to the window and tilted slightly so my voice would carry through the gap. "I *do* believe it, as I overheard them talking. Were you wonderfully surprised?"

She chuckled. "*They* were surprised anyway," she told me, "and not very wonderfully. We came back from our holiday early—Shahlyla had a work emergency. Big pile of rubble and junk and a lot of colorful language in our backyard. They're cross with us, but we've promised we'll roll our luggage down our front path again when the work is finished, and do our best to act amazed. That might be hard, though," she added, "as we won't be."

"Perhaps you could practice," I suggested.

"We have been," she told me. "We're watching YouTube videos about acting techniques for surprise. Anyway, trying to cheer up the TV people, we've been telling them how *perfect* the backyard is going to be, and how *delighted* we are—I mean, all that is true, of course. We don't need to act that. And we told them how the little girl next door made a wish that we would get everything we wanted? Remember when you made that wish, Lillian?"

I frowned, doubtfully. Had I?

Helen smiled. "You said, *I wish you could have all the things you want—the hot tub and the pergola, the patio and rosebushes, the herb garden! Everything!* Shah and I thought that was the sweetest thing. And now it's all come true! We think you must have used your birthday wish for us! It was your birthday the other day, wasn't it?"

I agreed that it had been.

"So the TV crew are now hoping to do a little interview with you as part of their story," Helen concluded. "About how you used your birthday wish for us. I mean, it's just a joke, of course—I'm sure you used your birthday wish for what *you* wanted, on your *actual* birthday, when you blew out the candles on your cake. And obviously, well, birthday wishes don't *really* come true, sorry to say. We're just being a bit silly and whimsical, and the TV people love it. So that's the favor we wanted to ask. No pressure—only if you like the idea. And we'd have to get your grandmother's permission, of course. Do you want to have a think about it?"

"I don't need to have a think!" I said, staring. "A *television* interview! How marvelous! I'll do it!"

Helen chuckled. "All right, I'll come back later when your grandmother is home and hopefully she'll like the idea too. When do you expect her back?"

"Around five thirty," I told her faintly. She gave me a thumbs-up sign, waved goodbye, and strolled away, back to her place.

"Good gracious," I whispered to myself—about the whole thing.

CHAPTER 71

"CERTAINLY NOT," GRANDMOTHER said.

It was later that evening, and Grandmother had arrived home with a paper bag of groceries. She thumped this down on the kitchen bench and gave me a look over her shoulder. I took a step back.

"You should not have opened the door to the neighbor—" Grandmother began.

"I didn't open the door, Grandmother! Did you not just hear me? I only spoke to Helen through the gap in the window!"

"Essentially the same as opening the door," Grandmother said sharply. "Do not interrupt me, child. Do not suggest that my hearing is defective. And do not attempt to evade house rules. Can I no longer trust you to be home alone? Is that it? Must I resign from my employment, although it brings me joy? And pays for these groceries?" She waved her hand at the paper bag.

"No, Grandmother," I whispered. "I mean, yes, Grandmother. I promise you can trust me. You may keep going to your job."

"Oh, I *may* keep going to work, may I? You are going to give me *permission*, are you?" Grandmother was slamming tins and packets into the kitchen cupboards as she spoke. She placed a carton of milk in the refrigerator and placed her hands on her hips. "You say the neighbor plans to return tonight, to ask my permission for you to be on television?"

I nodded.

"Speak, child. Do not nod."

"Yes, Grandmother."

"Continue preparations for supper and I will go next door at once and tell them it is out of the question." She wiped her hands on a cloth, stepped through the front door, and closed it firmly behind her.

CHAPTER 72

THE NEXT MORNING, shortly after Grandmother had left for work, there was another knock on the door.

I froze.

Moments ticked by.

"It's all right," called a man's voice. "I'll let myself in."

And there was Mr. Turtelhaze standing right beside me.

Once again, I was so startled I flung my chair back. It crashed to the floor.

Mr. Turtelhaze chuckled. He was dressed casually—jeans, sneakers, and a sky-blue jumper—and seemed cheerful. He knocked his knuckles against the table, glancing down at my schoolwork.

"Hard at work, I see," he said. "I think you've made an error on question four there, but otherwise, it's looking good. I won't take up your time. Just here to collect the gold coins you owe."

"Good morning, Mr. Turtelhaze," I said politely, lifting my chair up from the floor. "You startled me! I do owe you gold coins, however, I am prohibited from letting people into the house, so I am going to have to ask you to leave."

Again, Mr. Turtelhaze chuckled. He reached across the table for my jar of coins. "I let myself in, remember?" he told me, unscrewing the lid. "No rules broken." He began to tip coins into his palm, counting rapidly as he did.

"I think that might be . . ." I tried to remember Grandmother's exact words. ". . . I think that might be *evading house rules*. Please, Mr. Turtelhaze. I'm very sorry. I'm not allowed visitors. Although, of course . . . I do owe you coins . . . and I've had such marvelous, brief adventures! And it *was* Grandmother who gave me the jar of coins for my birthday. I can scarcely believe it's only Wednesday—only six days since my birthday! So much has taken place since then! I feel like a different person! And I know that Grandmother knows you—Oh." I stopped. He was raising his eyebrows at me. I hadn't meant to admit I'd been spying through the window and seen him leaving the house. "Anyhow, perhaps Grandmother wouldn't mind awfully that you're here. Still, if you would be so kind as to leave the moment you have all your . . ." He was still counting quickly. "I do hope there are enough coins, Mr. Turtelhaze."

He looked up at me. "More than enough," he said, and he tipped a few coins back into the jar.

"Still ten coins left," he said, sounding surprised. "It's five coins per wish, *so*, tell me, the next *two* times you visit the Kingdoms and Empires, do you wish to stay?" He smiled in such a friendly way.

I smiled back automatically and then felt my smile grow larger. Two more visits to the Kingdoms and Empires!

How wonderful!

"Oh!" I began—only something made me stop. I felt my heart fluttering oddly. *Five coins per wish*, he had just said.

Five coins per wish.

Suddenly I remembered my conversation with Oscar, the boy at the coach station.

"Mr. Turtelhaze," I said shyly, "are you a Genie?"

He bowed. "Indeed, I am!"

"And does that mean . . ." I felt even shyer. I looked away from him to the jar with its few remaining coins. "And does that mean that I could wish for *anything*? Not just to be able to stay when I visit the Kingdoms and Empires?"

He sniffed. "There are some restrictions," he said. "No wishes about where and when you go to the Kingdoms and Empires—I mentioned that earlier. No vague wishes like wishing that 'all is well' or that 'somebody is okay.' How am I supposed to define those terms? Has to be precise. And, of course, no wishes for extra wishes."

"Of course," I agreed.

"Otherwise," he said. "Yes. You have two wishes remaining. Wish for anything you like." He gave me an encouraging smile.

"All right." I tugged at my sleeves as I considered, then stopped at once. Grandmother grows very cross when I stretch my sleeves. It is an unseemly habit.

"I wish . . ." I began.

I did want to return to the Kingdoms and Empires, of course—at least for one final visit. But perhaps there was something else—something more important—I should do with my final wish?

"The *next* time I go to the Kingdoms and Empires," I decided, "I wish to stay for a very short—"

I stopped myself. Why was I always wishing to stay for a very short time? Originally that had been because I didn't want to break Grandmother's rules, or upset her. Yet no time seemed to pass when I visited the Kingdoms and Empires! Grandmother never even knew that I was gone!

Why had I carried on wishing for it?

I was always worried that time *would* pass, I realized. That the system would suddenly change, and Grandmother arrive home from work to an empty house.

"Well?" Mr. Turtelhaze prompted.

If I'd been braver, I could have stayed long enough to save the little boy at the circus the first time I saw him.

"The next time I go to the Kingdoms and Empires," I repeated, "I wish to stay for . . . *two hours*."

I took a deep breath. I'd taken a real chance.

Still, if I left at morning teatime, I would be back well before Grandmother returned from work, even if the time did pass.

Mr. Turtelhaze shrugged. "All right," he agreed, and he picked up the jar again and tipped five coins into his hand.

"And your other wish?" he asked, jingling the last few coins. He glanced around the room. "I bet you wish this house were bigger," he suggested. "Wish for a mansion? Or how about a swimming pool in your garden? As a surprise for your Grandmother when she gets home?"

I giggled. It *would* be a surprise. She might not like it though.

Mr. Turtelhaze rocked back and forth on his feet, watching me.

I'd always wanted to go to a regular school. That was my greatest wish. I took a deep breath, ready to speak that wish aloud.

"I hear you have a chance to be interviewed for a television show," Mr. Turtelhaze said suddenly, "and your grandmother will not allow it?"

Gosh! How did he know that?

"I bet you wish you *could* do the interview," he continued, his hands in his pockets now, grinning at me. "I bet you wish your grandmother *would* give you permission!"

Oh!

Of course!

That should be my wish! I'd get to visit Helen and Shahlyla's house while the interview happened! After that, they might start inviting me over regularly for afternoon tea! And children all over Australia might watch the television interview! *Those* children might become my new friends! Perhaps Fiona and her husband, Carl, might see me on the program in their new home up in Sydney? They might say, "Oh, there's Lillian from next door! Look how grown-up she has become! We ought to go and visit her!"

Then they would come and visit me!

Yes. That would be my wish.

I looked up at Mr. Turtelhaze. He raised a single eyebrow, still smiling.

"That the one?" he asked, reaching for the jar. "Television interview?"

I smiled. "I wish—" I began.

And stopped again.

I looked across at the jar. It seemed sorrowful now, only those few coins remaining at the very bottom.

A jarful of wishes was one thing. A single wish was another.

You should take that sort of thing very seriously. You could do something vital with a single wish.

I looked up at Mr. Turtelhaze. "May I have a little time to think about it?" I asked.

He studied me. "All right," he replied, speaking softly. "You can have until tomorrow morning." He looked pointedly at the clock on the wall. "What time do you and your grandmother ordinarily have breakfast?"

"Eight o'clock," I replied.

"Always eight o'clock? Each morning? Including your birthday last week? So your grandmother gave you the jar of gold coins at eight? At eight, precisely?"

"Yes."

He frowned. "Tell you what, I'll be here at seven tomorrow morning for an early breakfast with you and your grandmother. I'll arrange that with her. I'll even bring some friends along! It was your birthday last Thursday, wasn't it?"

I nodded.

"I'll bring a birthday cake," he said. "We can make it a birthday breakfast. Exactly one week late. And you can make your wish. Do we have a deal?"

I smiled. "How lovely," I said. "It's a deal."

CHAPTER 73

"WHAT A *PERFECT* day," I said to myself.

Mr. Turtelhaze had granted me one more visit to the Kingdoms and Empires, and I was going to have a birthday breakfast and a final wish in the morning! What could be better!

After he left I completed my schoolwork, took my meal breaks, practiced piano, and began dinner preparations. All day, I felt agitated. A part of me wanted to take my visit *immediately,* before I found myself shoved to a random destination, such as a sewage treatment plant. Another part of me was saying: "Slow down, Lillian, use this visit wisely."

It was almost time for Grandmother to be home when I finally decided where to visit.

The circus, of course. That way I'd be able to see all my friends in the Mettlestone family, and also make certain the little boy was all right.

In my room, I reached for the bottle and was about to take the stopper out but hesitated. Whenever I'd tried to reach the circus before, I'd gotten it wrong. What if I tried things a little differently?

First, what time had it been when I'd seen the little boy asleep in the enclosure?

The grass had been frosty and the stars high in the sky. Music had played from the circus tent while crowds of people wandered about, buying food from the stalls.

And then I'd heard bells jangling and people had begun streaming back into the tent.

That was it then.

Intermission.

Close to the *end* of intermission actually.

All right. That was the time.

I knew the date—just last Friday, the day after my birthday.

The place?

Gainsleigh Showground.

Bronte had suggested I write my destination on my hand. This made me giggle. You didn't usually get places by writing on your hand.

So how did you get there?

Suddenly I remembered Oscar in the waiting room of the coach station, the ticket seller behind the glass.

You bought a ticket.

You told the ticket seller—or the driver, or the conductor—exactly where you wanted to go.

I felt myself blushing. I had an idea, only I was embarrassed to try. It couldn't hurt though, could it?

I looked directly at the Genie bottle standing on my bedroom carpet, placed my palm against it, and said in my clearest, most polite voice: "Good morning. I would like to go to the Gainsleigh Showground, in Gainsleigh, Kingdoms and Empires, as the circus intermission is just ending, on the Friday of last week—that is to say, Friday, the twenty-fifth of May, please."

Shove.

REPORT 12

GAINSLEIGH SHOWGROUND, KINGDOMS AND EMPIRES
—Friday, May 25

* * *

It was intermission at the circus.

Crowds poured out of the tent, the Mettlestone family amongst them.

The color and swirl, the dazzle and gasp of the performances—acrobats, trapeze artists, clowns—gleamed in every eye. Fingers were clicked and shoulders jiggled in time to the music that still played.

Parents handed out coins to children, who flew toward the stalls, promising to bring back hot dogs and doughnuts, popcorn and fried potatoes, for everyone.

Little Benjamin sat up on his uncle Patrick's shoulders, perfectly safe. Isabelle, Franny, and Carrie, the three eldest Mettlestone sisters, had visited the circus grounds earlier that afternoon. They had informed the manager that a child would be in danger that very night. Isabelle was probably the most respected resident of Gainsleigh, and Franny the most intimidating former resident. (Something about the way she looked you hard in the eye while she bit off the top of a carrot.) Carrie, meanwhile, was so warmly friendly, you wanted to please her. Together, the three women were a powerful force. The manager had nodded vigorously. He swore to be vigilant. He would employ additional security guards. He would issue strict instructions. No load of gravel would be delivered, no storage container filled, without a thorough check for sleeping children. Satisfied, the sisters left the manager's office. Quickly and quietly, Carrie had also cast a Spellbinding ring right around the circus grounds, to prevent the intrusion of Shadow Mages. Then they'd all returned to Isabelle's apartment.

Nobody was worried. Nothing would happen to Benjamin—or to any other small child—at the circus that night.

Now the long-lost Mettlestone grandparents stood side by side, smiling over their grown-up children and their newfound grandchildren. The moon was high in a sky scattered with stars. The grass glittered with frost. There was still the second half of the circus remaining, and then several days of holiday with their family.

"What a *perfect* day," Jacob Mettlestone murmured.

"Careful," said Ildi, teasing him. "Always a dangerous thing to say." Still. It did seem pretty perfect.

REPORT 13

GAINSLEIGH SHOWGROUND, KINGDOMS AND EMPIRES
—Friday, May 25

* * *

"*And* it's our anniversary today," Jacob added, drawing Ildi closer to him. "Did you choose the circus for that reason, Isabelle? It's very thoughtful of you."

Isabelle was licking neat little swirls into her ice cream. She squinted at her father. "Your anniversary is in October," she said.

"And why would she have chosen the *circus* for that reason?" Franny asked. "You got married in the Gainsleigh Botanical Gardens."

"He means the anniversary of the day we first met," Ildi clarified. "We actually met at a circus when we were children. Have we never told you about that?"

A few of the others moved closer, curious to hear.

"As you might remember, I grew up on a farm just near here," Jacob began. He glanced around at his new grandchildren, reminding himself quickly which was which—Bronte in her yellow dress belonged to Patrick and Lida, Nancy's three girls with their braids (Imogen, Esther, Astrid), Sue's four boys from the countryside, who never seemed to stay still—although little Benjamin, the youngest, was still astride Patrick's shoulders, getting sticky toffee in his uncle's hair—Oscar from another world, the cheeky lad with bright eyes, and pale young Billy—still holding Alys's hand.

He addressed these children now. "My parents were farmers who adopted me when they discovered me, a little baby, in their wheat field one morning," he told them. "It was a bumper wheat crop, apparently, and nature celebrated by creating me."

The children gazed at him in wonder: they were still very impressed by his Wheat-Spriteliness.

"That's even though they already had three older boys," Jacob added. "Anyway, the circus came to town on a Friday in May, as it did every year—and still does, looks like—and I skipped school and hung around all day. I was only a little fellow at the time."

"Meanwhile, *I* had run away from home and joined the circus," Ildi contributed. "I lived up north with my father, who ran a pet shop. He'd asked me to deliver a cage full of rabbits, and I'd lost them. I was only six myself, and very frightened of getting in trouble. Spellbound a few Witches, and then took off." She chuckled. (Astrid, who can read moods, thought: *She doesn't really find that funny. She was truly terrified of her father, poor little girl.*)

"I spotted one of our neighbors walking through the circus grounds with her goat," Jacob said, resuming the story. "I hid, of course, so she wouldn't see me—but next thing a little skulk of Sterling Silver Foxes were threatening her! I went rushing up, thinking I could somehow protect her by shouting at them. They took off, and the neighbor and I thought I'd scared them away! She said I was so brave that she wouldn't tell my parents I was skipping school. What we didn't know, though, was that those Foxes had put a deep sleep spell on me. I wandered off again, and ended up curling up in some kind of . . . I don't know . . . storage container. Came mighty close to being crushed by a huge load of gravel, only someone dove in and dragged me out of there just in time."

The faces around him, he noticed, had stopped smiling. Instead, they were frowning, perplexed. Perhaps they didn't know what "gravel" was.

"Like rough-edged stones," he tried instead. "Very heavy."

Ildi, also puzzled by the youngsters' expressions, took over the story. "Jacob had no idea his life had just been saved—he was still under the sleep spell. The girl who'd rescued him had vanished, and the circus folk dumped him into a wheelbarrow and asked me to wheel him around and look for his family. I was the circus odd job girl, you see. So I wheeled him around until someone told me where he lived. When I reached his place, his family invited me to stay for dinner. Well, by the time we'd finished eating, the spell had worn away and Jacob was awake. He and I made friends instantly, and spent the next few days playing every chance we could. We became best friends!" She gave her husband a kiss on the cheek.

"We did," Jacob agreed, "and then—" He stopped. Wasn't this a sweet little story? Why did his family seem visibly distressed?

The music had increased its volume and changed its pace, signaling the end of intermission. All around, people were tossing their wrappings in the bins, wiping their hands, and heading back into the tent.

The Mettlestone family, though, remained frozen, staring.

"What's wrong with everyone?" Ildi demanded. "Is it because you want us to stop talking and get back to our seats? Just ask!"

Carrie's voice was hoarse. "Father was a small child sleeping in a storage container as a little boy?" she asked. "And he was almost buried by a load of gravel?"

"Yes," both her parents replied, bewildered by her tone.

"But that's the danger that Lillian warned us would happen *tonight*." Carrie's voice had grown stronger. "Right, Bronte?"

Bronte nodded, wide-eyed.

"So is it a coincidence?" Isabelle asked. "Or does Lillian Velvet have the wrong night?"

"And if she *does* have the wrong night," Carrie said slowly, "what exactly does that mean? That she's the person who was supposed to save Father, and she hasn't?"

"But Father *was* saved," Nancy argued. "He just told us! And he grew up, married Mother, and had twelve children! It's a coincidence! Everybody, just relax."

Still, a strangeness swept across the family then, like a wind that blows in from the ocean and turns the air to ashen gray.

CHAPTER 74

AND THERE I was!

A flash of pure joy struck me. I'd done it! Directly before me was a giant circus tent. Around me were swarms of people, along with the scent of damp grass and of sugary drinks—and tomato ketchup and corn on the cob—the sounds of tambourines and trumpets. Above me, a starry sky; beneath my feet, frosty grass—and most important of all? Gathered together just a short distance away?

The Mettlestone family.

Some I recognized from when they'd rushed down the staircase to stop me at Aunt Isabelle's place. Others, I knew well. There was Bronte and her cousins, the Staranise sisters; Billy and his beautiful mother, Queen Alys; Lida too, with her waterfall of hair; Sophy, the dragon vet. An aunt was crouching to study Astrid's finger: she was holding it as if she had just hurt it. The aunt kissed the finger, straightened again, and ruffled her hair. Astrid smiled. Oscar had just taken a bite of a sausage and then, eyes opening in amused panic, fanned his mouth, as if the heat of the sausage had startled him. A tiny boy sat up on a man's shoulders—could that be the little boy Bronte had mentioned?—Benjamin Mettlestone? Safe from being crushed by a load of gravel? He looked the right size!

An elderly couple at the center of the group appeared to have everyone's attention.

"Hello!" I called, taking a step in their direction.

The entire group turned to me. Some did this quickly, some slowly, some with a smooth motion, some more jerkily—but the moment they caught my eye, every single face wore the same strange and frightened expression.

And then they were gone.

There was no *shove*. I did not move. It was only that everyone else, and everything else, simply vanished.

As if someone had torn along a perforated line around my body—*rip!*

Or no, it was like that game Etch A Sketch that Fiona-next-door used to play with me when I was small. You slid a knob along the bottom of the screen and erased every mark on the screen.

It was still night, and I was still on the field, only there was no circus tent, no stalls, no crowds of happy people.

The field itself was more a swamp. I was ankle-deep in muddy water. A wind was blowing in that noisy, angry way that wind will sometimes blow. A piece of cardboard slammed against my face, and then the wind, apparently furious with me for having tried to steal its cardboard, tore the piece away and tossed it onward.

Quite close, I could hear dogs howling. High-pitched bells jangled. Enraged voices shouted.

I turned around slowly.

Across the field to my right stood a row of four or five rickety wooden houses. Each was raised on stilts. A lamp swung from a nail at the front of one of these houses, and the dim light revealed flaking paint and boarded windows. The angry shouts seemed to be coming from the first of the houses.

Across the field to my left, the silhouettes of a small group of adults paddled slowly through the water. Each held a broomstick aloft. As I watched they began to lift and twirl the brooms in unison. *Witches?* I thought, alarmed, and spun around again.

Behind me, there should have been a road. Instead, there was a river. Two boats raced along in the water. The figure of a child emerged from the hold in one of these boats. Instantly, a man's voice shouted, "GET DOWN!" and the child slipped under again.

Another turn and all I could see was darkness. I squinted.

Silver blades were spinning through the air directly at me.

CHAPTER 75

I FLUNG MYSELF to the ground.

Facefirst in mud and ice-cold water. Flattened myself. Held my breath. *Zzzip, zzzip, zzzip* sounded directly over my head. The breeze of the blades stirred my hair.

Zzzip, zzzip, zzzip.

I had to breathe! I had to get up—I had to—*zzzip, zzip!* I buried myself even further, nose pressed deep in the mud. Chest burning, lungs aching.

It stopped.

I wrenched myself up, gasping for air. Automatically, I wrapped my hands around my head and ducked. My whole body juddered.

Nothing.

Slowly I let my hands drop and looked around.

In the darkness, I could just make out the shapes of short, solid people, stomping along across the field. Every few steps, they sent blades spinning through the air. Steadily, they moved away from me.

I stood up cautiously. Muddy water poured from my clothes. I shivered and shuddered.

What had happened? Had I somehow been transported to a terrible future?

I had to spend two hours here.

I sighed a deep, trembling sigh and peered around. Should I try to run to the rickety houses and seek shelter? As I squinted in that direction, though, the angry shouting started up again. Thumping sounds too, and sudden crashes.

Should I simply crouch here in the muddy water for the next two hours, hoping nobody would notice me?

Or make my way to the river, and call for a passing boat to take me in?

Again, I squinted around. The darkness was taking shape as my eyes adjusted. Was that a hill rising up in the distance behind the rickety houses? Yes, I remembered there'd been a little hill beyond this field. Its peak was now covered with some kind of rock formations, like wafers stuck all over the top of a cake. One spindly tree stood in the center of these.

I would make my way up the hill.

From there, I'd be able to watch out for danger. Hide in amongst the rocks, or perhaps climb the tree.

It was an endless journey. The darkest nightmare. I splashed through the water at an awkward run. I hunched over and waded. When I reached the houses, I fell to my hands and knees and scuttled between them, the cold, muddy water slapping against my face, even into my mouth.

All around me the high-pitched bells jangled, the heated voices shouted. A child shrieked and then was abruptly silent.

"Her fever is too high!" a woman's voice cried.

BOOM! A distant explosion. I froze, and felt it vibrate through my body. *BOOM! BOOM!*

Flashes of light out of the corner of my eye. A howl of laughter; another of pain.

I heard a low, quick voice and realized it was my own—I was muttering to myself. "*Hurry, Lillian. Hurry, Lillian. Hurry, Lillian.*" My teeth chattered violently.

I reached the base of the hill and began to climb. It was quieter here, which only made the darkness more ominous. A figure emerged from the shadows, hurrying directly toward me, and I screamed.

The figure stopped. I squinted and made out the dirty face of an elderly man, dressed in torn and ragged clothes.

"Go home, child," he told me.

"Where am I?"

"Just outside Gainsleigh," he replied. "The old Gainsleigh Showground is behind you."

The old Gainsleigh Showground? So I *was* in the future?

"Please, what date is it?"

The old man winced. "Has the fever got you, child? Go home." And he carried on, calling over his shoulder, "It's the twenty-fifth of May."

"What year?" I pleaded.

I only just heard his reply.

It was this year. I hadn't traveled to the future. I was still here. It was still the day after my birthday—only everything had changed.

As I climbed higher, the water level fell. Now I was only splashing through puddles. Shadows loomed at me from every direction.

When I'd almost reached the rock formations, I realized what they were—gravestones.

It was a cemetery.

The moon emerged from behind the clouds, and now I could see across the landscape around the hill. It was a network of rivers, lakes, and ponds, estuaries snaking between them. Tiny patches of land held little gatherings of houses on stilts. Otherwise, the rivers ran all as one toward a vast ocean.

Silhouettes of ships and boats were dotted all over this ocean.

BOOM! BOOM! Flashes of light and sound from one of the ships. Nearby, another ship lit up with a burst of orange, tilted sideways, and began to sink. Shot by cannon fire.

Near the horizon I could make out the shapes of dragons in the sky. Bursts of golden light as they breathed their fire.

BOOM!

A dragon spun in zigzags in the air and plummeted toward the ocean. It disappeared. Shot from the air.

I hurried on into the cemetery.

It covered the peak of the hill and ran down its other side. Thousands of gravestones, crowded together, higgledy-piggledy. Here and there were larger sculptures—monuments, I realized.

In memory of Gainsleigh souls taken in the Whispering Wars, said one, followed by rows and rows of names in tiny print.

Remembering those Gainsleighians Drowned, said another, this one made of rough-hewn wood and scrawled upon.

I moved amidst the gravestones, catching sight of inscriptions as the moonlight touched them. Many were crumbling and overgrown with weeds.

Soraya Karim, taken by Whisperers, aged six—lost but never forgotten.

Idris Ravenswood, killed by Pirates, much-loved father to Jack and Matilda—gone to join his beloved, Stella (killed by dragons).

Another three makeshift monuments—some only inscribed with a leaky marker—each *Remembering those Gainsleighians Drown'd.*

So many drowned! So many people of Gainsleigh lost to the Whispering Wars, to pirates, to dragons! And here were the graves of people of all ages lost to fever, and lost to starvation.

I realized I was not breathing. I was numb with confusion! I was in Gainsleigh but it was so different!

On and on I stumbled between the gravestones. I reached an older section—much more weed-covered and faded. The inscriptions here suggested that these people had lived longer lives, and died of more regular causes—sickness or accident. Here was the grave of an old man who had succumbed to consumption in his ninety-sixth year. A woman of sixty had died in a cart accident. Still very sad, but less shocking. There was a cluster of graves all marked "Spellbinder—lost in the great Gainsleigh Sterling Silver Fox battle."

Most of these Spellbinders were grown-ups, but one was a girl named Ildi, aged six.

More elderly people who'd died of illness.

And then I stopped.

Mettle, said a gravestone.

I crouched and cleared away the dirt and weeds. My heart pattered peculiarly.

Another brush of moonlight, and I could just make out the words.

> *Jacob Mettle, aged six, killed by a load of gravel after bravely defending his neighbor from Sterling Silver Foxes; desperately missed by his parents, his older brothers, and his beloved dog, Angie. Our little hero.*

The date was Friday, May 25.

Sixty-five years ago.

REPORT 14

GAINSLEIGH SHOWGROUND, KINGDOMS AND EMPIRES
—Friday, May 25

* * *

Sixty-five years earlier, Jacob Mettle, the local Wheat Sprite boy, went missing. Eventually, he was discovered crushed beneath a load of gravel.

At first it was assumed that he'd simply curled up to sleep in the storage container and a dreadful accident had occurred. Quickly, though, it was discovered that the boy had been placed under a sleep spell by Sterling Silver Foxes when he'd attempted to save a neighbor from their taunting.

Local Spellbinders, along with Jacob's parents and three older brothers, hunted down the Sterling Silver Foxes, seeking revenge. A battle ensued. The Sterling Silver Fox skulk turned out to be much larger and more powerful than had been assumed. It was joined by other Shadow Mages. The local Spellbinders and Jacob's family were killed—as was a little girl, Ildi, who was trying to help, using her own Spellbinding powers.

Shadow Mages took control of Gainsleigh.

The annual May circus was canceled.

Years passed.

The Whispering Wars began. A few Spindrift children tried to infiltrate the Whispering Kingdom and failed. A Spellbinding was cast around the kingdom. However, the binding was frayed and uneven. Whisperers continued to escape, roaming the Kingdoms and Empires, stealing children. Eventually, the Whispering king defeated the Spellbinding altogether. The Whispering Wars resumed.

Years passed.

Dragon babies were hunted for their jewels. In revenge, the dragons burned acres of crops. Dragons were routinely shot from the air.

Years passed.

Pirates ruled the oceans, and criminal gangs the land.

A fever swept across the Kingdoms and Empires, killing countless children.

Years passed.

Disease infected fruit orchards throughout the Kingdoms and Empires, causing food shortages and vitamin deficiencies.

Shadow Mages roamed the land.

Years passed.

A mighty Ocean Fiend emerged, having hidden away for the last thousand years. It woke several other Water Fiends across the Kingdoms and Empires.

The Fiends sent a great flood across the Kingdoms and Empires. Thousands drowned. Those people who survived built rickety houses on stilts, or fought each other for the few remaining boats.

Gainsleigh, like much of the Kingdoms and Empires, was a wasteland of flooded waterways. Its people spent their days fleeing the vicious Fiends, the Shadow Mages, the fever, pirates, angry dragons, and starvation.

Gainsleigh Showground was just a swamp now. Its signposts and gateposts long gone—either washed away by floodwaters or taken down for firewood or building material.

In the graveyard above that swamp, Lillian Velvet stood at the grave of little Jacob. She looked out across the town, the harbor, and the ocean.

She understood.

She had failed to rescue the boy at the circus.

Somehow, this was the result.

CHAPTER 76

I FELT FURIOUS.

That surprised me. You'd think I'd have felt disappointed or distressed or devastated—any number of d-words. Instead I was overcome with anger. My shivering with cold transitioned to trembling with rage.

I bellowed at myself: "Over and over you have tried and STILL you have failed? Child, what a fool you are!"

How had I failed to realize that circuses can take place in different *years*, even if the date and month are the same!

Right, how are you going to fix this? I demanded of myself, fuming.

Fix this? I replied, rubbing my eyes. *I don't see how . . .*

Now! Fix it now!

I shook slightly, frightened by how searing my anger was. I could almost feel it singeing the edges of my heart.

Well, I thought uncertainly. *Soon two hours will be up and I'll be shoved home. I'll wait until I see Mr. Turtelhaze at breakfast tomorrow, and ask him to allow me one final visit to the Kingdoms and Empires for my final wish?*

I stamped my foot. *Foolish child! Fix it now! This suffering cannot continue another moment! Fix it now!*

I blinked.

Fix it now? It's true that I was *in* the Kingdoms and Empires at this moment. If I could somehow move to another time *within* this world, and within my two-hour limit, perhaps I would not have to wait until tomorrow?

How long had I been here already? Lying flat when those knives were flung over me. Making my way slowly across the swamp. Climbing this hill, reading memorials and gravestones.

So long! I thought in dismay. *It must be two hours already! Or very close to two hours!*

In that case, move fast! How are you going to get back to the correct time, the correct circus? To save that boy?

How?

Think faster!

I hadn't even started thinking.

All right. I folded my arms tight, hoping that would help with thinking. It only seemed to make me colder—if I could just change into dry clothes, I thought, I might be able to solve this problem.

I needed my Genie bottle. It contained all my memories. When I had the Genie bottle, I only had to open the stopper and watch the memories fly out.

My Genie bottle was in my bedroom.

What if . . .

What if I imagined my Genie bottle? Imagined holding it up and imagined the memories pouring out of it?

It didn't seem enough. It seemed unlikely.

Think faster, child! What is it about the Genie bottle? Why does it allow you to travel in time and space?

I felt my brow crinkle—and then clear.

"It's because it's empty!" I said aloud. Again, I was astonished, but I knew my words to be true.

The Genie bottle was special because it was empty. It allowed me to pour all my memories and thoughts inside it, and then it contained them with its stopper.

Very well. Find something else that is empty.

I looked around. I was trying to be calm, but my heart knew better. It was pounding frantically, like a toddler set loose on a drum kit.

There was nothing here that was hollow.

"Look *harder*!" I roared. "There *must* be!"

My eyes roamed the gravestones and memorials and snagged at that spindly tree. It was scarcely a tree at all, I realized. It had been burned badly and was blackened, its trunk hollowed out by—

Hollowed?

I ran splashing through puddles and skirting around graves until I'd reached the tree.

Oh, poor tree, look at you. Your thin, charred branches; your hollow trunk. I placed both palms on the rough bark.

"Please," I said to it. "May I fill your hollow trunk with my memories?" Even as I asked the question, I felt myself lighten, as if I was a teapot being tipped sideways. I even slanted my body, in the manner of the game that Fiona-next-door used to play with me. *Tip me over, and pour me out!*

Then, my palms still on the tree trunk, I said, "Please, may I visit the Gainsleigh Showground on twenty-fifth of May, sixty-five years ago, as intermission at the circus nears its end?"

CHAPTER 77

AND THERE I was.

A silver moon shone in a big sky that was scattered with stars and wisps of pale cloud.

Lively music played, tambourines clashing: a rapid tempo, lots of brass instruments and pounding drums.

Across the field, an immense tent stood, striped in blue and gold, its roof strung with fairy lights. Around the tent were splashes of golden light from little stalls. A bell was ringing. People were streaming toward the circus tent.

Closer to me, in the darkness, were the faint sounds of horses nickering and the deep shadows of caravans and other small structures. It was very cold. My clothes and shoes were still sopping wet and muddy. I shivered.

And then I saw the storage container.

"Back up!" called a voice.

There were the horse and cart, slowly rolling backward. There was the man with the lantern.

"Wait!" I shouted, and I took off at a sprint. The grass crunched beneath my feet. Lights grew stronger, sounds louder, tents larger.

"Halt!"

"Halt!"

The lever was being pulled. The cart was tilting up and up.

"STOP!" I screamed.

My legs were flying, my arms were pumping.

Any moment the gravel would crash down. *Creeeaak*—the cart was almost vertical. The gravel was on the very *verge*, the very *precipice* of falling.

The gravel began to topple.

I was almost there.

"STOP!" I shrieked.

They took no notice. I flung myself forward into the darkness, grabbed the arms of the little boy, *dragged* him out onto the grass.

BOOM!!!

The gravel landed with a sound like a thunderclap.

"What the . . ." said a voice.

The two men were on either side of me, staring down in wonder at the sleeping face of the boy.

"He was *in* there?" one breathed.

And: *shove.*

I was back in my room.

REPORT 15

GAINSLEIGH SHOWGROUND, KINGDOMS AND EMPIRES
—Friday, May 25

* * *

Sixty-five years ago, little Jacob Mettle, the Wheat Sprite boy, was dragged out of a storage unit a split second before being crushed by a load of gravel.

The girl who pulled him out then vanished.

The circus manager asked the new odd job girl, Ildi Stone, to take the sleeping boy to his family. She did so, wheeling him to his farm in a barrow. Ildi and Jacob became friends. (Privately, Ildi also tracked down each member of the Sterling Silver Fox skulk responsible for placing Jacob under a sleep spell. One by one, she dealt with them—they all left town. Unusually for one so young, Ildi was already a Spellbinder and had dealt with Witches in her own hometown. She was destined to have children and grandchildren who inherited her skill.)

The circus moved on. Little Ildi Stone and Jacob Mettle parted tearfully.

Several years later, the pair met again, by chance, at a grocery store in a seaside village where both were vacationing. They fell in love, married, and became the Mettlestones.

Working together, Jacob and Ildi captured some of the most dangerous Shadow Mages in the Kingdoms and

Empires. They were especially busy in the time of the Whispering Wars, when Shadow Mages joined forces with the evil Whispering king. They were pivotal in the negotiations that led to the K&E Shadow Mage Treaty, under which most Shadow Mages agreed to reside in specially delineated Shadow Realms.

Jacob and Ildi had twelve children: eleven daughters and one son.

Isabelle, the eldest, became a spy. Along with her butler, and from their elegant base in Gainsleigh, she has apprehended and captured some of the most sinister criminal overlords of the Kingdoms and Empires.

Carrie, having trained with her mother from a very young age, grew up to become Carabella-the-Great, the most powerful Spellbinder in the Kingdoms and Empires. It was Carrie who constructed the Majestic Spellbinding, which replaced the flimsy Spellbinding around the Whispering Kingdom, effectively ending the escape of Whisperers and the kidnapping of children.

Franny traveled across the Kingdoms and Empires, becoming mayor of the town of Spindrift, where she played a significant role in bringing the Spindrift children together. This helped to end the Whispering Wars.

Maya and Lisbeth became captains of the *Riddle and Popcorn* cruise ship. They spent years doing vital work assisting the Anti-Pirate League to pinpoint the location of the worst pirates.

Nancy grew up to chair several committees that enforce the K&E Shadow Mage Treaty, and that advocate for a safe and healthy balance between the rights of humans, nonhumans, Shadow Mages, Spellbinders, True Mages, and sundry others.

Sue became a farmer. While working in her orange

orchard, she noted early signs of a disease with the potential to infect fruit throughout the Kingdoms and Empires. Inventing a simple method for eliminating this disease, she quickly brought it under control.

Alys became a rock star who later applied for, and secured, the position of Queen of the Mellifluous Kingdom. There, she ruled with sense and compassion. The Mellifluous instruments played more beautifully than ever, sending ripples of harmony and love throughout the Kingdoms and Empires.

Claire became an event manager, organizing numerous conferences, including a medical convention at which doctors developed a cure for the mysterious fever that had begun infecting children.

Emma became an artist whose work inspired profound and magical thinking.

Sophy became a veterinarian specializing in dragon care. She was instrumental in promoting understanding between humans and dragons, and in preventing all harvesting of baby dragons for their gemstones.

And Patrick was such an optimist that he, like the Mellifluous instruments, sent ripples of cheer and laughter throughout the Kingdoms and Empires.

In addition to these accomplishments, some of the Mettlestone children also had children of their own.

Bronte Mettlestone, amongst countless achievements, defeated the evil Whispering king, allowing the Whisperers to return to their former excellent selves.

Her cousin Esther Mettlestone-Staranise became a Rain Weaver and conquered an Ocean Fiend *just* before he implemented his plan to flood the entire Kingdoms and Empires.

Esther's younger sister, Astrid, although still very young, knows whenever somebody is lying, and exactly how people are feeling. She has already worked with her local mayor to uncover lies and deception at every level of power.

Esther's older sister, Imogen, formed a connection with Oscar Banetti, a boy from another world. A short time ago, this connection led to the release of an Elven city from a shadow spell that would have destroyed all the Elves. These Elves have already quietly unpicked several shadow spells that might otherwise have spread new waves of hunger and disease.

Time, meanwhile, has remarkable achievements in store for the other grandchildren: Prince Billy and his farming cousins.

* * *

Today, in accordance with the Gainsleigh tradition for the month of May, a circus performed at the Gainsleigh Showground.

Intermission was over.

Jacob and Ildi Mettlestone had just told their family the story of how Jacob was rescued from the storage container when he was a young boy.

A strangeness had swept across the family, like a wind that blows in from the ocean and turns the air to ashen gray.

Then, for a breath of a moment, every member of the family was plunged into a savage darkness, a darkness crammed with images of floods, fires, and furious dragons; sounds of cannons booming, sirens blaring, children sobbing, adults screaming; smells of fetid mud and decaying garbage; sensations of fierce hunger, freezing cold, fever, and terror—a darkness that spiraled them through locked, unlit basements; starless, cloudless nights; deep black chasms in which their bodies splintered, their minds dissolved—*they ceased to exist.*

And then, impossibly, each saw the distant figure of Lillian Velvet standing on a hillside by a gnarled, broken tree; Lillian sprinting across frosted grass; Lillian swooping—

And the darkness dissolved.

Most of them stumbled in place. Their faces were gray and slack with shock.

"What just happened?" whispered Bronte.

"I *think,*" her grandfather replied, "that Lillian Velvet just saved our world."

"Not just our world," Carrie remarked heavily. "Our lives. Our very *existence.*"

At this, a lightness, almost a giddiness, washed over the family. They smiled around at each other. More than ever before, they were suffused with joy—how good it was to be out and about this evening!

"Anyway," Ildi said, resuming her story shakily. "I was so sad when the circus moved on and I had to say goodbye to Jacob and his family."

"Same," Jacob declared. He lowered his voice. "That's when I used my Wheat Sprite wish actually—to wish that Ildi and I would meet again one day."

"Ridiculous." Ildi sighed. "We could have just arranged a meeting place."

"So we did meet, some years later, at a grocery store, and the rest, as they say, is—"

"Yes, yes, history," Ildi agreed.

It was time to return to the tent for the second half of the circus. Yet the family stood a moment longer, taking each other in. They felt powerfully grateful to be part of a family, this family, to love and be loved—to exist.

"Righto," said Franny, twirling a carrot between her fingers. "Let's head in."

And they all filed back to their seats.

CHAPTER 78

I SAT ON my bedroom floor in the late afternoon light.

The silver moon seemed still to shine, the lively music still to play, the frosty grass still to glint—and all of it was inside my heart.

I was elated.

I'd done it. This time, I'd *truly* done it, and the little boy was saved. That strange, dark time I'd seen, of flooding and violence and petrified children—somehow that time line had spooled out from the little boy's death. Now that he was all right, the time line would vanish. Perhaps it would be like the cord of Grandmother's vacuum cleaner? When you finish using it, you press a button and, with a mighty *phhhht!* the cord is sucked inside the machine.

I felt the way characters in my storybooks feel on the morning of their birthday or a picnic. Just like those characters, I clapped my hands gleefully, and leapt to my feet.

How to contain this excitement?

I would open my bedroom window. Like all the windows in our house, this is locked in position so you can only raise it slightly. Today, I decided, I would force it higher, letting the breeze flow through my room in celebration. I pressed my fingers under the frame and lifted.

Nothing happened.

I gathered my strength, set my feet firmly on the carpet, and *wrenched.* With a creak and a rattle, the window began to rise! Very slowly, but it was working! I rested a hand on the sill, getting my breath back, ready to try to force it further up, and—

WHOOSH!

The window crashed straight back down, landing on my hand.

My fingers were pinned in place.

For a moment, I stared in shock, not understanding what had happened. Then it struck me like a slap across the face: a terrible pain in my fingers. My body reacted in panic: my face burned, nausea struck my belly.

I tugged my hand but it was jammed in place.

"Help!" I cried out. "Help me!"

But who would hear me?

At that moment, a key sounded in the front door. Grandmother was home!

"Grandmother! Help!" I shouted. "My fingers are jammed! It hurts! It hurts!"

The jingle of Grandmother's keys, the swishing as she hung her coat on the rack, the soft thud of her setting down her bag.

Why was she taking so long? Could she not *hear* me?

"Grandmother! Help!" I shrieked, as loudly as I could. "Help! *My fingers are jammed in the window!*"

Her footsteps down the hall. At last!

The footsteps passed my door. Continued on to Grandmother's room. The sound of her door closing.

"Grandmother! Grandmother!"

Oh, my fingers burned! I did not know it was possible to hurt this much. I tugged my hand again, trying to release them.

No, that wouldn't work.

Calm down, Lillian. Figure this out.

I tucked my free hand under and tried to lift. Nothing.

"Help! Grandmother!"

Tried lifting again. Still nothing.

Come on, Lillian. You just have to get the angle right. I twisted slightly. Steadied my legs. Grasped with my free hand as tight as I could, and *wrenched*!

And *wrenched*!

Cre-a-ak.

The tiniest, slowest agony of movement and the window lifted *just* a fraction—and I slid out my hand.

BANG!

The window fell back into place, shuddering as it did.

I grasped my aching hand with the other and hunched over, rocking back and forth. The jammed fingers were a brilliant pink color.

Outside my bedroom, I heard Grandmother walking back down the hall to the kitchen.

I hobbled out to join her.

"Child," she said, turning from the sink.

"Didn't you hear me calling?" I asked. "My fingers were jammed under the window! Look how red they are! It was agony! It took *all* my strength to use the other hand to get it free."

"I certainly heard the dreadful racket you were making in there," Grandmother replied. "Never make that noise again. I was ashamed. If you jammed your fingers this was your own fault for tampering with the window. You know perfectly well not to do that. And look at yourself, child. You are filthy. Go and wash up immediately."

I looked down.

Of course. I'd forgotten that I'd crawled through mud in that terrible world.

"Sorry, Grandmother," I began, feeling guilty—and then I stopped.

Grandmother was scowling. My fingers were throbbing. Muddy water was dripping from my clothes to the floor.

And a curious thing happened: all the emotions inside me—my earlier elation, my shock at the falling window, my guilt about dripping mud—they all slipped away from me, like a wave sliding back from the shore.

I felt empty.

Empty all the way to the horizon.

Not empty like the Genie bottle, or the hollow tree—not full of possibility. This was a different, frightening empty.

"Stop it!" I told myself. "You saved the boy! And tomorrow you are having a birthday party! And there will be another wish! Yes, Grandmother is angry, but this is your own fault!"

A shiver ran through me. Memories flew unbid into my mind.

Queen Alys calling up to Billy: *You're tremendously brave and patient! I'm proud of you!* Bronte and her cousins hugging me. The old lady wanting to play with her grandchildren even though they'd blocked her front door with their boat. The aunt at the circus crouching to kiss Astrid's finger and rustle her hair.

"*Go and wash up,*" Grandmother repeated, staring at me.

Slowly, I turned and walked down the hall to my room. I closed my door.

Another memory: the Mettlestones shouting at me to *get away from that window*! when they thought I might be harming their family.

The Mettlestones storming the jewelry store to save Queen Alys.

This memory rolled over in my mind and blended with another: Grandmother storming in from outside when I'd washed her bedroom window to surprise her.

Would Grandmother shout at a stranger who meant to harm me? Would she storm into a jewelry shop to save me?

I found that I was crying.

"Stop crying," I instructed myself.

The crying only turned to sobbing. It was a violent sobbing, and shocked me. I hadn't known that crying could sound like this—a harsh, low tone that seemed to claw at my throat, as if the emptiness was trying to claw its way out.

"*Stop it, stop it,*" I gasped. "*Grandmother will be angry*!" But I only cried more violently.

"*Why are you crying*?" I demanded of myself, trying to smother my mouth, to make it stop.

Because Grandmother walked by my bedroom door while I cried out for her help. Because she did not say, "Oh, poor you!" and kiss my crushed fingers. Because Grandmother has never once hugged me. Because Grandmother did not say, "You managed to get the window back up by yourself? I'm proud of you!" Because Grandmother has never once played with me, or given me a treat.

Because the pickle jar of coins is the first gift that Grandmother ever gave me. I've never had a birthday cake or birthday wish before. Because I long for Fiona next door. Or the kindness of Helen and Shahlyla. Or the love of the Mettlestone family.

"Who speaks to you in this way?" Reuben the Genie had asked. *"And how does it make you feel?"*

"You are the most frightened person I've ever seen," Astrid had declared.

It was Grandmother who spoke to me like that. Very often, too.

How it made me feel was terrified.

Astrid had been right. Grandmother frightened me more deeply, more completely than any of the dangers I'd faced in my adventures.

Of course she would never storm a jewelry shop to save me! The idea almost made me laugh as I rocked back and forth, and howled.

CHAPTER 79

I GATHERED MYSELF together and changed into dry clothes. I put the wet, muddy clothes in a bucket in the laundry to soak, rinsed off my shoes as well as I could, and set these on the back porch to dry.

The sounds of machinery and hammers, talking and laughter still came from behind the fence. I hurried back inside and closed the door. I washed my face and brushed my hair.

Grandmother and I ate supper—she did not mention my crying in my room—and then I bathed and went to bed.

The next morning, Grandmother knocked on my door to wake me early.

When I came down the hall, I gasped. The table was set for eight people. There were paper napkins and colored party hats at each place. A cake sat high on a stand in the center of the table. I counted ten candles.

"*Grandmother,*" I breathed.

She was in the kitchen, wearing her apron over clothes I hadn't seen before: a crocheted pink cardigan and a knee-length skirt with tiny flowers printed all over it.

"Oh, *Grandmother,*" I said.

Grandmother took no notice. She was frowning at the frying pan, pushing slices of bacon around.

A loud knock sounded at the door, and I saw Grandmother give a little jump.

She set down the spatula, removed her apron, and hurried

to the door. Suddenly our living room was filled with hearty adult voices and movement.

I stared in wonder. A few of the adults were tall and thin, wearing smart dresses and suits, their wrists and throats glinting with jewelry. A few were more sturdily built, their clothes a little more worn, the colors more autumnal oranges and browns. These wore beads strung around their necks, and long socks with sandals.

"Ah, this must be the birthday girl!" one of the sturdier ones said, clasping her hands and gazing at me. "Happy birthday!"

"It's not . . ." I began. I cleared my throat. I felt I had to be honest. "Thank you, but it's not my birthday today. My birthday was exactly a week ago."

"Indeed it was," said a voice, and Mr. Turtelhaze strode into the room. At this, the others burst into laughter—which was unexpected.

"Come," Grandmother said. "Everyone take a seat and I will bring in the breakfast."

"And then Lillian will make her wish!" one of the strangers exclaimed, and the others said, "Oh yes, so she shall. So she shall!"

Good gracious, I thought, sitting up at the table.

It was both strange and exciting.

CHAPTER 80

DURING BREAKFAST, THE adults spoke about weather and politics. Now and then one of them would direct a question at me.

"And what do you think of a nor'easterly breeze?" they might ask.

"Oh," I'd say, my heartbeat quickening. How did one behave at a birthday breakfast when a stranger asked about a nor'east breeze? I had no experience of birthday breakfasts and, honestly, no real opinion about breezes from *any* direction.

"I suppose it would please me," I ventured, "if the day were warm and the breeze cooled me down."

The interlocutor nodded. "Indeed," she said, seeming pleased.

We ate bacon with fried eggs and drank glasses of apple juice.

"And who did you vote for, Lillian? In the most recent state election?" a thin, elegant man inquired. He had a diamond-studded wristwatch with a gold band, and his ears ended at very fine points.

"I'm not old enough to vote," I whispered.

The man laughed, and so did everyone else at the table.

"Speak clearly, child," Grandmother told me sternly. "Of course you're not old enough to vote! Our guest was making a joke."

"Oh!" I forced a little chuckle.

They all laughed again.

Although I had no experience of birthday breakfasts, I was

beginning to feel very uneasy. Surely there was something strange about this one?

"Time is getting on!" Mr. Turtelhaze said suddenly. Everyone looked at the clock. It was half past seven. I supposed Mr. Turtelhaze needed to get to work.

"Yes, it is time for the birthday cake," Grandmother agreed. She rose, went into the kitchen, and returned with a box of matches.

One of the guests reached out to gather the used plates, stacking these in a haphazard pile at the end of the table. Grandmother lit the candles.

My first ever birthday cake.

"Have you prepared your wish, Lillian?" a guest asked.

"You don't have long," Mr. Turtelhaze added, looking at the clock again. "So you'd better have!"

They all laughed again.

My wish. Of course. In the oddness of the birthday party, I'd forgotten. What should it be?

REPORT 16

THE LUMINOUS FOREST, OUTSKIRTS OF GAINSLEIGH, KINGDOMS AND EMPIRES
—Thursday, May 31

* * *

Isn't it strange how time seems to collapse in on itself?

One moment you're sharing a welcome breakfast, holiday stretched out before you—the next, you're saying farewell. Days that had fanned out like a deck of cards are snapped into one neat stack.

It was Thursday morning and many of the Mettlestones were departing on the 6:00 A.M. coach: Maya and Lisbeth to their freshly repaired cruise ship; Nancy and her girls (Imogen, Esther, and Astrid) to meet up with the girls' father before returning to school; Sue and her boys back to their farm; Claire to a conference; Patrick and Lida to the Whispering Kingdom, to deal with glitches in its ongoing political transition.

The remaining Mettlestones waved them off from the sidewalk. Then they put their hands in their coat pockets and sighed.

Who were the remaining Mettlestones? And why were they *not* on the 6:00 A.M. coach?

Well, Bronte and Oscar planned to leave at midday for their schools in the mountains; Alys and Billy would be collected by Mellifluous security that afternoon (security weren't taking any more chances with the queen); Carrie was staying an extra week to assist investigations into the Shadow Mage gang; Franny wanted more time with her long-lost parents (under the toughness, Franny is all heart); Emma was *still* (dramatic fling of the arms into the air) waiting for her island to be rebuilt; Jacob and Ildi hoped to visit their old friends ("Hold up, you're dead, aren't you?" the friends would exclaim)—and Isabelle and the Butler needed no excuse. They lived here.

This group of eleven now walked to the Luminous Forest for an early-morning breakfast picnic. (Oscar and Bronte didn't walk—they rode their skateboards. Billy jogged alongside them.) Picnic blankets were spread out and baskets of pastries and fruit distributed.

The family were more relaxed, and more sunburned, than they'd been a week ago. Also, Jacob and Ildi were now referred to as Granfy and Grandma (at their own request), and their voices wove seamlessly through the family chatter.

Mostly, the chatter consisted of recountings of the delights and mishaps of the week—the time Benjamin fell from the dock into the harbor and was scooped out by his uncle Patrick with a fishing net; the night they'd all crowded into a glowworm cave and the girls had sung a rude version of their school song; the day they went hiking and Theodore, Billy's dog, had rolled in cow manure.

Theodore, recognizing his name, stood abruptly. He'd been relaxing on the grass alongside Billy. Now he looked very noble, eyes bright and expectant.

"Ah, he reminds me of the dog I had when I was a boy," Granfy Jacob said, not for the first time that week. "Her name was—"

"Angie," several family members put in.

"Billy," their aunt Emma said at the same time.

"Nope, not Billy," Franny said gruffly. "There's Billy. He's your nephew, Emma. Not a dog."

"Indeed, I am," Billy agreed, brushing grass from Theodore's fur.

"Yes, yes." Aunt Emma's hands fluttered. "Only, listen, I've just remembered—Billy, aren't you . . ." She paused for dramatic effect, ". . . *allergic* to dogs? Your mother mentioned it in a letter to me! And yet here you are . . . *with a dog*!"

Alys had been gazing up at the canopy of leaves. "I remember, Emma," she said, turning back. "I wrote to you that Billy had decided he'd grown out of the allergy. Turns out, he was right." She herself stroked Theodore now, and he pressed his muzzle into her hand.

"It happens," a few people chorused. "It's perfectly possible to grow out of allergies."

"Or maybe Theodore's fur doesn't have the same allergens as other dogs," Carrie suggested mildly. "Relax, Emma."

Emma was irritated. "Nobody else thinks it odd that Billy grew out of his allergy *just* as the heroic Theodore turned up at his door?"

"Oh, as to that," Billy said, "that's thanks to Lillian Velvet."

A startled quiet fell over the group. Even the birds in the trees paused in song. Oscar stopped trying to hide the raspberry jam that he'd just spilled onto the picnic blanket.

Everyone turned to Billy.

"When Lillian appeared in my room, I showed her my painting of a dog," Billy explained. "I told her I was allergic to dogs and liked to pretend the painted dog was my own. She was awfully kind. She said, *Oh, I wish you weren't allergic and that this dog was your real dog!* I thought that rather sporting of her. I didn't know she was a Genie child, of course, so I didn't realize just *how* sporting! As time went by, though, I felt more and more strongly that her wish was coming true. It sort of tingled in me, do you see? And then? Right after Mother disappeared? Theodore appeared at my door! Looking *exactly* like the dog in my painting! And never once making me sneeze. Allergy"—he clicked his fingers—"gone."

"Ohhh," everyone said, very pleased by this story. "How lovely that Lillian Velvet used one of her wishes for you! Or perhaps that was *two* of her wishes?"

"And how *lucky* that she did!" they all chorused next—for Theodore had traced Alys across the Kingdoms and Empires, leading to her rescue.

"I wonder if Lillian Velvet has become a Genie yet?" Isabelle mused.

"She told us that her tenth birthday was Thursday, the twenty-fourth of May," Bronte remembered, "which is . . ."

"Exactly a week ago," the Butler confirmed.

"And she received her gold coins at breakfast time on her birthday," Bronte continued. "So she might be becoming a Genie at this exact moment!"

At this exact moment!

Again, everyone said, "Oooh!" delighted by the idea.

"I wonder if she used up many of her wishes," Billy mused.

Everyone agreed that Lillian would have taken *great* care not to use many wishes.

Then somebody mentioned that the blueberries were excellent, weren't they? And a mild discussion followed about whether blueberries were better when large and plump, or when tiny, sweet, and hard.

CHAPTER 81

THE ADULTS SANG "Happy Birthday" to me in rich, deep voices. I looked around in wonder, forgetting for a moment that I was supposed to be thinking of a wish.

"Now blow out the candles," Mr. Turtelhaze commanded, once the song was over, "and state your wish."

It took a few moments to blow out the candles, as I'd never done this before and wasn't sure how.

The final flame wavered and disappeared. Smoke formed a cloud above the cake.

A pause.

Did most people feel as edgy as this when they were having birthday parties? There was such tension in the room!

"Well?" Mr. Turtelhaze prompted.

They all hunched forward, smiling at me.

"It's only . . ." I began shyly. "It's only that I want to use my final wish properly."

"Child," Grandmother said sternly. "Our guests are waiting. Choose a wish, please."

Mr. Turtelhaze touched Grandmother's arm. "What do you mean by using your wish properly?" he asked me.

"There are probably people who need it more than me," I explained. "I've just had a lovely breakfast and I feel quite well, but there are people about who are very hungry, and perhaps . . ." An image of soldiers marching in the Whispering Kingdom jumped into my mind—thin wrists and bony necks, bandaged arms and wounded legs. ". . . and perhaps wounded," I added, falteringly.

Grandmother reeled back. "People who are hungry and *wounded*?" she repeated, her eyes flashing. "What nonsense! You know no such people!"

One of the broad-shouldered women fingered the beads around her neck. "As a matter of fact," she said slowly, "I have a husband at home who is *very* hungry and quite wounded. You could wish for a fruit basket and basic medical supplies, and I could take it to him. You'd be most welcome," she added graciously.

"Thank you!" I said. "All right, I . . ." Again, I stopped. I did not mean to be impolite but was *that* the best use of my final wish? It was difficult to concentrate with this panicky feeling in my stomach. Even though I was surrounded by smiling faces, I felt exactly the way I'd felt when I was eight and accidentally knocked Grandmother's tea over so that it stained the cloth—and heard her footsteps coming down the hall.

I forced myself to breathe deeply.

"Perhaps you could take some breakfast leftovers home for your husband," I suggested. "And have you considered taking him to the hospital for his . . . wound?"

The tall, thin man beside me clicked his fingernail against the prongs of his fork. "Tell you what," he said. "I have a dodgy knee from an old skiing accident. It aches every time I walk! Doctors can't do a thing about it. Use your wish to repair it, perhaps? *That's* not something that can be fixed with breakfast leftovers or a trip to the hospital!"

"Oh!" I said. "Thank you! That sounds *very* worthwhile!"

"Right," Mr. Turtelhaze said, leaning back in his chair and glancing toward the clock. "Is that your wish?"

REPORT 17

THE LUMINOUS FOREST, OUTSKIRTS OF GAINSLEIGH, KINGDOMS AND EMPIRES
—Thursday, May 31

* * *

Breakfast was almost over.

Everything was slowing down: the way people reached for pastries, how they chewed, how they brushed ants from the blanket, the spaces they left between sentences.

They were promising to write to each other regularly until their next reunion—which would take place much sooner than in twenty years!

"And the children will write to their newfound grandparents," Isabelle declared, "once a week at least."

"We *will*?" Billy demanded in horror. (Letter writing was not his favorite pastime.)

There was laughter. Billy muttered, "Seriously, though. Must we?"

People resumed eating.

"I have a question," Bronte said suddenly, "about letters that one *has* to write." She seemed hesitant. Everyone waited for her question. "Well, remember how I gave my Genie bottle to Lillian Velvet because she had a letter asking me to?"

Nods and murmurs of "Oh, I'd forgotten about that."

"I never said who the letter was from," Bronte continued. "You all thought Lillian had tricked me into giving her the bottle, and I was embarrassed to tell you more."

"Tell us now," her grandma Ildi suggested. "Who was it from?"

Bronte smiled. "Let me tell you exactly what the letter said," she offered. "I know it by heart." And she took a deep breath and recited:

Dear Bronte Mettlestone,

You will find this strange but I am writing to ask you to give your Genie bottle to Lillian Velvet, please. It's v.v.v. important that you do so.

Don't hesitate, be fearless, take this chance.

Yours,

Bronte Mettlestone

P.S. Yes, this is you, writing from the future. I'm an old lady by a lake now & very happy. Your life will be filled with adventure ☺

A short silence followed Bronte's recital, and then several slow gasps.

"No wonder you didn't tell us," Isabelle said drily.

"Why ever did you *believe* it?" Carrie wondered.

"A strange girl turns up with a letter claiming to be from *you* in the future?" Franny stretched out her legs. "And you hand over your Genie bottle? What are they teaching you in school, Bronte?"

"All right, all right." Bronte was growing annoyed. "This is why I didn't mention it earlier. I only mention it now because I'm wondering: should I make a note reminding myself to *write* this letter when I *am* an old lady by a lake? Or will it just happen? As for why I believed it . . ." She paused, embarrassed again. "It's partly that the handwriting looked exactly like mine. And partly"—she scratched her forehead quickly—"well, that line about *don't hesitate, be fearless, take this chance* is something that . . . I secretly chant to myself whenever I feel afraid. I've never told anybody that."

The mood changed again. Expressions softened. "Fair enough then," Franny said shortly. "I like your chant, Bronte. Keep it up."

Granfy Jacob made a growling noise in his throat. "Strange though," he said, "that Lillian used this complicated method of getting herself a Genie bottle. I understood Genie children were given bottles on their tenth birthdays, along with their gold coins. Actually, the gold coins usually come *inside* the bottle. So did Lillian lose hers? Break it? Fill it with fizzy pop and need an extra one?" He chuckled.

"Her gold coins came in a pickle jar," Bronte reminded him.

"The other thing that's strange," Isabelle added, "and that we haven't discussed, is the fact that Lillian Velvet was listed in the official records as the Queen of the Mellifluous Kingdom. The record's been corrected now, of course, but how did it happen?"

Alys shrugged. "My people back home are as mystified as we are," she said.

"Oh!" Billy cried suddenly. He had just taken a mouthful of juice and began to choke on it. Somebody thumped him on the back, which did not help. He wiped his face with a napkin. "Oh," he repeated, more calmly. "Do you know what I just recalled? When I met Lillian, I thought she was a local who'd been injured in the storm and had amnesia."

"Reasonable," the others said, a bit doubtfully.

"So I opened my curtains to remind her what her kingdom looked like. And do you know what she said?"

The others waited.

"She said, *Oh, I wish it* was *my kingdom! It's so beautiful!*"

Billy stopped and waited, expectantly. There was a pause and then a burst of laughter.

"Oh! It was an accident!"

"She was just delighted by how beautiful the kingdom was! And accidentally wished herself its queen!"

The laughter carried on for a while, and then faded.

People returned to their own thoughts. A few frowned. A couple tugged at their lower lips thoughtfully.

"That whole thing with the Genie bottle," Granfy said eventually, brow crinkling. "I can't figure it out. Why *did* she need Bronte's?"

"I'll tell you what confuses me," Bronte put in. "Lillian has a Genie guide, right? Mr. Turtelhaze? But she didn't know *why* she was being transported to the Kingdoms and Empires."

"She called it being shoved," Oscar put in, "and yep, she was pretty clueless."

Granfy plucked at the grass behind him, troubled. "Maybe Genie guides *don't* explain things. They just warn the child not to use all their wishes?" he suggested.

"She told *me* that Mr. Turtelhaze charged her gold coins to see me," Billy said. "I thought she had a concussion and was muddled."

Grandma Ildi drew her knees up to her chest and wrapped her arms around them. "You know, it seems a bit . . . *careless* of Lillian," she said, "to make that wish about the Mellifluous Kingdom. She surely knew that her wishes would come true? And that she only had limited wishes? And that if she *used* all the wishes inside the week, she'd end up . . . well, dead?"

All this while, a slow and terrible realization had been creeping through the group. It seemed to pounce on them all at once.

"She didn't know," Carrie breathed. "*She doesn't know.*"

CHAPTER 82

"I MEAN," I began. I felt myself blushing terribly.

It seemed cruel not to help this fellow with his knee, but honestly, the world was probably full of people with dodgy knees. There were people suffering from much worse too—serious illnesses, unjust imprisonment, desperate unhappiness.

"*Child*," Grandmother snapped. "Make your wish at once! Your manners are appalling! I am ashamed!"

Everyone shuffled uncomfortably and lowered their eyes.

"I'm awfully sorry," I whispered, trying not to cry.

"Come now," Mr. Turtelhaze coaxed. "It *is* a difficult decision. Let's sort this out, shall we? First of all, remind us: what time did your grandmother give you the gold coins?"

"Eight o'clock," Grandmother replied. "On the dot." Everyone's eyes swung toward the clock. It was quarter to eight.

"Very well," Mr. Turtelhaze continued. "You have fifteen minutes. Not long. It would be a dreadful shame to waste your final wish. Perhaps I could help you to decide?"

I looked at him gratefully. "Yes, please."

"You'd like to use your wish to benefit as many people as possible. Correct?"

I nodded eagerly. Even though I could sense Grandmother's anger like fire against my shoulders, I felt relieved that he understood.

"In that case, may I humbly suggest that you wish for a new hospital in Bomaderry? One with all the latest equipment, comfortable beds for patients, and funds to employ excellent doctors, nurses, and physiotherapists? *That* will help *thousands* of wounded people, *and* people with dodgy knees! What a wonderful use of your wish!"

Now the relief was overwhelming!

"Thank you!" I cried. "That sounds perfect!"

"Is that your wish then?" Mr. Turtelhaze demanded.

I considered. Perhaps I could tweak the wish a little. Add a special wing of the hospital for orphaned children? Include a window onto the street where hungry people could collect free soup and crusty bread?

Powerful impatience blazed around the table. I was taking too long.

"We'll light the candles again," Mr. Turtelhaze decided. "You blow them out and then make your wish aloud."

"All right," I agreed. "Will you sing the happy birthday song to me again before I blow out the candles?"

That way, I could finalize my wish in my head while they sang.

Mr. Turtelhaze reached for the matches. I thought perhaps his hands shook a little.

"Deal," he said.

REPORT 18

THE LUMINOUS FOREST, OUTSKIRTS OF GAINSLEIGH, KINGDOMS AND EMPIRES
—Thursday, May 31

* * *

The picnic seemed to burst into vigorous life, a little like a classroom after the teacher has departed.

Everyone was talking at once. Everyone was distressed. "We must warn her!" and "It might be too late! What if it's too late!" These were the key phrases shouted.

Isabelle spoke in the voice she used to penetrate chaos. "Quiet, everyone," she said.

The group fell silent. Her parents looked at her, impressed.

"We must remain calm," she said. "Quite possibly, Lillian *does* know she must not use all the wishes. However, if there *is* a chance she doesn't—and if there *is* still time"—she paused, her eyes flashing—"we need to warn her immediately. Oscar"—she turned to him—"I know that Lillian is from your world, and that your wheeled board can take you there. Do you think you could go and find her?"

Oscar blinked.

"His world is quite big," Bronte apologized.

Smoothly, Isabelle swung around to address her father. "In your university course on Genies, did you learn a way to contact the Council of Genies?"

Granfy Jacob nodded. "It's pretty tricky though," he said. "One must step outside reality to reach the world of Genies."

There were splutters of greater distress.

Granfy raised both hands. "The simplest way is to fall asleep and dream," he said. "I'll lie under this tree. It will take time, though, and may not work." He and his wife exchanged troubled glances. "I fear this issue may relate to the enemy who kept us in hiding. If you can reach Lillian Velvet directly yourselves, please do."

He marched across to the shade under a tree, lay down, and closed his eyes.

"I know!" Emma cried. "Contact Lida and tell her to whisper a message to Lillian!"

"Good thought," Carrie said, "but how do we contact Lida on the coach?"

"It wouldn't work anyway," Bronte said regretfully. "My mother's whispers would not carry to another world."

"When I met Lillian as a child," Carrie said, "she *told* me where she lives. If only I could remember that far back!"

Suddenly, Oscar jolted upright. "She told me too," he said. He tapped his forehead, trying to wake the memory. "Small town. South. Near my mate's holiday house," he muttered. "Bomaderry! That was it. Carmichael Street . . . she didn't give me the number though." He blinked. "But she said they have a letter box shaped like a hair dryer!"

"A what?" the others asked, but Oscar was on his feet, looking around for his skateboard. He found it, leaning against his backpack.

Bronte jumped up too. "I'll come along—help to track her down."

"Grab your board." Oscar nodded, and he reached to take her hand.

Carrie was watching them gravely. "Go as fast as you can," she said. "And please"—she spoke for all of them—"please stop Lillian Velvet from using all her wishes."

CHAPTER 83

TEN LITTLE FLAMES flickered on the candles. Drops of wax melted onto the icing.

Grandmother and her guests sang the birthday song even more heartily, and rather more rapidly, than the previous time. Several eyes darted to the clock and back to me.

My heart fluttered. I composed my wish.

I was ready.

REPORT 19

CARMICHAEL STREET, BOMADERRY, AUSTRALIA, THE WORLD
—Thursday, May 31

* * *

Oscar and Bronte slid from one world into the other, hand in hand. Their wheels hit the surface of the footpath at noisy high speed. Their hands parted.

They were at the top of a steep street. From up here, they could see the small but sprawling town of Bomaderry. It was set in a picturesque rural landscape—green fields, patches of trees, cows, rolling mountains—cut through with roads, large and small.

Carmichael Street itself was long and wide, and lined on one side with little suburban houses and the other with fields. They were on the field side.

"We need to cross over," Oscar said, one foot on the footpath, one on the board. "And look for the hair-dryer-shaped letter box."

Bronte looked at him blankly, so he drew a hair dryer shape in the air.

She nodded—

Vvvoosh!

A car had just driven by them down the street. The force of it shivered in Bronte's spine.

Cars here were nothing like the curvy new automobiles that were becoming popular at home but would never replace horses and carriages. These were sleek, shiny, low to the road, and unthinkably fast.

"Dangerous," she said grimly—as she always did when Oscar brought her and her cousins here.

Oscar sent her a quick, crooked grin.

"You right?" he checked. "Stay close. Look both ways. 'K, now."

And stepping back onto his board, he took off across the street.

Bronte took a trembling breath, steeled herself, and followed.

CHAPTER 84

FOR A SECOND time, I blew out the candles. I was more efficient now, understanding the amount of breath required and how to direct it at the flames.

Once again, there was a haze of smoke that quickly cleared.

"I wish—" I began, and stopped.

Several of the adults *tched* in irritation.

I knew I was being annoying, but something had occurred to me. "Mr. Turtelhaze," I said, "the other day I wished aloud that my neighbors could have their dream backyard. And now that has come true. I thought that was just a coincidence—Helen and I laughed at the idea that it was my birthday wish. Now, though, I wonder. *Was* it because of me? Was that one of my wishes?"

Mr. Turtelhaze nodded. "It was. It cost you five gold coins."

"Good gracious," I breathed. "Perhaps you ought to have . . ." Again, I did not wish to be rude. I started again: "Perhaps it would've been better if you'd let me *know* that any wish I made aloud would come true?" I suggested. "I could have accidentally wished for something dangerous! Something that *harmed* somebody!"

More shuffling around the table, and sighs of annoyance.

"You'd never have done that," Mr. Turtelhaze said heartily.

"But why didn't you tell me?" I persisted, "so that I might be careful?"

Again Mr. Turtelhaze looked at the clock. "You have ten minutes," he said briskly. "The reason I did not tell you was because wishes should not be overthought—as you are doing now." He smiled, lifted his chin, and looked at me directly. "Make your wish," he said.

REPORT 20

CARMICHAEL STREET, BOMADERRY, AUSTRALIA, THE WORLD
—Thursday, May 31

* * *

Two skateboarders hurtled down the footpath.

Oscar, who was known among locals up in Sydney as a speed demon, had never skated so fast. His eyes were nearly closed against the wind. Vibrations buzzed through to his fingertips. Any moment, he knew, he could get the speed wobbles and crash.

Following closely came Bronte, her hair flying behind her, her face tense, knees slightly bent.

A car reversed out of a driveway. Oscar swore, executed a power slide, and *just* swerved around it, skimming the bonnet. The driver braked hard, wide-eyed and shaken.

Further down, a woman wheeled a baby in a stroller. A patch of pavement was scattered with loose gravel. A ridged crack in the concrete was marked with orange traffic cones.

They skated through these obstacles, the sound of their wheels against the concrete like thunder.

"It's there!" Bronte shouted, pointing further down the street.

Oscar didn't answer. He saw the hair-dryer-shaped letter box. He focused, skating even faster. *Too far,* he was thinking. *It's much too far.*

CHAPTER 85

I NODDED.

I felt very solemn.

"Child," Grandmother said, her voice low and ominous. "Hurry."

I took a deep breath.

"I wish—" I began, and they all leaned toward me. "I wish that there—"

And the front window smashed with a mighty crash, shards of glass showering in every direction, adults leaping to their feet, chairs falling, voices shouting, legs and fists pounding, a skateboard swinging, and somehow I was hustled through the chaos and onto the front porch. "MAKE A WISH!" a voice boomed. "MAKE IT *NOW*!"

But hands gripped mine and I felt myself lifting—higher, and then higher, and then higher still—until there I was, soaring in the blue.

PART 16

CHAPTER 86

LITTLE PIECES OF sky had caught on my clothes.

Well, this is no good, I thought, sorrowfully. *The sky will have holes in it now! Like the leaves of a plant being eaten by a caterpillar.*

Then I woke up properly.

I was lying on a bed, beneath a white blanket that was decorated with little blue flower buds—not pieces of the sky.

Relieved, I sat up and studied the room. It was small with pale pink walls, a rocking chair, and a bookcase. There was a window, but a heavy curtain was drawn across it. I was wearing a nightgown I did not recognize.

Where was I? And however had I come to be here?

I squinted, thinking back to my last memory. I'd been at my birthday breakfast with Grandmother, Mr. Turtelhaze, and their friends. Suddenly, there'd been smashing glass and shouts. Oscar had taken one hand, Bronte the other, and we'd soared into the sky—I beamed at that memory. Oh, it had been magic! Magic! The quiet of it, a flock of birds skimming by, occasional clouds, a damp dewiness on my face.

I recommend it to everyone.

Then what? A muddle of several voices cut off almost instantly by silence—and sleep.

Someone must have put me to bed in this pleasant room. Was I in my own world or the Kingdoms and Empires? Had I been shoved?

Ah, I thought, my mood plummeting. I'd never be shoved again. No more adventures in the Kingdoms and Empires. No more visits with the Mettlestone family.

And I'd wasted my final wish! Those last minutes must certainly have run out by now. There would be no local hospital to help wounded soldiers and people with dodgy knees! Mr. Turtelhaze and Grandmother would be angry.

It was a shame, I thought, that Oscar and Bronte had chosen that moment to smash through the window and take me flying. I did not blame them, of course. They can't have known how badly they had timed their visit.

I swung my legs over the side of the bed. The carpet was soft under my bare feet. Then, as I was about to stand, there was a knock on the door.

"Come in?" I called, uncertainly. I hoped I was not inviting some sort of villain into the room.

Or a vampire. They only enter if you invite them, and here I'd gone and done that. That was just my joke with myself, as I knew vampires were not real. Although, of course, I'd known *dragons* to be "not real" only a few days earlier. Suddenly, I was frightened.

It was not a vampire though. It was a bearded man.

"Please," he said. "Don't get up. You need your rest. May I chat with you, though, Lillian?"

He sat down in the rocking chair, and suddenly I recognized him.

"Reuben!" I said. "Hello! Am I in the Kingdoms and Empires then? How marvelous! I didn't think I'd ever get to come back. Is this the Kingdom of Kate-Bazaar? That's where I met you when you were in the cave. I have to confess something. I broke my promise. You asked me not to help anybody, as that would change history. I *did* help people though. After you'd left, I—"

"Yes, the little twins, Eli and Taya," Reuben agreed, smiling. "You rescued them from the ocean. I certainly do not blame you. You did well. I was mistaken in my advice. Your actions during the week after your tenth birthday are folded into time—they are 'meant,' so to speak. I did not know who you were back then, you see. Can we start in a different way, though, Lillian? I'd like to tell a story if I may?"

"You may," I agreed. I pulled my legs back up onto the bed

and leaned against the headboard. I do like stories. Fiona next door used to tell them to me.

"A drink? Something to eat? Before I begin?" he inquired.

"No thank you," I replied. "That is kind of you, only I just had breakfast."

I faltered. Had I just had breakfast? How long had I been sleeping?

Reuben, however, only nodded and rocked slowly back and forth in his chair. He began to speak.

"The story begins over twenty years ago," he began.

"Wonderful," I said. "I love historical fiction."

He chuckled briefly and then his face became serious. "Relax, Lillian," he said. "All you need do is listen."

He said this so gently that I felt oddly sad. Rather than asking me not to interrupt, as most people do, Reuben had told me to relax. It felt like a neat trick somehow, or a surprising inversion.

I settled back into the pillows and listened as Reuben told his story.

CHAPTER 87

"OVER TWENTY YEARS ago," Reuben repeated, "in the time of the Whispering Wars, Jacob and Ildi Mettlestone discovered something extraordinary.

"The pair had spent many years working in Shadow Mage control. They excelled at this: both had fine diplomatic skills. Jacob was a True Mage—a Wheat Sprite, actually—and Ildi, a powerful Spellbinder. Most people don't come into their spellbinding skills until they are twelve or thirteen, and then they require training. Ildi realized when she was five, and was self-taught.

"At any rate, just over twenty years ago, Jacob and Ildi observed a handful of Shadow Mages with sharply increased powers. They were baffled. Bewildered. Word on the street was that something or someone was *helping* these Shadow Mages. Equipping them with new and better powers. Who or what could it be?"

Reuben touched his foot to the floor to stop the rocking for a moment, and he leaned forward.

"It was a Genie, Lillian," he said.

I gasped. A Genie! I was very caught up in the story.

"Yes." Reuben nodded and resumed rocking. "This was extraordinary because a Genie's essence is starlight. It should be *impossible* for a Genie to enjoy wickedness—and yet, this one clearly did. The impossibility meant nobody else had seen the truth. Jacob, however, had studied Genies at university. And Ildi had been raised by a violent father who presented himself to the world as a kindly pet shop owner. She knew about hidden evil. Hence, the pair *could* see it. They alerted Genie authorities. The wicked Genie was captured."

"Phew," I said.

Reuben looked at me with interest. "Yes, phew," he said, "or perhaps not phew. You see, it's also impossible to capture a Genie. There are stories in your world about Genies being captured by bottles. That is a misunderstanding. Genie bottles do have a hold over their Genies, in that they send out strong signals, calling the Genies to them. And they soothe and comfort their Genies. Yet, they do not *literally* hold Genies. A Genie's essence is outside of life, you see, outside of reality and time. How *can* you hold such a person? You may place a Genie in a prison, and the Genie may *seem* to be trapped—but the essence of the Genie might continue to roam between worlds, causing trouble."

"And that's what happened with this wicked Genie?" I guessed.

"Exactly. His name was Gianni, by the way. I'd met him briefly years before this, when he was running for election to the Council. He was a brilliant Genie and held strong views on Genie rights. The Council has strict rules, you see. If, for example, a Genie grants wishes or time travel in a way that dangerously alters the time line? The Council will restrict that Genie's power until the Genie finds a way to repair the time line—and to convince the relevant Board of Timekeepers it's been done. You see, the Council believes that serious alterations to the time line will tip the universe upside down, causing terrible death and destruction. Now, *Gianni* claimed that that was nonsense. As Genies are *meant to be,* he said, any changes we cause to time or reality are *meant to be* too. And he thought that the Council and its timekeeper boards were power-hungry bobbleheads."

Reuben paused and twirled his thumbs thoughtfully. "You know, I actually wondered if Gianni might be right? I even considered voting for him. Next thing, though, he was declaring that evil has just as much right to exist as good, and that we should be granting wishes to Shadow Mages, and promoting sadness and despair! He lost a lot of votes that way. Also, lost a lot of friends. This meant he was isolated. Lonely and angry, he started to play with his own ideas—granting wishes to Shadow Mages, giving them extra powers. He formed his own little team of Shadow Mages. He threatened to take down the Council itself and was setting this plan in motion when Jacob and Ildi Mettlestone discovered his wickedness.

"And thus, he ended up in prison. Imagine how angry he was! Of course, the Council restricted his powers—but there was still the risk I mentioned. That his essence could roam between worlds. The Council advised Jacob and Ildi to stage their own deaths and go into hiding, in order to protect themselves and their family from Gianni's fury."

"Oh my," I murmured.

"Meanwhile," Reuben continued, and I snuggled into the bed a little more. I love it when a story says *meanwhile*.

Reuben smiled at me kindly. "Meanwhile, a Genie child was born," he said. "Genie children are very rare. This one, as is the custom, was placed in a basket on the doorstep of a kindly couple in another world. She was raised by that couple, as their own child. On her tenth birthday, a package was left on her doorstep: it contained a Genie bottle filled with gold coins, along with a note explaining that she could spend the coins on wishes. Five coins per wish. The note warned her that she must *not* use up all her coins within the next week."

"Hmm," I said. I rubbed my nose and leaned forward, listening.

"Over the next week," Reuben said, "as is the custom, the child was transported to various places and times in the Kingdoms and Empires. On each visit she met with a person who needed help—for some reason, this was generally a person connected with the Mettlestone family—little Jacob Mettle, asleep and about to be crushed by gravel; the drowning twins who'd later become Spindrift children and play a small, important part in the lives of many Mettlestone family members. And so on. Sometimes, the child used quick thinking to help the person, and sometimes she used one of her wishes. Occasionally, she met up with a Genie guide named Reuben. All Genie children are allocated a Genie guide. Reuben advised her, and reminded her to take *great* care not to use all her wishes."

"Reuben is *your* name," I pointed out, thoughtfully. I was very interested in—and a little puzzled by—the story of the Genie child, but Reuben's name had distracted me.

He nodded. "It *is* my name, Lillian. In fact, it was I. *I* was the guide for this child. Anyhow, the Genie child completed the week with plenty of wishes remaining. That week is a test, you see, and helps the Genie child learn to treat their powers with respect. This child had *certainly* done that. She had helped all the people in trouble. Yet she never used her wishes recklessly. She had plenty of wishes remaining. She had passed the test. All it took then was a week's orientation with the Genie Council and her certificate was granted at a ceremony. She was an official Genie. She now had the power to grant as many wishes as she liked."

I was pleased for the Genie child, but a great itchiness was growing all around my mind.

"You know, that sounds a bit like what happened to me," I said, "only I received gold coins in a pickle jar, not a Genie bottle, for my birthday. And no note. Also, I didn't use *wishes* to help people who were in trouble—I didn't even know I *had* wishes—not until recently. I spent my gold coins to stay in the Kingdoms and Empires when I was shoved there. And *I* didn't have to be careful not to use all the wishes. In fact, I was *trying* to use my last wish just before Oscar and Bronte crashed into my house. I hope I haven't"—the itchiness intensified—"I hope I haven't accidentally stolen a Genie's gold coins somehow, and used them as my own?"

Reuben shook his head. "You have not."

"Well." I decided to change the subject. "And meanwhile, the other Genies properly captured the wicked Genie, so he couldn't hurt the Mettlestones anymore? So Jacob and Ildi Mettlestone could come out of hiding?"

Surprisingly, Reuben shook his head a second time.

"The Genies *thought* they had properly captured the wicked Genie," he told me solemnly, "and they told Jacob and Ildi that it was safe to emerge. The family held a week of celebrations in Gainsleigh to welcome them back. But the Genie had tricked the other Genies—he had *pretended* to be fully captured. In fact, a part of him was still moving about between times and worlds. He took the form of a minor Genie—a secretary to the Council who was busy at a meditation retreat outside time."

I wasn't sure what a meditation retreat was but let that go.

"He had an evil plan," Reuben told me. "To carry it out, he needed the help of his team of Shadow Mages, as he was without his full powers. Do you want to know what his evil plan was?"

"Yes, please."

"First, to take revenge on Jacob and Ildi—starting by having his team of Shadow Mages attack and kill all the Mettlestone children and grandchildren. He wanted Jacob and Ildi to suffer those losses before they died themselves."

I took a deep breath. "He doesn't sound a pleasant chap."

"Not in the least. But second—and this was his master plan—to destroy a Genie."

"Oh no!" I gasped.

"Yes. That way he could declare himself the most powerful Genie of all. And take control of the Council—essentially making himself universal ruler of Genies and of time."

"Gosh," I said.

"Destroying a Genie was an impossible plan, for as I have mentioned, Genies exist outside of time. This puts them beyond life and death—they cannot be destroyed."

"Phew," I said.

"However," Reuben continued, "there *is* a devious way you could destroy a Genie *child* if you wanted."

"Oh dear," I said.

"If you could get a Genie child to use all their wishes within a week of their tenth birthday, that Genie"—Reuben snapped his fingers—"would disappear."

"Disappear?" I whispered. "Where to?"

Reuben pressed his fingers to his temples. "*Disappear* is not the right word," he said. "I mean that the Genie is extinguished. Like a candle blown out. Gone."

I thought of the smoke fading away after I'd blown out my birthday candles (twice).

"He chose the Genie child I've just mentioned—the one who was somehow connected to the Mettlestones," Reuben continued. "This was the *perfect* Genie child to destroy, as far as he was concerned."

I didn't like to jump to the end of the story, but I couldn't help it. "But you said that that Genie *completed* her week without using all her wishes!" I said. "And she became an official Genie! So it was too late for the wicked Gianni! His wicked plan was thwarted!"

For a little while, Reuben simply rocked back and forth in his chair.

"Yes," he agreed eventually. "She *did* complete her week. However, Genies can, of course, travel in time. And do you know what Gianni did?"

"What did he do?"

"He traveled back in time to the day that the Genie baby was placed in a basket with a note at the door of the lovely couple. He took—"

"Hold on, if he could travel in time, why not just go back and kill Jacob and Ildi *before* they discovered his wickedness?" I suggested. "That way he'd never have been found out in the first place."

"Excellent thinking, Lillian. But the Council takes important information like that outside time. Once Jacob and Ildi had told them about Gianni's evil, the Council knew it and would always know it—no matter how twisted time became."

I nodded, more or less understanding.

"So," I prompted, "he traveled back in time to the day the Genie baby was at the door?"

"And moved the basket next door instead," Reuben finished. "Placed one of his Shadow Mages into *that* house and had *her* raise the baby, as her grandchild. When the bottle of gold coins arrived for the Genie child's tenth birthday? The Shadow Mage simply collected it from the correct house next door. She gave the coins to the child in a different container—a pickle jar—and hid the Genie bottle so the child would never have its power. She threw away the note."

I frowned.

"Gianni, meanwhile, changed the register of guides allocated to Genie children—easy to do as he'd taken the form of the secretary, of course. He deleted *my* name and replaced it with the secretary's name. Mr. Turtelhaze."

Something caught in my throat.

Reuben was gazing at the ceiling though and didn't seem to notice. "Even though I was no longer the Genie child's guide," he said meditatively, "I remember feeling a peculiar urge to travel in space and time. I was exploring a cave in Kate-Bazaar one day, wondering what I was doing there, when I *met* the Genie child. I didn't know she was a Genie child then. I could see that she was from another time—Genies can see time—but only the official Genie guide can see that a child is a Genie child. Otherwise any Genie who ran into them would be tempted to help the Genie child with their challenge. *Only* the guide can help."

He blinked and looked back at me: "As Mr. Turtelhaze, Gianni became the child's guide. During the week after her tenth birthday, he was notified whenever the Genie child traveled, and had the power to visit her himself whenever he liked. He did *not* tell her that she couldn't use all her wishes. In fact, he tricked her into wasting wishes each time she was transported to the Kingdoms and Empires, by asking if she wished to stay or not. He failed to mention that anything she wished for would come true. This meant she accidentally wasted wishes. And then, when time was running out, he even *urged* her to use her last wishes. He—"

"Stop it," I ordered. "I'm tired."

The itchiness had become overwhelming. My skull crawled with it. I squirmed around in the bed, trying to scratch at the inside of my head. At the same time, my eyes were heavy with weariness. I'd never been so tired.

"I *do not like this story,*" I half-shouted. "I'm tired! I need to go to sleep!"

"Lillian," he said. "Lillian, the Genie child was you."

I glared at him, squeezed my eyes shut, lay down, and fell asleep.

CHAPTER 88

OVER THE NEXT few days, I slept often.

Reuben checked on me regularly, but I did not speak. One morning, he brought me a glass of freshly squeezed juice. After I had tasted it, I spoke: "What's in this juice, please?"

"Orange, apple, pineapple, and watermelon," he replied, "with ice cubes and a touch of mint."

"Delicious," I said. Then I set the glass down and fell asleep again.

Another time he gave me a caramel milk shake, and once a frosted cupcake. All delicious.

"I can't think why I'm so tired," I confessed, after the cupcake.

"It's the shock, Lillian," Reuben replied calmly. "Your grandmother—the person who raised you—tried to help a wicked Genie destroy you."

"Be quiet," I said and fell asleep again.

After a week of this, I began to wake properly. Reuben told me I should continue resting, and he pointed to the bookcase by my bed. It turned out to hold children's books I hadn't read: *We Didn't Mean to Go to Sea* by Arthur Ransome, *The Westing Game* by Ellen Raskin, *Dragon Skin* by Karen Foxlee, *Lirael* by Garth Nix.

"These stories are *magnificent*!" I told Reuben when he arrived with a mango smoothie one day. He seemed pleased but admitted he hadn't read them himself.

"You should," I said.

After that, he often sat in the rocking chair reading, while I read on the bed. It was very companionable. Occasionally, Reuben would chuckle or gasp and I would say, "Which bit are you up to?" and he would tell me. Then I'd say, "Oh, yes, I love that bit."

One day I knelt up on the bed and opened the curtains.

I saw a picturesque garden with an emerald-green lawn, rosebushes, and apple trees. In the distance, snowcapped mountains.

I gazed at this view for some time.

I began to ask Reuben questions. I avoided mentioning Grandmother and Mr. Turtelhaze, focusing more on the Mettlestones. Reuben explained how the family had realized the truth about me, and how quickly Jacob had dreamed his way through to the Genies, so that they could dispatch Reuben to help. And how Oscar and Bronte had rushed to my world to protect me.

"They saved me just in time," I realized. "I was about to make a wish."

He nodded gravely.

I began to feel drowsy again. I picked up another book and read.

Not long after this, Reuben brought me a dressing gown and slippers and suggested I read in the sitting room. This room was comfortably furnished with lamps and squashy sofas. Its large windows looked onto the garden. There was also a desk in the corner with an old-fashioned typewriter sitting on it.

"If you like," Reuben offered one day, "you could write the story of what has happened to you since your tenth birthday, Lillian. It would be very useful to the Genies. It might also help sort out the tangles in your mind."

I agreed. That is how I came to write these chapters, dear reader. My typing is getting faster now. The first chapter took me *days*. Reuben inquired politely whether I might prefer pen and paper, but I persisted.

"One branch of the Council is working on capturing Gianni—or Mr. Turtelhaze, as you know him," Reuben told me.

"Another is working with the Board of Timekeepers on the time line. Your chapters will help them make any necessary repairs. The Council is in charge of time, you see, and reality, and all that."

"Gosh," I said.

CHAPTER 89

NOT LONG AFTER this, I discovered that the wardrobe in my room was filled with dresses and coats, sunhats and bathing suits, in rainbows of colors and all in my size. I began to dress each morning, rather than staying in my nightgown and slippers.

One day, when Reuben and I were sharing a plate of grilled cheese on toast in the sitting room, I told him that I'd be perfectly all right if he needed to go to work. I had already taken up too much of his time, I said. I could stay here alone and do my schoolwork.

"Schoolwork!" He sounded startled. "I'd forgotten all about that." The corners of his mouth turned down as if to say, "Oops!" This made me giggle.

Then he wiped some cheese from his beard and said, "As for time, you have taken none of that. You see, we are technically *outside* time."

It seemed he had whisked me straight out of time the moment Oscar and Bronte brought me through to the Mettlestones. Most Genies have a little cottage outside time, he added, and this was his.

"*Inside* time, it's still nine minutes before eight o'clock on Thursday morning," he told me. "Mr. Turtelhaze and your grandmother are still shouting at each other amidst the broken window glass."

I stared at him.

"You'll have to go back into time eventually," he continued. "You're not an official Genie until you make it through those last nine minutes—and then the orientation week and ceremony, of course, but those are outside time."

Oh! For a moment, I was pleased, thinking I could still wish for that hospital after all.

I blinked. I was being nonsensical.

"Must I return *home* for the last nine minutes?" I asked. "Back into the shouting and broken glass?"

Reuben shook his head. "It doesn't matter where you are," he said. "You can spend the minutes in the Kingdoms and Empires if you like. Just as long as you don't make a wish."

"I'm sure I can manage that," I said softly.

"Yes, I'm sure too," he agreed. "However, we'll keep you here until we're certain that Gianni Turtelhaze is under control."

"Thank you," I said.

"The very least we can do," Reuben said heavily. He stood and carried the empty plate into the kitchen. "Meanwhile," he said, "we're expecting company!"

"Company? Should I hurry and bathe and go to bed?"

"Certainly not," Reuben replied, surprised. "Come into the kitchen and help me bake a cake."

It turned out that our visitors were members of the Mettlestone family. Reuben was bringing them outside time so he could interview them. He would then write "reports" to be sent to the Council along with my chapters.

The first to arrive were the Staranise sisters, braids swinging with interest. Reuben said we children could spend some time together once he'd conducted his interviews.

So we ran into the garden and began playing games I'd read about in books—running and chasing, or jumping over ropes, or elastic bands, or hedges. There was laughter and the sun was warm. Reuben emerged and suggested he turn the sprinklers on so that we could splash about and cool down. We became very wet and muddy.

Back inside, we ate a pile of sandwiches that Reuben had prepared with fresh, crusty bread.

The girls called me "darling" and offered me hugs. That was funny, as we were still wet and muddy from the sprinkler. Dripping on the floor, actually, and leaving big damp marks on the couch. This frightened me suddenly; however, Reuben said it didn't matter a bit.

"Listen," Imogen said, chewing on a sandwich, "if this wicked Genie went back in time and switched Lillian to the wrong doorstep, why can't *you* time-travel right now, Reuben, and switch her back to the correct one? Wouldn't that fix everything?"

"A good thought," Reuben replied, "but the time line has already been disrupted too much. When Gianni switched Lillian's basket, he not only caused Lillian to suffer a difficult childhood but also caused extensive damage to reality. The change nearly undid the entire Mettlestone family! At nine P.M., the day after Lillian's birthday, she was sent to a circus years earlier, and was unable to save Jacob. At that moment, the time line unraveled and the Mettlestones disappeared—along with the Kingdoms and Empires as you knew it. It was only Lillian's determination to rescue little Jacob—as she had in the previous time line—that saved you all."

"*Thank you*, Lillian," the Staranise girls all cried. "You darling!"

"But it was my fault for *not* rescuing him," I argued. "I wished to stay for a very short time and so I wasn't there long enough. I do not deserve your thanks."

"Why did you wish to stay for a very short time?" Reuben asked, studying me closely.

"I was afraid Grandmother would be angry if she found me gone," I replied.

"And whose fault is that?"

"The evil Genie's fault!" the Staranise sisters cried. "And Lillian's grandmother's fault! Plus, she didn't know she was meant to be there to help someone. You were so brave, Lillian. You tried and tried until you *did* fix it for us."

After that, we shared slices of the Golden Caramel Cake that Reuben and I had baked, along with cups of tea.

The following day, Oscar visited. I thanked him for having rescued me.

"No worries," he said.

The three of us made homemade pizzas in the kitchen while we chatted. Oscar seemed relaxed with Reuben, as if they were old friends. He asked a question that surprised me.

"So what about Lillian's biological parents?" he asked. "Where were they? I mean, where does Lillian *come* from?"

Reuben was rolling out dough. He paused, holding up the rolling pin. "Ah," he said, smiling. "A Genie child is formed of broken starlight."

"Stars are just big exploding balls of gas," Oscar said promptly.

"I'm glad to hear your new school is educating you, Oscar," Reuben retorted, "however, as I said, a Genie child is formed of broken star*light*, which—"

"Mainly hydrogen and helium," Oscar was saying, "and the star*light* is just electromagnetic radiat—" Oscar began. Reuben raised a floury palm in the air, silencing him.

"You know how people wish upon stars," he said sternly.

Oscar chuckled. "Now you're going to say that a wish upon a star creates a Genie child? Dude. I love this world."

Reuben collapsed into a chair in an exaggerated way that made us laugh. "There's a certain kind of wish," he said—and then his voice lowered and softened, so that Oscar listened.

I listened too, of course, feeling strange.

"Most people wish for gold, say, or a puppy, or for their grandma to stay healthy," Reuben continued. "But *sometimes* a person is miserable and despairing. The person lies flat on their back in a grassy field, gazes at the stars—and there is *no wish*. Instead, there's a sudden burst of wild determination, from deep within that person, a burst so powerful that it shoots up to the sky, sends a star spinning through space and time, sends the star*light* cartwheeling, cracking into pieces—before looping and twirling back into the heart of the person on the grass. Do you know what that is?"

"What?" I whispered.

"It's a *wish upon yourself.*"

Reuben stood again and resumed rolling the dough.

"And the broken starlight turns into a Genie child?" Oscar asked, wonderingly.

In reply, Reuben nodded once.

A little later, while we were scattering peppers, salami, and cheese on the pizza base, Oscar asked another question: "So a Genie baby is *always* put in a basket at the door of nice people?"

"Yes." Reuben nodded.

"How do you know they're nice?"

"Oh, certain homes shine with kindness," Reuben explained. "They're only ever occupied by kind people."

"Fiona and Carl *were* kind," I confirmed, "and now Helen and Shahlyla, who live in their house, are also lovely."

"At whatever point the basket was left on the doorstep," Reuben said, "the people who lived there would have raised you as their own."

Oscar was carefully removing mushroom slices from the pizza—he doesn't like mushroom. "You know that's not how it works in our world, right?" he said.

"What do you mean?" Reuben asked.

"If you find a baby on the doorstep you're meant to go to the police," Oscar said, "and the police try to track down the mother. The baby would go into the foster care system, most likely. Maybe get adopted in the end."

"Good gracious," Reuben murmured. "I must notify the Council."

A dimple appeared in Oscar's cheek, and he shot me a quick wide-eyed look that made me laugh.

"Still," Reuben mused, "Fiona and Carl must have either broken the rules or become official foster parents themselves in the original time line—which has now dissolved—because they *did* raise Lillian. And if she was left on that doorstep today, I've no doubt that Helen and Shahlyla would find a way to raise her too."

I stopped laughing then and began to cry. It was very sudden. It was the idea that Fiona and Carl might have been my parents, or Helen and Shahlyla.

Imagine that.

I couldn't stop crying for some time. Reuben and Oscar were tremendously kind. After the pizza, we had ice cream for dessert.

CHAPTER 90

WHEN BRONTE METTLESTONE visited, I thanked her too, for rescuing me, and she said, "My pleasure."

We found a rope swing attached to a tree in the garden and took turns pushing each other. We talked about Bronte's Genie bottle, and about the Genie dressed in shades of red, whose bottle it had once been.

"I wonder who that Genie is," Bronte said. "I remember she was very beautiful and graceful."

"She was," I agreed, thinking of my dream.

Reuben brought out glasses of lemonade for us. "I've been wondering myself," he said. "I don't think I know her."

Then he sat on the bench near the swing.

"It's fortunate that you had that bottle, Bronte," he said next, "and that you gave it to Lillian."

Bronte smiled. "So I must remember to write that note when I'm an old lady and meet Lillian?"

"You must," Reuben agreed. "You will."

Bronte hopped off the swing and picked up a glass of lemonade.

"Has Mr. Turtelhaze been captured yet?" she asked.

Reuben glanced at the sky. "Come inside," he told us. "There's going to be a thunderstorm."

I will not describe all the Mettlestone visits. Several aunts arrived in groups, and tended to be noisy, with either arguments or laughter. Billy came along with his mother, Queen Alys, and his dog, Theodore. We painted a mural of a beach scene on an outside wall together while Theodore watched, puzzled but supportive.

They were all kind and grateful to me, for saving their family—especially the Mettlestone grandparents. Ildi even thanked me for setting the rabbits free.

"If you hadn't, I'd never have been frightened into running away to the circus," she said. "I was upset at the time, but you actually saved my life." Then her voice softened and she said, "Not everyone gets handed the best parents, Lillian. Only a few days before I met you, I'd been lying in the middle of that very field miserable, gazing up at the stars. The strangest thing happened. I felt as if the universe turned inside out for a moment. Anyway, luckily, as life goes on, you can choose new families. You'll always be a part of ours, if you like."

"You certainly are," Jacob agreed, gripping his wife's hand, and mine too.

Reuben raised an eyebrow at me. "No *wonder* you're connected to the Mettlestones, Lillian," he said. "You are one. Because of you, Jacob exists. And turns out, because of Ildi, you exist."

Ildi and Jacob were puzzled so Reuben explained and, surprisingly, they both cried.

Carrie Mettlestone's visit was strange. She is a large, well-dressed, grown-up woman and yet, when she grinned at me, there was the girl who had been my first friend. We talked about the magic of the Sparks.

"I returned to the forest often after you vanished," Carrie said, "long after the Hurtlings moved on. I had liked you so much!" Over time, though, she said, she had grown up, and become a busy Spellbinder, and the memory of that one afternoon had faded—until Billy's painting reminded her.

"I hope we can be great friends now?" she suggested.

I agreed, although privately I didn't see how I could be "great friends" with a grown-up—even Fiona-next-door had been more like a pretend mother than a friend. However, as the day went on, Carrie told such funny stories, and sang such loud, thumping songs—somehow persuading *me* to join in—and I saw how she could be a wonderful friend. The best grown-ups, I realized—recalling Fiona again—are the ones who remember how to play.

While the three of us ate dinner together, the conversation turned to Shadow Mages. As Carrie is a Spellbinder, she was interested to discuss the Shadow Mages who had helped Mr. Turtelhaze with his wicked plans.

"The Genies have now rounded most of them up," Reuben told her, "including those who were arrested after Alys was rescued. It seems that Gianni had given them the power to hide their shadow magic so that Spellbinders could not bind it. They had to capture Alys when she realized it *was* shadow magic behind the storm, to stop her from revealing this to her sisters. They brought her to that jewelry shop meaning to entice the family over there, where they could destroy you."

"Which they almost did," Carrie nodded grimly, "except that Lillian helped us." She shook her head admiringly at me, and I felt embarrassed.

"And a small group of Witches and Sterling Silver Foxes were living in Lillian's world, helping him out there?" Carrie checked next, adding salt to her roast potatoes.

Before Reuben could answer, I asked, "What was my grandmother?"

They both turned to me.

"A Witch or a Sterling Silver Fox?" I prompted. "Which was she?"

"Oh." Reuben swiveled his chair around so he could face me properly. "Neither, Lillian. Your grandmother was the human form of a rare and original kind of Shadow Mage. Ordinarily, this Shadow Mage consists only of sound, shadow, and energy, but Gianni gave it the gift of human form."

"What's it called?" I asked.

"A Hurtling," Reuben said.

There was sharp intake of breath from Carrie. I only stared.

CHAPTER 91

WHEN METTLESTONES WERE not visiting, Reuben and I continued our pleasant days, taking turns at the typewriter. Reuben's reports were coming along, and so were my chapters. (Reuben's typing was so fast it was like hailstones on a tin roof.)

One day, I was fetching a glass of water from the kitchen, and it slipped through my fingers and crashed to the floor.

"Oh!" I said and moved toward a cupboard where I knew the dustpan and broom were kept.

"*Stay where you are!*" Reuben said sharply. He had appeared at the kitchen door.

I froze.

Reuben stepped carefully around me, swept up the broken pieces, and threw them away.

He placed a hand on my shoulder. "Your heart is beating a million miles an hour," he said softly. "I'm so sorry, Lillian. I didn't mean to frighten you. You were about to step on a shard of glass. I spoke sharply because I did not want you to cut yourself."

"I'm sorry I broke the glass," I said.

"I care nothing about the glass," he replied promptly. "I care about you."

Not long after this, I asked Reuben if gravity was different here, outside of time.

"How do you mean?" he asked.

"Oh, it just feels . . . lighter than at home. My legs feel springier, and my shoulders don't drag as much."

"Lillian," Reuben said, looking at me directly. "You grew up with a Hurtling. A Hurtling's goal is to crush life of all kinds."

I blinked.

"Whereas now you are safe," he added, giving a sad little shrug.

Dear reader, my narrative is drawing to a close.

Reuben has just told me that members of the Genie Council will arrive any moment to speak to me. He is excited. He believes this means they have captured Mr. Turtelhaze—properly this time—and that I will be able to return to time and continue life.

"With Grandmother?"

"No, Lillian," he replied. "We will find you a new family. When the nine minutes are complete, and even once you've been certified as an official Genie, you will still be you—Lillian—a girl of ten years. Would you like to live in the Kingdoms and Empires with the Mettlestones then, do you think? Or in the world where you grew up?"

I told him I hardly knew the world where I grew up and that I'd like to explore it a little. I said that it was my world, and that I missed it—the mandarin trees, the birds, the cows in fields, the corner store. "So if there was a family that would take care of me there," I finished, "that would be my choice. Although I'd like to remain friends with the Mettlestones and visit them sometimes?"

"Absolutely," Reuben agreed. "All right, once you're an official Genie, we'll see what we can do. Just promise me you won't use your wish in those last nine minutes?"

"Of course I won't!" I laughed.

My final thought is this: I like the way people keep calling me Lillian. I know that's my name, but still.

Dear reader, I hope you have people who call you by your name, and that they do so with love.

All my wishes to you,
Lillian Velvet

PART 17

REPORT 21

MY PLACE
—Outside of Time

* * *

I am shaking with rage.
I am pure anger.
Fury.

The Genie Council came here, to my place. I am Reuben, to be clear.

They spoke to Lillian without me. They led me to believe they were here merely to tell her that Gianni was captured. I expected they'd apologize for failing to secure him properly in the first place, praise Lillian for teaching herself how to use the Genie bottle, and even a hollow tree, to help her move in time and space, and thank her for restoring the time line, broken when young Jacob was not rescued.

But no. None of that.

While I happily gardened, they were in my living room asking Lillian Velvet for a favor.

A favor.

(Yes, I know these reports are meant to be "objective," but this trembling rage is itself *objective truth.*)

Still, they had not secured Gianni. Their efforts had failed.

Yet they were close—very close. The outline of

an elaborate enchantment was in place. All they needed was a way to distract him while they filled it in.

This was the favor they required.

Would Lillian return to time, please? And distract Gianni, leading him to believe she was going to make her final wish?

Gianni was obsessed with the idea of destroying her.

All Lillian had to do was keep him chatting, while *not* making a wish. As far as Gianni knew, just a moment ago, Lillian had been whisked away by Oscar and Bronte. As her Genie guide, he could find her easily.

Now she would simply take a short walk in the Luminous Forest.

Gianni would pounce.

The Council would be nearby, working rapidly to enchant Gianni while he was preoccupied. They would keep an eye on Lillian. No harm would come to her!

Easy! She would be helping to save all the worlds, and all the time, from a wicked and powerful Genie.

Of course, Lillian agreed at once.

And then what happened?

I cannot type for my anger.

REPORT 22

THE LUMINOUS FOREST, OUTSKIRTS OF GAINSLEIGH, KINGDOMS AND EMPIRES
—Thursday, May 31

* * *

S (Still shaking with rage.

My fingers are bruised from bashing at the keyboard.)

"Absolutely not," I said, when I learned from the remaining Council members what they'd planned. "I forbid it."

But it was too late.

Several Council members had taken Lillian back into time. She was in the forest, not far from where the Mettlestones were picnicking. Crouched by the brook, she was scooping water into a tin.

It was eight minutes before eight o'clock on Thursday morning, exactly a week after Lillian's birthday.

The Council members were huddled amidst nearby trees. Self-enchanted, they could not be seen or heard.

Upon my arrival, they enchanted me. I could not move. Otherwise, they knew, I'd have swooped Lillian back outside of time.

"I forbid this," I said. "I will *not* allow you to risk Lillian."

A few Council members chuckled; most ignored me. They do as they please.

"Shhh," CM# commanded. (They go by code names, usually "CM" followed by a punctuation mark.)

"It's already working," CM_ added. "He has located her. See? Here he comes now."

We fell silent and watched as Gianni approached Lillian. To our surprise, the Hurtling who had raised Lillian accompanied him.

Lillian, of course, knew this pair as Mr. Turtelhaze and Grandmother. I will refer to them as such from this point.

"Child!" Grandmother exclaimed. "What were you thinking, running out on breakfast like that?"

Lillian looked up and smiled.

"Hello, Grandmother!" she said. "Hello, Mr. Turtelhaze! I do apologize. My friends Oscar and Bronte surprised me and brought me here to join *their* breakfast party in the forest! I'm just fetching some water for the group."

She straightened up, the tin of water swinging in her hand.

"Your friends smashed our window," Grandmother said sternly. "Inconsiderate. And you yourself have behaved very rudely indeed to our guests."

Mr. Turtelhaze stepped around Grandmother.

"You startled us," he said, speaking mildly, "rushing away like that. And didn't you promise you'd make a wish? What about the hospital?"

"Oh, of course!" Lillian said. "Again, I apologize."

There was a brief silence. Mr. Turtelhaze was studying Lillian's face. She held his gaze, innocently.

"Well!" he said abruptly, and he dropped to the ground by the brook, crossing his legs. "Let's finish the party right here, shall we?" He patted the grass on either side of him. After a moment, both Lillian and Grandmother sat too—Grandmother, a little awkwardly.

"A slice of birthday cake each while Lillian makes her wish," Mr. Turtelhaze announced and, with a flourish, he took a packet of cake slices from his pocket and handed one to each of the others.

What was he up to?

The Council members were muttering to each other. They kept glancing over at Lillian, then up at the trees, and then at each other, muttering. This is how they build their enchantments.

"Work fast," I told them, under my breath.

"We are," CM: replied, calmly. "We almost have him."

Over by the brook, the three munched cake. Only five minutes of wishing time remained. Mr. Turtelhaze was cutting it close.

"Now then," he said, brushing away cake crumbs. From his other pocket, he drew out the pickle jar. Five gold coins clinked against the glass. He unscrewed the lid and tipped these into his hand. "Go ahead and make your final wish," he prompted.

"I will," Lillian agreed. She bit her lip, as if considering. "Only, may I double-check that I can't wish for something bigger? Such as world peace?"

Mr. Turtelhaze spoke evenly. "We've been through this. That's too vague a concept. Your hospital wish is perfect."

"Thank you," Lillian said. "I'll add a special wing to the hospital where sick children can paint and play—perhaps sing songs?"

"Indeed," Mr. Turtelhaze said, and although his

voice remained mild, I could hear a change in tone. "Tell you what," he continued. "I've an idea for a *different* wish."

I felt myself go cold.

"He knows," I barked. "Get her out of there."

The Council members ignored me.

REPORT 23

THE LUMINOUS FOREST, OUTSKIRTS OF GAINSLEIGH, KINGDOMS AND EMPIRES
—Thursday, May 31

* * *

"Let's say your grandmother was extremely ill and about to die," Mr. Turtelhaze said, "wouldn't you wish her to be cured?"

Lillian blinked and swung toward her grandmother.

"*Are* you ill, Grandmother?" she asked.

Grandmother, confused, tried to catch Mr. Turtelhaze's eye. His gaze remained fixed on Lillian. "Well," Grandmother hedged.

"Your grandmother is a Hurtling in human form," Mr. Turtelhaze said amiably. "Do you know what is fatal to Hurtlings?"

Lillian's brow crinkled. Grandmother's face paled.

"Fridaberries," Lillian recalled. "Have you eaten one, Grandmother?"

"Indeed, she has," Mr. Turtelhaze declared. "Many. In the cake she just ate." Grandmother gasped, but he spoke over her: "If you do not use your wish to cure her, she'll be dead in moments. You'd best hurry. Make the wish. Save your grandmother."

I swung around to the Council members. *"She'll do it!"* I snapped. *"Get her out! Now!"* I struggled against the enchantment.

Perspiration had formed on the Council members' foreheads.

"She won't make the wish," one argued. "Why would she sacrifice herself for that cruel woman?"

"She absolutely will," I bit back.

"We've almost got him," CM# murmured. "Can't stop now."

By the brook, Grandmother squirmed. "Gianni," she moaned. "She won't make that wish. I've *never* been a loving grandmother to her!"

Lillian's face grew thoughtful.

"You fed me," she told her grandmother, "and educated me at home. And taught me manners. You must have been a *little* bit loving?"

"Mr. Turtelhaze provided money for the food," Grandmother snapped. "I only educated and taught you manners because I could not *bear* to live with you otherwise. Home schooling was essential so I could keep an eye on you."

Lillian nodded slowly.

"Four minutes to make the wish," Mr. Turtelhaze murmured. "And less than four minutes to save your grandmother. Look at her face and hands. See how the veins are turning purplish? That's the poison rushing toward her heart. You'd best hurry."

"Grandmother." Lillian's voice was almost dreamy. "You sent me to stay with Fiona next door when I was small, knowing how happy that made me! You must have loved me a little to do that."

"That was only so you'd stay connected to the house where you were *supposed* to be," Grandmother growled. "The Council monitors Genie children occasionally for their first few years. The moment that monitoring stopped, Gianni arranged for Fiona and Carl to be sent to Sydney for their work—they might have interfered with the plan otherwise. They liked you too much. Fiona wrote letters and sent you presents for years! I hid them all in my wardrobe."

"Oh." Lillian's face fell.

"You see," CM: murmured to me, in an aside. "Lillian is stalling. She won't make the wish." The Council members moved even closer together, sharing rapid words.

"She *will,*" I roared. "*Rescue her!*"

Two Council members snapped their fingers, silencing me.

"Is that why you didn't want me in your bedroom that day?" Lillian ventured. "When we were washing windows? I remember I felt drawn to the wardrobe. Could it be because Fiona's letters were—"

"No, of course not!" Grandmother was scornful. "Your Genie bottle was hidden in the wardrobe! That's what was calling you! After that, I buried it in the garden!"

"Well, you could have destroyed it?" Lillian suggested. "And you didn't. That was perhaps a loving—"

Grandmother cut her short, irritated. "Some of our group thought it should be destroyed, but a Genie bottle is *much* too valuable," she said. "We planned to draw on its power ourselves once you were eliminated!"

"You have two minutes," Mr. Turtelhaze told Lillian, still perfectly calm. "Look at your grandmother's eyes. Do you see the streaks of purple? She must be in considerable pain."

Grandmother scowled at him. "She won't do it," she said. "Cure me yourself, Gianni. Have her make a different wish."

The Council members spoke feverishly.

"Almost," muttered one. "Almost."

I fought violently against their enchantment of me. I swore but my voice would not sound.

"On the day you gave me the pickle jar of coins," Lillian said to her grandmother, "you left me a note saying, *Don't spend all your gold coins in one day.* Why would you write *that* if you actually *wanted* me to use them up? Perhaps it was a warning? Which suggests you do love me?"

"Nonsense," Grandmother growled. She was writhing, tugging at the collar of her dress, panting in pain. "We worried the Council would be alerted if you began spending coins too speedily! That's why I wrote that!"

"Ah." Again, Lillian studied her fingernails.

"You've less than a minute," Mr. Turtelhaze told her. For the first time, his voice seemed to snag.

Lillian looked at him. She glanced back at her grandmother. Suddenly her face cleared. "Oh!" she said. "Grandmother, you keep insisting you never loved me! You don't *want* me to use my final wish to save you! So you *must* love me, just a little!"

A split second in which horror crossed the faces of the Genie Council members, and—

"I wish that Grandmother would be cured," Lillian said.

Snap. Mr. Turtelhaze was captured.

He smiled anyway. Not quite eight o'clock and Lillian had used her final wish.

PART 18

REPORT 24

THE LUMINOUS FOREST, OUTSKIRTS OF GAINSLEIGH, KINGDOMS AND EMPIRES
—Thursday, May 31

* * *

"Let me go," I whispered.

Dazed, the Council members released me from the enchantment.

I took myself outside of time.

I had to. I was pure anger.

Lillian is about to vanish.

It won't happen instantly—reality can take a few minutes to form when it's in shock.

And it *will* be in shock at this turn of events—the loss of a Genie child.

I want to be composed for Lillian's last few minutes. I want to honor her strength rather than blaze at the Council members who caused this.

Writing these last few reports has released a little of my rage so that now, instead, I am calm with grief.

I will return to time now.

"Goodbye, Lillian," I'll say.

REPORT 25

THE LUMINOUS FOREST, OUTSKIRTS OF GAINSLEIGH, KINGDOMS AND EMPIRES
—Thursday, May 31

* * *

Back in time, I rushed to Lillian's side.

"Oh good," she was saying, as she studied her grandmother's face. "Your eyes are clearing up. Are you feeling better?"

Grandmother's mouth opened and then closed again. She was staring wildly.

Next, Lillian looked across at the Council members. Between them, they were holding the essence of Gianni Turtelhaze in the air. The effect was of several people gripping a single marshmallow with toasting forks. Their shoulders strained with the effort.

"Put him in the pickle jar," Lillian suggested.

She stood, holding out the jar. The Council members glanced at each other, then nodded and shuffled toward Lillian, holding Mr. Turtelhaze aloft. Slowly, they navigated him into the jar. The moment he was in there, Lillian screwed on the lid.

"Who wants him?" she asked.

I took it from her.

The essence of Mr. Turtelhaze grinned from within the jar. You could feel his glee warming the glass. I could not stand it. I passed it to a Council member.

Most had gathered close around Lillian. Their

faces were very grave. "Dear Lillian," they murmured. "You have done well—but we are so sorry."

Each in turn, they shook her hand.

"Excellent work," one muttered. "You stalled him for exactly long enough for us to capture him. If only you hadn't . . . if only you . . ."

"You did beautifully," another added. "Such courage. It's a real shame that you . . ."

They kept glancing at Grandmother, who had shifted herself along the brook. She was hunched over, staring at the water like a moody teenager. Was she glum because her boss, Mr. Turtelhaze, had just been captured and would therefore be unable to reward her years of work, as he had promised? Or because Lillian, the child she had raised, had just sacrificed herself to save her?

When I turned back, the Council members had all fallen silent. They stood about, awkward. Lillian seemed very small. She smoothed down her dress.

"Is there nothing we can do?" I pleaded suddenly. I knew there was not and yet—"Is there no loophole? She used her wish so bravely, and while helping to capture an evil Genie! Shouldn't that count for something? Can't the rule be overruled this once?"

The Council members looked at me. Their expressions are usually brisk and bossy—sometimes amused. It was strange to see them heavy with sadness instead. "If there was a way," said one, "I swear that we would use it."

"It's out of our hands," said another.

"She has very little time," said a third.

They all shook their heads.

"Well!" said a hearty voice. "If you only have a little time, why not use it wading in a brook?"

REPORT 26

THE LUMINOUS FOREST, OUTSKIRTS OF GAINSLEIGH, KINGDOMS AND EMPIRES
—Thursday, May 31

* * *

The voice was that of a middle-aged woman who herself was wading in the brook.

We had not noticed her there.

At first I believed it was a Mettlestone sister—there are so many of them, and I knew them to be picnicking nearby. Upon closer inspection, however, it became clear that she was a stranger.

A tall, lean woman, she had dark brown skin, made darker by the sun, and long, sinewy arms and legs. She wore a simple shift, and her feet were bare. The water glinted and splashed around her as she approached us. Her forehead was lined, but her smile was large and bright.

"You're a Sprite," I realized, sensing the true magic in her.

"Not a Water Sprite, though," one of the Council members put in, studying the woman, "although you're in the water."

"No," she agreed. "My name is Belvaan and I am a Tree Sprite. Love to get my feet wet whenever I can." She kicked the water about, and it tumbled and sparkled. "Good morning, all," she concluded, looking up again.

"Good morning," we chorused.

It was very surreal to be exchanging polite greetings with a newcomer at such a time.

"Lillian, I already know," Belvaan continued, "although we've not yet met. I've been watching the drama from over yonder and now I've come to introduce myself."

Lillian's face wore the expression it carries when she is confused but wishes to be polite. "You know me?" she asked carefully. "Although we have not met?"

"Long ago you were here in the forest, Lillian," Belvaan continued, "with the girl Carrie Mettlestone. There was a split oak. It was dying. You wished for it to live."

"I did?" Lillian was now openly baffled.

"You did." Belvaan nodded. "You said: *You poor thing. What happened to you to split you like this? I wish you could be healed somehow.* And of course, as you were a Genie child, your wish came true. You spent one of your wishes to heal a tree! Thank you, Lillian! Truly!"

Lillian beamed. "I'm so glad!" she said. "Although I don't deserve your thanks—I didn't know my wishes were coming true. I'm glad the tree was healed though. Were you nearby when it happened? I don't remember anybody else being about?"

Belvaan shook her head. "Not nearby," she said. "I didn't even exist. The tree was healed, and in its joy, it created me. I am the Tree Sprite of the once-split oak. Thanks to *you,* Lillian, I exist!"

Lillian's smile grew broader. "Well, that's perfect," she declared. Indeed, it seemed a perfect way to say goodbye.

"It's thanks to her that *I* exist now too," another voice broke in, sounding very cranky. It was Grandmother, still hunched over the brook. "I'd be dead from the fridaberry poison if you hadn't used your wish to save me, child! Why would you do that?" She rubbed her face vigorously. She was confused by the emotions she was experiencing, and this made her angry. "Using your last wish! Sacrificing yourself! I certainly did *not* deserve it! I don't know—I don't even—"

"Oh, that wasn't Lillian," Belvaan interrupted from the brook. We looked back down at her. "I mean, Lillian *tried* to do that—but, well, I hope you don't mind, Lillian." She sounded very apologetic. "Sprites have a single wish and I just now used mine to cure your grandmother. Didn't like to see you throw away your own final wish—not after what you'd done for me! I hope you're not annoyed," she added anxiously.

Everyone was silent, staring at her.

"Hold up!" The sprite had now crouched and was groping around in the water. "Here, these fell as you were capturing that Genie."

She straightened, holding out her hand. Five gold coins lay on her palm.

REPORT 27

THE LUMINOUS FOREST, OUTSKIRTS OF GAINSLEIGH, KINGDOMS AND EMPIRES
—Thursday, May 31

* * *

Lillian was safe.

She was *not* about to vanish.

She had *not* used up her final wish.

Eight o'clock had come and gone, and Lillian had *not* used up her wish!!!!!

I would like to type those words over and over, for pages and pages: *She had not used up her final wish. She had not!*

She was safe.

Ah, Lillian. You are safe.

You should have seen how the pickle jar lit up with fury as Mr. Turtelhaze—stuck in there, gloating—realized the truth!

Silly fellow.

That's what you get for an obsession with revenge and power, am I right?

I apologize.

I am giddy.

I know I'm not writing with the calm formality expected of a report.

I'm still angry with the Council members, of course—they should *never* have risked Lillian in this way. It was *pure* luck that the Tree Sprite was passing, and used her wish to save Lillian. Of course, the Council members are already starting on about how they *sensed* she'd be there, or they predicted it, or it was all folded deep within their plan . . .

Nonsense.

They were just as relieved and astonished as I was.

I mean to say, they embraced Belvaan in effusive thanks and whirled her in dances of gratitude! She became quite embarrassed.

"Honestly, it's the least I could do," she kept repeating, and at one point she declared: "I'm relieved to be rid of that wish, actually. It was always hanging over my head—'Is *this* the right moment to use it? Is this? How about this? How should I use it? What's the wisest way to use my wish?' And so on. Now I'm just free to be me."

A wish can be a gift and a burden.

CHAPTER 92

GIFT.

Definitely a gift.

Between us, I was *very* glad not to disappear. When I hear the name *Belvaan* now, my heart glows.

It was very strange, having cake by the brook with Mr. Turtelhaze and Grandmother while the Genie Council built an enchantment nearby. They'd allowed me to hear and see them despite their spell so I'd know they were there. Each member of the Council seemed to have a favorite color, and to dress in several shades of this color, so I kept sensing swirling pinks and turquoises, magentas and indigos from the corner of my eye. As if lolly wrappers were blowing about in the wind.

Snatches of what they were muttering kept floating by me too. It was difficult not to giggle. It really made no sense.

Later, Reuben explained that enchantments are composed of memories, music, mathematics, and dreams—the sorts of things that exist outside of time. I didn't know that though and was confused to hear humming mixed with "Oh, remember the day lamb chops were on special at the grocery store, only they were already past their sell-by date?" and "The square root of 181," and "I dreamed I was swimming in a cup of tea. *Quack!* I said. I was a duck."

Anyhow, when Mr. Turtelhaze told me he'd poisoned Grandmother, I knew I would wish for her to be cured. I was trying to hold off until the Council's enchantment was complete.

During the Genie orientation week (conducted in Reuben's house, mostly boring, but they did teach me how to move in time and space very easily), people kept looking at me strangely. They wanted to know *why* I'd wanted to save Grandmother. She'd never been kind to me!

But listen, dear reader. She's a *Hurtling*. Her whole nature wants to destroy life! Imagine how difficult it was for her to live with me! And yet, somehow, she did live with me.

Mr. Turtelhaze, on the other hand, was a Genie, so his essence is starlight—yet he found a way to turn evil! When you think about it, both he and Grandmother had tremendous strength of character.

Reuben gaped like a goldfish when I told him this.

"I don't mean I want them to get certificates of merit or anything," I said. "I actually hope Mr. Turtelhaze stays in the pickle jar."

"Nobody's planning to release him, Lillian."

"And do I really not need to see Grandmother again?" I asked.

"Of course not. Unless you want to."

That made me pause.

Saying goodbye to Grandmother had been very peculiar. For a long moment, we had only stared at each other.

"Goodbye then," she said eventually, very stiffly. (She was being taken by Council members for interrogation.) "Thank you for . . . that."

"Goodbye," I replied. "I . . ."

What was I going to say? *I'll miss you?* Surely not.

I feel terribly betrayed by you?

I don't understand?

In the end, I said this: "I was always afraid, Grandmother. I don't think that is normal in a childhood. You were cold, cruel, and uncaring toward me all my life, and now, in helping Mr. Turtelhaze try to destroy me, you have shocked and hurt me deeply. I think perhaps you were afraid of him yourself. Still. You have behaved very improperly. I am ashamed of you."

Grandmother's face crumpled like old lettuce. She bowed her head. She was marched away.

"Perhaps one day I'll want to see her again," I told Reuben.

"I think she really did love me a *teeny* bit, you know. She was even crankier around my tenth birthday, perhaps distressed about what was happening?"

"Plausible," Reuben replied. "After all, it's impossible not to love you, Lillian."

Then he turned his attention to the subject of afternoon tea.

REPORT 28

THE LUMINOUS FOREST, OUTSKIRTS OF GAINSLEIGH, KINGDOMS AND EMPIRES
—Thursday, May 31

* * *

A couple of final admin matters.

The individuals known as Fiona Wynne and Carl Tan, currently residing in Sydney, have been notified that their old neighbor—known as "Grandmother"—is deceased, and that they are named in her will as the guardians of Lillian Velvet.

They'd barely finished reading the letter before they were speeding down the highway to be by Lillian's side. They are overjoyed.

Upon their arrival, they will learn that the house in which Grandmother resided with Lillian has been left to them too.

To be clear, Grandmother is *not* deceased. That's just for legal formalities. In fact, she has reverted to her original Hurtling form and is in talks with Franny Mettlestone, who is experienced in the reform of Shadow Mages. Grandmother says that Lillian's generosity gave her such a jolt it has sort of "shoved" her toward the bright side. We shall see.

* * *

These reports commenced with a description of the Mettlestone family farewelling their parents at the docks by moonlight.

I conclude now with the happy assurances that the Mettlestones are well, engaged in their various occupations and hobbies, happy in the knowledge that Lillian Velvet is safe—and that Gianni/Mr. Turtelhaze, the fearsome enemy of Jacob and Ildi, is locked inside a pickle jar at the back of the pantry in the Genie Council kitchen, behind the fermented fish.

* * *

I trust that my reports will be useful to the Council of Genies, and to all Boards of Timekeepers, and I remain,

Yours truly,

Reuben
Genie 2388

CHAPTER 93

THESE DAYS I live with Fiona and Carl in the house where I grew up.

It's not exactly that, though. The walls have been repainted in bright colors, carpets replaced by floorboards, and the lace curtains by plantation shutters. Huge plants in pots stand in the corners, and the couches are deep, squashy ,and covered in colorful throws. Fiona's photographs of sea horses—she loves to scuba dive—line the hallway. Carl's muddy work boots stand by the door.

My own paintings are pinned to the refrigerator with magnets. Fiona has even framed two and hung them in the living room, which bewilders me, as they're *not very good*. Yet Fiona's whole face breaks into a smile when she looks at them.

The fence between our house and next door has been torn down—Fiona and Carl became instant friends with Helen and Shahlyla, who insist we enjoy their marvelous backyard any time.

"After all," they told Fiona and Carl, "Lillian wished that it be built!"

All four adults chuckled, as if that was a joke, and then stopped chuckling, and looked at me. They know I'm a Genie now. Reuben said I may tell those closest to me. So they looked at me, and they realized that it *had* been my wish that built their backyard, and this made them laugh properly.

Over cake and coffee at my place, Reuben explained to these four adults that I should have a regular childhood now, please, with my true Genie life beginning when I'm grown up.

"It's a difficult balance being a Genie," he told them. "As much as possible, Genies should avoid granting wishes, instead guiding people to help themselves. To do this, Genies need to learn to value them*selves*. Do you think you four can help Lillian do that?"

For some reason, all four of them became teary. They promised they would.

(Reuben has told me separately that I'm allowed to grant tiny wishes, here and there, if I like.)

Often, in the afternoons, I visit the Kingdoms and Empires to see my friends. Fiona and Carl insisted on coming the first time, so they could meet the Mettlestones and ensure I was safe. We went to Isabelle's fancy penthouse apartment in Gainsleigh, where they met Aunt Isabelle and the Butler, as well as Bronte's parents and grandparents. The adults had wine and cheese and played lively games of charades.

Fiona and Carl came home very cheerful and said the Mettlestones seem lovely, and very funny, and that I may visit whenever I like. I should reciprocate, they said, and invite the children to play at my place, or for sleepovers. They themselves are planning to invite the Mettlestones to a barbecue soon.

They're still thinking about whether I'm allowed to accept Aunt Sophy's invitation to visit Dragon Great Damian. Apparently, he wants to take me flying, to thank me for saving his life. I can tell by the spark in Carl's eye that he's keen to meet a dragon for himself.

Although I'm friends with all the Mettlestone children, I sometimes think I have a particular connection with Bronte. The other day, she and I were hiking in the mountains near her boarding school. I was telling her how the Genie bottle is still soothing to me, and how it calls to me when I'm away from it for long.

"Reuben says it will stop having such a hold over me one day," I said, "and then I'll want to give it away."

Abruptly, Bronte stopped. She stared at me strangely.

"That's a lovely red coat you're wearing, Lillian," she murmured (unexpectedly).

"Thank you! Fiona bought it for me. See, I love the color red, and—"

At that point, I stopped too. We held each other's gaze for a while. The same thing was occurring to us—that perhaps one day *I* would be a grown-up Genie dressed in shades of lipstick red, and would travel back in time, meet a man who runs a stall in a market. I'd give the man my Genie bottle to sell at his stall, telling him it no longer had a hold over me—and later, I'd return to the stall to meet Bronte herself, a slightly younger Bronte. "This bottle," the stallholder would tell her, "will help you dream the dreams you're meant to dream."

"And you'll visit your *own* younger self," Bronte said, wide-eyed, "and shove yourself into the dream of little Jacob Mettle! You're going to be so elegant and beautiful!"

"She might not be me," I said, still doubtful.

"It makes sense," Bronte argued. "Anyway, you're definitely going to have adventures, Lillian."

"So will you have adventures," I reminded her. "We know that from your letter to yourself."

Remembering this, she lit up with a smile, and we carried on with our hike.

In the meantime, my days spin with adventures anyway, and with wishes come true—such as going to school (as marvelous as I knew it would be), and doing homework (not all it's cracked up to be—Oscar says, "It was never cracked up to be anything, Lillian, you did that with your own cracked-up mind"), outdoor guitar concerts, amusement arcades, skating at an ice rink, learning to ride a bicycle, and to roller skate, afternoon tea in a shopping mall, joining a net ball team, watching Carl's soccer games, a seal show at Taronga Zoo in Sydney, and Fiona calling me into the kitchen: "Lillian! Lillian! Look what I've done!"

It turned out that a packet of flour had slipped from Fiona's fingertips onto the countertop, where it burst open, covering her in flour. She had only called me in so that I could laugh with her, about how funny she looked with her face and her hair all covered in white powder. It really was funny. We laughed and laughed, and then she said, “Let’s have fish and chips at the beach for dinner—what do you think?”

That sort of an adventure. Imagine it.

Some Notes on This Book's Production

The art for the jacket and title lettering were hand-drawn by Jim Tierney using a Cintiq tablet and Adobe Photoshop. The text was set in GazetteLTStd Roman. The Gazette font family was designed with newspaper print in mind, to withstand high-speed presses and coarse newsprint and to guarantee legibility despite long press runs. The initial caps are set in Rough Cut; a sturdy gothic font designed by Simon Walker and the illustrated framings for each initial cap were created by Jim Tierney as well. It was composed by Westchester Publishing Services in Danbury, CT. The book was printed on 78 gsm Yunshidai Ivory uncoated woodfree FSC™-certified paper and bound in China.

Production was supervised by Freesia Blizard

Book design by Paul Kepple

Edited by Arthur A. Levine and Arely Guzmán